One-Man Boat:
The George Hitchcock Reader

WORKS BY GEORGE HITCHCOCK

PLAYS
The Discovery and Ascent of Kan-Chen-Chomo (1954)
The Magical History of Dr. Faustus (1954)
The Ticket (1956)
The Counterfeit Rose: A Baroque Comedy (1957)
Whistle Stop (1957)
Prometheus Found (1958)
The Housewarming (1958)
The Busy Martyr (1959)
The Devil Comes to Wittenberg (1980)
Five Plays (1981)

LIBRETTI
Trial by Jury (freely adapted from Gilbert and Sullivan, 1949)
The Impresario (a new libretto for the Mozart singspiel, 1963)

POETRY
Poems & Prints (1962)
Tactics of Survival (1964)
The Dolphin with the Revolver in its Teeth (1967)
A Ship of Bells (1968)
Twelve Stanzas in Praise of the Holy Chariot (1969)
The Rococo Eye (1970)
Lessons in Alchemy (1976)
The Piano Beneath the Skin (1978)
Mirror on Horseback (1979)
The Wounded Alphabet: Poems Collected and New, 1953–1983 (1984)
Cloud-Taxis (1984)
Turns and Returns: Poems and Paintings (2002)

TRANSLATIONS
Eight Poets of Germany and America (with Heiner Bastian, 1967)
Selected Poems of Yvan Goll (translated with Galway Kinnell,
    Robert Bly and Paul Zweig, 1968)

SHORT STORIES
Notes of the Siege Year (1974)
October at the Lighthouse (1984)

NOVELS
Another Shore (1971)
The Racquet (1993)

ANTHOLOGIES
Pioneers of Modern Poetry (with Robert Peters, 1967)
Losers Weepers: An Anthology of Found Poems (1969)

EDITORSHIPS
San Francisco Review (associate editor, 1958–1963)
kayak (editor, 1964–1984)

One-Man Boat:
The George Hitchcock Reader

EDITED BY
JOSEPH BEDNARIK
MARK JARMAN
ROBERT McDOWELL

Story Line Press
2003

Published by Story Line Press, Three Oaks Farm, PO Box 1240, Ashland, OR 97520-0055, www.storylinepress.com.

This publication was made possible thanks in part to the generous support of the Nicholas Roerich Museum, Mr. Robin Magowan, and our individual contributors.

Cover design by Lysa McDowell.
Cover art: "The Poet" (1999), oil crayon on foam board (15½" x 19½") by Jorge Hitchcock, from the collection of Clemens Starck.
Author photo courtesy of Jens and Petra Herrmann.
Interior design and typesetting by Sharon McCann.

Library of Congress Cataloging-in-Publication Data

Hitchcock, George, 1914–
    One-man boat: the George Hitchcock reader: poetry, fiction, magazine editing, interviews, and drama / by George Hitchcock; edited by Joseph Bednarik, Mark Jarman, and Robert McDowell.
        p. cm.
        ISBN 1-58654-022-X
I. Bednarik, Joseph, 1964– II. Jarman, Mark, 1952–
III. McDowell, Robert, 1953– IV. Title.

PS3558.I8 A6 2003
818'.5409—dc21
                                    2002012759

ACKNOWLEDGMENTS

This book exists through the generosity of many people, including: Fred Muratori, who helped locate *kayak* rejection slips; Lawrence Smith, for permission to reprint his interview from *Caliban*; Dr. Michael Peich, for access to transcripts of his interviews with George Hitchcock; Robert Bly, for permission to reprint his attack on *kayak*; to Philip Levine, for his Foreword; and to the taxpayers of the United States, who support the publication of the *Congressional Record*.

Special thanks are due to Catherine Powell of the Labor Archives and Research Center at San Francisco State University and Dr. Michael Basinski of The Poetry/Rare Books Collection at the University at Buffalo, New York, where the *kayak* archive resides.

For Marjorie Simon

Asleep there were just these dreams and no others. Awake there were these actions only. Only these deeds came into being.

—Kenneth Rexroth

❦ CONTENTS

FOREWORD

A Means of Transport

by Philip Levine

*a*side from comic books, the first publication that obsessed me was *Life* magazine. I was probably only nine or ten when I discovered its riches, which were then available for a dime, a sum I could earn in an hour. No, it wasn't the politics or vision of Henry Luce, the booster of unrestrained capitalism, that grabbed me; the last thing I did was read the articles. It was the photographs, at first the war photographs from Spain and China and later those from Europe, North Africa, and the Pacific as well as the great photographic record of an America stumbling through the blighted peace of the Depression with its bread lines, dust-bowl nightmares, and industrial cities going to ruin. Until I discovered the poetry of T.S. Eliot, the images of Robert Capa, Margaret Bourke-White, Dorthea Lange, Carl Mydans, Edward Clark, Alfred Eisenstaedt and their colleagues were the most powerful I knew. When in high school I got into poetry the word began to replace the photographic image, and by the time I discovered at eighteen "The Preludes" by T.S. Eliot the process was almost complete. Little wonder that two decades later I hit upon a magazine that fascinated me almost as much as *Life* had and certainly more than any other literary publication. It was, of course, George Hitchcock's *kayak*, the first poetry journal I knew that was dedicated to the image and the only one I've ever ransacked with the same feverish anticipation I had those early issues of *Life*. In the very first issue from a poet I'd never heard of, Louis Z. Hammer, I stumbled across, "Investigators are prying into the American bloodstream; / In Wyoming a horse dies by a silver river, / Two maiden sisters in Los Angeles have torn open their hands. . ." And from the editor himself:

> America, beneath your promise
> there are underground lakes
> full of morphine
> and broken carburetors!

Doors open and close on my shadow.
My intestines burn. I am expelled
from various academies.

(The writing alone—even without the gas—would have gotten him expelled from any number of academies.) This was something new and different: it was neither the self-righteous rhetoric of the thirties protest poetry nor the overheated rant of the literary victim. Impossible to locate its origins in the American poetry of the forties and fifties or English poetry since the fall. This was a surrealism, or better an ultra-realism, whose fathers and mothers were unleashed Americans and whose uncles were Europeans, Iberians, and Latin Americans. There's a myth that American poetry was asleep during the Eisenhower years; American poetry has never been asleep; however the best known contemporary poetry during the post-war era was certainly powerfully sedated. The poets wild enough to be truly American were underground only because the official organs of reproduction were too sterile to allow them life anywhere else. What *kayak* did was collect these separate writers into a national movement and then sic them on the *Hudson* and *Sewanee Reviews*.

All you had to do was look at the magazine to know it was something new. (It's been copied so often that today someone first stumbling upon it might not recognize how striking it was in 1964.) Bound in heavy cardboard and voluminously illustrated, it sold for only a dollar or $3 for a two-year subscription of four issues. The paper itself had a crude substantiality, "target paper"—I was later told—that George got cheaply. The illustrations were mainly engravings taken from odd and magical sources. For example, *kayak* 2 was dedicated to *America's Underground Channels and Seams* and the engravings were mainly taken from *Boston's Main Drainage* (1888) and Andre's *Practical Coal Mining* (1879). Each issue bore the following motto as an indication to possible contributors and readers of the magazine's ambition:

A kayak is not a galleon, ark, coracle or speedboat. It is a small watertight vessel operated by a single oarsman. It is submersible, has sharply pointed ends, and is constructed from light poles and the skins of furry animals. It has never yet been successfully employed as a means of mass transport.

If you hoped to appear in the magazine you had to paddle your own boat; where you were headed was your business. The epigones of

Lowell and Wilbur were not welcome. From that first issue it was a place for me to discover new poets as well as a new vision of our poetry. It was here I first read John Haines, David Antin, Bert Meyers, Lou Lipsitz, Dennis Schmitz, Kathleen Fraser, Herbert Morris, Margaret Atwood, Charles Simic, Bill Knott, Margaret Randall, Adrien Stoutenberg, Shirley Kaufman, James Tate, Adam Cornford, Steve Dunn, Mark Doty, William Matthews, Mark Jarman, and Brenda Hillman. Within a few issues well-known poets as diverse as Tom McGrath, David Ignatow, Louis Simpson, W.S. Merwin, John Logan, Wendell Berry, Hayden Carruth, Paul Blackburn, Donald Justice, Gary Snyder, Anne Sexton, Charles Wright, Raymond Carver, Stephen Dobyns, Charles Hanzlicek, Kenneth Rexroth, Peter Everwine, and Richard Hugo made appearances, and curiously none of them seemed in the wrong neighborhood: they sounded like themselves and like one of the voices of *kayak*. I can still recall Mark Strand telling me over thirty years ago, "I've got a poem coming out in *kayak!*" Clearly it had become *the* place to appear. I seriously doubt this was George's ambition for his eccentric journal, but for years the poets had been starved for just such a meeting space and finding it we found it irresistible. I haven't mentioned translations, which became a regular feature of the magazine. Except for Rexroth's superb versions of the Chinese, they were largely of twentieth century European poets not yet discovered by many Americans—Rafael Alberti, Benjamin Peret, Odysseas Elytis, Vincente Huidobro, Hans Magnus Enzensberger, Tomas Tranströmer, et al.

By 1969 it had become a quarterly and was regularly publishing prose; not just prose poems—for they were there from the start—but prose-prose, critical essays, reviews, and visionary opinion pieces representing utterly conflicting views. The reviews could be tough, sometimes even tough on regular *kayak* poets. (I was one who got bombed, although as I recollect not as badly as Dan Halpern in a review titled "Short Order Cooks of Poetry," which savaged Halpern's anthology of the younger American poets.) And the letters. One must not forget the letters, for they became for many a source of great wonder. An early one from Shirley Kaufman, a response to the kayak press book *Pioneers of Modern Poetry* edited by George and Robert Peters, brought to our attention an all but unknown though masterful poet, Alexander Raphael Cury, whose poem "Enquiring About the Way," Kaufman demonstrated, had inspired Kafka, although the poem, unlike either *The Trial* or *The Castle*, ended on a note of hope:

I am going home.
Go home.
What is the name of this place?
Square
Street
Lane.

Equally delicious were the gripes. One from Rodney Nelson of San Francisco began:

I hope you will excuse me for being direct: I see no point in sending *kayak* any more poems or articles. The fact that you, as editor, are free to interpose your own personality between me and the readers is a sure indication that your magazine is socially unhealthy....Why should an editor steal a stamped, self-addressed envelope from a writer.... Because nothing else matters but sly harassment, when the world is falling down around your ears. Into this picture fit you and your incredibly silly magazine, neither of which would last a minute in a people's society.

If this was the idiocy George was getting from the left, it's hard to imagine how much worse the complaints from the right were. From the start *kayak* presented found poems. I don't believe they were there only for laughs. The poets of that era—perhaps the poets of every era—had a tendency to exaggerate their social and spiritual significance. There was a lesson here for all of us who hoped to survive the violence and pain of the sixties: without a healthy and ribald disrespect for authority we were doomed. Like his great forbearer Walt Whitman in the preface to *Leaves of Grass*, George was telling us in his own writing and in the sassy and irreverent entity that was *kayak* to take off our hats to no one.

I first met George Hitchcock in the spring of 1965. He'd come to Fresno as one of two poets reading on the Academy of American Poets California Circuit, which was then in its infancy. (Unfortunately it never lived into its teens.) The other poet was my old friend Henri Coulette. For the students at Fresno State it must have been something of an eye-opener; if they'd had any notions regarding the nature of the poet, his or her appearance, style, character, and writing, these two would have blown it. Henri was perhaps half a foot shorter than George and very slender—an ex-distance runner, he still looked as though he could do a mile in four minutes and change—he dressed in the style of an under secretary of state on the threshold of a promotion: for day wear (and the reading took place in the early afternoon) he favored light gray suits, bright ties, ox-blood loafers. His dark hair was cut so short that its natural curliness was barely visible. His complexion was a light olive; he was, he claimed, in spite of his name a "black Irishman." George is a big man by any standard and he carries himself with the exuberance of a very big man. Back in '65 he probably weighed a solid 230; his style of dress is hard to describe for no extant term quite gets it. I'll call it post-Hemingway baroque. For day-time wear it could include anything from a foundry-worker's coveralls to a purple tuxedo. His hair was just going gray and was so thick, long, and wild it looked as though it had never faced the shears of a trained barber. I thought immediately of Theodore Roethke during his greenhouse years.

Though both were superb readers their styles had almost nothing in common. Coulette read from his wonderful first book, *The War of the Secret Agents*, with an almost icy precision that beautifully suited the work. Essentially a shy man, he spoke little between poems, which was a shame for he possessed a fine sense of irony. Fortunately it came through in the poems. Then it was George's turn. First he thanked Henri for the reading and for his companionship during their tour, and then he turned to his poems and opened up his enormous voice and let go. Nothing was more obvious than that he liked performing; he put his whole self into it. First his poems, serious and visionary, driven forward by the fury of his energy, original, surreal and unpredictable:

> I celebrate the swans with their invisible
> plumage of steam, I pursue fragrant bullets
> in the blue meadows, I observe in the reeds
> the sacraments of cellulose, I seek
> my lost ancestors.
>
> (from "How My Light is Spent")

He followed them with a short collection of riotously funny found poems: Yes, this was truly the editor of what was becoming the most original and readable American poetry magazine in decades. I had asked myself before what was it that gave *kayak* such a potent and unified vision of the America of the sixties in spite of the fact it seemed to have room for almost every talented poet not writing Petrarchan sonnets (although George had published a wonderful parody of one), many poets who couldn't even speak to each other: The answer was here in the character of George Hitchcock. Before the reading ended George did something I have never seen another poet do: he turned to the audience and asked if there were anyone among us who would like to come forward and join the reading. No one took him up on it, so he turned to me and said, "Come on, Phil, you must have something to read." I was so startled I declined the invitation. Generosity of this nature is not something one encounters very often on the reading trail, which is, unfortunately, where one is apt to see poets at their very worst, full of self and empty of a sense of others. George, I realized, was entirely sincere, and a word came into my mind that I have rarely brought to bear on anyone, much less a touring poet: Bountiful. This guy had a lot to give and the energy and character not to tire of giving it.

Everything I learned about George that first day I never unlearned, for he is exactly who he is: an adult in total possession of himself. There is no pose, no effort to charm—indeed he is naturally likeable and charming—and his personality is so rich that every time I've been with him for a day or more I've been rewarded by new discoveries. The man who founded and edited for two decades a truly great poetry journal had to be tough at times, had to possess high standards and his own vision of the poetry that mattered. As a non-academic he had no experience with committee decisions regarding artistic merit. George is a strong man with strong beliefs, one who is able to live with the dislike of others. (Have a look at his testimony before HUAC, and you'll get an idea of what he thinks of committee decision and of courting dislike when it's worth treasuring.) You could say of George that what you see is what you get, but it wouldn't be true: you get more than you ever see.

Some years later George asked me if I'd like to do a book with kayak press. By this time he'd done books by Charles Simic and Raymond Carver, so the press—though a small one—was on the map of poetry. He warned me that it would be illustrated and that I would have no say in the matter as well as no say in the choice of the cover or in any aspect of the design. He wouldn't fool with the poems and I wouldn't fool with the production of the book, which was fine. I was by this time a devoted reader of the magazine as well as a delighted contributor, so I had a clear notion of just how eccentric his sense of illustration could be. I'd been having a terrible time finding a publisher for my third poetry collection. It had wandered from editor to editor collecting rejections. George had already printed the poem "They Feed

They Lion" in *kayak*, but the manuscript of that title was sleeping in the editorial offices of Wesleyan University Press where it would be awakened to a second rejection, but I had another collection, which I gave George. The submission and acceptance took place through the mail and required no contract or paperwork. I received a copy of the new book, *Red Dust*, a month ahead of schedule. It looked like no book I'd ever seen before, and I liked it. I even liked the poems; I hadn't had time to tire of them. In the letter that came with that first copy was a check which amounted to my royalties: he didn't want the trouble of screwing around with the bookkeeping; he was sure he'd sell all the copies, so here it was in dollars. That too never happened before or again. It may be a first in the history of poetry.

For many years I did not take George's poetry as seriously as it merited. I think I may have been so enraptured by his presence that I assumed that was the entree of the feast he is. In 1984 he sent me a copy of a large collection, *The Wounded Alphabet*, which contains several extraordinary poems in his distinctive voice, poems as extraordinary as anything being written. Here is one, "End of Ambition," though I could have chosen "There's No Use Asking" or "His Last Words":

End of Ambition

when I get there the last
mail has been sorted
my friends gather
in their arctic parkas
they speak a language
I don't understand
they've put off their
togas I don't recognize
the pumping station
or the grimy collier
docked at the pier

I'd waited a long time
I sat in the tower
for months weaving
these wings out of rage
& envy I'd almost

forgotten the song
of the parapet &
the green vision
we saw from the cliffs

perhaps it's too late
perhaps they no longer
care the tide is out
the rules of flight
have been altered and
maybe there's no way now
to get beyond the clouds
of white corpuscles
and the tongues
darting & skimming
over the parched
mud-flats

To understate the matter, George gave the American poetry world
three priceless gifts: his own writing, *kayak*—the finest poetry magazine
of my era—and his complex and unusual presence, which served as a
model for so many of us: the model of the poet as a total human being
(as my mother would have said, a *mensch*). I've heard poets not a frac-
tion as dedicated and gifted as George whine about how much they'd
given America and how little it had given back. I've heard others liter-
ally cry for the lack of fame and fortune they'd suffered because they
chose to be poets. I can't imagine anyone who'd been mentored by
George, officially or otherwise, crying over his or her lack of celebrity.
He or she would be much more likely to greet the closed door to fame
with suitable defiance and if words were required they'd likely be "Live
free or die." George is one of those Americans who spring up all too
rarely, those originals who make you proud of your birthright: he loves
this country so much he's spent his life trying to make it a place worthy
of its stated principles, its land and its people. Like anyone struggling
to make his or her America a decent society, George has known a his-
tory of losses; meeting him you would never know it. His years in the
labor movement have taught him all a person needs to know about loy-
alty, independence and human dignity. His years as a gardener and an
actor taught him the value of beauty and new growth. Those of us who
shared his years as an editor and writer learned by example that a per-
son can give his energy and heart to worthy ventures even in a corrupt

society and never compromise. For those of us to whom he has been both mentor and friend—a huge portion of my generation of American poets—the gifts have been enormous and no doubt different for each of us. I believe we all learned that the age-old conflict between art and life was nonsense: in George's case nothing was more obvious than that art was his life and his life was an art. His laughter—like a totem against depression and defeat—I carry with me always, and his lesson that hard work in the service of a good cause is like poetry, its own reward.

POEMS

Lead Kindly Light

I stand with the elect,
seat-check in my hand,
one eye pressed
to the keyhole
of heaven.

There are holes
in my knickerbockers;
it is 1929 and raining.
No seats, the usher
tells me, are available
till the Second Coming.

Messrs. Pusey and Keble,
you have failed me:
your compasses run down
the mice have eaten
the Doctrine of Real Presence
and God no longer resembles his photographs.

In my pockets
the marzipan saints turn to syrup.

The Quarrel

then there was the noon of salt
when the yellow bird rose
and stayed transfixed in the sky
the light burst the windowpane
everything was plain enough:
what you'd drawn in the dust
with your stick the unspoken
verbs and the sky in bits
like a dropped dish

but words won't help
what's broken's broken and speaking's
but a gloss you had your sorcery now I have mine
and neither mends that gold bird
so why dispute? the pattern's
in the cloth—why unravel
that which soon enough will fall apart
from its own damned contrariness?

Vexatious Aphorisms

God's in his heaven, says
the man in the abandoned tower
whose tongue is covered with bees.

A rose falls into self-analysis;
nothing now can revive it.

Autonomous hands grow
from the rusted vibraphone.

A simple diet wards off constipation.

Count the soldiers hidden in my glass,
says the mirror to the overstuffed chair.
What now?

Any unbuttoned anchovy will do in a storm.

From thread to needle will do in a storm.

From thread to needle to needle from thread
the argument proceeds. No one is the loser.

The self-critical hairbrush
surveys its monstrous goiter.

To speak in gobbets of sperm
is the ambition of all novices.

From the windows of heaven a damsel leans;
her tears form a chain to lift
the scorpion to ecstasy.

Saying Goodbye

what we had raised in the night
disappeared soon enough in daylight

its cornices crumbled
the heavy weight of its worn arch

fell into the floodstream.
stones. broken stones.

I could not know that your eyes
limned with kohl and sapphire

would lie there gazing up
into the hot sun of the desert

I could not foretell the twin
columns of that lithe statue

aging into steles
from yet another ruin

another Persepolis
commemorating foolishness.

Botanizing again

on Big Diamond long
vista deserted farms
brambles the sawdust burners
of Hilt Lumber and later
the hot walk down through
manzanita and deerbrush
to the spur track

> traffic of birds in
> the summer air
> flights and hoverings
> rustle of
> lizard or grouse

thrown backward I was
into runes of leaf and blood
memory of hot creosote
under my bare feet in
August of 1928 railroad
ties and yellow path
of dust sparrowmarked
and spurting at footfall
botanist's press banging
at my knees with its
absorbent papers and
burden of slain flowers

> racing down those tracks
> three ties at a leap
> what a scorn of time
> I bore then
>   held
> in those blotters
> between rock cress
> and Indian Warrior

dried and flattened
for those coming after.

The Orchard

Grackles over the wild mustard:
black on gold. Water lies
stagnant under the wood bridge.
The pond has a heavy skin
of dust: a chub floats belly-up
silver in the sun. My ladder
walks through the orchard,
its head among white blossoms
its coarse feet crushing the run-
ways of gophers. I stand on its stilts
and prune to the outside bud.

The questions which occur along this dreamflecked avenue

Who is it tears open the traffic arrow
and dissects its white shadow? Which pale
waiting room full of spies and spinal
taps will contain the man of gourds?
What knife shall cut the diseased testicle?
If you question the hummingbird will it
tell you where it's going? Will the conductor
of this train punch my ticket of smoke?

History is more opaque than we expected.
The Neo-gnostic Age, the age of Burnt Aspirin,
draws nearer. All plants are monoecious,
the last gilt has peeled from the Blessed
Virgin. Porcelain athletes swim
across the lake to their beach umbrellas
and half-eaten sandwiches. The autumn wind
stretches its arms. Only the moon won't admit
defeat. Like an old sponge I must wring it out:
    it drips on the oil cloth, then to the floor,
    lambent, mucilaginous, a dying periscope.

The public monuments sneeze. Man has become
a bandit to his brother. Night drops
in the corner pocket. Night will redo
its fingernails. Night will settle
all tabs. Yet each
enigmatic dawn
the cats return.

Fourteen Stanzas in Search of

1

What's there? she asked.
He told her behind blue is seven
over summer heat the soldier's
eyes, back of the sabre lies
a land of forbidden roads
and heliotrope; don't joke
she said, I have to know
in whose throat the song
lies hidden, what tongue is
already clothed in glass and
in the bones of which bird
I can read your departure.

The sky broke out in sweat;
a gull dropped its shadow.
I found it, she said, putting
the lens in his hand
and so he began

2

I'm not alone he thought,
I have the wolf and the manatee
the icy flames of the Pleiades
infinity's railway
and the hand with its calluses
which climbs toward me out of
this mineshaft. I don't know why
I'm crawling across the plain
of burrs and pyramids (Teotihuacán
or Tibet?) glaciers and ivory
needles, wild pigs
in every gutter, but I know
I'm not alone

3

The others were there as usual
at the usual street-corner: the one
with the limp and his brother with the brass
nose-ring, the old one who had grown blind
waiting for it to happen, the one with the tiny
box in which he kept insects
and he of the blue cowl, the beard and the falcon.
They asked the usual questions, what
became of fire, who kept the key
to the vaults and why the lace had all
evaporated; not much was different—
the one in the kaftan was apologetic
just as he'd been before and the one
with the steel blade drove it deeper and
deeper, smiling much
as he'd always done

4

They showed him the ladder he had to take;
it leads, they said, into the kiva.
He went down it one foot at a time
gripping the rungs, feathers in his eyes
lightning around him, harsh smoke
nailed to his ribs. Where you're going
you won't need poker-dice or that dented
tin-whistle, you're not looking
for coins or French kisses, they said
this ladder leads to the smokehouse
the earth's asshole
and you'd better be quick about it

5

You're done for now, said the man with the hawk
hanging there between heaven and nothing at all
your clothes ripped, beard singed, one bloody hand
on the middle rung, not up not down but nowhere much
                         a puppet
                         a scarecrow
                         rag doll of butterflies
                         emperor of what's half-done.
Hang in there, she said, you've seen the worst.

6

God help him till the red axes come!
There's no bed like air, falling's
another language entirely, short on conjunctions
what happens happens, no use arguing;
anyway, beneath him the inevitable committee waits
they with their wreaths and baskets
they'll pick up the pieces, they always do
they with their sappy odes
and crocheted blankets

7
                    "No point in all those place
mats
                    no one's coming to dinner,
only
                    the tattooed man from
Otaheite
                    the lady with the waxed mous-
taches
                    and her little dog the wind"

8

You can't stay there, she told him
you can't drink wine from that skin,
that's reserved for tears, only
the suffering can take up that guitar
only the witnesses without rifles
are allowed on these walls, there
where the carriers walk with their gourds
full of grace notes. It doesn't matter your
credentials are signed by an archduke
they're not important your visas and boxes
of dust, the answers to your questions
aren't at home, even the ice-chimes
won't take up your echo, won't
carry your insincere song

9

He tried the Queen of Pentacles:
that is your fate, she said
a darkened lighthouse, a rotted elm tree.
But what does it mean? he asked
the maggoty elm, the lighthouse shut?
The blade of a knife the barb
of an arrow, the gypsy said,
you'll dance a lot then come
to that end; no use cursing
pour your seed where you like
in the end it'll be as if
you hadn't lived at all
the lighthouse shut and every
last leaf gone from the elm—
bright steel and the barb of an arrow. No use grousing.
He paid up and left

10

On Thursday they came to the ocean
it didn't open up, not like the Red Sea,
if anything it closed in—water
on all sides, spratling and anchovies
in their shoes, herring gulls screaming
fishnets rubbish and kelp and the same sullen boatman
tinkering with his outboard.
Yet they had to pass, their way
lay over the straits to the marl cliffs
and the clocks all chimed Deafness
or Guilt, and the skies with their fluffy garlands wouldn't
stay that way forever

11

What the boatman said:
kelp-trees is worst they tangle the prop
shark got no bones only gristle and teeth
a full moon makes the sand thirsty
you can never lead a south wind by the hand
no use mopping the clouds it only leads to hail
to catch eels you bend the thorn of a cactus
the Holy Ghost hangs over us all like a
                              billowing jib
let Him have his head he knows where the fish are
                        when the radar don't
that's what the boatman said

12

If on the other beach they should meet
themselves coming back twenty years
will have passed and he still asks
what's for breakfast? And she still says
I've lost it, my contact must have
fallen between the floorboards
but their hair is gray now
and their grammar disheveled.
I hardly knew you, he tells himself

whatever happened to...?
But already she has forgotten
the end of the sentence

13

To have come so far and to find nothing
and in the heart of that Nothing still
another: Himalayas of emptiness
ice-leaves lost fragrances
moon craters Glagolithic runes
deserted shrines made of oil drums
dolphin-shadows spume-castles
menhirs dolmens stonehenges
of the imagination

To have come so far...

14

                                    one eye for weeping
                                    one eye for sight
                                    and this one fixed
                                    like a carbuncle
                                    in your forehead

put there to reflect

                                    the vanishing god

In This Third Year of a Useless War

On Sunday in this third year of a useless war,
Released for this day from calendars
And the scent of cities
I walk on the Pacific slope
Looking for mushrooms.
Off the coast, from Bolinas Point to Mile Rock
The Japan Current runs southeast.
There is no sun
A trawler beats through the swell
The sea has a reddish look
The wind whistles gently out of the west
Smelling of almonds and gasoline.

High in the pastures I find a fresh clump
Of lactaria, good eating. Farther on,
Under the live-oaks, boletus
Push through the leaves.

The rivers of Korea are red
The rivers encarnadine the sea
Redden Kuroshiwo, the Japan Current,
Not like Sargasso with algae
But with the blood of mothers.
Kuroshiwo flows eastward first,
Then fingering the littoral of Alaska
Turns south past Cape Blanco
And lays its burdens
On the wholesome beaches of California.

Kuroshiwo
In other years you brought warmth to our scalloped coast
Deposited banners of kelp
Palm trees, driftwood,
Glass balls curiously netted,
     peaceful commodities of flotsam.
I looked to you, Kuroshiwo,

16

As a bringer of messages from afar
A trafficker in remembrances
A traveler
Mother to seaweed
And the warm womb of plankton and starfish:
All these things you were to me, Kuroshiwo,
And I loved you for them.

But today I see human bodies in the surf
Numerous as jellyfish after a storm
And I hear the sucking whistling roar
As the seas retreat down the sands.
Below me you draw back, Kuroshiwo,
Baring the side-scuttling crabs in their dark pools
Laying open the discreet chambers of cuttlefish
The brown algae flaccid on the rocks
The sea anemones bewildered.

In the distance
Beyond the Farallones
Beyond the last gull
Product of eruption
Of napalm
Of dive-bombers
Of the geology of the insane,
There appears the tidal wave.

Kuroshiwo, angry brother,
What do you hurl at my coast?
What is this wave
Which sends the sandpipers
Screaming through the skies?
Which fills our coves and inlets
And inundates my land?

It is blood, blood, blood,
Blood that breaks over Stinson Beach
Blood that drenches the oaks and redwoods
And stills the astonished hikers
Blood that covers Fort Cronkhite
Covers the gun-emplacements and the cow-pastures
Covers the radio towers on Bolinas Point
Covers the anxious dairymen.

My America, can you not see the wave
Which is so clear before my eyes?
Can you not see the bodies floating in the surf
Numerous as jellyfish after the storm?

We choke on blood.
Surely we shall drown in the blood of our creating.

In this third year of the war
In the light misty rain of early January
I walk gathering mushrooms.
Under the madrones I find a deadly amanita
White-cauled and beautiful, the least piece
Decomposes the pancreas. I see
Amanitas lofty as sequoias
Spread over my land like carpetweed
White
Viscous
Suppurating poisons
Initiating the gestures of death.

Kuroshiwo, angry brother,
Tell me I have not come too late
Tell me what actions will reverse this horror
So that I, an American, may once again know you
As the messenger of warmth and driftwood
And may unobstructed search in your baggage
For those curious netted glass balls.
        —*San Francisco, 1953*

Twentieth Century Argosies

Some think by godlessness the world's betrayed
    And, strapping on celestial parachutes,
Take aim, push off, and, undismayed,
    Drop—into their fishing boots.

Some heed instead *The New York Times*
    Or Mrs. Eddy's *Monitor*,
Walk grimly for the March of Dimes
    And take the kiddies on a tour

Of Disney's latest horror. All fails—
    Eckankar, EST and Tupperware
Can't give us a hint what it entails
    When Clio the Muse lets down her hair.

Jason sets sail from Mamaroneck
    In search of something or other;
A golden fleece transformed to dreck
    Seems hardly worth the bother.

At dawn the bandaged weathervanes
    Illude the Grecian baromancer.
And should Mercator fail there yet remains
    The tight-rope dancer—

Equilibrist who treads a sigh
    Stretched from curb to garbage pail,
His elbows akimbo and one eye
    Cocked on the morning's mail.

Shipwrecked without their compasses,
    The Baedekers are out to tea;
Doctor Spock may have clipped our prepuces
    But he can't do much with history.

There's only the vertical ice-dream man,
    The oath of the necromancer,
The leaf, the sequin, the unforeseen élan—
    There's only the tight-rope dancer.

The Barber of La Paz

He leaned upon the bedroom table,
A sparrow chirping in his vest;
He felt like Joseph in the stable,
Loved and unloved, the pointless guest.

Something or other dimmed his sight.
A tugboat hooted on the shore.
His fingers felt the morning light,
His ivory combs whispered, "Restore."

The sofa gave a little squeak,
The razor cut was clean and deep,
He left her bleeding, as a creek
Might leave a snowbed in its sleep.

He walked along the *malecón*
Bearing a ringlet in each hand;
He felt as if God alone
Had such kingdoms at his command.

He walked his cell on polished feet,
Thankful his shirt had worn so well.
They hanged him in Salvatierra Street—
You ask in vain for Manuel.

Three times he'd curled her hair,
Fourteen years old or thereabout.
No point in calling for him here,
The *peluquero* Manuel is out.

Drinking Song

Travel a road one time only, then
    Give it away.
    Cross a fresh sea
Before breakfast and never drink
From the same tide twice. Think:
Use each road one time only, then
                 Level it out.

Shovel a wave bare-chested, then
    Toss it away.
    Civil you'll be
To ravenous dahlias gorged on ink.
Never wear skates outside the rink.
Dishevel a bed one time only, then
                 Sluice it out.

Level a glass one time only, then
    Drink it all down.
    This Beaujolais
Is better off dead in a wink.
What's undrunk now goes down the sink.
Level your glass one time only, then
                 Toss it out.

Interrogation

where do you come from?
> *the belly of the parenthesis*

who are your relatives?
> *the grandfather of shadows*
> *the dog inside the razorblade*

what is your passport number?
> *three*
> *only three*
> *always three*
> *for a total of three*

nationality?
> *clandestine*

place of residence?
> *at present?*

yes at present
> *the menagerie of yeast*

and proposed?
> *somewhere in the sea*

please state your occupation
> *I buy and repair ripples*

repeat that please
> *I restore straw*

your means of support?
        the keel
        the garlic
        the two-headed wave

what are your plans if accepted?
        to build holes

and promoted?
        holes within holes within holes

Group Portrait

the family is gathered here in this picture
Uncle Ted on the left smoking consonants
Aunt Beth in her mechanical nightgown
father on his motorbike mother getting
refueled the sons and daughters busy
becoming monuments   grandfather the lion
of lounge bars grandmother who took in
the sky on laundry-lines and hung
her money out to dry under heat lamps

they've got style this family
with its epaulettes and sciatica
they're thinkers they make fans
to cool the ants and teach bees
how to pomade their moustaches
originals that's what they are
their faces waxed like apples
their gloves cut off at the knuckles

they study they learn to turn leaves
into lighter fluid they parse sentences
from almanacs they become famous
flying about the moon on mothwings
when they grow old they embroider
sparks and go to Victor Herbert on
Wednesday afternoons trailing innocents
behind them kites on umbilical cords

The Prophet

when he came back from the war
he had a dry cloud on his tongue

he said the ounce is more discreet
than the pound the days

are little baskets of confetti
guilt spreads in the night no one

pays it to grow it just does
the mystery of skin isn't

appreciated he said the pious
bite cats to death god is handing

out sugar in the wrists of hurricanes
the cathedral tower has sunk

in the snow but no one marks
the place where it stood the trees

are all whitehaired now and quartz
crystals grow in our lungs

they didn't listen he's mad
they said and turned over the page

now no one can interpret these chancres
and the dead quail in the streets—

The Hero

he stopped in the first town just
inside the emperor's walls

he saw the foot about to crush
him the gallows they'd built

for dreams he pulled his hat down
low and walked into his fathers

he had second thoughts about swords
they'd been left in the plaza

heirlooms something he'd rather
do without he was built to stand

perpendicular to lightning
but the world was horizontal

his disciples hid in bells
they put on coats of stone

you'll find him in a whisper
glued to the bottom of a trumpet

what he feels about it I don't
know he never told me

it's been left up to the author
to fill in the blanks any

way he can but there's no
way to translate

the apple tree growing
from his forehead

He Didn't Ask Much

it was only the bird in the helmet
he wasn't asking much just

the blue haystack and its rosary
of dew he said we haven't a lot

not even weeds in the brown-bread
not even the first star

over the garden he wanted to see
between the dunghill and the town clock

a city of chimeras he said
the nearer you get to courage

the more leaks there are in the bag
he said tomorrow I'll be back

the day after I'll measure
out the portions

they took him by the neck
when he started to applaud the trees

they twisted it he
let out a squawk as for them

they sit on the courthouse steps
passing judgment

Death of the Race Driver

the crowd surrounded him
he'd been dragged to death
they weren't indifferent
some even made speeches
said the tangle of smoke
from his ruptured ribcage
was prophetic they said
his flesh would be reborn
in the sunflower others
cursed the gods called
him Hector said that was
life no use complaining

I couldn't say all I knew
was that dust drifted
over his face and an old
watch its case smashed
lay on the dirt track oozing
second-hands and that Priam
wept and the children's
broken toys were picked up
and duly photographed

now it's all been filed away
was it a masquerade or
were those swollen eyelids
really opened on something
more dazzling than the
twisted manifold the
mangled wheel spinning
idly in the hot noon?

His Last Words

the cold wind hums its little tune
in the blasted trees the stars

are shimmering fish they flick
their tails and are gone

you can't find their be-
ginning nor their end

this afternoon there's a column
of black ants going ceaselessly

up and down the staircase of leaves
what can you make of the ale-

wives dead on the oily sand?
or the shadows' mouths gaping

for all our manifestoes? I
leave you this amulet and its

mirror-image asleep in the *logos*
it may help you some day

if you stand in the same light
now tear up reputation it's made

of tissue paper and soon enough
they'll replace it with the firing

squad drawn up stiffly in the bleak
unequivocal dawn

Mirror on Horseback

the mirror creates its own mythology
it takes circular journeys not mistresses
it gazes benignly from the walls of inns
and blesses the lips of the wanderer

the philosophic mirror practices yoga
while riding the back of a tiger
it destroys its ancestors
and proclaims the godhead of arson

the debauched mirror sleeps
with its own sisters and echoes
the melodies they chant
in the seashell's nacreous ear

the hungry mirror gathers fragments
of the rainbow with its glass teeth
it devours cathedrals and eyebrows
indifferent to pleas for immortality

the athletic mirror rides bareback
it disdains saddles locking its thighs
about the sea

The Picnic

first lift the ceiling off by its ears
send home the moon it won't be on call
arrange the clouds in asymmetrical pairs
caution the brooks against running uphill

then spread out the cloth of cannabis
with painted eggs at each of the corners
lecture the ants set them to reading this
caveat to carnivorous sojourners

for the sun will be there smoking cheroots
and passing out luminous whirlers
the sea was invited but sent regrets
the trip's too long and her hair's in curlers

bring in the sturgeon and its edible roe
the lamb chop dressed in paper pantaloons
call up the cook who saws water in two
and the manic-depressive with his talking bones

the tipsy magician will utter his tricks
while the lady in suede makes love to the breeze
the guests will all pirouette in their tracks
and the caterers waltz with the birch trees

There's No Use Asking

it's not in the books not in
the documents you won't find
it in any phrase balanced on
edge like a spinning coin

look if you like in your mirror
it won't be there nor under
the shaving mug either
it's only visible
in the face drowned

in the lake or deep in the glacier
grinding the iron mountain you'll
find it where the fog erases the beach
or in the driftwood's insane leer

look, the politician's watch
has stopped an embolism attacks
the Christmas tree its ornaments
glitter and go out the mannequins

have lost their motors and stand
motionless in the empty shop-windows
in the museum of wonders
the woman with the wax knife

stands ready to strike her fatal
blow while Marat naked and pustulent
squirms in his four-legged tub
he is ready to enter the black house

he is already rehearsing the secret
code-words I promised to show you

Splitting

I wanted to leave
I'd been there too long
wandering around in the museum
of goiters
looking for the geometry
of flowers and never
quite finding it

the eggs all wore spats
and had their hair in inverted commas
the professors walked through the studio
with Significant Form on a leash
looking they said for the root canals
of dog violets all that analysis
got to me I said it's time
to float on my back
in the lake of silence

too many curators
not enough curlews
time to go

Dream Sonata

seven mirrors are perched
like crows in a burnt tree

they preen their feathers
and gossip of sunlight

sirens of glass they've led the drop
of blood through a maze of veins

and showed it the erect spine
but it refuses to climb that ladder

it wants to put on a mask of water
and sleep in the well it tugs

at the well-rope and the mirrors
answer like wind chimes

a hand crawls up the wellside
stone by stone its fingers blunt

and palped the nails scratching
out messages when it gets

to the top it will fall back
someone always sends down a mossy

bucket after it but it's no use
the hand is lost the blood too

they remember when they ran wild
over the mirrors and danced

at the banquet of smoke but now
all the hand can do is climb

stone by stone up the wellside
only to fall back

while the drop of blood slowly
coagulates on the ground

Hammer, Nails, Saw

a hammer goes to the river
looking for nails
the fish dart away they're
not illiterate those fish

a saw comes by on the back
of a swan singing:
we must learn to nail the water
we must learn to saw the air
we must learn to undress clouds
there are gods inside waiting
to get out

the bulrushes snicker
the smart fish hide in deep pools
they know a thing or two those fish
they've heard that talk before

this life isn't easy
says the hammer to the saw
I'm just doing the job I was hired to do
says the saw to the speechless river

the river with a rip down its back
not even nails can mend

Silence Please

the alphabet sings
in a drop of blood

the power of verbs
is just a pious memory

take up the mountains
in hands of lace they're

a bargain no one
will give you as much

for your poems don't
say a word just let

the leaves speak for
you the raindrops wag

their tails and the sad
beaches talk with their

fellow atheists the surf
this is the way to ill

ustrate our origins
not with ink and disquiet

but with an almost im
perceptible shiver

Solitaire

all that winter you were gone
the skylarks went on crutches
I woke up every dawn
to crows quarreling in ditches

I'd been there before I knew
that landscape of demented kings
I'd seen the courtiers in blue
masks and idiot posturings

when you're nailed to a scar
you don't care for fine words
the juggler at the bazaar
or the chap who eats swords

the world's deceptive—too many
crafty smiling bones
eyes masquerading in money
and loquacious spoons

so I say goodbye to the foxtrot
and to badminton in the park
I shuffle the deck and deal out
snowflakes in the dark

The Years

one day drives out another the red sun
a hammer the cold stars the heads
of breathing nails

the seed is slaughtered the meadows
turn black from old fires
the singing birds nailed up on rustic crosses
a warning to travelers

the weeks are eaten by swarms of ants
the months open their vegetative maws

malice grows fat simplicity
leans on its snow-shovel hopeless
against each day's tide of paper

the day which presents us with its gifts
of calluses and magnetic warts

I close my eyes and see the manes of lions
entangled in the exhaust pipes
of glittering Porsches

every hour a suicide
buried unshriven in its mailslot

I awake in the night my window open
the shadows of mountains afloat in the air
dripping amethyst and sapphire
from the great field of gravestones
gleaming in the Milky Way

Victim

they told him the time was all wrong
the harvests weren't in no one
had mastered the antler dance or learned
how to talk to the walking waterfall

he said he didn't mind his eyes
had run down the lashes singed
he'd walked a long way the temple
was still far off and the perfect orison
would probably never be heard

so if the arrowhead in his side took fire
he'd share the blame they shouldn't
feel guilty there was too much
of time anyway too many drunken hours
and nobody to roll up the tent-cloth

all right they said and took him by the wrists
and shook the rain out of his hair
one of them nailed him upside down
to the afternoon and the others wrote
his name over the gate in letters of blood

you won't be forgotten they said if that's
any consolation the bees will remember
you'll be a fragrance in their language
and horses will come running
at the gong of your name

The Ladder

the ladder is largely illiterate
and until recent times practiced
parthenogenesis

the ladder does not wear pockets
or nurse its young

accustomed to heights its rungs
are often found
at great altitudes
commonly amidst the detritus
of downspouts or growing
in crevices at the summit
of mansards

the ladder is readily domesticated
but reverts on occasion
to predatory ways
promiscuously devouring
footsteps and birds' eggs

a flight of ladders
loping over the veldt with
awkward though leisurely paces
is a noteworthy sight

shy when alone
a pride of ladders is capable
of a show of bravery
particularly
when protecting its young

the ladder is often entangled
in awnings where it may
by the amateur
be mistaken for the lesser scaffold

the distinctive mottling
however
differs sharply

the throat of the ladder suffers
from parasitic growths but
its only known natural enemy is
the high voltage wire

contrary to tradition ladders
do not commonly
lead to heaven

Ultima Thule Hotel

philodendrons rotting the carpet
the bellman picking his nose

in the lobby elephant ears
in the powder room no pets

no women no guests after ten p.m.
cooking in rooms is forbidden

considerations of health prohibit
random expectoration

the armchairs are spavined
the desk clerk pours corrosive

sublimate in every bathtub
the awnings rot the corridors reek

of gin and garlic the tenants
rattle in their cells like dry beans

in a gourd yet the rooms are all full
reservations won't be honored

book early or don't come at all
this is the end this is Armageddon

in leatherette the party favors
have exploded your number is up

your credit card lies dead
under an egg-stained napkin

Exordium

butter the blade of the axe
pour cream on the necessary knife
teach us, masters, to relax
with the consolations of belief

kind words can often charm
the whip's abrasive lash
and mitigate the harm
the scalpel does to flesh

death by jellied gasoline
is sweeter far with prayer
while vivisection's not obscene
with Bartok on the record player

the general grips the testes
of the guerrilla in his vice
the chaplain assures him the best is
to strive for inner peace

speak courteously as you drive
the spike in the peasant's brain
compassionate sentiments relieve
otherwise traumatic pain

teach us, masters, the prospectus
for the Well-Considered Life
so illusion may protect us
as we raise the knife

An Exorcism

The squid prevail: already
they mount our verandahs
invoices in their tentacles
their breath sweetened with sen-sen
their eyes moist with sympathetic rheum:

they mount with moustaches
they mount with a plethora of cuffs
they mount with prefabricated flowers
patented cures for ambition
and plastic sleep.

The doorstop is broken
barricades are useless
the muezzin dozes in his deserted tower.

Therefore
let me wave before their menacing gloves

> the rose the wand the snowflake
> the whale the wind the breath of spume
> the boot the jonquil the leaf
> the chair the ice the teeth in the leek
> the hammer the wings the stone the plank
> the seed the arrow the coil of joy
> the individual tear.

Lessons in Alchemy

1

The season advances.
Forgotten shoes litter the sandboxes.
Ice floes appear in the Tunnel of Love.
In the bare twigs the ideograms of thrushes
and over my shoulder I see the teeth
of the carnivorous sun.

2

           To wash brick
one employs hydrochloric acid and
asks forgiveness. How else in this century
shield one's self from rotted mortar?

3

The season advances. Our prayers
spank in the wind like a loose sail.
Convolvulus overruns the carburetors:
the chain comes loose from its sprocket
and in the fretful brain
speedometers whir like window blinds.

4

Exchanges will not be honored.
There will be no rebates.
The Kingdom of Heaven is permanently closed
to tourists wearing stilts.

Fugue and Variations

So it's you?
Yes it's me.
I thought so.
You did?
Yes I did.
Did what?
Thought so.

Heliotrope. Patchouli.
Delineations of wet nooses.
The door risen from the dead; the throat
which has choked on lace.

It's a matter fabricating the seething feet.
It's a question of the gold-rimmed warts.
Of authenticating the least follicles.

This lamp has been—
Reserved?
Yes, reserved.
Now?
Or presently.
By whom?
Does it matter?
By whose order?
Does it matter?

Does it matter?

Dusk comes over the horizon like a cowboy.
In the vestibules of soap darkness is king.
The Choctaw nations are tipped into the sea,
while each April another government
evaporates at the Finland station.

You shrugged?
Unavoidably.
Noncommittally?
Unavoidably. The fact is—

The fact is there are terrorists in the player piano.
They have exploded our dentures.
They openly boast of chromatic fantasies.

Chopin appears in the mahogany frame.
Berlioz inaugurates the Stadt-Theater;
he is giddy from the long sea voyage.
The curtain has opened on the insect comedy:
the flies, saturated in musk,
sing in tender silver voices heavy with torn vodka:
Voi sapete, quel che fa.

Now everything bursts into light—
the scabbard the spool the swollen flag
the stone guest on the phosphorescent stair.
It is not the destruction of the dream but the dream itself.
It is not the epoch of Saturn but the slaughter of smoke.
The key turns twenty times.
The walls will not open.
The walls will never open.

I hold out my hand to incoherence.

Villa Thermidor

He sits in a deckchair reading Colette
and fanning himself with a pair
of shoelaces. In the rose garden

giant snails copulate in rhythms
undulant and infinitely beguiling.
His ancestors lie snoozing

in the family urns. Fog has lately
attacked the poinsettias. On the pier
by the lake there are adenoidal

swellings—the boathouse no doubt
is ill. Umbrellas are descried
gliding above the local peaks.

Undulant and infinitely beguiling.
Next year, says the *Oakland Tribune*,
snowshoes may be taxed

for their illicit oils. Stingrays
flap in the sand like wounded moths.
Infinite and undulant.

Cocktails are served from five
to seven at the bottom of the pool.

Directions

I am in the forest looking for
fragments of speech, the betrayed
holy words which cannot utter themselves.
I have been lost for days.
There are many moons; the time
is at the crossroads of autumn.
In my mouth are burnt poppyseeds,
at my elbow December's shadow.

I ask for directions; you answer:
"Somewhere, in some house far from here,
a man is weaving the rope in which
this day shall be hanged."

The Potter's Hand

The wall of yellow brick, the kiln,
dripped glazes, a row of empty wheels,
the niche which holds the magic
lembick (from which, I'm taught,
all fogs, miasmas, melancholy rise).

Two men in leather aprons
take my coat; one bears
a rod of glass rubbed
till it glows; the other,
a curved machete.

They nod to me.
The stove itself is porcelain,
a man's height, pierced
with a dozen vents.
Its door swings open.

The Lady waits within,
seated in obedient flames.
I sprinkle dust from left
to right, mutter some formula.
Silence perhaps is best.
In a moment now she'll
see me, rise, and
brushing fire aside,
offer me my appointed seat
in that great chamber.

All That I Should Have Seen

To speak simply is the straitest art
demanding the most of its practitioners;
speech stripped to its essential part,
chaste and unarabesqued.

But no sooner is this maxim written out
than rococo and rebel eye and ear
reject what's straitly clear:

for is what seems mere ornament
perhaps in its own self the sacrament
of speech? Mariposa tulips,
moth wings, that slanting rain—
rare details, rare beauties—
gestures overlooked, greenveinéd stones
I should have stooped for but ignored
intent as I was on bare bones.

Quits

So that this spring we will be quits
let me declare my indebtedness,
for the streams now are full again
and the first dog violet's on the path.

I thank you because you instructed me
(you who could not look on loveliness
without tears) in beauty's pain
and were yourself such a vase of it
as no spring cataract will fill again.

The yellow pollen comes off on my hands
as I brush the alder catkins.
I think of you.

The trillium and adder's tongue
spring from the moss
too sharp and sudden for philosophy.
I give you thanks.

The new buds of azaleas
grow to birds in flight.
Goodbye.
I would be quit of you.

Mission Dolores, Its Squadrons
of the Dead

Blackberries rise through
this city, veils of grass
drop over its stone teeth.

The pious enter preceded
by gifts, their tears
fall inward and dissolve.

O thickets of granite ships
sailing across the earth,
your funnels gray as rain,

your lookouts standing erect
in crowsnests of bone!
The sun drops. The angels

spread their wings, on their
stone feathers the tracks
of snails with satin lips.

I watch the sunlight decay
and the carved elegies
bleed into that dark becoming.

Off Season

In the sea, kelp;
in the sand, the roots
of a broken umbrella.

A tern:
oil slick:

the surf stinks
of dying jellyfish.

Single
wooden
sandal.

Under the boardwalk
last year's newsprint
weddings
and wars
in the forgiving mold.

Rain:
the long
walk home.

The Years

Crossing the old trestle I stare between
the ties at the scarred face of the river.

A storm is coming up from the south,
the fir trees stir in expectation.

A boy kneels among the rushes
his hands cupped in the house of trout.

How familiar this bridge is: there's
a broken flume which drips water,

a sawmill on the plank road beyond,
the fragrance of new bracken

and from my wet hands the sunlight spills
like an unending stream of fish.

The Swim

Gravel
a broken seawall
the red buoy
barnacles adrift
on a thatch
of water Dredges
piers & pilings
arthritic with shells
the odor of oil
varnished waves
with fingers of
kelp Caws Cries
& Silences &
over all the
glittering shell
of heaven

A whiskered
seal rises
beside me
like a drowned
prophet

The Rehearsal

Under the frost, new grass;
in the sky small clouds
round as daisies. Spring
unfolds: inside her soft corolla
bees hum. The sky,
stiff as iron, supports
the gold wings of finches.

I walk past the rotting ciderpress.
Grouse explode in the air about me.
The voice of the wind issues
from a wooden throat
with its old moanings
and hairy pressures.

Now it will all begin again.

Fields near Pendleton

their crests of wild flax
their troughs filled with shadow
the long groundswells the wind makes
under a froth of grain.

A combine comes over the horizon
full-rigged, leaning into a gale of chaff.
A flock of pilgrim geese undulates
in the cloudless sky.

Waiting for some message I sit
in the shade of an old oak
but the birds have gone
and I hear the creaking only
of that ghostly immense ship
which harvests the waves.

A Hot Day with Little Result

The fish have grown torpid.
They avoid me.
I rest in the shade of a covered bridge—
its planks thunder beneath the logging trucks.

The stream breathes softly
in the roots of the cottonwoods,
it sends out secret messages of dust
to the suave rushes.

A farmer on a red tractor
spreads corduroy on the hill opposite me.
The meadow-rue is in bloom.
There is no use fishing.

I sit in the shade and think
of that great tortoise who carries
the Bay of Naples on his back.

Alarm

Fire! Fire! I hear
at the edge of my dream.
The horses whinny.
The dry ferns curl into flame.
The animals paw the earth.
I run.

Yes, always I run:
backward through old fevers
leaving these heavy years
and meaningless bridges.
Vaulting the stile
I shout, fire! fire!
in the field of the red bull.

Home Town

My uncle sets me adrift
in a box on a pine plank.

I voyage to the land
of eagles where I
marry and grow firm.

In my suit of feathers
I fly to the Township
of Complacency
where my uncle fishes.
I seize him by the hair.
Vengeance, I say.
Aieee! my uncle cries.
His wife runs from the house,
grabs him by the ankle.

With my new wings
I pull them both aloft.
My cousin comes from
the schoolhouse, catches
the hem of her mother's dress.
Vengeance, I say.
Come down, she answers.

One by one all the people
of that wretched town
run out of their houses.
They grab each other
by ankles, knees, trousers,
shawls, dresses, fish-lines,
toes and members.

Their weight is nothing
against the strength
of my eagle's wings.
I carry them, a great chain,
out over the Bay
of Forgetfulness
and let go.

(after a Tlingit Indian myth)

The Cormorant

Past Fort Point we came in running,
the fishermen clustered on the black rocks
and the air full of improbabilities.

Running with the wind, a beam wind,
fair all the way, the air
speaking the sails, the sky full

of paper wings, your eyes afire
with wonder. But halfway in you cried out
and I turned and saw the sick cormorant.

Drifting on slack tide it came past,
flotsam, what life left paid out
in barely keeping afloat;

oiled down, that veteran of nautical
heaven fell here to die; deep diver,
that far seer, surveyor of mistrals,

knowing on spring's fairest day
what it is to die; come
from the myriamorphic kiss of winds

to drown in the oil slick spread
by some tanker from Martinez
or Crockett or Richmond.
                        Helpless,
it drifted by.
             The fog rolls under
the bridge. Some little while we float
then sink in seas of chemistry.

The Act

Bareback, she balances on a wisp
of steam. I hear her magnetic voice,

I see her eyes which are thistles,
the creased poppy of her sex.

Her whip cracks. I sing my campaigns
of grace, my legends of sawdust,

recounting the loves which flew
from cisterns of rust, my meetings

with masks and dragonflies, forays
into those gardens under the sea.

The voice of the phonograph dies
on the dying air. My histories

collapse like fans. I see them now
for what they are—mists, maggots,

odd corners of old trials
that ended in fog. The whip cracks.

The children's hour is over. Again
I'll leap through that paper hoop.

Records

Another
Russian
has returned
after
2,000,000
miles
in orbit.

Today I sat
motionless
for
28
minutes
while a
butterfly
folded its
trembling
wings
and rested
on my knee.

FROM PIONEERS OF MODERN POETRY (1967) AND LOSERS WEEPERS: AN ANTHOLOGY OF FOUND POEMS (1969)

These found poems operate on one simple principle: they must have been discovered somewhere amidst the vast sub- or non-literature which surrounds us all. In some instances I may have cut up and rearranged a found object to suit my own tastes, but in no case has original material been added. The interest which so many accomplished poets have shown in the Found Poem demonstrates, I think, its importance to us as a source of wonder, laughter, and enlightenment.

—George Hitchcock, from *Losers Weepers*

Mark Out the Rocking Horse
(with Robert Peters)

1. Members of a Set

Say:

Look at the set of houses.
Draw a ring around one house...

Look at the set of seesaws.
Make an X on one seesaw...

Look at the set of sailors.
Draw a ring around two sailors...

Draw a ring around two wheelbarrows...
Draw a ring around one sail.

Look at the set of rocking horses
Mark out all but one...

2. Counting to Ten

How many grownups
are at the party?

How many horns are there?

Discuss the sets that have
two members:
two children without party hats
two X's on the score pad

Discuss the sets that have
three members
three plants three darts

Have the child count to ten
Tracing
the numerals on the banners

3. *Distinguishing*

Which one
is the hat with
the feather?

Cake with candle?
False face
with beard?
Butter-
fly with spots?
Last
jump
rope?

(from *Discovering Number Concepts*, a practice work-
book for the pre-school child, 1966)

Distinguishing Ru from Chu

Give the sounds of the curved mated Phonographs.
Give the sounds of the straight mated Phonographs.
Name the six vertical Phonographs.

What caution should be observed in writing Lu, Ur, Wu
    and Yu?
What are the two ways of writing Hu?
How may Ru be distinguished from Chu when alone?

How is Iss joined to a curve?
How is Iss joined to a straight stroke?
What rules apply to Sez, Steh and Ster?

What is the effect of lengthening Emp?
What is the effect of lengthening Ung?
What is the effect of halving a stroke?

When should the Eshun curl be used?
What should you be slow to adopt, and why?
How may a vowel be written when alone?

How long should the ticks be made?
After what stroke is Ul always used?
What are the small final hooks?

(poem assembled from the review questions in *Barnes
Shorthand Lessons*, 1885)

The Call of the Eastern Quail

What is the hewie chirp?
How written by note?
    What is triple-tonguing?
    The reverse chirp? How expressed?
What are the quittas?

Define the whit-cha.
Define the e-chew.
What is the chut-ee?
How made? How expressed?

Define the ascending and descending yodels,
    dipped yodels and quivers.
What are the two liquid bird figures?

What is the lup-ee?
What is the e-lup?
How made? How expressed?
What is the call of the Eastern Quail?
What is the call of the Western Quail?

With tongue and teeth whistlers
    what can be substituted for
    the yodel, lup, hedala and cudalee?

What is the wave?
On what pulsation do we stop?

(from the examination questions in Agnes Woodward's
Whistling as an Art, 1923)

Standing Around

Painful Heel is found
Among persons who do
Constant standing.

It is frequently
Known as Police-
Man's Heel.

Painful Great Toe,
also known as flexus,
Hallus Rigidus and

Hallus Dolorosus,
Is attended with great
Pain in the first

Metatarso-
Phalangeal Joint.

Morton's Toe begins
With burning, tenderness
And swelling through the Dorsum;

Weak ankles, loss of balance
And elongated foot
Are also found.

Onychauxis is hyper-
Trophy in which the toenail
Is overgrown.

Vascular corns are very painful.
Hallux Varus, also known as
Pigeon Toe,

Is of little importance.

(from *The Human Foot*, by Dr. W.G. Scholl)

What to Say to the Pasha
(being a dramatic monologue in twelve parts)

1

Shall I assist you to alight?
Procure for me a little milk and honey
Pitch my tent and spread out my carpet
The wind is keen today
We may have a storm tonight
It lightens
It thunders

The air is very temperate
The trees are beginning to be covered with leaves
Autumn is the season for fruit
The sky begins to get cloudy
The nights are short and the days are long
The snow is fast melting from the ground
The enemy has advanced as far as Kafr-dawar
Of what advantage will this be to me?

2

Whose?
Not yet
We want
I will give you
Wait patiently
Leave it alone
Go away
Why are you here?

3

In which direction is the wind?
It is an easterly wind
It is a westerly wind
It is a northerly wind
It is a southerly wind
I have been very much occupied

4

How many men has the Pasha?

5

Is the proof of this news strong?
They are hidden behind the mound
They are advancing from the rear
Be quiet
Don't make a noise
It seems that the enemy is restless

6

Do not the mosquitoes trouble you?

7

Undo it
Tie it up
Turn it over
I hope you are better
Is it not so?

8

What is your name?
Who are you?
I am a Bedouin
We are Bedouins
What are you doing here?
We have come to fight and to loot

I am anxious to return to the camp

9

It is enough
How far is it from this place?
Do me the favour
Do not forget
How do you do?

Mind your business
It is painful
This is painful

10
Bring in the rebels
Tie their hands and feet
You have done it well
Joseph, bring in the dinner
Will you please sit next to the lady?

11
I am wounded
  I am shot

  Shot in my arm
  Shot in my leg
  Shot in my foot
  Shot in my chest
  Shot in my head

  Bind up my wound
  Give me something to drink, for
  I am thirsty

12
Have pity on me
Spare my life

I surrender myself

(poem assembled from the Rev. Anton Tien's *Egyptian, Syrian and North African Hand-book, A Simple Phrasebook in English and Arabic for the Use of the Armed Forces and Civilians*, exact provenance unknown but obviously early Kiplingesque)

The One Whose Reproach I Cannot Evade

She sits in her glass garden
and awaits the guests—
The sailor with the blue tangerines,
the fish clothed in languages,
the dolphin with a revolver in its teeth.

Dusk enters from stage left:
its voice falls like dew on the arbor.
Tiny bells
sway in the catalpa tree.

What is it she hopes to catch in her net
of love? Petals? Conch shells?
The night moth? She does not speak.
Tonight, I tell her, no one comes;
you wait in vain.
              Yet at eight precisely
the moon opens its theatric doors,
an arm rises from the fountain,
the music box, face down
on her tabouret, swells and bursts
its cover—a tinkling flood of
rice moves over the table.

She smiles at me, false believer,
smiles and goes in, leaving
the garden empty and my thighs
half-eaten by the raging twilight.

Serenade

What
         do you want   You
whistle at me from your perfumed window

                         I bring you a gift of flax
                         I bring you a gift of steam
            You translate them into sleep

I go from door to key to door and then back again
apparently we are caught in ice you and I like
the spirits of Indians

Come
            the streets are full of poultices
            the streams flow with rivets
            I traverse bridges which end in fire

            What
                         do you want of me
Come
            I bring woven moons
            You answer me with dust and lemon peels

Yet today you smile and I put down again this pack
full of ribbons and gold teeth

Come
            in the century of my birth I
            hurl myself from parapets of grace
            spiked plants grow from my ribs
            I leave at dusk for Bokhara

What
          is your Christian name   Why
          do I see you in the knees of stairways

Have patience
          some muezzin huge as smoke
          calls me into your prayers

The Death of Prophecy

The moon passes its zenith
its secrets guarded by devout
archers; nostrils ablaze,
the planets spin in silver
polyhedrons.

    The glaciers have melted.
    The sundials have fallen.
    The genitals of insects
    are imprinted in stone.

O mountain with eyes of green malachite,
the moon is enmeshed in the folds of your breasts!

    The rockets sputter and go out.
    The egret stands alone in the sedgy stream.
    In its cave of water
    the sacred snake hisses and moans.

Who shall distinguish the sun
from the gold bee of artifice?

The United States Prepare for the Permanent Revolution

The green shingles of rest homes unfold revealing
    innumerable blonde attics each with a pair
    of pining eyes and an old phonograph
    playing *Nights in a Spanish Garden;*
Women's handbags open their beaded mouths and utter
    bulletins of rouge and used cleaning tissue;
Various ambiguities take flight from the telephone wires
    and are descried flying southward
    over Cairo, Illinois;
Gospel singers assemble beneath the veiled balconies
    which jut from decayed sopranos;
Dark mornings fall over Seattle.

Terrorists are seen skulking in the public latrines,
    their feet wrapped in soggy vermicelli;
Parking meters rise to heaven chanting the praises
    of unnatural leisure;
tied to a rope of frozen milk a blind man leaps
    from the parapet of Equitable Trust and
    parachutes to safety his descendants hidden
    in the crannies of his venerable beard;
Mauve fungoids scraped from the undersides of pool
    tables are
    traded for Green Stamps in the Farmers' Market;
Viscosity is proclaimed the prime law of the Universe.

Lighted cigars fall like meteors on a deserted football field
    in Pierre, South Dakota—their entrails are
    officially examined for signs of cancer;
Canvas doorways open in the sails of fishing smacks
    and emit a sour wind;
Groves of carefully marcelled kelp sprout from the armpits
    of the Statue of Liberty;

Flaming poems are inscribed on the groins of mysterious
    black women in straw capes whose thighs
    smell of creosote;
A puma is discovered cowering on the shelves of
    a suburban lending library—in the floodlights
    his tears turn to opals.

A railway flare burns in the bowels of a cuttlefish
    trapped at Sarasota, Florida;
Cases of pomade opened at Nogales for inspection
    are found to contain smoked ice;
A pair of Anglo-Saxon hips is placed on display at
    the Museum of Modern Art.

Dry boards lie at the edge of the road:
Centipedes enter their knotty throats.

What is the recommendation?
Deliberate excision of proud flesh.

        A woman stops me in the corridor.
        Her tongue has been replaced by
        a single mute camellia.

The Oxidizing Illness

Fever sits on my forehead.
I break the bindings of streets
and embark upon aimless crusades.
The sidewalks disgorge their
processions of drunken boots;
on the stained walls I see
the degenerate faces of statesmen
and the thwarted loins
of mysterious polymaths.

Bandaged women accost me;
I flee the terrible cavalry of their
eyelashes. Guides in gauze masks
lead me into mint-smelling quarries.
Waters hiss and fall.
The knives congregate.
My tongue becomes liquid glass.

I run through the breath of the juggler
I run past the left hand of ferro-concrete
past the garden of leather wheels
through the tensile strength of crystals
to the green asp which coils in the snow.

Awakened, I ascend ladders of thanksgiving.
I enter the sunlight through the gills of leaves.
My body, whirling in a nest of sutures,
burns in the bright day.

Recovering from Despondency

The long war is over, the bullets
go to bed with their nurses, the chorus
of stubborn chancres is silent at last.

Clouds open their windows to breathe again.
Alone on the sidewalk, I write my name in ice cream
and listen for the overdue trellises.

The bronze songs of the leaves
float over the lawns as
gently as shadows.

Women pass from door to door carrying
covered wicker hampers; the attar
of peace drips from their hands.

My friends, miraculous survivors,
stand with their feet in ruined cellars,
and reflected in their compassionate eyes
I see the torches of distant weddings.

Messages

In the distance the violet bay;
above my head various sopranos
floating in spasms of miraculous
sunlight.
     There are fires on the sea
and wandering tongues in the meadow.
The telephone wires whisper together.
The white breath of the apple trees
hovers in a net of twigs.

I walk alone through the wet fields
carrying an aging life. The swallows,
felicitous surgeons, present me
with their airy sutures. I shall lean
into the calligraphy of new wheat.

Lying Now in the New Grass

the wind falls the fields
fold in upon each other
like wings on a sleeping
insect. The house heavy
with the day's sweat sighs
beneath the hand of dusk.

All things sleep:
lilac iris bracken
windmill & anvil
the stones which dream
of moss the cold stars
in endless heaven.

Now may all rutting lovers
under this lace of leaves
lie down in comfort.
Let them not hear the dew form
over the pastures nor foresee
its sharp hooves in the loam.
May the plow of night
pass over them.

Afternoon in the Canyon

The river sings in its alcoves of stone.
I cross its milky water on an old log—
beneath me waterskaters
dance in the mesh of roots.
Tatters of spume cling
to the bare twigs of willows.

The wind goes down.
Bluejays scream in the pines.
The drunken sun enters a dark mountainside,
its hair full of butterflies.
Old men gutting trout
huddle about a smokey fire.

I must fill my pockets with bright stones.

Annus Mirabilis

Night rises like a liquid
in my window. A woman
lies moaning somewhere
in the buckthorn.

Children run through the streets
with torches of Indian tobacco:
take care! they shout,
the sick are abroad!

Look!
The stars turn smokey
in the thighs of the god.
The century burns
with a slow fever.

The Noose of Apathy

I saw the executioner and in his hands he bore
the noose of apathy to tighten at my throat.
Always had I imagined him otherwise
and had not thought in this guise
to see him come,
a sober and fastidious pedant
proffering tedium.

Now when I think of death I know its modes—
the lasso in the teacup, the angel
driven from the door;
and most of all that deadly daily
itching sore
which corrodes and corrodes.

May All Earth Be Clothed in Light

Morning spreads over
the beaches like lava;
the waves lie still, they
glitter with pieces of light.

I stand at the window
& watch a heron on one leg,
its plumage white in the green banks
of mint. Behind me
smoke rises from its nest
of bricks, the brass clock
on the kitchen shelf
judges & spares.

Slowly the bird
opens its dazzling wings.
I am filled with joy.
The fields are awake!
The fields with their hidden lizards
& fire of new iris.

Three Portraits

1. The Peddler

In the *zócalo*
a one-eyed salesman
offers me a gourd
wrinkled
dried
with the face of God
painted on it
in cochineal & indigo

God is dead,
I tell him.

You are right,
he answers,
but it is only one peso.

I shake the gourd;
the seeds rattle
like thoughts in a dry brain.

O unfortunate country!

2. *An Old Man*

An old man with
tears on his cheeks
spoke to me in the park.
"Where can I buy shingles?"
is what I thought he said.

But I must have been
mistaken
because
his teeth were gone
his green eyes homeless
and his hands
cupped about some tiny animal—
a moth, perhaps.

3. *Student*

In her mind
peach blossoms
and the Villa
Farnese
on her breast
the deuce of diamonds
and firm/oh firm
in her white hand
the Palo Alto bus schedule.

The Lake

Waternymph . dragonfly
indescribable fisher of the secret places
relieve me of all ambiguities
cleanse me . silent onlooker
of reluctance.

    Relieve me of that 2-headed lion which resides
                        under the spleen;
    Unburden me of the waiter bearing the icetray
    of the locked room . the overdue train
    and all scents & memories of leather.

Runnelled   muddied   bespattered lake
take me unhesitant in your avenues
let me set fire to the chimneys of lilies,
entangle me in your slippery gutters of trout
the boudoirs of watersnails . the alleys of pike.

    Lake which among the reeds sings endlessly
    lend me your sedge voice
    and permit me with your wet teeth
    to devour the marsh-marigolds.

And you . old witness . comrade-in-arms
who does not forget, will you sing with me
among the rushes?
Dragonfly . waternymph
clandestine fisher of the secret places?

Figures in a Ruined Ballroom

The chandeliers hemorrhage, Tritons
weep for the plaster dolphins, the pheasant
in its glass bell feeds on candle droppings:

apothecaries cannot heal the wax dogs,
sutures will no longer save Apollo
nor violins awake the stuffed ospreys.

Roses in this carpet grow from a soil
of forgotten shoelaces and those eyes
which gleamed at cotillions now jostle

the glands of mendicants. Dust is king.
Neptune burns in the sea, on a sepia cliff
Aphrodite sits, plaiting a braid of tears.

These statues turn by concealed levers:
their hinges fold in on mortality.

SHORT STORIES

❦ THE STONEMASON'S DAUGHTERS

*a*t Bandon on the Oregon coast there is or was a cave or gallery or grotto which runs ninety feet beneath the sea and from which the surf can be heard beating against the basalt ramparts above. On certain days, said Busoni's nephew in jest, those attuned to it could hear the chant of mermaids bemoaning their lost Atlantis, and on stormy nights the intemperate sea growled to break in so that all inside lay under its constant threat. Yet despite that menace, in the room with the gold and green and aquamarine of a thousand inverted bottles and the nacre and scarlet of conch and oyster and scallop shells set in mortar, there were rough benches and a table and—on the landward wall—a painting of Malaga as it must have seemed to the departing Moors. Don't forget to put in, said Thornton Gale, the wineskins on the wall. He had an eye for detail.

All this splendid digging with its stone architraves and trove of antique bottles and majolica shards was the work single-handed—well, almost single-handed for Carlos and I were there too, as you shall see—of the Catalan Luís Canseco, Bandon's stonemason, called in the village Louie the Mex or Crazy Louie or sometimes after his patronym Thirsty-Dog, but to me always and thus henceforth Maestro Luís with the accent on the final syllable. When he began it I don't know but he was already at least fifty when Thornton Gale and I came to Bandon and his two daughters were just finishing high school and Carlos away in the army, so he must have been at it a long time. It's forty years later now and he's gone—certainly the way he wanted to, into the sea—and I think the mortar and tile and bits of bottle must have gone on nearly to the end, for Maestro Luís might lose his sight but I can't imagine he would ever lose his faith—

—Or run out of liquor. That, of course, is the voice of Busoni's nephew, mocker and skeptic. He had never been in the caves, indeed was one of those whom Maestro Luís went to great pains to keep out—a Captain of the Infidels, he called him in his kindlier moods—but he knew everything and everybody. I think his febrility of soul sprang from the fact, and it was an uncontestable fact, that he was the nephew of a very great man although today remembered if at all for his piano arrangements of what old Bach had written for the church organ. At any rate, *that* Busoni was his uncle and the consanguinity had colored, and perhaps poisoned, his life forever after. A man with six fingers on his right hand, Maestro Luís said. But this is in the future, I only learned it after Hewett West had virtually given me Bandon. At this time Busoni's nephew was our patron, he had taken us in when Thornton Gale and I came out of the mountains back of Gold Beach, sheltered us, fed us and introduced us to everyone in Bandon he thought we should know. I was seventeen, Thornton a year or two older, sun-tanned and boisterous. It turned out he had other interests in us as well but at the time that hadn't entered our minds. We ate his food, drank his wine, and listened to him play Bach partitas on his gilt cherrywood harpsi-chord in his uncle's transpositions. He was our friend and I feel a twinge even now for the jokes we made at his expense.

—You got to hold blade up and down. Straight. And dig fast before he get away. So. That is Carlos speaking, the first day we met, clamming, of course, and complete duffers at it. Carlos was still in uniform with sergeant's stripes and service ribbons and though he was no older than Thornton he seemed perched on an eminence of worldly wisdom, immensely attractive. And sinister. Pachuco, said Thornton under his breath and that trisyllable evoked a world of slicked-down hair, switch-blade knives and motorized menace. He was friendly enough but defi-nitely not the sort you took home for tennis on the family court in sub-urban Portland. Still, his advice was good, we *did* catch more clams almost immediately, and Thornton and he entered that afternoon upon a wary alliance that was to lead us to Maestro Luís and all that makes up the heart of my story.

But what drew Carlos to us, a pair of lubberly gringo boys who wore their hats Digger style but kept Keats and J.K. Huysmans in their rucksacks? Don't show him your gold nugget, Busoni's nephew warned us, he can throw a knife, but it was too late for that, the nugget had already been Thornton's first ploy in the war over the turf of man-hood—Carlos' service bars versus our nugget, tiny but authentically discovered while panning along the Rogue River. —Man, he is leetle! (Carlos again.) Hold your breath or you blow him away. But I could see he was impressed all the same. Not by the nugget of course, for as I was to learn, Carlos never valued *things*, but by what he saw inside it or superimposed upon it. Semi-literate as he was, Carlos had a truly metaphysical mind; when he looked at you, you knew he saw consequences and that always made one shiver a bit. Carlos is a soldier in the Lord's army, Maestro Luís was fond of saying, and then after a drink from the wineskin he added, but not a big one.

Carlos and I—Carlos and Thornton and I: I see the three of us digging side by side, not for clams now but to extend the Lateral Gallery, deep underground, pouring with sweat, the sea omnipresent beyond the thin rock walls, first Carlos then I with the steel digging-bar cutting into the sandstone, Thornton behind us with the broad shovel we used to load the little car which the two girls, hauling on the frayed manila rope, dragged up the long incline to the surface.

—Yo ho ho and a bottle of rum, sang Carmelita.

—Fifteen men—cried Laura.

—On a dead man's chest—yelled Carmelita.

—Drink and the devil had done for the rest, sang Laura and Carmelita together, with a lusty tug on the rope.

Two cartloads of rubble and sandstone in an evening, no more. Maestro Luís was not in a hurry; to work too fast is to offer an insult to the stone, he said. Besides two cartloads were all he could count on the tide to carry off each night, for when we had the rubble aboveground that was only half the job—then we had to lay out the twin tracks of planking from Canseco's stoneyard out to the cliff's edge and maneuver the ungainly cart down to the dumping spot. Beneath ground we had the luxury of lamps but once we were out under the canopy of night there could be no lights to reveal our work to the neighbors. Bandon must sleep, Bandon must not know of the secret digging in her entrails. By morning the absolving sea would wash away our detritus, the planks would be piled again amidst the mason's scaffolding, a wreath of smoke would ascend peacefully from Crazy Louie's tile-kiln, and there would be no trace remaining of the night's secret labors. That was the way he wanted it.

Do I seem to be boasting of my share in the grottoes? I don't mean to. Actually, the part we played that summer was not an important one; others might have, and no doubt in preceding years did as much. And for the finished work—the mortaring, the setting of arch and spandrel, the tiles, bottles and shards of pottery—all that was done privately by Maestro Luís and his daughters. Thornton and Carlos and I were not even permitted to watch that work. —Later, when the leaves fall, he told us with a smile. But later, when the leaves *did* fall, we were gone, all three—Carlos, his leave up, went back to Fort Lewis, Thornton took a job on the Klamath Falls newspaper, and I—well, my father drove down the Coast to pick me up and take me back to Portland where I was to start pre-medical schooling. My father was shown the nugget that didn't visibly impress him and was introduced to Busoni's nephew—His Eminence, Thornton had taken to calling him—who did. We said nothing at all about Maestro Luís but secretly swore, all three of us, to meet again in Bandon the next summer. Those were golden days.

We kept the promise, or at least two of us did, for from the moment of his arrival I could see that something had changed with Thornton. For two years he had been my mentor, we had read Plato together, drank, argued and swore over Baudelaire and Rimbaud. But now he had encountered a real murderer—a deranged sheepman who had killed his boss and tried to dispose of the body by burning it in a vat of sheep-dip; Thornton had covered the trial for his paper—and he claimed it had shown him the cruel face of reality. I laughed at him and said that no one could live more than three weeks in Klamath Falls without succumbing to the general idiocy. He had to admit that but kept on talking of money and blood, blood and money, as if they were all that truly mattered and he began to keep away from Master Luís and his projects. I didn't reproach him—we had long ago agreed on the odiousness of moral judgments—but I could sense that we were drifting apart and that it was only a matter of time until we would pass each other with indifference. But in the intricate ordering of the universe every weight has its counterweight; the loss of Thornton's affection freed me to be drawn by other magnets—first to Carlos and the Master and then, later on, to the stonemason's daughters.

First, Carlos: during the inaugural summer of our friendship we had been puzzled by his relationship to Maestro Luís. Busoni's nephew said, clearly, he was the old man's bastard; but now as I came to know him better, Carlos told me his own story: Maestro Luís was that and nothing more—his master. They were actually of two continents although a single tongue. Carlos was Mexican, from Oaxaca where at six he had been a shoeshine boy, at eight an apprentice thief and at ten a jailbird, so swiftly do careers ripen in the tropics. —Then I think hard, he told me. This path it lead to a throat cut in the *barranca*. So I take another turning. On that turning he apprenticed himself to a tile setter where he demonstrated his talent, sought further instruction, and emigrated to the United States with the address of Luís Canseco pinned inside his sweater. Thus he came to wet windy Bandon in a November so miserable that he nearly died of pneumonia.... But wait a minute— Maestro Luís, why and by whom was he known in Oaxaca?

—Maestro Luís, he is known *todo el mundo.*

—For what?

—*Las cuevas.*

—And yet no one here knows they even exist.

Carlos shrugged. It was a gesture of resignation in the face of that impenetrable stupidity he had to recognize as the hallmark of the blind, non-metaphysical *norteamericano* world; it said at once everything and nothing at all. If Northamerica chose to ignore its masters and saints that was none of Carlos' responsibility. Still, he came to be proud of the army discharge and attendant citizenship Northamerica gave him.

—Now I can work daylight, he said with a laugh. He lived with his Master, carried hod for him on bricklaying jobs, toiled in his grotto at night, drank from his wineskin and escorted his daughters to the heavily chaperoned dances at Bandon High.

But there is Thornton again, pale and shaken as I have never seen him.

—You've got to help me cope. It's getting to be more than I can handle. We were walking on the stone jetty that shielded the fishing boats and a stiff wind blew the words back in our teeth. In weather like this we were grateful for our Down-Easter coats and knit watch-caps.

—He says he loves me.

—Loves you? Who?

—His Eminence, of course. He's threatened to kill himself if I don't....

I was stupefied; this was all new to me.

—Love you? You mean...?

—Yes. That's what I damn well mean! Thornton exploded. Rimbaud and Verlaine, Willie Shakes and Mister W. H., Michelangelo and the whole of Cupid's circus! That's what I mean, and what the eminent composer's nephew means I leave to your imagination. Grade A buggery, I should say. But what do I do about it? I'm into him for eighty dollars worth of piano lessons, he's my host, and my parents think he's the second coming of Ludwig J. C. van Beethoven. It's a godawful mess. How do I get out of it?

I suggested that he could either smash His Eminence in the teeth—

—They're false. He'd have a heart attack.

or resign himself to a life as an Imperial courtesan in the style of Antinous and Tiberius.

—God knows I've thought of it, Thornton laughed, it would solve a lot of my problems. He shied an angry rock into the curled-back waves. But, aesthetically speaking, he just isn't my dish of tea. And with

Thornton the aesthetic judgment was always the final one from which there was no appeal. So he went back to Klamath Falls and lives there still. Six months ago, when I set out to get the testimony of all the survivors who had known Maestro Luís and his caves I called on him there. He had grown very stout, married a Dutch wife, and owned seven hundred acres of reclaimed lake-bottom that had brought him a Mercedes-Benz and an authentic Archipenko bronze. I suppose he was the most genuinely cultured man in Klamath Falls but I came away from our interview rather more saddened than enlightened. Strive only for glory when you are young, Maestro Luís said, then in old age you will have the young on your side. That hadn't happened to Thornton.

In retrospect (infallibly wisest of the spects) what I feel most is how cruel we were to Busoni's nephew, the only one of us who loved and suffered for his love. We should have rejoiced that beneath that facade of witty indifference there was a heart after all; instead, we only laughed at his crippled passion. And I often think that if Busoni's nephew had really been Tiberius and able to command his Antinous it might have saved Thornton Gale in the long run. Thornton needed to be shipwrecked and instead he was wafted ashore at Klamath Falls where the only trauma are those of murdered shepherds and the only blessings those of the Kiwani.

But his departure had one agreeable consequence: apparently Maestro Luís had thought Thornton a bad influence on me and now that he was gone I was taken from the digging and hauling and given a job with more creative possibilities. Further, I could now work in daylight, above ground and pretty much set my own schedule. This was convenient since as a concession to my father I had taken a summer job with his friend Lars Gustafson who had the Bandon ship chandlery and I was supposed to be on call at various odd hours to demonstrate his antifouling paints and his various shellacs and varnishes. I don't remember making many sales or working very hard at it that summer, but I was around the harbor a lot and got to know a lot of Yugoslav and Italian fishermen. There weren't many pleasure boats—the Depression was on and most of them had been run aground and pirated for firewood.

Anyway the Maestro thought enough of me, as I've said, to let me share in decorating the caves and I felt that this was a high honor. It was the first time anyone had recognized the artist in me and I was proud and began to walk in a new way.

—Jorgito is getting stuck up, said Carmelita.
—Hot shit, sang Laura, he thinks he's hot shit.

They pulled their cart up from the caves and rode it down hill to the beach, screaming and dodging the boulders in their path.

Here I want to describe the job Maestro Luís gave me even though it may seem trivial or inane, because it was my Rite of Initiation and hence will be forever sacred to me: On a sheet (four feet by eight feet) of heavy plywood the Maestro drew an irregular figure. I then bent strips of three-inch sheet metal to follow his lines. Inside the space thus enclosed I put one layer of old newspaper, lightly glued to the board, then tacked down various bits of salvaged or stolen chicken wire and metal netting. On another plywood sheet nearby I mixed gravel, sand and cement with enough fresh water (sea water wouldn't do) to make a stiff paste. This I shoveled into the metal forms, leveled with a screed and pounded and probed and shook until it filled every curve or nook. Now began the most delicate work: five-eighths of an inch of fine plaster spread with a trowel and wooden float over the still wet concrete and then the mirrors—what glittering bouquets of them! I had seen Maestro Luís returning with his bronchitic flatbed truck from excursions up the coast to Reedsport and Marshfield and Florence loaded with cracked and peeling mirrors from which once-youthful images of lips, chignons and moustaches had now departed, leaving only vacant pieces of sky. These fragments it was my splendid duty to place in magic circles, ondelets and necklaces across the wet plaster. But first to break! And there lay the beginning of art; I will not soon forget Maestro Luís' look of scorn when he discovered me breaking a mirror with a ball-peen hammer.

—No, Jorgito, no hammer. Force at a single point makes the isosceles triangle. He picked up one of the sharp splinters that sprang from my hammer blow.

—God loathes one thing only more than isosceles triangles and that is parallel lines. Here—he picked up a fresh mirror and with a thoughtless motion as if he had merely stumbled, let it fall. It shattered in four different directions. —That is the way you must break mirrors. Without purpose, gently, so as not to offend the glass. That is God's way—he works through accident, and not by malice.

He had the habit, not unusual among seers, of marshalling God behind his own arguments. Not that he was particularly devout—I have heard him give God plenty of abuse, usually obscene, when His planning went awry. Maestro Luís dealt with God as one prince might treat with another: with respect but never with any hint of subordination. I always thought it a very workable arrangement, though I've never had the temerity to try it for myself.

107

But back to our mirrors. —Place them according to deep impulse, Maestro Luís instructed me.

—And if I have no impulse?

—Then you have not lived enough. Of course, he added with a smile, it will help if you are a little drunk. I followed his advice and I think the work improved.

Afterwards Maestro Luís colored the plaster interstices, using fresco paints chiefly in magenta, ochre, chartreuse and violet. —Avoid blue, he warned, that color is the sea's and it will be angry if we steal it. When the plaques had dried we stripped away the metal forms and carefully turned them over; the backside was then waterproofed and after nightfall he and Carlos would carry the finished piece deep into the caverns and affix it to one of the corridor walls. I was never allowed to watch this part of the work and consequently could not tell how my part of the decorations fit into the total design.

—You are the larva, Maestro Luís said. Do you foresee the butterfly? I do not think so. All the same I think he was pleased with my progress because toward the end of that summer he gave me a special project: an eye four feet in diameter, an eye for a serpent made out of a mosaic of mirrors.

—Very small pieces. Very close together. They must glitter.

—Is it evil? I asked.

—Do not think evil, Jorgito. Think glitter. This is to be a very great snake and all the glitter in the world must be in his eye. Perhaps he is good, perhaps he is not. This does not concern you. You are to think of the stars. Millions of them. And so close together you cannot get a toothpick between them. Then you will have glitter.

Against this voice I hear that of Busoni's nephew drawling the line from Cowper:

—Where every prospect pleases, and only man is vile.

It was the end of August and he was giving a party, a party to which I was invited solely to placate Thornton. The nephew had hoped that Thornton would drive over to the Coast (he didn't) and Thornton's friends were an obligatory part of the mise-en-scène. There were also a couple of dozen other people from up and down the Coast, students of his and visitors from Portland or Seattle who had summer cottages among the sand dunes. The guest of honor—you could tell that from his position in His Eminence's prized Eames chair—was Redfern Mason who wrote on music and art for the *San Francisco Examiner*. Steamed clams and a wine punch concocted out of a sweetish sauterne and ginger ale (a nightmarish drink) were served, and Busoni's nephew played

Bach partitas for four hands with one of his students and then cruised about through other members of the Bach family—Carl Philip Emanuel and Johann Christian are the ones I recall but I'm sure there must have been others too; it seemed to me at the time that that family specialized in boredom but no doubt that opinion was only an index to my own callow iconoclasm. And to tell the truth I didn't hear much of the music anyway, I was so occupied with watching Busoni's nephew and fantasizing about what he wanted to do with Thornton and whether it would be an advantage or disadvantage to take his teeth out that he could have played "Kitten on the Keys" and I wouldn't have noticed.

Afterwards there was applause, more wine punch and clams, and Redfern Mason made a nauseating little speech about the universality of genius and how fortunate we were in Bandon to have a representative of a great artistic family to keep the flame alight *ex partibus infidelum*, and so on and so forth.

No doubt I had taken too much of the sweet sauterne but something else was at work too: I was in paint-spattered dungarees and dirty espadrilles among a relaxed, well-dressed crowd of summer visitors, my knuckles were raw from the abrasion of fresh lime and cement, the year was 1939 and suddenly I felt irrevocably proletarian. Busoni's nephew wasn't the only genius in Bandon, I said in a very loud voice, and a ten minutes' walk would take them to a man of no high-flown pretensions who was the equal of any artist in America.

—And who is that? asked Redfern Mason with remarkable patience considering my rudeness.

—His name is Luís Canseco.

—Canseco? He riffed through his ever-ready mental card file of Important Figures and came up empty. —The name escapes me.

—Because you won't look, I said in a gratuitously nasty tone.
Busoni's nephew scented a massacre and intervened.

—Canseco is our local stonemason, a Spaniard, I think, a *naïf* painter. He spoke in a manner designed to be judicious but only achieved the patronizing.

—His friends (here a gentle smile to me) say he has talent, but the rest of us really have no way of knowing, since Señor Canseco never exhibits. He is—how would you say it?—an original.

This of course was just the provocation I needed. Very rapidly and with a fluency I had never before possessed, I said a lot of things about the middle classes' blindness to real art, the fraudulence of museums and galleries, the artist's variation on Kant's categorical imperative and all the bouillabaisse of ideas in which I had been swimming the past two years, some my own, some Thornton Gale's but most transposed out of Maestro Luís' conversations. It was a wild, vehement farrago that I certainly meant to be offensive. Yet when I finally brought it to an end there was nothing but silence, then a single burst of applause, from Redfern Mason. Since he was guest of honor the other guests dutifully joined in applauding the experience of being insulted.

—Beautifully put, Redfern Mason said. I found myself agreeing with every syllable.

To which Busoni's nephew contributed, This young man fancies he is our local *fauve*.

Alliteration here took over: if I'm your local *fauve*, then you're our local faggot, but I had sense enough to hold my tongue. —Thank you, Mr. Busoni, for your clams, I said. And left. If they wanted me to be Bandon's wildman, I exulted in the role. Better that than my earlier billing as the kid who sold foul-weather paint to the Yugoslavs.

Unfortunately, that wasn't the end of it. The next day I had to strip the forms from the snake's eye and scrub it with a ten percent hydrochloric solution. But the gate to the yard was locked. Maestro Luís' flatbed truck was in the driveway so I went to his house for the key. The girls were on the front porch clipping each other's toenails.

—You're in for it, Jorgito, said Laura.

—Papa's boiling mad, Carmelita said.

—Where is he?

—Gone fishing. Carmelita pointed to the sea where a brisk wind was plowing the water. Look!

—He's taken Carlos with him, Laura said.

—Out there, Carmelita said. Beyond the pelicans. One more tack and he falls over the edge, she added with relish.

I peered into the glaring sun and made out, in the far distance, the orange speck that was his lateen sail.

—Papa only goes fishing when he's mad, Laura said.

—Poor fish, Carmelita said. They'd better watch out. And she handed me a note from her father, a note that I still possess. Since it is the only surviving scrap of paper in his handwriting I include it here, though its contents are far from flattering:

Sir:
Even a coyote does not shit in his own den.
Be gone.
            L. Canseco

I was devastated. What had I possibly done to deserve this contemptuous dismissal? The girls, back at their toes again, did not hesitate to acquaint me; like a pair of Furies they were at their merriest and most vocal in the face of catastrophe—anybody's catastrophe. If the world should end tomorrow, as I hear widely prophesied, I truly think you would find Laura and Carmelita holding a party in the prompter's box.

—That man you sent to see Papa, said one of them (it doesn't matter which).

—Is a journalist, sang the other.

—Papa hates journalists.

—Particularly from the Hearst papers—

—Because Papa hates Mr. Hearst—

—Who supports General Franco—

—And Papa hates General Franco—

—Really, *really* hates Franco! (this in unison)

So there it was: from me to Redfern Mason (who was personally what they used to call an avowed anti-fascist) to W.R. Hearst to General Francisco Franco—the chain was inexorable and complete, and I was its proximate victim. I said goodbye to the sisters (I noticed that farewells excited them too, with their whiff of irretrievable loss) and left Bandon. I thought it wisest to seek my rehabilitation at a safe distance.

From Portland I sent Maestro Luís a long and (I thought) tactful letter of apology. I did not bear down heavily on the innumerable hours of free labor I had contributed to his grottoes but wrote chiefly of my good intentions and my sure knowledge that Redfern Mason detested Franco and, in general, of the value of a good press to an important master such as he unquestionably was. There was a lot more that, thankfully, I have now forgotten. With my savings I bought a case of very good red wine of Seville and had it shipped to him. After about a month I received the following letter from Bandon:

Dear Jorgito:
Papa says he was wrong to lose his temper when you only wished to do him a kindness. Papa says to ask you to do him the courtesy of forgiving him. (Those are his words.) The wine you sent came without breaking and we drank some of it. Papa says it is good but corky but that is because it comes from Andalusia where all the wines are corky. Papa says it reminds him of why he left Spain but not to tell you that. You see how wicked I am?

111

We have painted your snake's eye cadmium yellow and it glows in the cave. It is very beautiful and frightens Laura a lot. We look forward to seeing you next summer.*

> Your true friend,
> Carmelita Canseco

*Carlos does too.

So the rift was mended.

But not really, completely. I had been hurt too much and as Heraclitus said you never step in the same stream twice anyway. I think I continued to respect Maestro Luís just as much as an artist and a thinker but was a bit more perceptive of his human failings. I guess what I am trying to say is that the period of youthful hero worship was over and a tentative new realism (the Age of Hewitt West I was later to call it) was gestating.

Besides, there were plenty of distractions: that was the year Europe went to war; it was the year I finally and irrevocably told my father I would not participate in the organized conspiracy of the medical profession (with what a family uproar you can well imagine); and it was the year I went to the quarterfinals of the National Intercollegiate Handball Tournament. Obviously, it was the kind of year when hardly anyone gave a thought to art and one's responsibility toward it. (Parenthetically: my absorption in handball remains one of the great unsolved mysteries of my life. How I could have run morning after freezing morning, around the draughty, splintery old courts of the Multnomah Athletic Club in pursuit of that brutal hand-stinging rubber pellet is beyond me—I must have been endowed with unguessed reservoirs of masochism. Yet I kept at it for a dozen years and was six times club champion, although the honor now seems to me a dubious one.)

I made it to Bandon only once that summer. Maestro Luís was the soul of cordiality; he seemed determined to regard our differences as over and done with or perhaps he had really forgotten them. He had certainly drunk all the wine, corky or not, and on the day of my arrival Carmelita and Laura fixed us a marvelous paella which we washed down with cheap California zinfandel. Carlos was there too, and it was obvious that he was now the heir apparent; which was only natural, since he was devoting his life to the Master's Way while I had been, at best, a summer soldier. Still, I thought he was beginning to get a trifle pompous about his role as the Apostle Peter, and said so: he smiled gently in response. A soft word turneth away wrath—that was Carlos.

After dinner Maestro Luís said, It's time Jorgito saw the eye of his snake, and we descended into the caves. Carlos had run a power line in and there were light bulbs every twenty-five feet so the going was not too bad. For the first three hundred feet our path followed a natural cave, the discovery of which had no doubt prompted Maestro Luís to begin his own excavation, first as a mere enlargement; this part he had left undecorated except for some natural stalactites and piles of clamshells left by generations of Coast Indians who had found refuge here. It was only after we had descended three tiers of hewn stairs that the paintings and mosaics began, and then only when we were plainly below sea level did I make out the snake. It was not the eye but the jeweled tip of its tail that we saw first—a shock, because I had always envisaged the great serpent as rising out of the cave whereas the Master plainly saw it plunging even deeper into his kingdom. Perspective, Maestro Luís had often enough told me, is what distinguishes the ant from the antelope.

And had it not been for that old buccaneer Hewett West that might have been all, for when I left Bandon the next morning I was not to return for over ten years. Or perhaps never. The eye? Yes, it was there, a thousand resplendent mirrors glittering deep beneath the sea. But staring in the wrong direction as far as I, the ant, was concerned.

—Captain, said Hewett West, I have a project that might interest you. How would you like to be president of the Port Orford and Bandon Gas Company?

We were standing, brandies in hand, overlooking San Francisco from an eighth floor suite in the Mark Hopkins Hotel. Hewett West called me Captain as a familial courtesy. The war over, the Army had sent me back to graduate school to get an M.B.A. but I soon had enough of Columbus, Ohio, and resigned my commission, thus in my father's eyes burning the last bridge which might have led me to the Naugahyde isles of respectability. But I had published my first stories by then and eight years as an officer and so-called gentleman seemed enough penal servitude to expiate my guilt toward my family.

—Of course, said Hewett West in his new role as Satanic tempter, it's not quite as impressive as it sounds. The company has four trucks, five employees and a part-time auditor, a lot of expensive leasing contracts that aren't worth a damn, and a negative cash flow of twelve thousand a year. But you might have fun turning it around.

I greatly admired Hewett West. The diabolic side to my soul found its perfect echo in him. When I was a child he would arrive on the City of Roses, traveling parlor-car, take off and brush his gray fedora, and pause in the center of his spiderwebs to visit us for a day or so. His arrival always meant a gleaming ten-dollar gold piece for me and his departure was effected in wafting breezes of *eau de cologne*. He was my father's first cousin and he bought and sold utilities—not as an occupation, nothing so mundane ever clouded his image—but as an amusement, a jest, a regal folly. His coats had detachable fur collars, his cigars wore opulent paper rings. His cigars? Yes, when I first read Shakespeare's great tragedy *Antony and Cleopatra*, the odor of my cousin Hewett West hung heavy between every line. Those were the cigars—Antonio y Cleopatra—that he invariably smoked! It was as if he had written, or at the very least, inspired, the tragedy. There was a breadth and sweep to his character, to his mysterious comings-and-goings through the sedate fabric of our family, that reminded me of the Morgans, whether the freebooter Henry or the financier Pierpont it didn't much matter. And it was this romantic pirate who was now offering me my return to Bandon, the lost kingdom of my youth, as one of its ruling princes. If I hesitated a moment before accepting, I took care not to let him see it.

So I returned to the Oregon coast. I have written elsewhere of the comedy and tribulation involved in trying to supply those two towns with butane so I am not going to repeat that story here. Suffice it to say that though I had to report to Hewett West's holding company they left me pretty much alone; I don't recall my cousin visiting Bandon once— he obviously had larger fish to fry, and as long as my quarterly balance sheets showed improvement (and they did, narrowly, until the denouement of my career as utilities magnate) no one interfered. As for myself, I acted as I imagined Hewett West might have done: the purchase, distribution and collection for my butane became an outrageous game to be conducted above all with a sense of style, while the bourgeoisie of Port Orford and Bandon were to be the natural if unwitting victims of my *compradore* cynicism. When ethical questions arose between me and them I told myself I was collecting material for future novels and asked what Balzac or Stendhal might have done in my place. No wonder that when the whole structure finally collapsed no one seemed surprised or very sympathetic; Julien Sorels are never appreciated by their contemporaries.

The company's main office was in Port Orford which is a couple of hours' drive south along the coast, but I was in Bandon two days a week and promptly drove out to Maestro Luís'. The beat-up old flatbed with its portable cement mixer was in the driveway and nothing seemed changed except for a new, carefully lettered sign: Canseco and Gutierrez (that was Carlos, a partner at last), Masonry, Brick and Tile Work—All Types—Reasonable. I parked my gas company pickup, got out, started up the driveway, hesitated, then turned back and drove away. Not now, I told myself, I'll go later when I'm settled. But that later soon stretched out to six months. The truth is I was afraid of the questions Carlos and the Master would ask me. What had happened to my devotion to art? Where had the calluses on my fingers gone? What was I, the trumpeter of revolution, doing with propane and monopolies? And since these were questions I often asked myself and could never answer I drifted into absence from my troubling conscience, Luís Canseco.

Finally, we were brought together by accident. South of Bandon, on the Port Orford road, there is (or was—it has since burned down) a creamery at Langlois which made the finest Danish-style blue cheese in America. I took to stopping there and one day the young woman who had been selling me my blue for weeks whispered over the counter, Father knows you are here, Jorgito. He would be glad to see you. It was little Laura Canseco, almost unrecognizable in her mask of maturity.

So once again I entered that house above the cavern:
—It is Jorgito, Papa.
—*Mi casa es su casa*. He did not turn from his chair in the window where he appeared to be gazing out at the ocean. A storm was coming up, the sea was black and we could hear its artillery pounding unmercifully on the beach. Hundreds of gulls circled over the cliff looking for refuge.
—You've come to see your serpent?
I reminded him that he had already shown it to me. —Oh, he said and lapsed into silence. Carmelita stood beside him and I thought she looked somber and worn.
—Jorgito is back from the war, Laura ventured.
—It isn't over yet, Maestro Luís said flatly. *He* is still in Madrid. And all the others are still out *there*. He waved a gnarled fist at the ocean as if each wave were his personal enemy and turned about in his chair to face me. Then I realized why Laura had said he was changed: his eyes were milky with cataracts and resembled nothing so much as those on the marble bust of Homer that my grandfather kept in his study. Maestro Luís was blind.
He must have sensed my dismay, for he said in a kindly voice, No more stones for Canseco. Carlos is master now, I am the apprentice. I am learning all over again to hear. It is very exciting, Jorgito, I am like

115

a baby just born—so much to listen to!

Carmelita followed me out to my car.

—He speaks a great deal in Catalan, she said. Naturally, no one here understands it, so there are problems.

I took her hand impulsively. —Listen, I said, tell Carlos not to pay your gas bills.

She laughed. —We haven't, for three months.

—Don't pay them. Ever. They will fly away, you understand?

She squeezed my hand. —I understand, Jorgito. God has given us wings and we must use them.

—Exactly, I said.

After that I began seeing quite a lot of Carmelita. Misty mornings we walked on the beach picking up driftwood, went dancing and drinking at Pierre's out on the Point and once spent a week together at Crater Lake. I was fond of her and she of me but both of us in a way that avoided questions of commitment; Carmelita had had quite enough of family obligations in her life with Maestro Luís, and I had gone through a rather sticky marriage while I had been stationed overseas. I had fallen in love with an actress, married a British woman on the rebound and suffered through a divorce—no, let me be honest about it: I had married Alison, *then* fallen in love with Trudy, and *then* Alison walked out on me, in that order. Anyway, I found Carmelita relaxing and a lot of fun. Spontaneous, mercurial, unpretentious—those were the adjectives recollection assigns her.

I was in Port Orford on the day Maestro Luís drowned so whatever I say about it is second hand and, by the rules of evidence, suspect. The story his daughters gave out was that he had gone sailing alone, been caught by a sudden gust off the point of the jetty, and went down. The boat—*mirabile dictu!*—had then righted itself and been driven on the beach by the onshore winds. No mention was made of the fact that Canseco was virtually stone blind and was never, to my knowledge, crazy enough to sail that dangerous coast in such a condition. There were a lot of other things wrong with the official story. The daughters, who stuck together on all the details, said that Carlos had taken the truck and gone to Mexicali to pick up a load of tiles; perhaps, but three days later I saw the truck abandoned behind an old garage in Yachats; I couldn't be mistaken about it, I got out of my car and checked. The license plates had been stripped and someone had painted over the emblem on the cab door but I would know that chassis anywhere. And

Carlos never came back.

This leads me to the ugliest surmise of all: was that really Luís Canseco's body in the coffin at the Bandon Chapel? Or was it Carlos? I was puzzled—or paranoid—enough to try to see for myself on the morning of the funeral but the undertaker wouldn't let me near the casket. —The deceased was in the water for three days (the daughters said a day and a half). It isn't a pretty sight; there has been a lot of disfigurement. So I had to let it go at that. After all, Canseco's next of kin swore it was their father's body, so who was I to raise my voice against them? But as you will see, there was more there than met the eye, to borrow a cliché from detective fiction.

Oregon winters can be ghastly and particularly on the coast, where for weeks on end every describable variety of rain falls with scarcely an intermission. It was on one of those cold blustery drizzling days that they buried Luís Canseco if indeed it was he in the coffin. At the gravesite we stood in a damp shivering row like crows in a muddy cornfield while a gaunt hatless man said a few words in Spanish. The daughters of course were there and perhaps eight or ten old laborers and masons with their relentlessly dripping wives. Naturally there were no priests or ministers—the old man's strained relations with God's houses were far too well known for that. It was all very depressing. *Sic transit gloria mundi*, I thought, although in Maestro Luís' case he had had little enough *gloria* during his lifetime. Perhaps he would get a better shake in the hereafter.

When I walked away from the cemetery there was Busoni's nephew emerging from the throng.

—Too bad he couldn't swim, he said sardonically, he would have been spared this.

I hadn't seen him for a dozen years but he looked exactly the same, rather like Dorian Gray with dentures. I felt that I had been unkind to him in the old days so when he proposed a drop of sherry at his studio I accepted.

—We had our differences, Busoni's nephew said, but he was cut from the authentic granite, that one.

Which summed up the way I felt. Busoni's nephew played me Ravel's pavane in the manner of Rameau (for once, no Bach!), we sat in the dusk for a few minutes, then wordlessly shook hands and parted. I guess you could call it a reconciliation.

My own Waterloo followed soon after. I came to my office one February morning to find a very official looking seal-cum-padlock on the door and two sheriff's deputies parked in an old Chevrolet in front of it. They had their windshield wipers going to preserve their steady view of the Port Orford and Bandon Gas Company and its officers.

—You're closed, Doc, one of them said affably. Might as well go home and get an extra forty winks. Orders of the Superior Court.

The other one asked me in an equally friendly manner where in this godforsaken town he might get a decent ham sandwich. I told him, then went home and called Hewett West's office in San Francisco. It took nearly an hour before I got anyone who was willing to say anything at all; finally one of the executives with whom I was on drinking terms came on the line.

—Listen, George, he said a bit breathlessly, the shit has really hit the fan down here. The chief isn't in and I don't know when he will be. I think he's up at Tahoe thinking things over but I wouldn't try to get him on the horn cuz they won't put you through. My advice to you, old chum, is to batten down the hatches and get ready for a bumpy ride. It ain't going to be sweet, the laundry is all coming back dirty.... And so forth.

I drove all night to Lake Tahoe. Driving has a wonderfully narcotic effect on me; when I left Bandon I was furious but when I pulled into my cousin's summer place in North Lake Tahoe I had daydreamed myself into a chapter from *The Charterhouse of Parma* and was feeling almost serene. *Que sera, sera*, the old song goes.

Hewett West, in a plaid logger's shirt, was outside splitting pine logs with a double-bladed axe. I had never seen him look more fit or relaxed.

—Good morning, Captain, he said cheerfully, how are things in Port Orford? I explained how things were and he began to whistle, not in surprise, but musically, like a meadowlark. It was a talent of his I had never suspected. Of course he knew how things were in Port Orford and Bandon far better than I. And in Redding and Billings and Crescent City and Walla Walla and a dozen more towns as well, things weren't going too well. In fact, his whole empire was lumbering into bankruptcy and its generals faced probable criminal charges, so the anguish of a minor pro-consul in a distant and unimportant province didn't count for much, but you wouldn't know that from Hewett West's remarkable aplomb. If Rome was sinking (and it was) His Serene Highness was going down with a smile on his lips.

—The vicissitudes of business life, he said amiably, and added, time for a brandy, Captain.

So we stood under his majestic pines and drank brandy and soda, my cousin and I, and by the third glass we were roaring with laughter. After all, he was doing me a favor, wasn't he! We both knew that in the long run I wasn't cut out to be a business tycoon and now, unhampered by balance sheets and butane, I could get on with the real business of living.

This is where this history should end. But in life there are always so many untied ribbons, unanswered questions, letters turned inside out and left in plain sight, and the novelist's eternal temptation is to answer the unanswerable and place the final lantern in just the coign from which it will cast a sudden revelatory light on what has hitherto been inexplicable....

Let me tell you a dream, a dream I have had at least once a year over half of my life: I am in the caves of Bandon, sometimes with Carlos, often with Carmelita or one of the other women in my life. The dream starts with a great sense of euphoria: the cave is mine and I am displaying it to someone I wish to impress. We go down stairs, stair after stair, many with hand-ropes, far more stairs than there ever were at Bandon. At last we reach the great room of the serpent's eye. But something is wrong—one of the glittering bits of mirror has fallen from its place in the mosaic. I scratch the plaster behind it with my fingernail and instantly water spouts from the wall, first in a trickle and then, inexorably, despite my every effort to stanch it, in a growing stream and at last a deluge, as the sea takes over the cave. Here I awake in terror.

Of course this dream is based on (or prophesies? the sequence no longer seems certain to me) a possible event in the waking world. It long ago occurred to me that Maestro Luís, plagued by his blindness and inability to finish his masterpiece, might have drowned himself in his own caves. The scenario I had worked out had him descend into the grotto with dynamite or blasting caps, seek out by touch and echo the thinnest part of the wall and then with one explosion let the sea in. And Carlos? It was inconceivable to me that Maestro Luís would wittingly involve Carlos in his death, but I fantasized that the disciple might have seen the entrance (normally hidden under a pile of scaffolding) disturbed and followed his master in hopes of saving him. If that was indeed Carlos' body in the coffin, then his was the only one the daughters had been able to recover, since he was closer to escape when the blast went off. And why would Laura and Carmelita then go to such lengths to fabricate the supposed drowning at sea? Since childhood they had been drilled to preserve the secrecy of the caves; or perhaps the grotto had come to symbolize their shameful bondage to their father's dream, which they could not possibly reveal to all Bandon. Preposterous? Maybe. But it certainly seemed more likely to me than the story the two sisters persisted in asserting.

The last time I dreamed of the sea entering the cave was six months ago. I woke up with the immediate resolve to go back to Bandon and assemble the pieces of the puzzle if I could. The time was right: I was between assignments, I had just sold the European television rights to a story and had money enough. So on impulse I flew to the West Coast, rented a car and drove down from Portland over the once-familiar route. Let me stick to a simple narrative of the next few days and you can decide for yourselves whether I found the key or merely revealed a new puzzle within the puzzle:

I spent three utterly depressing days in Bandon. It is always a mistake to go back to the scenes of your youth with sentimental expectations, but it is particularly so in the towns of western America. The trouble is that they have no memory, and the present is so preoccupied with becoming the future that there is no opportunity for crystals of recollection to form around it and give it a semblance of grace. Thirty years had passed. No one I talked to had ever heard of Canseco or the grottoes of Bandon. I searched in vain the telephone book and tax records for any Canseco or Gutierrez. Busoni's nephew was dead, the creamery at Langlois had burned down, and where the stonemason's yard had once been there was now a motel flanked by a 7–11 convenience store which dispensed beer and razor blades twenty-four hours a day. Even the beachfront cliffs had eroded into unforgivably alien contours.

The owner of the motel was particularly unhelpful. Yes, he had been there when it was built. Canseco? No, the land had been bought from a man from Reedsport who ran a wrecking yard there. And caves? Not that he knew of. He had had soil samples taken to a depth of ten feet before he had built (Don't want no land-slips out here, you know) and he was positive that if there had been a cave it would have shown up on the engineer's report. I was overcome with frustration; it was as if Luís Canseco, his family and his great work had never existed, or had receded into the Stygian depths of the collective unconscious from which they had for a brief moment risen and glimmered.

Then I had a stroke of luck. I walked to the harbor and there, just where I left it so many decades before, was Lars Gustafson, Ship Chandlers, the windows full of dusty cordage, old spinnaker booms and running-blocks innocent of oil for thirty years. I trembled and went in; it seemed a miracle. As miraculous as the row upon grimy row of paint cans filled no doubt with the same varnishes and anti-fouling paints I had once foisted upon the Yugoslavs. And the miracle was compounded—not that my old employer was still there (Dad's in San Diego these days; couldn't stand the rain any more) but before me stood Peter Gustafson, stockboy when I was salesman, and now an authentic if balding memento of a past whose very existence I had begun to question. After a little prodding he was brought to recollect me and then, on the off chance, I asked about Laura Canseco; he had had, I remembered, a high school crush on her.

—Laura? Of course. She's living up in Eugene. (To authentic Bandonites everyplace outside their city limits was always "up.") Married to a lawyer there. Came down for the school reunion two years ago looking very trim. Wait, I have her address here somewhere.

I gave him my (mental) benediction: sturdy Peter Gustafson, faithful to past and its relics! I asked him if he remembered Laura's father.

—Sure, he said with certitude. Crazy old Greek who fell off the pier and drowned. Used to buy water-sealers from Dad.

Of such data are folk-myths created. I said yes, that was the one, took the address he offered me and left Bandon in such a flurry of nervous anticipation that I forgot to turn in my motel key. I have it to this day, a souvenir of a voyage into futility.

In Eugene I looked up Laura under her married name. She herself answered the phone. Perhaps she was surprised but she didn't give that impression. Yes, she remembered me. I had been her father's apprentice for a time many years ago. And what did I want? I explained in as few words as possible. No, she was afraid she couldn't help me; it was all many years ago and her memory was poor. She was terribly sorry but she was quite sure she had no recollections of any value to me. And now I must excuse her, she was late for a hairdresser's appointment. It had been delightful talking to me, but...and hung up.

But I wasn't going to give up so easily. By dint of three more phone conversations, one of them with her husband, I was granted a brief personal interview. —Although I'm afraid, said her husband, the answer is going to be the same.

Laura lived in a pseudo-Norman villa in Washburn Heights. A colored maid let me in. As I waited for Laura to come down I studied my own reflection in the baby grand piano; it gave back every wart and scar. There was a volume of Chopin Études open on the music rack and in the exact center of the Brussels lace runner a single red rose in a Sung

Dynasty bud vase. Outside, on the lawns, I could hear the *click-click-spat* of a Whirlybird sprinkler measuring out the afternoon. All that's lacking, I thought with a touch of my old malice, is the set of Great Books in hand-tooled Morocco bindings.

We shook hands formally all around and then sat down, Laura and her husband side by side on the sofa facing me. The husband was a large florid man who might have been considered handsome next to a tarpon. Laura looked amazingly young, flawlessly dressed and coiffed, and quite unlike anyone I could ever have known in Bandon. She repeated in a carefully modulated voice almost word for word what she had told me over the phone. I only half listened—she's been cloned from one of those elegant chatelaines in *House Beautiful*, I was thinking. When she had finished all the reasons why she couldn't remember a thing about her father, the husband took over.

—You have to realize, Hancock, that my wife has painful associations concerning her former way of life. We think it would be better for all concerned if you didn't stir up old worries. He paused significantly and then concluded, in a sense, that is a legal opinion as well.

—I understand perfectly, I said and got up. Obviously I was being threatened; it was time to bow out. But I had one other card up my sleeve: Peter Gustafson was keeper of the Bandon H.S. class records and he had given me Carmelita's address, too.

—I'm sorry to have imposed on you, I said directly to Laura and watched her eyes for any flicker of response. There wasn't so much as a blink.

—So good of you to have called, she trilled and swept me toward the door. Behind my back I could hear the Whirlybird dispensing benevolent rain to the lawn.

Next day I flew to Klamath Falls, spent a sentimental afternoon with Thornton Gale and then made my way, mostly by feeder airlines, to Gillette, Wyoming. As we circled the town before landing I saw a regiment of dung beetles below me, scarifying the land into diseased furrows and blisters. Gillette is the center of open-face coal mining in the Rockies and it is hard to imagine a more consummately hideous town.

—What ever brought you here? I asked Carmelita.
—My work.
—It means that much to you?
—Yes.

She taught drawing and painting to eighth graders, an occupation I thought she could follow pretty much anywhere but I refrained from saying so; it occurred to me that Gillette, Wyoming might represent some form of penance to her.

—You haven't changed, Jorgito. I would have recognized you anywhere.

—And you, I responded, are even more beautiful than I remembered you.

Which was only partial flattery in the Spanish manner; she really looked thirty-five at the most although my arithmetic told me she was closer to sixty. Everyone who had touched or been touched by Maestro Luís seemed to have been granted the gift of youth.

She divined my thoughts. —You are going to write about Papa?

—Perhaps.

—I thought some day you would, she said, as if this meeting had been preordained.

—Let's go to dinner and I'll tell you about it.

—All right, but only if we split the check.

She took me to one of those ubiquitous Old West Beef & Grog houses with rusted hayrakes hanging from the rafters and began to talk.

Unlike her sister, Carmelita wanted to talk, seemed eager to talk, although in the end I think I was even more confused by her volubility than by Laura's frozen reticence. First she talked about her children, the children in her classes, that is; then, in the middle of a sentence, she asked me my astrological sign (Gemini) and offered to do my horoscope. —Not that I believe in it, she laughed, but it gives me a chance to do character analysis and that I do like. A moment later she was describing the bison in Yellowstone Park, then she got on backpacking in the Grand Tetons. Meanwhile, we had drinks and then more drinks and then some food and then still more drinks. I didn't much care where her loquacity carried her—I was warmed by it, just as I had been chilled by Laura's icy gentility. I decided that Carmelita was for me and I would relax and enjoy the evening and let her get to the heart of the matter in her own good time. Which of course she did.

—My father was a real bastard, she ultimately said out of nowhere. He wasted his life on a monomania. And he would have wasted mine if I hadn't broken away.

The caves beneath the sea? They didn't exist, she answered coolly, they were only in his head. I reminded her that when I first saw her she and her sister had been pulling a heavy cartload of rubble up from those caves.

But she was adept at changing the subject. —That cart! I remember it all right. Do you know, when I was six years old my father made us

—literally forced us—to pull that cart all over Bandon collecting old bottles and broken dishes, like beggar's children.

I brought her back to the caves. Oh, there was an underground studio right enough—her father's secrecy of character was so great that he hated working by daylight—but it was merely an old wine cellar. In Bandon's archaeology apparently you could work your way from the Sea-Drift Motel through the wrecking yard and stonemason's compound back to a grand Victorian seaside mansion which once stood there. Its builder, a Portland land speculator, lost his money and his wits and ended his life in the madhouse. The castle burned to the ground in 1914. Canseco bought it for the thousands of bricks in its chimneys and foundations. The price? Three hundred dollars, and, since Bandon was desolate during the war, the land was thrown in free. And from those simple wine cellars were to germinate his insane dream of descending beneath the sea.

—What you've got to realize, Carmelita said intensely, is that my father was a species of monster. Oh, he had charm, I don't deny him that. But he was a monster just the same. I've been reading a biography of Richard Wagner, and what immediately struck me was how like Papa he must have been—arrogant, vain, cruel, egotistical, suspicious, tyrannical, it's all there. The difference is, Wagner had talent as some sort of justification. My father had none. Only words.

I was alternately dismayed and fascinated, not only by a daughter's willful destruction of her father's image but by her tone of passionate sincerity; she was a woman who could hate, that was clear.

—His mosaics? All of the best ones were stolen from Carlos. He picked people's minds. He had the ability to bring out talent in others— you must have noticed that, Jorgito—but really none at all himself. He was a master at only one thing (this bitterly)—the art of getting others to work for him.

We had finished dinner and moved to the lounge, where gas flames flickered over plastic logs and a pianist sank slowly under the weight of the "Yellow Rose of Texas."

—And when I think of what that man did to my mother, Carmelita said and audibly ground her teeth. I had heard this story before, years ago, during the week she and I had spent at Crater Lake, but had forgotten it. Now it came out again, the simple farm girl who worshiped her Luís, the life of sacrifice and humility, her tuberculosis and his apparent indifference to her and hatred of her illness, the death that a more considerate, less preoccupied, husband might have averted....

But now I was only half listening. There are some people who put so much vitality, so much dramatic intensity into their speech that you become enamored of their gestures and no longer hear what it is they are saying. Carmelita was like that. No doubt it was all the whiskey I had taken, too; at any rate, I began creating a fantasy world of my own. If only I had not left Bandon when I did, consigning Carmelita to that drawer in the memory where you dip when you send out Christmas cards. This woman had once been mine; I had heedlessly thrown away a treasure to seek out goals as illusory as her father's. Perhaps, even now, it was not too late to capture that human warmth again. Emboldened and flushed, I took her hand in mine and, under the wagon wheel in front of the fake bonfire, said with all the tenderness I could muster, —You know, Carmelita, I was once very fond of you. I think I teetered on the brink of falling in love.

—That's very sweet of you, Jorgito. She squeezed my hand affectionately. But I am not Carmelita.

—Not Carmelita? I thought the whiskey had affected my hearing.

—No, she said simply. I am Laura.

—Really?

—Really. Do you think I wouldn't know? She spoke casually but with complete conviction; if it was acting, then she was the finest actor I had ever met.

And I was checkmated. If she was playing a game, then she obviously felt only contempt for me; if she was telling the truth then I had made an utter and unforgivable fool of myself.

—Carmelita lives in Eugene, she said in the tone she no doubt used to explain primary colors to one of her backward students. You visited her Tuesday. Surely you didn't think she was Laura?

—She phoned you, then!

—Yes. She warned me you might be coming. I think you frightened her, Jorgito.

—I? I was a perfect gentleman. Too perfect.

—But it wasn't you she was frightened of.

—*Entonces?*

—It was herself. I think she was afraid of how much she might still care. Suddenly she exploded, upsetting her drink on the wagon wheel.

—Twenty years married to that pig! You don't know what a swine he is. Carmelita is a passionate woman, Jorgito, and for twenty years to be penned up with that—that soulless golf-cart! I don't know how she has survived.

Suddenly I grew dizzy, and it wasn't altogether from the whiskey. I wanted to cry out that it wasn't for her sister I cared, but for the voluble, inspired, demented woman across from me at that moment, whether Carmelita or Laura or ghost of my old desire, but, lacking the will to break a lifetime of inhibition, I fired instead one last shot in the dark:

—Tell me, was it you who found Carlos' body?

She stared at me as if I had suddenly gone insane.

—That night your father drowned, didn't Carlos go down with him? Did he try to save him?

There was a long pause and then Laura/Carmelita broke into a warm forgiving smile.

—Why don't you ask him?

—Who? Carlos?

—Of course, she said in the friendliest possible manner and scribbled an address on her drink-stained coaster. Give him my love, Jorgito. They say he is doing very well.

She called the waiter and we split the check down the middle.

Alamos, in Sonora, Mexico, is a town de Chirico would have loved. It is sewn together out of arches, colonnades, knife-edged shadows and silence. I arrived there at noon and the honey-colored streets were deserted. In the *zócalo*, a solitary dog lay panting in the shade of the bandstand. It was incredibly hot.

Artesanos de Alamos the sign said. The shop looked closed but the door opened under my touch. There was no one in the *tienda* but a steady *slap-slap* with a continuo of creaking led me into the studios. And there, half in shade, half in sunlight, absorbed at his potter's wheel, I saw, in a momentary epiphany, Master Luís Canseco himself, his sight restored, his bare feet on the kick wheel, a world of perpetual surprise flowing from his fingertips. Then a lattice fell, the light shifted, and Carlos Gutierrez sprang up to greet me.

—Laura said you might come. I would give you *un abrazo*, Jorgito, but you see—He held out his hands, slippery with wet clay. But come, let us talk. He led the way to the inner courtyard. It is wonderful I see you again. You have no change. Juancho! Juancho! A boy appeared from a pile of clay sacks where he had been napping. This is my son, Juancho, he is a lazy devil. He gave Juancho rapid instructions in Spanish and the boy took his place at the wheel. He needs practice, that boy. Come, follow me. *Cierra tu boca*, Sam! This last to an orange macaw which had joined in the excitement. I would talk to him in *Inglés* but he is from Panama and knows only dirty words—cunt, balls, fuck off. The parrot obliged us by repeating that message in full voice.

126

A number of dogs from the next patio responded with yelps and howls; for a moment I thought all Alamos was springing to life, but then the racket subsided as quickly as it had risen and everything was somnolence again.

—Now, said Carlos, knocking the cap off a bottle of cold beer. What do you want to know? I am here, I tell you everything. Of course he meant that in exactly the same sense Maestro Luís used to say, My house is your house. What he meant was, he would tell me what he chose to tell me and we would both pretend out of good manners that that was the complete truth.

So I asked him if he thought it possible that Maestro Luís could have sailed that boat alone in his condition.

—Only if he no longer care whether he come back. But who says he was alone?

I told him that was the official story.

—No, no, he could not have been alone. That is not possible. He paused, then peered at me sharply. I see what you think, Jorgito, but I was not in that boat. On our friendship I swear it. And he added with a trace of bitterness, If I had sailed it, I would have known how to bring it about and pick the Maestro up when he fell out.

—Then who *was* with him?

Carlos spread the palms of his hands toward heaven. *Quien sabe?* Lots of people knew how to sail that boat.

—And what about the truck? The day you left for Mexicali for a load of tiles, how far did you get with that truck?

—Ah, the truck! He wiped the foam from his lips with a sleeve. That truck, Jorgito, it was no damn good. I take the bus.

—All the way to Mexicali?

—Farther. Guadalajara, Morelia, I do not remember. There are tiles everywhere in Mexico. Even Zamora.

—And you didn't come back?

—It was too rainy in Bandon. Always rain and cold. Brrr!

—Did the girls send you away, Carlos?

He considered the question carefully. —Maestro Canseco's daughters have been very good to me, he said at last, very *simpatico*. They buy out my share. I have money enough to come back here. You see?

I let it go at that; we could both read between the lines. But there was one other question—Yes? I said that Laura claimed that there was no cave at Bandon, that the galleries where he and I had spent so many hours of labor were a mere illusion. What did he think of that? What could possibly be her motive in denying the simple truth of experience?

He answered my questions with others.

—Why should it trouble you, Jorgito? Look into the heart. You have anguish, no? Because they do not see what you see? Because their pain perhaps has taught them another truth. Is that it?

We were silent for a long time. The faintest hint of breeze began to stir the leaves of the banana tree in the courtyard. A burro brayed in the distance.

—It is enough the caves for you are true, Carlos said. What do you gain by asking more?

—And for your part? Are they true for you?

He stood up and stamped the dried clay from his feet.

—Me? I am artist, I believe in everything. It would be foolish not to. Besides, Luís Canseco has seen them. And Luís Canseco was a great man, perhaps what you call a genius, *es verdad?*

—*Claro*, I said. That he was.

On the way out Carlos showed me his pottery. I thought it very good. In the summer, he explained, there were few visitors and time for uninterrupted work; in winter it cooled off and the tourists came, customers perhaps. Juancho was still at the wheel and Carlos paused to check his work. My eye caught a large oval platter with a cerulean blue snake curled about its edge. The snake had no eyes; instead, in the very center of the plate, glazed in violet and magenta, there was a single disembodied eye.

—From inside it peers out. That is why it is bigger than it should be, Carlos said. Do you like it?

—More than like.

—It is yours. He handed me the plate.

But I had learned how to match his manners.

—I should not dare eat from it, I said, unless I had rewarded the creator for his labor.

Carlos smiled at me and with the most delicate of shrugs indicated rather than said, As you wish.

I paid for the plate and left.

—La Paz
January, 1984

✈ THE SKI BOOT

Some time after sullen noon Mrs. d'Arcy mounted the mustard-colored stairway and called Lewis to the hall phone. Lathered, a towel around his neck, he was trimming his moustache to a Bach English Suite on the record player. The towel was marked Hotel Belmar, Mazatlán, and the lather was vaguely green—by a miscalculation fathered by last night's wine he had begun shaving with chlorophyll toothpaste.

"Now whoever it is, Lewis," Mrs. d'Arcy said, "please for the love of Jesus remember it's my telephone and be polite."

"I'm a perfect gentleman," Lewis said.

The voice at the other end of the phone was loud and aggressive.

"Lewis Epp?"

"It is." There was a pause, then a fresh attack:

"Is it left or right?"

"What?"

"Is it left or right?"

Lewis put the receiver down and wiped the lather out of his ear.

"Is *what* left or right?"

"The boot."

Mrs. d'Arcy whispered over his shoulder, "If it's the income tax people you won't gain a thing by being belligerent."

"Left," Lewis said, "I think."

"Don't let anybody else touch it," the voice answered. "I'll be right over."

"And don't tell them any more than you have to," Mrs. d'Arcy added in her corrugated voice.

"He's hung up."

"They always do." She began taking the curlers out of her dyed red hair. "That's their way of intimidating you. Phone you up at all hours, then hang up when you answer. They're rotten."

"You've got it wrong. It was somebody about a boot."

"A what?"

"A ski boot. I found it and placed an ad."

"You must have been drunk."

"It was in the men's room at the Palace of the Legion of Honor. Where they're showing the Matisses. When you find something like that you've got to answer its challenge."

Mrs. d'Arcy gazed at him with benevolent disbelief. "Well, I wish you'd stop picking things up. Who knows the germs you bring into this house just by picking things up."

"Art," Lewis said, wiping his face, "is a meeting of accidentals at a certain place in a certain light. I might go on to add that life itself is pretty much the same sort of gig."

"A ski boot in a lavatory?"

"You're beginning to think like a painter." Half way up the stairs he was seized by an apothegm that he could not resist sharing with her; he leaned over the banister and said, "The world is full of lonesome shoes looking for each other. Excuse the soap on the phone. And send the man up when he comes."

In fact, the painting was going fine. *Objets trouvées* No. 37 was already printed in the lower right hand corner—starting from the title gave him a firmer grip on the content, he felt—and the upper foreground was working itself out smoothly. This time he was using surgical gauze dipped in plaster of paris instead of the burlap that had been the feature of No. 36 and the new material was full of exciting possibilities. He ignored the first knocking and when it was repeated he went to the door in irritation; he had already forgotten the phone call and today promised to be the first in weeks when he might make a real breakthrough into new and higher ground.

A tall man with a heavy paunch, sad brown eyes, and the fallen face of an old Saint Bernard stood in the hall.

"Campendonck," he said. "Arne Campendonck." It sounded like a seal barking. They shook hands. "I live in San Jose but I drove up the minute I read your ad. It's costing me a day's work."

"I'm sorry."

"It's no skin off your ass," Campendonck said and put the shoebox he was carrying down on a chair, then wiped his bald head with a yellow handkerchief and looked around the room. It was jumbled with old paint cans, stretching-frames, easels, a sick philodendron, dirty blankets, *The Decline of the West* in paperback, seven loose bricks, the complete length of a rusted Studebaker exhaust pipe and muffler suspended from the ceiling, and three sandstone boulders full of holes bored by marine molluscs. An electric hot-plate stood on the floor in the false fireplace, a pot of sizing glue cooking on it.

"Artist, eh?"

Lewis shrugged. He was used to the question and no longer rose to the bait.

"Done a bit of it myself," his guest said. "When I was younger, of course. Dry point etching. I used also to indulge in a bit of *La Vie Boheem.*"

"A gas, isn't it?"

"You ever read Schopenhauer? Or Bodeller? Great poet, Bodeller. 'Where are the snows of yesteryear?'" He winked broadly. "Ask Bodeller. He knows."

"Lewis!" It was Mrs. d'Arcy calling from the stairway.

"Excuse me," Lewis said. "Make yourself absolutely at home." He went out into the hall. Mrs. d'Arcy stood at the stairhead in the red-and-gold kimono her brother-in-law had brought her from Yokohama.

"What is it now?"

"Don't act so tortured, Lewis. I just wanted to remind you that your room is a mess."

"Thanks. Thanks a lot." They went through this at least three times a week and it was getting to be a drag.

"If it's someone important you can entertain him down in the music room." The music room was another of Mrs. d'Arcy pretenses—it held an untuned upright piano, an old Victrola and any number of scraggly African violets that were always rotting holes in the carpet.

"It's not *that* important."

"You're sure it's not the income tax people?"

"No, it's a man from the Ford Foundation. They want to buy my paintings for a memorial exhibition."

Mrs. d'Arcy put a solicitous, kimonoed hand on his arm, "I know that sort of laughter, Lewis, it's just whistling in the dark. If you bring him downstairs I'll serve sherry. You're alone here in San Francisco, Lewis. I want you to think of me as you would your mother."

"You never met my mother. She used to be in the Ice Follies."

Mr. Campendonck's bald head appeared in the doorframe. "Is there anything you can do about the smell from that glue?" he called. "It's an olfactory menace!"

"Okay, okay, I'll get it," Lewis said angrily and ran back into the room and turned the burner off. The glue was dripping down the side of the pot and had made a free-form puddle on the linoleum.

"Who's the doll?"

"My landlady."

"Girls, girls," Campendonck said with a sly wink. "You artists got it luxurious. In my own case I am in the bonds of matrimony going on sixteen years and cherish nothing but fond memories of *la dolce vita*."

Lewis opened the window and set the dripping glue-pot amid the chlorotic parsley in the windowbox. The sky outside seemed a uniform blank wash of gray. "Everybody thinks a painter's got nothing to do but ball with the models," he said bitterly. "Why don't we drop the subject. You came here about a shoe."

"Son, Campendonck is a philosopher. A shoe to him is a shoe. And a boot? Likewise. But a friend, when I got a chance to acquire a friend, somebody who has insight into life, an artist, a free-thinker, do I talk about shoes, which are after all only the external dross on the human pediment if I make myself clear?"

Now I'm in for it, Lewis thought, another day is going the way of yesterday and the day before, and just because I'm too damned tolerant with people. He retracted his head from the window in time to see his visitor pull a ski boot from his box.

"Just so you don't think I came here under false pretenses. Is this the mate to the boot you found?"

"I'll see," Lewis said wearily and brought his own discovery from the closet. Campendonck set them side by side on the floor. They were obvious mates.

"Mr. Stanley, meet Dr. Livingston," he said triumphantly.

"Tea time!" Mrs. d'Arcy called from the stairwell in a voice dripping with sugar.

There seemed to be no way out.

"Property?" asked Mr. Campendonck, ladling a spoonful of hot tea into his brandy. "As the philosopher said, *la propriety est vol*. To translate, it's nothing but bloody robbery. I scorn it."

"I used to be a Christian Scientist myself," said Mrs. d'Arcy warmly. "Please have some more of the Korn Krackles."

"They're delicious," Mr. Campendonck said. "The main thing is you've got to recognize we are all human and all got our weaknesses, rich and poor alike. As Bodeller said, *C'est la vie*. To translate..."

Lewis drank two glasses of brandy in a row and then said, "The ad cost me $6.80. I don't want any reward but I think I ought to get my investment back."

"You won't lose a thing, son. It's a real pleasure to meet an honest man."

Beyond the arched and leaded windows of Mrs. d'Arcy's music

room the fog appeared; an afternoon wind had sprung up, racking the old house with random creaks and shudders. The African violets shivered gently in the draught.

"We'd better finish the brandy," Mrs. d'Arcy said with a giggle. "My daughter will be home from school any minute."

"I'm always observing things other people don't notice," Lewis said. "There must have been perhaps a hundred people passed by that toilet and thought it was occupied because they could see a boot under the door, but I was the first one to notice that there was no shoelace in it. It's an eye for detail, you're either born with it or you aren't..."

Now Mr. Campendonck rose to the challenge of his surroundings: "Caruso! There was a voice! Nobody like that any more."

"I have some old records of Galli-Curci and Tito Schipa you must hear," Mrs. d'Arcy said. "I had no idea—"

"Just tell me where you dropped it and the boot is yours," Lewis persisted.

"Be a dear, Lewis, and don't set your glass on the piano. It makes rings..."

"Galli-Curci? No!"

"I've got to finish a painting today. I mean, it's a privilege meeting you, Mr. Cameldock, but I'm really supposed to be working—"

"Son," Campendonck said benignly, "I drove all the way from San Jose for this occasion. You can certainly spare the few minutes required for another drink."

The logic of this appeal was irrefutable. Lewis held out his glass to be refilled. The doorbell rang.

"Don't answer it," Mrs. d'Arcy said brightly, "It's only Bev. She's forgotten her key again."

"Just a short one."

"She's learning to be a dance instructor."

Mr. Campendonck stood majestically by the glossy Victrola and gazed in nostalgic rapture at the worn black disk in his hands.

"Galli-Curci! Now *there* was a voice! Call me a liar if you want, she could break a wineglass with her high C!"

They were crowded in the back of a cab, bound for the Green Lemon Grill. Mr. Campendonck, flushed, was sharing a pint of Jim Beam Bourbon whiskey with the assembled company; Mrs. d'Arcy wore a tall black Spanish comb in her hair, and Lewis had her daughter Beverly on his lap. Outside, in the drizzly streets umbrellas popped up like early mushrooms.

"*Bonne chance!*" cried Mr. Campendonck with a goatish laugh and tilted the pint aloft.

"Are you comfortable, Lewis?" Mrs. d'Arcy asked solicitously. "She's a heavy girl."

"He's squeezing my tit."

"Watch your language, Bev."

"My language? And what about *him?* Don't think he isn't leading me on!" And, turning about in his lap, she placed her thumbs in Lewis' ears and gave him a wet and lingering kiss on the mouth. The cab turned sharply onto Sutter Street; a number of buildings seemed about to fall on them, and Lewis' hand, lately resting in the warm curves of Miss d'Arcy's bosom, gripped the door handle, braced against catastrophe.

"Ooops!" cried Mrs. d'Arcy sliding down on them across the slick imitation leather, "Here we go again!" Then, righting herself, admonished, "Don't be a tramp, Bev. What will Lewis think?"

"Lewis isn't thinking, are you, Lewis?"

"Relatively speaking," Lewis said, coming up for breath, "I am not."

Mr. Campendonck, teetering on the jumpseat, gazed from a fog-streaked window at the phantasmagoria of Sutter Street and said softly, "Those were the days, those were the days! Do you remember them?"

"I never remember anything," Mrs. d'Arcy said with a sigh of resignation and let her flaming orange hair with the black tortoiseshell comb fall back gracefully on the upholstery. "That's my trouble. I never remember a damned thing."

The afternoon went as afternoons did. At the Green Lemon Grill the jukebox played mambos and sambas while Beverly demonstrated her foot-work and Mr. Campendonck grew loud and sweaty and called for whiskey sours all around. Lewis danced with Beverly and then with a lean blonde in a fringed jacket who had been a rodeo rider at the Pendleton Round-up and then with Beverly again. "Cha-cha-cha!" he whispered in her ear.

"Mother's had her eye on you for months," she said. "Watch out for her. She's sticky."

"I can take care of myself."

"I'll say you can."

"What I mean is, yesterday at the museum I was perfectly sure it was going to lead to something unexpected. You should have seen it. All by itself on those white scrubbed tiles. It was a fantastic picture! I suppose I could have walked off and left it there, but the whole gig is yin and yang, don't you think?"

"I sure do." She snuggled closer. "Like my perfume? It's Scandalous."

"Mmmm."

The jukebox ground to an end. She gave his hand a squeeze and said, "I've got to run to the sandbox. Don't wander."

At their table Mrs. d'Arcy was awaiting him, a gallant rank of whiskey sours before her. "Such a spender," she cried. "And Lewis, just imagine, I thought he was from the income tax! How wrong can you be?"

Lewis felt it was time to take a firm grip on events. "I've got a statement to make. I'm through being a Good Samaritan."

"Drink up, Lewis, I saved one for you."

"Just let him give me the $6.80 and I'll go home. Presumably you think I've got nothing better to do than hang around gin mills all day, but you're mistaken. I'm a serious artist."

"Of course you *are*." Mrs. d'Arcy moistened her handkerchief in a whiskey glass and removed a smudge of lipstick from his cheek. "But wait a minute or two. He's thinking of giving you *both* the ski boots. Outright. Why should he keep them, he says, he's too old to go to the Sierras any more."

"Tantivy, tantivy, tantivy!" cried their benefactor, emerging from behind a potted elephant-ear plant, a French horn in his hands.

"He can keep his damned boots," Lewis whispered fiercely under the Spanish comb. "I'm giving fair warning, that's all." He tossed off the whiskey sour and got to his feet.

"Ahunting we will go, ahunting we will go!" Mr. Campendonck sang with feral gaiety.

"Oh, there you are!" Beverly called across the waxed floor. "I was looking all over for you." The jukebox renewed its Latin rumbling.

"Finders keepers, losers weepers," Lewis said.

"You're really *with* it." They slid into each other's arms; the room whirled around them with a lovely centripetal force while the music seemed to spread over the floor like maple syrup. "I mean, *really* with it," she whispered. "Like, where have you *been* all my life?"

But he had not yet fully surrendered to the sweet haze of yet another evening. "What would *he* be doing at the Matisse show, anyway?" he asked.

"Who cares? Mother's always picking up icky types like that. Forget him. Live in the present tense is my motto."

There was a long and magical silence between them during which evening at last succeeded the drab afternoon, the chairs, tables, bar and chandelier of the Green Lemon Grill evolved from random groupings to configurations of compelling beauty, and Lewis himself, gyrating skillfully on the dance floor, became part of that miraculous, swaying tapestry. "I'm floating," he said at last. "I mean, floating."

"You're a doll."

"Let's go outside."

"You're gassed."

"No, I'm not. It's love or something."

"It's raining out there."

"I wouldn't care."

They danced behind a wicker hall-tree verdant with coats and scarves, and in its protective shade, exchanged priapic kisses. The jukebox emitted a sweet, viscous tango.

"Lewis."

"Yes?"

"Imagine, all this time you've been living upstairs, practically right over my head, and we never knew."

"Mmmmm."

"Put my blouse back in. And now, just by accident, we found each other."

"God's design."

"I mean, if it wasn't for that ski boot we might have gone for years just nodding to each other in the hall and never really *knowing*."

"Nothing happens by accident," Lewis said fiercely. "Not the sparrow, not the wave. Nothing and everything. There's a design everywhere. Ink spots, oil puddles, the crack in the plaster, bloodstain on the sheet, it's all there. You've got to have the goddamned eye to find it, that's all." Then he bumped into a table and upset it and there was a confused argument with two men who had been playing chess and insisted that the pieces be put back exactly as they were but of course no one knew where they had been. Somehow the others became involved in the argument, too, for the last Lewis recalled of the Green Lemon Grill was Mr. Campendonck shouting "Olé! Olé!" and executing veronicas with a tablecloth. Mrs. d'Arcy followed them to the door. "Isn't he a scream?" she said. "So generous." She leaned her head against Lewis' corduroy jacket and began to sniffle.

"Cut it out, Mother," Beverly said, putting on her coat.

"I'm such a rotten sentimentalist! I always have been."

"I've got to finish that painting," Lewis said unsteadily but with the profound conviction that the statement explained and justified the whole afternoon.

"You dear children, you dear children," Mrs. d'Arcy sobbed. "Now watch out you don't catch cold."

"Don't worry," her daughter said cheerfully. "Not with me he won't."

Mrs. d'Arcy adjusted the comb that had come askew in her orange hair and, drawing Lewis toward her, whispered wetly in his ear, "You're a sneaky sonofabitch, Lewis Epp. A mother's curse on you."

"I'll keep it in mind," Lewis said.

Outside, the city was clothed not in rain but a damp fog. Night closed around them and the tatters of fog rose over the harsh neon and the cruel quadrangles of concrete, lending them a soft and accidental grace. Rather like chiffon, Lewis thought. He must try that tomorrow on No. 38.

MISCELLANY

❦ TESTIMONY BEFORE THE COMMITTEE ON UN-AMERICAN ACTIVITIES

United States House of Representatives, Subcommittee of the Committee on Un-American Activities, Hearings Held in San Francisco, California, June 18–21, 1957

PUBLIC HEARING, TUESDAY, JUNE 18, 1957

A subcommittee of the Committee on Un-American Activities met, pursuant to a call at 10 a.m., in the Board of Supervisors' hearing room, City Hall, San Francisco, California, Hon. Francis E. Walter (chairman) presiding. Committee members present: Francis E. Walter, of Pennsylvania; Gordon H. Scherer, of Ohio; and Robert J. McIntosh, of Michigan. Staff members present: Frank S. Tavenner, Jr., counsel, and William A. Wheeler, investigator.

Testimony of George Hitchcock accompanied by Counsel Charles Solomon

MR. TAVENNER: Will you state your name, please.

MR. HITCHCOCK: George Hitchcock.

MR. TAVENNER: Will counsel accompanying the witness please identify himself for the record.

MR. SOLOMON: Charles Solomon, 38 Pacific Avenue.

MR. TAVENNER: When and where were you born, Mr. Hitchcock?

MR. HITCHCOCK: I was born early on the bright June 2, 1914, in Hood River, Oregon, where the delicious apples come from.

MR. TAVENNER: Where do you now reside?

MR. HITCHCOCK: San Francisco, California.

MR. TAVENNER: How long have you lived in San Francisco?

MR. HITCHCOCK: Twenty-two years.

MR. TAVENNER: What is your occupation or profession?

MR. HITCHCOCK: My occupation is a gardener.

MR. TAVENNER: What is your profession?

MR. HITCHCOCK: My profession is a gardener. I do underground work on plants.

MR. TAVENNER: Mr. Hitchcock, upon the change of the propaganda issued from Moscow, this committee invited a number of specialists who have had experience in foreign countries and in this country in the field of Communist activities to give this committee their views regarding the objects and purposes of the change in the Communist Party line. The committee issued a pamphlet, a symposium on these matters entitled "The Great Pretense." I believe there are as many as 39 people who contributed to it, and it is significant that a number of those who did contribute to it were of the opinion that the Communist Party which had refused prior to that time to accept the Trotskyites—in fact, they were at war with the Trotskyites—and who had refused to accept Socialists, because they thought Socialists were mere reformers are now endeavoring to form a united front to take in those which had been its former enemies. For instance, Harry Schwartz stated:

> World communism is now embarked upon the most skillful and seductive foreign policy in its history. It appears to the world wearing a mask of friendship, benevolence, and love of peace as never before. It stretches out the hand of friendship to Socialists, ignoring the past Communist attacks upon and murders of Socialists. It appeals to every element in every country that can possibly be induced to turn against the United States.

Another prominent individual in this field, Mr. Anthony Bouscaren, stated this:

> The leaders of the Soviet Union have launched a new tactical maneuver which is fraught with dangers for the United States. As a result of the February 1956 meeting of the Communist Party of the Soviet Union, the forces of international communism have adopted new tactics to accomplish three objectives: (1) Appeasement of discontent within the Soviet sphere; (2) extension of neutralism abroad through a united front with socialism; (3) weaken and discredit anti-Communists within the United States.

Another, Mr. Gerhart Neimeyer, stated that among the new lines which Khrushchev's announcement portrayed is this:

> ...the idea of cooperation with other Socialists and especially Socialist Democrats.

Now, there has come to my attention an article from the *Militant*, dated March 10, 1957, at page 3, which is an official organ of the Socialist Workers Party, and I read:

> San Francisco. The third meeting of the organizing committee of the Independent Socialist Forum was held last month. Chairman was George Hitchcock, a playwright connected with the Interplayers Theater Group of San Francisco. Mr. Hitchcock is recognized as the chief organizer of the Independent Socialist Forum.

Were you the chairman of the Independent Socialist Forum at the time that I mentioned, March 10, 1957?

MR. HITCHCOCK: Yes.

MR. TAVENNER: Were you a member of the Communist Party at that time?

MR. HITCHCOCK: On this question I should like to say first that I am not now a member of the Communist Party, as the committee well knows, and all my friends know. However, I shall decline to answer any further questions of my past associations or political beliefs on the following grounds:

The first ground is under the protection afforded me by the first amendment which stipulates that Congress and committees shall pass no laws interfering with my privileges for free speech and rights of assembly and the like.

The second is the ground of the fifth amendment which says that I may not be forced to testify against myself, and the third is the grounds that this hearing is a big bore and a waste of the public's money.

THE CHAIRMAN: That is the biggest audience you have ever played before. Go ahead, Mr. Tavenner.

MR. TAVENNER: Mr. Hitchcock, you say you are no longer a member of the Communist Party. Were you a member of the Communist Party in February 1956?

MR. HITCHCOCK: Counsel is not so naive to expect me to answer the question. I have already given my grounds.

MR. SCHERER: I ask that the chairman direct the witness to answer.

MR. HITCHCOCK: I must decline to answer the question on the grounds previously stated which involve my protection under the first amendment and the fifth amendment and any other amendments that may be relevant.

MR. TAVENNER: Are you aware of any plan of the Communist Party to propagate the line which these specialists have stated in their opinion it was the purpose of the Kremlin to accomplish, namely, to unite with the Communist Party Socialists, the Trotskyites, or we may say the Socialist Workers Party in a united front with the Communist Party?

MR. HITCHCOCK: Really, Counsel, you do not expect me to answer that one, either, do you?

THE CHAIRMAN: You are directed to answer the question.

MR. HITCHCOCK: I must decline to answer the question on the grounds already stated, including the first amendment and the fifth amendment. I may further add as an Irishman though—

MR. MCINTOSH: As a matter of curiosity, you said with the rather broad gesture that all of your friends know you are not a Communist today. How would they gain such knowledge?

MR. HITCHCOCK: I must decline that one, Mr. Congressman, also on the same grounds.

MR. SCHERER: When was it that this article said he was chairman of this Socialist group?

MR. TAVENNER: March 10, 1957.

MR. SCHERER: Were you a member of the party on March 10, 1957?

MR. HITCHCOCK: Am I directed to answer that question?

THE CHAIRMAN: Yes; you are directed to answer the question.

MR. HITCHCOCK: Congressman, I must decline to answer that question on the same grounds as I have already indicated, the first, second, third, fourth, fifth, and other amendments.

MR. SCHERER: Did you resign from the Communist Party so you could assume the chairmanship of this Socialist Party group?

MR. HITCHCOCK: Am I directed to answer that question?

THE CHAIRMAN: Yes; you are so directed.

MR. HITCHCOCK: I must decline to answer that question on the grounds already cited including the first, second, third, fourth, fifth sixth, seventh, eighth, ninth, and tenth amendments, including the fifth.

MR. TAVENNER: You have posed a very interesting situation here. You say that you and your friends know that you are not a member of the Communist Party now, but you decline to state whether or not you were on March 10, 1957, just a few months ago.

MR. HITCHCOCK: Counsel knows perfectly well—

MR. TAVENNER: Wait just a minute. What has occurred or transpired since March 10, 1957, that would cause you to make such wide and divergent answers as to those two dates?

MR. HITCHCOCK: Counsel knows perfectly well that this type of questioning is an attempt at entrapment and I have no intention of answering.

MR. SCHERER: I think the testimony of what these men said in the symposium is true.

MR. HITCHCOCK: That is your inference, Congressman.

MR. SCHERER: Were you a member of the Communist Party yesterday? You said you are not today.

MR. HITCHCOCK: That is a delightful question. Am I directed to answer it?

THE CHAIRMAN: You are directed to answer it.

MR. HITCHCOCK: I must decline; I wish to decline; I do decline.

MR. TAVENNER: The article I referred to states that this was the third meeting of the organizing committee of the Independent Socialist Forum. Will you tell me when the other two meetings occurred?

MR. HITCHCOCK: I don't remember the specific dates but they were earlier this year, prior to that.

MR. TAVENNER: Your position calls for further questioning about this. When you became active in this work apparently your position in the Communist Party changed.

MR. HITCHCOCK: That is an inference.

MR. TAVENNER: Just a moment.

MR. SCHERER: Is his inference incorrect?

MR. HITCHCOCK: Am I directed to answer that?

THE CHAIRMAN: Yes, you are.

MR. HITCHCOCK: I must decline to answer that question on the grounds of the first, second, third, fourth, and fifth amendments.

MR. TAVENNER: I think it is of interest and importance to know where the leadership of the Communist Party here in San Francisco fell out with you over your work in the Socialist Party or that they were unwilling to go along with international communism, the line of which was pretty well indicated by Khrushchev.

MR. HITCHCOCK: That is a statement. You said it. It would be interesting. I don't doubt it.

MR. TAVENNER: You can supply the answer to it, can't you?

MR. HITCHCOCK: I shan't.

MR. TAVENNER: You said you shan't?

MR. HITCHCOCK: I shan't if I could. You are putting hypothetical questions in my hand—I mean my mouth.

MR. TAVENNER: What *did* happen between you and the Communist Party?

MR. HITCHCOCK: Am I directed to answer that?

THE CHAIRMAN: Yes.

MR. HITCHCOCK: I must decline to answer on the grounds of the first, second, third, fourth, and fifth amendments. Anything more?

THE CHAIRMAN: Be patient.

MR. TAVENNER: Prior to your taking the position of chairman of the Independent Socialist Forum, did you have a considerable period of training within the ranks of the Communist Party?

MR. HITCHCOCK: Really, Counsel, that is a naive question. You do not expect me to answer.

MR. SCHERER: I ask that you direct the witness to answer.

THE CHAIRMAN: Have you completed the question?

MR. TAVENNER: Yes, sir.

MR. HITCHCOCK: I must decline to answer the question on the grounds previously stated.

MR. TAVENNER: Is this information regarding you correct? It appears from the *Western Worker*, the issue of July 12, 1937, as early as that date, you were elected the educational director of the Young Communist League.

MR. HITCHCOCK: You are certainly going a long way back, aren't you, Congressman, Senator?

MR. TAVENNER: We would like to know how experienced you are in the field.

MR. HITCHCOCK: Am I directed to answer it?

THE CHAIRMAN: You are directed to answer it.

MR. HITCHCOCK: I decline to answer it on the grounds of the first, second, third, fourth, and sixth amendments.

MR. SCHERER: What is the third amendment?

MR. HITCHCOCK: I am not a lawyer. I leave that to you. I just throw it in.

THE CHAIRMAN: I must again remind the audience that you are here as guests of the committee. This is serious committee business. You may think it is funny, but we do not. Go ahead, Mr. Tavenner.

MR. TAVENNER: In the year 1937 while a member of the Young Communist League were you editor of *New Frontiers*, the official yearbook of the Young Communist League?

MR. HITCHCOCK: I again have no intention of answering it. Are you directing that I answer?

THE CHAIRMAN: Yes; you are directed.

MR. HITCHCOCK: I must decline to answer on the grounds of the first, second, third, fourth, and fifth amendments. You are going a long way back, Senator.

MR. SCHERER: We come up to date. I put it to you as a matter of fact, and ask you to affirm or deny if it is not a fact, at the direction of the Communist Party in accordance with its new programs outlined by these writers, you did not resign from the Communist Party and accept the chairmanship of the Independent Socialist Forum.

MR. HITCHCOCK: Am I directed to answer that question?

THE CHAIRMAN: Yes; you are directed to answer the question.

MR. HITCHCOCK: I must decline to answer that question on the grounds of the first, second, third, fourth, and fifth amendments. My attorney just told me that the third amendment has to do with the quartering of soldiers during time of war.

MR. TAVENNER: According to the investigation that the committee has made, you have been very experienced in the field of education, of a certain character. For instance, according to the *People's World* of September 4, 1946, it is reported that you had been appointed trade-union director of the California Labor School. Is that correct?

MR. HITCHCOCK: Am I directed to answer that question?

THE CHAIRMAN: Yes; you are directed to answer that question.

MR. HITCHCOCK: I must decline to answer that question on the grounds previously stated, including the first and fifth amendments.

MR. TAVENNER: We find that the 1947 catalog of the California Labor School lists you as a member of the staff of that school during that year; is that correct?

MR. HITCHCOCK: Am I directed to answer that question, Congressman?

THE CHAIRMAN: Yes; you are so directed.

MR. HITCHCOCK: I must decline to answer it on the grounds previously stated.

MR. TAVENNER: *The Daily People's World* of February 6, 1948, discloses that you had evidently changed your position at the California Labor School and were now teaching comparative philosophy at that school and, according to the issue of April 6, 1948, of the same paper, you were still teaching at that school, your subject being modern philosophy. According to the issue of June 7, 1948, of the same paper, there were a number of seminars to be held by that school and, on August 13 and 14, you were part of a panel. An issue of the same paper printed announcement of the summer program for 1948 and that, on August 6, 7, and 8, you were to participate on a panel organized by it, and then again on December 28, 1949, and in January 1950 you were to conduct courses at the California Labor School. Is that record of your teaching at the California Labor School substantially correct?

MR. HITCHCOCK: I think, learned Counsel, I would decline to answer that on the grounds previously stated.

MR. TAVENNER: I have no further questions, Mr. Chairman.

THE CHAIRMAN: What is this Independent Socialist Forum, Mr. Hitchcock?

MR. HITCHCOCK: It is a forum devoted to nonsectarian and nonpartisan discussions and education around Socialist questions. The members of the committee are welcome to be of any political persuasion on the left. We try very carefully to see that it is not controlled by any party or organization on the left. It is simply a forum for discussion for people who are interested in radical ideas in the city of San Francisco to get together in public and discuss those ideas for any audience that cares to come. We would be happy to invite you Congressmen, if you would like to come.

MR. MCINTOSH: Has your forum had occasion to discuss the recent announcement of the Chinese Communist dictator of the liquidation of some 800,000 Chinese citizens between 1949 and 1954?

MR. HITCHCOCK: That has not come up yet, but there is no reason why it should not be.

MR. MCINTOSH: Is it on the agenda?

MR. HITCHCOCK: I did not say it is on the agenda, but people have full opportunity to discuss any point of view, the only general limitation being that they be of interest to the Socialist public or people interested in ideas. We entertained as our guest, for your information, at a very recent meeting, the west-coast director of the National Association of Manufacturers who wished to discuss the question of socialism—against—and that is the sole function of this organization.

It is completely public, and if you would care to appear on the platform I am sure you would be very welcome to appear. That is all. There is nothing else. We don't take a stand and we don't have any position apart from that.

MR. SCHERER: When Mr. Tavenner asked about your occupation you said you are a gardener.

MR. HITCHCOCK: That is correct.

MR. SCHERER: Do you have any other occupation?

MR. HITCHCOCK: I have hobbies. It was released to the newspapers that I am an actor but if I am supposed to be a pillar of the entertainment business in San Francisco, they are barking up the wrong tree. I have acted in the theater occasionally for the fun of it.

MR. MCINTOSH: We pay $9 a day for it.

MR. HITCHCOCK: I thought I would get some in on the television people.

THE CHAIRMAN: The witness is excused.

INTERVIEW FROM DURAK: THE
INTERNATIONAL MAGAZINE OF POETRY

The inaugural issue of Durak: The International Magazine of Poetry
featured the following interview with George Hitchcock. It was con-
ducted by Robert Lloyd, a co-editor of the magazine, on June 3, 1978,
at George Hitchcock's home in Santa Cruz, California.

DURAK: What were you doing before you began writing poetry?

HITCHCOCK: From the age of nineteen to about thirty, I was trying to
write novels. Realistic novels in a large structure. I wrote four and I've
thrown them all away. In those days, I was writing what the Germans
call *Bildungsroman*—novels of the educational development of a young
man. Rather classically modeled. One of them was going to be pub-
lished but the war came along and it all evaporated. Then I threw the
manuscript away. It's burnt.

DURAK: Where were you educated?

HITCHCOCK: I took a B.A. degree at the University of Oregon in the
middle of the Depression. After that, I dropped out of school com-
pletely; I mean, I never went back.

DURAK: How were you able to afford college during the Depression?

HITCHCOCK: Well, my father and grandfather both helped me and I
lived in the town where I was brought up—Eugene, Oregon. I didn't
wander away. I suppose it was expensive to go to school. It was diffi-
cult because people didn't have a lot of money. On the other hand,
things didn't cost very much either. I think my last year of college, I sup-
ported myself, chiefly, by playing poker.

DURAK: Did you enter the war?

HITCHCOCK: I was in the Merchant Marine. I can't say I had very hair-raising war experiences. I felt the war should be won, but I also was not about to get myself killed if I could avoid it. I've always been, as Shaw said, a revolutionary you could find in the back row during an actual riot looking for the nearest exit. From 1950 until 1967 or 1968, I worked first as a construction laborer and then went into landscape gardening and was doing general landscaping for many, many years. Of course, I deliberately chose landscape gardening because the work was seasonal. You can work hard during the summer, and then in winter-time, you have a good deal of time to write.

DURAK: Haven't you also been connected with the theater?

HITCHCOCK: I've been very seriously committed to the theater and I did a great deal of acting. I've had about twenty-five different productions of original plays—San Francisco, off-Broadway, community and university theaters around the country. As an actor, I think I've had sixty or seventy leading roles mostly in classical plays.

DURAK: When did you first become interested in poetry?

HITCHCOCK: In the late thirties, I'd been exposed to a lot of modern poetry. I was a good friend of Kenneth Rexroth. He used to read his early manuscripts—before he had his first book published—to me. He really introduced me to contemporary poetry.

DURAK: What was your first introduction to Surrealism?

HITCHCOCK: Well, in the thirties, I was a great admirer of Neruda, García Lorca and—strangely enough—the Surrealist stories of Philippe Soupault. Those are the ones I'd read by the time I was twenty or twenty-one.

DURAK: How did it happen that a young American kid in Oregon was reading Neruda in the thirties? It wasn't popular then, was it?

HITCHCOCK: It wasn't popular at all, but it was accessible. H.R. Hays brought out his *Twelve Latin American Poets* in 1937–1938, something like that. I ran across Neruda in 1940, I guess. I had read Lorca before that. I was very much involved in the fate of the Spanish Republic in 1935–1937.

DURAK: Were you reading Breton and Soupault's *Littérature?*

HITCHCOCK: No. I don't read French for any enjoyment. I can read the French newspapers, but I don't read imaginative work in French. Breton is hard enough to read anyway, let along trying to translate, too.

DURAK: In Matthew Josephson's *Life Among the Surrealists—*

HITCHCOCK: We had dinner with Matthew Josephson three months ago, and two days later he died. I'd never met him before and I spent the whole evening talking to him. It was quite fascinating because I'd admired not only his *Life Among the Surrealists*, but also his biography of Stendhal which I'd read years ago. But alas, after one evening's conversation, to die.

DURAK: You don't think the two were related?

HITCHCOCK: I hope not! Pray to God, no!

DURAK: He refers to the feeling Americans have that Surrealism is a widespread artistic hoax—

HITCHCOCK: But then there are people who run around saying that Picasso was a widespread, international hoax. One ignores it. I don't care what the American people think of Surrealism. It doesn't make any difference to me.

DURAK: So the idea of national recognition doesn't appeal to you?

HITCHCOCK: It's at the back of my mind... very far removed from the surface. I'm not primarily concerned with that, no. Well, you know, one has to write and create according to one's own lights, as best you can. The poet, hopefully, does not have to lead the life of a huckster or a promoter. I think when you create, you create with all the integrity and all the ability you can according to your talent. You leave it to other people to worry about whether you're any good or not. It's nice to be published. One tries to get read by people for whose opinions one cares. I'm not exaggerating when I say that as a poet, I write for the good opinions of two hundred people in the country and I think almost every other poet—who's a good poet, in his heart of hearts—does the same thing.

DURAK: Can you tell me who one of those two hundred people is?

HITCHCOCK: They are fellow poets mostly. A few readers you meet. People whose opinions you value. Otherwise, you might as well become a rock star, if you want publicity. Publicity is terrible. Most types of publicity are degrading. So you're not interested in that kind of exposure. I'm not. I hate it. I'm afraid of it. That kind of popularity doesn't interest me at all. I think it's too bad—you see a person with some talent (at least, I thought Erica Jong had talent) who surrenders herself completely to the American success story. She's in a bad way artistically. I think people who accept transitory popularity for a mass audience in preference to sticking with, working with what they know, never minding about all that, I think invariably they burn themselves out and become corrupted. It's the history of a great many talents in this country. I don't think it's an accident that we have the highest of all possible suicide rates among writers in this country in this century. It relates to a surrender of integrity to the American success story. This is the only country in the world that has such an exaggerated sense of success. Success in this country isn't viewed as a lifetime of steady work, little by little putting the bricks on some edifice we may not know what it looks like until it's through. It's viewed as winning a mass audience, courting a mass audience, getting the kind of money and lifestyle to loaf on that money. Getting popular acclaim. I don't think that has anything to do with good writing.

DURAK: Do you think there's a sufficient audience for poetry today?

HITCHCOCK: There is a good audience. You just can't take a Madison Avenue view of what an audience should be. There is a good audience in this country. God knows, there's ten times the audience there was when I started writing. There are all sorts of people reading poetry in this country. It's not a mass audience; if you compare it to the people who go to a baseball game or the people who tune into a television show every night, then it is minuscule; it doesn't exist. That's not the kind of audience one should be interested in. I'm interested in an audience to whom I can speak, to whom I would enjoy talking if I met them vis-a-vis—one-to-one conversation. That kind of audience is a good audience but that kind of audience is perhaps a thousand people.

DURAK: Would you like to sit in a room with those one thousand people?

HITCHCOCK: Oh no, no, of course not! I'm a terrible claustrophobic about things like that. No. No, I wouldn't do that. But the ideal audience—the audience I would like to consider I write for—is one that if there were one thousand people on one thousand consecutive nights, I would enjoy sitting and talking with each one of them. Or perhaps three or four at a crack. So this evening, I meet three members of the audience; the next night, three more; and the next night, four (so that we don't get too uniform). The next night, one.

DURAK: Is there Surrealism in life or is it strictly an artistic technique? Do you perceive Surrealist tendencies in the world?

HITCHCOCK: Well, obviously, there's a great deal that's illogical—according to classical Aristotelean logic—in the world in which we live. I suppose that's why Surrealism is a twentieth century phenomenon. To me, Surrealist poetry is an art form. It's the expressive form which certain Romantic impulses characteristically take in the twentieth century.

DURAK: Surrealism presents the state of the soul in this century?

HITCHCOCK: I suppose so. I think Surrealism is an outgrowth of the Romantic revolution both in England and on the Continent. In a way, it's a further development. You could start with Byron, through Baudelaire, through Gérard de Nerval and Lautréamont on down through contemporary Surrealists. I think Surrealism is just a part in that cycle.

DURAK: Why does American Surrealism exist?

HITCHCOCK: I don't think I can answer that question. Not because I wouldn't be willing to if I knew, but I'm not at all sure. I think when Surrealism first occurred in this country, it seemed highly derivative to many people. Many people chose not to accept the Surrealist way of looking at things.

DURAK: How would you characterize that way of looking at things?

HITCHCOCK: That's hard to answer, too. I don't know. It's one of those things I can recognize immediately when I see it, but it can be defined in a great many different ways. I suppose you took a look at the Edward Germain anthology *(Surrealist Poetry in England and*

America)? That's a very worthwhile book because it's the first time any-
one has systematically gone through the literature to try to extract a tra-
dition of Surrealism in British and American poetry. Although he
includes a lot of people I wouldn't. I think only accidentally they are
Surrealists or they wrote one or two poems. Tom Clark doesn't seem
very Surrealist to me. A very latitudinarian and catholic interpretation
of what is Surrealism.

DURAK: Who were the first generation American Surrealists?

HITCHCOCK: Harry Crosby, Charles Henri Ford, Edouard Roditi.
People who were very much in contact with the European painters.
They were either Americans abroad or New Yorkers who were in con-
tact with Dali, Breton, or others in the Surrealist movement. A second
wave of Surrealism emerged in the late fifties–early sixties with poets
who began to use American images and utilize some of the same tech-
niques and the same attitude toward the world as Breton and Desnos
had. They used American imagery and created American Surrealism. It
utilizes dreams, the subconscious, random association—all the well-
known devices of the Surrealists—but utilizes them with American
material, American consciousness, and elements of our American expe-
rience. The language and experience of the American people is certain-
ly different than that of Europeans. I can tell imitation French
Surrealism immediately. It's different than, say, Robert Bly's poem
which was written nearly twenty years ago on J.P. Morgan which was
a very Surrealist poem but uses the language and experience of
America. One in that series called "The Current Administration" which
was published in *kayak* in 1966:

> Here Morgan dies like a dog among whispers of angels;
> The saint is born among tincans in the orchard;
> A rose receives the name of "The General Jackson."
> Here snow-white blossoms bloom in the bare homes
> Of bankmen, and with a lily the Pope meets
> A delegation of waves, and blesses the associations
> Of the ocean;

Obviously a Surrealist poem, but he's concerned with American mate-
rial. It's very different in a way from the type of Surrealism of Desnos
or Breton. During the late fifties–early sixties, a number of people,
myself included, were writing poems with American material and the

American experience. A number of poems from *The Moving Target* and *The Lice* that W.S. Merwin published in the sixties... very Surrealist in that way. A great deal of James Tate's poetry which he started writing in the sixties was very Surrealist in that fashion. With the American experience and the peculiar American sense of humor, James Tate has written poetry which is not only Surrealist but is also full of one-liners and vaudeville gags. That material is perfectly all right. The French Surrealists of the 1930s venerated Charles Chaplin and the Marx Brothers and that material would've gone into their poetry if they felt at home using it. It certainly should go into American Surrealist poetry. There are a lot of things unique in the American experience; they're in our subconscious and if we let go, we utilize them.

DURAK: How do you begin a poem?

HITCHCOCK: I put myself in a position where I can be dictated to. What comes out, I write down. But what I write down, I don't treat as a sanctified text. I fiddle with it, rewrite it and try to find the center of it. In poetry, I always start with the idea of music. I enjoy writing poetry; when the day comes that I don't enjoy writing poetry, I'll stop it. The real task in my poetry is to discover the extent and geography of my own subconscious. And then put that down in the most intelligible fashion reconcilable with the subconscious. And I utilize all the words I know to do it. A lot of people say I use a lot of long words. If I use a lot of long words, it's because I'm familiar with a lot of long words. They're a part of my life.

DURAK: Are you being dictated to by something other than yourself? Are you saying it's mystical?

HITCHCOCK: The process of creation is mystical, all right, but I don't put mystical names on it. I'm not religious. I prefer to use the terminology of Freud and say: it's the subconscious dictating the content to the conscious. Then we argue about it. The conscious argues back and says that that doesn't make a very good poem. The process of the argument is worked out in successive drafts of the work. The conscious argues and then the subconscious asserts itself and argues back; each time, I get a new draft of the work.

DURAK: When the subconscious is dictating to you, are you aware of what is being written?

HITCHCOCK: I try not to be. Sometimes I am, but I try not to be. I start writing and just writing away and I never look at a word the moment I put it down. That's the only way you can induce and maintain that state of consciousness. If you stop and look, you're lost. The idea in this sort of writing—automatic writing—is to free yourself from all grammatical and critical worries. Just start writing and allow one word to discover the next word without thinking about it. Pretty soon one word leads to another. If you get expert at releasing your subconscious and releasing your sense of play or accident, it goes pretty well. When you go back and read it, every word is a surprise; you don't remember what you've written at all. If I start remembering what I've written, then I know I'm being too self-consciously creative and it's time to quit.

DURAK: Are you writing in lines?

HITCHCOCK: I'm writing in rhythms. Sometimes I'm writing in lines— it's hard to generalize. Sometimes I am and sometimes I'm not. But nearly always, the most important thing for me in writing a poem is to get some musical sense before I start to write. Some sense of the rhythm. Not the content. Not even the words. The rhythm of a particular line will appeal to me first. Then I will repeat that rhythm in variations and then I will start writing down—while thinking that rhythm, while feeling that rhythm—all sorts of nonsense. Anything that comes to my head. Then, when I've sufficiently covered or disfigured a page with these chicken tracks, the problem is to find the center of it—what it revolves around. The problem is to define what you now have so that it is communicable to someone else, but not overdefine it—what you have then is a prose statement. If you approach the conscious too closely, then it is no longer a poem. On the other hand, if you don't approach the conscious—if you don't touch the sores of the conscious some place or another—then it is probably not a communicable poem.

DURAK: And you never touch the rhythm?

HITCHCOCK: Obviously, one's ear is not infallible when you start writing things down. Frequently you get a lot of clinkers. I always write out of a strong sense of rhythm and that's what has led me, in the past year or so, to turn back to certain rhyme forms.
DURAK: Reading some of your new work, I was surprised to discover the rhyme forms—

HITCHCOCK: Why? You have a preconceived notion that the avant-garde and everything forward is away from rhymed structure. That was a perfectly valid idea in the days of the youth of William Carlos Williams and the middle age of Ezra Pound. I think the poet should be prepared to use any and all resources. I don't like clinking rhymes. I usually am wittier and have more fun playing with off-rhymes, bizarre rhymes and things of that sort. Those are all resources the poet can use with discretion. Why not? I don't see why you shouldn't. I've always felt that the distinction between rhymed verse and free verse was a dead issue. It's an issue of the twenties. This battle was fought out fifty years ago and free verse is definitely the predominant style of verse. What we have lost in the course of this is music in poetry. We have an awful lot of people writing poetry today who might just as well be writing prose; they have absolutely no ear and no sense of music. Music doesn't nec-essarily mean Algernon Swinburne and elaborate rhyme schemes. It has to do with rhythmic sounds. A great many American poets today pay no attention to that and, I think, their poetry suffers. At least to me, poetry is music.

DURAK: Is a line, then, a rhythmical unit?

HITCHCOCK: Not always. I think the rhythm rises out of the syllables and the words, and it doesn't make a great deal of difference where you put your line-stops. I like to use line-stops not to accent the rhythm, but to create a contrapuntal rhythm. I like to use what they technically call enjambment to create a syncopation like in jazz.

DURAK: However, you're not committed to rhyme—

HITCHCOCK: I'm not committed to rhyme. It's usually not my bag. I grew up writing free verse, but I'm fond of music and I think poetry without it is not good poetry. A lot of poets seem absolutely committed to a program or platform. I think the day of the programs and plat-forms—at least the fierce defense of Modernism—was fifty or sixty years ago! It meant something then. People took a chance if they stuck up for Imagism, free verse or Surrealism. It doesn't mean anything today. Those battles have been fought and Modernism won. But, to me, the poetic enemies today are no longer the little old ladies who are imi-tating Swinburne.

DURAK: Who are the poetic enemies?

HITCHCOCK: For me? I have lots of poetic enemies! I mean poetry which I don't care for and which I don't think is doing anything. We're getting a lot of flat poetry. We're getting poets who are highly venerated but I don't care for—Charles Bukowski, for example.

DURAK: You don't care for Charles Bukowski's work?

HITCHCOCK: No, I think he's terrible, but he has some talent. I was just reading the other day a Robin Skelton article: reading Charles Bukowski, he says, is necessary so people can see what would've happened to Henry Miller if he hadn't gone to Paris. It's easy to be cruel to Bukowski; he laps it up. He specializes in drunken readings and insulting everybody in the audience and all his contemporaries. He does have some talent, though. I just don't like his macho, racetrack and whore stuff. I don't like Ernest Hemingway for the same reason. Each of us has his own prejudices and the best we can do is to be honest about them.

DURAK: Bukowski is an authentic, working-class poet—

HITCHCOCK: Well, it's authentic. It's American, but it's a part of America I can do without quite easily. And since I was for twenty years a workingman and thus daily in contact with people just like that, it doesn't thrill me to make that discovery. To the generation of young, middle-class people who are not exposed to working-class culture, Bukowski is a great discovery. I dare say he is but, to me, he isn't. He talks with not a great deal more flair than characters I worked with in the shipyard. That's why he's authentic; he represents lumpenproletarian America. It's real and it's true but the whole thing is fatiguing.

DURAK: You've published many found poems and edited two *kayak* anthologies of found poems. How did Robert Peters and you begin *Pioneers of Modern Poetry?*

HITCHCOCK: In the early days of *kayak,* I was continually searching for materials for cut-ups—for collage cut-ups. In the course of getting Victorian engravings for that purpose, one runs across a great many crazy texts. I started saving some of those texts for found poems. I proposed to Robert Peters, who was at Cambridge at the time, to collaborate with me on the project. He discovered some, too, and we started writing learned and scholarly footnotes. Some people took it seriously, though. We had a long correspondence with some chap at the

University of Kansas, who thought they were very real and very serious. Well, the source material is all legitimate. We broke it up into lines, obviously. We didn't invent anything. It's all there. It all came out of the books it purports to come out of: Victorian physical exercises, marching steps, Indian clubs, farm manuals on the silo and dizziness in geese. Some of those are coming out, incidentally, in the new *Oxford Book of American Light Verse.*

DURAK: What characterizes a good found poem?

HITCHCOCK: I think one of the characteristics of really good found poetry is that it has bizarre and attractive language. Linguistically, there's something going on and rhythmically, there's something going on. That's why question-and-answer manuals and instructions for exercises are so good, because they have a built-in rhythm. The catechizing nature of some of them. Some of them are review questions like "Distinguishing Ru from Chu"—do you remember that? It's from *Barnes Shorthand Lessons* published in 1885. It's a series of questions, and a question test has set up a certain kind of rhythm; you repeat another question and another question and so forth. Anton Tien was the author of the *Egyptian and Syrian Phrasebook.* I think he was an Arab with a built-in poetic sense because his English versions of all these phrases you're supposed to learn in Arabic are just loaded with rhythmic variations. I think he had natural music flowing in his veins.

DURAK: Found poems also raise the distinction between poetry and prose. How do you characterize the difference?

HITCHCOCK: It's partly music and it's partly compression. I'm giving you my definition; it won't stand up in court. Prose has music, too—a steely, controlled music. If you read the prose of George Bernard Shaw you will see a strong musical sense in it. What poetry always has that prose doesn't is an elliptical sense—a sense of terrific compression so that it's full of lacunae, little leaps, which you have to bridge by projecting the reader into it, which you have to bridge by projecting your own fantasies into the line. The prose line will spout it all out; it says everything. Its objective is clarity. Its objective certainly must be that it needs to say one thing and not another. It has a logical clarity to it, whereas, the objective of poetic lines, to me, seems to be quite the opposite—ambiguity. The poetic line does not mean to say exactly what it says. If it did, it would be prose. It means to set up resonances around an idea so that a number of different things can be inferred from it. There's always that element of ambiguity. It's always up to the reader to determine if I meant this or meant that—or perhaps, I meant both at the same time.

DURAK: Your poems have drastically changed in the sixteen years since *Poems & Prints* was published. Your early poems were hermetic and sparse compared to the lyrical poems in *Lessons in Alchemy*.

HITCHCOCK: I'm not sure I agree with that. To tell the truth, I've never gone back and spent a lot of time analyzing where I was. Writing poetry, to me, is always a question of the present moment, so it's where I am right now that interests me. If my poetry has enough value that someone wishes to analyze it in historical terms, it's all right by me; I can't object. But, I never do it myself. I've never been concerned with poems I've already written and I'm always concerned with what I'm going to write next.

DURAK: Given the development of your work, it must have been difficult to revise the old poems that appear in *Lessons in Alchemy*.

HITCHCOCK: Well, there were a couple of poems I wanted to include in that book because they were out of print and I was very fond of them. As I got them ready and looked at them, I thought—well, you can call it *rewrite* if you want—it consisted of cutting a few things. I don't think I wrote any more, added anything or changed any words in any of those poems. In the ones I'd selected, a word or two seemed a little overly loquacious. There was not quite enough focus so I'd cut a bit. I don't hesitate revising something if I feel like revising it but, in general, I haven't done it. The only time when I review some of these poems is when I start using them in readings. When I do a number of readings, then I pick up a poem out of an early book and read it. Consequently, I hear it a lot; I hear myself reciting it and I feel the audience reaction to it—or lack of reaction. Sometimes, I reappraise a poem that way—as a performance piece, as some of them are.

DURAK: Is this reappraising the work of the conscious or do you try to recapture the imagination which was involved there sixteen years ago?

HITCHCOCK: That's not a long time for me. It might be a long time to you. As one gets older, he changes his perspective on what makes a long time. I think I'm a reader just as any other reader. When I go back to some of my poetry, I find it evocative. It is evocative not only of states of mind which existed when I wrote it, but it is evocative of something more than that. It's sometimes evocative of newly created perceptions. It becomes a new experience, too, even to the person who's written it. Suppose I haven't read a poem in three or four years—if that poem is any good, I expect it to evoke things which weren't there when I wrote it, since my consciousness has altered in the three or four years since I wrote it. Just as I would expect it to evoke different images and different experiences in the perceptive reader than those I may have intended—assuming I intended anything at all.

DURAK: What do you want to evoke for the perceptive reader?

HITCHCOCK: I want to create a sense of wonder and mystery on which the reader can project himself and fantasize. To do that, one must wrench accepted reality. You pull it apart. You throw it a little out of kilter, a little out of gear. This encourages the creative act of reading and the projection of fantasy on the part of the reader. That much I want out of a reader. Whether the reader evokes something happy or something sad—I don't think about it. Of course, if I'm fundamentally writing a poem in a sad mood, I dare say sadness is going to come across to the reader. I never start thinking of the reader except when I'm putting the final touches on a poem and working toward clarity; then, sometimes, I do. I think: no one is going to understand this. It's clear to me but it has, obviously, not been worked out enough because no one is going to be able to understand it, and what concessions can I make? A little clarity without destroying the fundamental ambiguity of the poem and the fundamental mystery of the poem. I think your imagination can be working at very high speeds and still nothing comes out that is an effective poem because the imagination doesn't make any allowance for the other denominator in a poetic experience. The poetic experience is like a spark which goes from one pole to another pole—it bridges and leaps. In order to make that flash which is the *frisson* of a poetic experience, there must be not only the mind that creates but there must be the mind that receives it. That mind is the reader's.

DURAK: In *Notes of the Siege Year*, you refer to the "epiphanies which elude logic." Do you think of epiphanies as manifestations of the divine?

HITCHCOCK: Well, I use it in Joyce's sense. It was one of his favorite words and, as he was very anti-Catholic, he didn't mean it in the divine sense. An epiphany to Joyce was a moment of illumination. Revelation. Where the revelation came from, you can call divine if you want. A sudden moment of transformation. You look all day at a tree and then, suddenly, in a moment of epiphany, the tree appears to you to be the hand of God, if you wish, or a burning bush or a flame or something. It's metaphorically transfigured and that occurs in a moment. The Japanese poet Basho felt in order to achieve what was his equivalent of epiphany he had to look at some object—in his case, in nature—so intensely that he almost felt himself transferred inside it. Without rationalizing about it, without thinking about it too much, but just trying to be with it and then, perhaps, an epiphany comes about and this object is transfigured by metaphor. It becomes something else quite literally. That, I think, is one of the acts of poetic vision.

DURAK: What concerns are important for you in poetry that you read and write?

HITCHCOCK: A loving attitude toward words is one thing that a poet must have. The poet cares for words and one word is distinctive, has a wonderful sound, is absolutely irreplaceable. It is the *mot juste*, as Flaubert said, while another word is hackneyed, clichéd, overworked. You have to develop that sensitivity to language. It's your language and as a writer you have to spend a lot of time working with it. You should be sensitive to it. The poet also ought to have a sense of rhythm and music. I said before, I think that's one of the great things lacking in contemporary poetry—a musical, rhythmic sense. I think any artist also has to have a real sensitivity to the nuances of psychological states. This is, perhaps, more important in the short story, the play and the novel than in poetry—I've read poetry by some people who are psychologically very obtuse—but then, I don't think of myself exclusively as a poet. I'm a writer; I've practiced all the forms of writing and will again. In all of them, the sense of nuance and subtlety of psychology of human behavior is extremely important. It makes all the difference between a really good writer and a person who's heavy and who doesn't understand behavior or, if he does understand it, doesn't know how to translate it into language. In the fiction I read, as in the fiction I write, that's a very considerable desideratum. It's something that is important to me. There are a lot of other things I think are important. I think the good writer should be, as nearly as possible, a universally cultured person. We all have our blank spots and things we can't really react to. We should know a good deal about painting; have a certain empathy toward nature and some knowledge of it. Be widely read. Widely read is, perhaps, not quite so important as to be widely sensitive. I think rich poetry comes from rich consciousness, a fantastic subconscious and relatively good linguistic control.

DURAK: You adhere very closely to the compositional techniques of the French Surrealists.

HITCHCOCK: Well, I've only been able to write poetry utilizing these techniques. I don't exactly know why but, at certain stages in my life, I've been so tied up psychologically with intellectual structures. Perhaps this sounds strange coming from a person who all those years was working with his hands, but I approached the art of writing only from an intellectual point of view. It was only in the process of a psychological and artistic re-evaluation in my thirty-fifth to fortieth year, I began to find benefits in letting go. No longer being fully planned and programmed, and finding a release in the non-rational actions and non-rational forms of thought. Then, I found myself able to write poetry. I remember when I was eighteen or nineteen, I tried some derivative verse which, fortunately, was long ago destroyed. It was only when I was able to break down my own personality structure and achieve more flexibility. This was, chiefly, not only through emotional experiences, but by trying to improve myself as an actor in an art form where you have to have great sensitivity, nuance and flexibility. In the course of becoming a good actor—which, I think, I more or less achieved—I certainly overhauled my personality a lot and my preconceptions of art forms. I came to place a great deal more faith in what you might call the instinctual, subconscious or non-rational elements in art.

DURAK: Do you consider yourself a Surrealist?

HITCHCOCK: I'm not a Surrealist in the sense that I agree with any more than thirty percent of what Breton or the authorized spokesmen of Surrealism had to say. I speak of it only as a method. For me, it's a method by which I can write poetry and feel at home with poetry. What comes out of it is largely Surrealist poetry, broadly, but that's because that's the only way I can write effectively. I tried the other ways when I was young and they don't work for me. Poetry, to me, is accompanied by a release of the imagination which I can accomplish by the methods of Surrealism. Thus far I am a Surrealist. No further.

DURAK: In many of your poems, there's often historical and technological imagery creating a counterpoint with the magical quality of your Surrealism.

HITCHCOCK: Yes. I read a great deal of history and a great deal of biography. And I read a good deal of science. I have mixed feelings about magic. I love to create magic, but magic which is just magic is likely to be cute-sy. It's likely to be fey. I like magic created out of the materials of non-magic. So that's why you find a lot of scientific words which belie magic.

DURAK: In your novel *Another Shore*, you say that we are educated within the structures of reality but "it's possible that they lack the modalities of the inspired." Would you ignore the structures of reality in favor of the structures of the imagination?

HITCHCOCK: Under certain circumstances, the structures of the imagination are the reality. The task of the poet is to revolutionize reality. It's not enough to simply mirror what passes for external reality. In so far as we are artists, we try to alter that by revolutionizing the nature of reality. And to do that, we must approach from some place... must have our foot on some point of support beyond that reality.

DURAK: Is the imagination in your work a perception or a creation?

HITCHCOCK: I think it's a way of creating another world out of the materials I have perceived in this world. Put it back together according to different laws. Defy gravity, for example. The laws of alchemy over the laws of gravity.

DURAK: Do you consider yourself relatively optimistic in your attitude toward the world?

HITCHCOCK: I don't feel one way or another about the world. The world is... my attitude toward the world? Well, most of the time, as you probably have observed, I'm relatively merry. Relatively optimistic. It's very difficult at times, considering the state of the world, to maintain that attitude. I would prefer to maintain that attitude all the time. I like to be optimistic because it makes me feel better. However, if one is chronically optimistic in a situation that doesn't call for it, you have a tendency to become sentimental and stupid. My own predisposition is certainly toward optimism. Poetry, for the most part, is an act of joy for me. I enjoy writing poetry and I get a great deal of satisfaction out of writing poetry whether anybody else likes it or not. I enjoy the act as I am describing it to you, and I enjoy the end-product enough of the time to keep me relatively pleased with myself.

DURAK: Do you have favorite poets whom you always enjoy reading?

HITCHCOCK: Not really. Not really. In the first place, I have to read a great deal of poetry editing *kayak*, so I don't read poetry for relaxation apart from that. I write poetry. I don't read that much, although. I've read an awful lot at one time or another. When I read poetry, my tastes are fairly catholic. I'm very fond of Yeats; much of Yeats I admire tremendously. I was brought up on the early poems of T.S. Eliot and I still have a great feeling of admiration for him. He's a wonderful poet.

DURAK: Some critics have argued that T.S. Eliot's critical and political stance set poetry back fifty years.

HITCHCOCK: Oh nonsense. That's absolute nonsense. Nothing sets poetry back fifty years. It's as if you're graphing a line of progress; as if each generation was getting closer and closer to the roseate goal of perfect poetry. And along comes some dastardly bastard who through his influence sets us all back fifty years. That's nonsense. Poetry isn't proceeding in that line anyway. No one can demonstrate to me that the poetry being written today is any better—generically—than the poetry Keats wrote. Our language may have changed, our concerns may have changed, but you can't demonstrate that. You can't demonstrate the myth of progress, that each decade poetry is getting better and better and better until some day there will be a millennium and everybody will write poetry that will be absolutely, ravishingly fantastic. It's utter bullshit. Any concept that any one poet or critic can set poetry back is all rubbish. Poetry isn't going any place anyway, so how can it be set back? On top of which, although I disagree with Eliot's critical and political stance as much as anyone does, some of his poetry is absolutely wonderful.

DURAK: If poetry isn't going anywhere, why does it keep going?

HITCHCOCK: Oh, because of each glorious moment that the poet finds himself in. That is what the poet is concerned with. I hate these people

165

who are more concerned with the zeitgeist, the spirit of the times, where something is going, and what is happening to American poetry, than the act of creation itself. To me, it is moment after moment after moment in which the poet creates something and alters reality in the course of it, which is the beauty of poetry even though nobody recognizes it. Still, the poet feels it and he does it. The poets who start saying, "Now I'm going to shape the course of American letters and after me everything will change"—now this is, of course, the attitude Robert Frost had for years and believed it—they're full of shit; they become pompous, pretentious and nonsensical. This is not a game shaping the course of history. The act of creation is everything. And when you create, your peers are Keats or Breton or name your half-dozen favorites from various schools. Or Yeats. Those are the people you're competing with. But you're not involved in some historical process which is consciously shaping the future of American letters. It's English Department talk. It's the talk of people who are more interested in the historical process than they are in the poetic moment. To me, the poetic moment is everything, and the historical process—I couldn't care less. When they come to evaluate the historical process and what's going on in this country, I'll be long dead. It will make no difference to me. But no one will take away from me the moments of poetic creation and reshaping of the world. Small as they may have been. Unimportant as they ultimately, historically, turn out to be, they are the heart of poetry. And this is what the poet ought to be concerned with.

CHRONICLE OF THE BEAT GENERATION FROM AMERICAN SOCIALIST

This review by George Hitchcock of Jack Kerouac's On the Road *and Allen Ginsberg's* Howl and Other Poems *appeared in* American Socialist *in 1958.*

Americans have a peculiar affinity for marking their history off in decades. Each decade in turn gives rise to its particular and often exaggerated zeitgeist, which literary and social historians promptly embody in a "generation." Thus we have had "the lost generation" of the twenties, "the socially conscious generation" of the thirties, "the war generation," and now in the fifties we have a rising aspirant for the title in the so-called "beat generation."

How much historical validity this categorizing actually has and how much it owes to our Madison Avenue habit of summing up every complex problem in a slogan, must remain for the time being open questions. But here in San Francisco, at least, we do have a very lively and vocal "beat generation" and the work of Ginsberg and Kerouac is the most illuminating guidebook to an understanding of it.

First, a little etymology. The word "beat" is, I take it, employed in three different senses, although even insiders don't appear to have reached agreement on the exact degree of its ambiguity. In addition to its obvious sense there is the jazz connotation and, finally, a sort of shorthand where it is assumed to stand for "beatific." The meanings are interlocking and more or less—depending on your mood—interchangeable.

The historians and publicists of the "beat generation" have been the poets Kenneth Rexroth and Lawrence Lipton, although it is arguable how much direct influence they have had upon writers for the most part twenty years younger than they and concerned primarily with the attitudes of their own contemporaries. Rexroth is a distinguished poet and critic who for nearly thirty years has nurtured and kept alive on California soil a sort of transplanted Chicago anarchism. He is a caustic, opinionated man who sometimes appears as if he were sitting for a statue of "the last Wobbly," but he is also a scholar of genuine ability and one of the few authentic poets the Pacific Coast has yet produced. Lipton is a midwestern anarchist who now preaches "total disaffiliation" from American society and urges his fellow-poets in Southern California to adopt a voluntary "vow of poverty" as a practical method of escaping from the corruption of the dollar sign. Both are vigorous pacifists.

If Lipton and Rexroth can be called the elder prophets, Allen Ginsberg certainly has every claim to be known as the movement's Jeremiah. For as the Lord is reputed to have revealed to Jeremiah in the wilderness: "And I brought you into a plentiful country, to eat the fruit thereof and the goodness thereof, but when ye entered, ye defiled my land and made mine heritage an abomination," so Ginsberg in a neon wilderness cries out against the corruption of America, lamenting the destroyed lives and blighted ambitions of his generation, not omitting those "who were burned alive in their innocent flannel suits on Madison Avenue amid blasts of leaden verse & the tanked-up clatter of the iron regiments of fashion & the nitroglycerine shrieks of the fairies of advertising & the mustard gas of sinister intelligent editors, or were run down by the drunken taxicabs of Absolute Reality."

The publication here of his *Howl and Other Poems* created the closest thing to a literary sensation the West Coast has known in many years. The title poem is a protracted cry of rage, Biblical in form and Surrealist in imagery, often turgid and at times hysterical, yet never lacking in explosive energy. It is the work of a literary dynamiter for whom anguish, marihuana and defiant homosexuality are all avenues of protest.

Orthodox society was quick to get the point. The Collector of Internal Revenue, a prominent Republican politician, ordered an entire edition of *Howl* seized in transit from its British printers to its publisher, Lawrence Ferlinghetti, a San Francisco poet and bookseller. Ginsberg's occasional use of un-bowdlerized Anglo-Saxon was given as the excuse, although Rexroth and others charged that the hand of the archdiocese was behind the seizures. Protests to Washington and the obvious lack of legal grounds resulted in the release of the edition.

The San Francisco police, perhaps with prompting from the same source, then got into the act. Officers of the Juvenile Bureau arrested Ferlinghetti and his clerk on very much the same charge that the officials of Athens brought against Socrates twenty-four hundred years ago—"corrupting the young"—in this case by offering *Howl* and a semi-anarchist literary magazine, *The Miscellaneous Man*, for sale.

The resulting trial attracted national attention and saw a nearly unanimous united front of the city's intellectuals in defense of Ginsberg and Ferlinghetti. A distinguished list of authors and critics took the stand in defense of *Howl's* literary qualities, while the District Attorney's office, largely staffed by Democrats, offered a somewhat shame-faced case for the prosecution. Judge Clayton Horn's ultimate decision for the defense surprised no one in particular, but his opinion was both literate and libertarian and should serve as a valuable precedent. In many ways it was an advance over the historic Woolsey decision (ending in 1933 the American ban on Joyce's *Ulysses*) as it emphasized in particular the importance of protecting the rights of social criticism.

Howl is at present selling merrily through another edition, Ginsberg was last reported sunning himself in North Africa, and the censors are presumably licking their wounds in the confines of the Olympic or Bohemian Clubs.

The second salvo in the battle of the "beat generation" has now been fired via the respectable Viking Press. It is *On The Road*, a novel by Jack Kerouac, a 35-year-old adopted San Franciscan who once played football at Columbia University. This last piece of information is not as meaningless as it sounds, for he approaches writing like a half-back on an endless touchdown run. He has already completed eleven full-length novels, of which *On The Road* is only the second to reach print, and if he can maintain his present pace is likely to set new mileage records for the medium.

He writes breathlessly in a potpourri of styles and with almost total recall of the materials of his own wandering life. *On The Road* is a sort of saga of a generation of rootless, restless lumpenproletarian bohemians who endlessly traverse the face of America in search of her significance. They live in defiance of the norms of our prosperity, working at odd jobs when they have to, but preferring, when possible, the alternatives traditionally available to the hobo. From New York to New Orleans to Denver to San Francisco to Mexico City—this is the track of their ceaseless hegira. Everywhere they seek the ultimate in ecstatic experience, whether it be in driving a borrowed Cadillac a hundred miles an hour across Iowa, in all-night philosophic discussions, marihuana, jazz, or copulation.

Kerouac's hero, a "jail-kid" from Denver, Dean Moriarty, is a sort of intellectual Elvis Presley filled with a frantic hunger for life who leaves a trail of burned-out automobiles and women behind him from one end of America to the other. His characteristic manner of speech can be conveyed only by an example:

He watched over my shoulder as I wrote stories, yelling, "Yes! That's right! Wow! Man!" and "Phew!" and wiped his face with his handkerchief. "Man, wow, there's so many things to do, so many things to write! How to even begin to get all down and without modified restraints and all hung-up on like literary inhibitions and grammatical fears."

Moriarty and his friends live in a souped-up world of continuous exhilaration as if the Second Coming is momentarily to be glimpsed around the corner. His psychological state could accurately be defined as approaching the manic. The philosophizing in which he and his friends are eternally indulging is all rubbish—and generally self-conscious rubbish. It is compounded of bits of Zen Buddhism, Saroyan, hop-talk, and Hemingway, with a generous admixture of the mystical primitivism of D. H. Lawrence's *The Plumed Serpent*. Nor do any of his characters ever really do anything or communicate with each other— they assume, instead, attitudes of angst which Kerouac apparently feels are proof of their uniquely inspired visions. "See, we are really MAD," he seems to be telling us over and over again. "Cool, beat, and MAD." Since the characters are precisely as MAD at the beginning as they are at the end and nothing else changes very much, we may be excused if we have grown to feel a certain weariness toward them.

But beneath the cultish nonsense and literary borrowings there is another aspect to *On The Road*, and it is this which gives the book its value. For in his naive outpouring Kerouac gives us at least one authentic picture—the picture of a submerged America, the America of an alienated, protesting generation which wanders from meaningless job to meaningless job in the depths of her psychic forests, a part of America expatriated in its own land. And this tragedy is not merely the personal one of Dean Moriarty and Sal Paradise—it is the tragedy of our society, glittering on its suburban surfaces and anarchic and despairing in its true heart.

Unlike Ginsberg, Kerouac feels no Messianic outrage at this tragedy; it might be argued, indeed, that he never gets the point of his own story, so enchanted is he by an "our gang is wonderful" feeling. But the point is there, and Kerouac's naive enthusiasm in the end proves an even more effective tool for laying it bare than Ginsberg's rhetoric. Kerouac should be distinguished from his gallery of hipsters. As a writer he owes more to the romanticism of Thomas Wolfe than he does to the "cool cats" of his own generation. He has warmth and compassion, and does not suffer from the pessimism or explicit homosexuality which limit Ginsberg's approach. Sensing his own expatriation within America, he tends to identify himself with his fellow outcasts in our society, particularly among the Negro and Mexican peoples:

"At lilac evening," he writes, "I walked with every muscle aching among the lights of 27th and Welton in the Denver colored section, wishing I were a Negro, feeling that the best the white world had offered was not enough ecstasy for me, not enough life, joy, kicks, darkness, music, not enough night..."

Romanticized as this version of Negro life is, it helps to illustrate one of the great differences between this generation of "expatriates" and those other expatriates of the so-called "lost generation" of the 1920s. For what has changed is not the philosophizing—all the "frantic" talk can't disguise the same old content—but the social position of these bohemians. The expatriates of the twenties—and here I think of *Tender is the Night* and *The Sun Also Rises*—nearly all had money or at least pretended that they did, and they rejected American materialism in favor of the more urbane values of a decaying European upperclass civilization. But the expatriates of Kerouac's "beat generation" are aliens within their own country and in their frenzied quest for inner truth are being drawn toward the sources of new life and hope within that country.

I hope that I have indicated that Kerouac is a remarkable writer, although not for reasons of which he himself seems aware. But as a document of our times his *On The Road* rises far above the cult which helped give it birth and may, in time, be that movement's chief justification.

PLAYS

Theater As a Way of Life

*t*he two plays which follow are the work of a playwright whose sole exposure to the New York theater is one April evening when he sneaked in at half-time to watch a production of Molière's *School for Wives* somewhere on East 47th Street. He went back to the West Coast the next morning and hasn't returned.

I make the point because when I was writing plays it was generally assumed that American theater and the island of Manhattan were roughly coterminous and that any script worth producing ultimately ends up on Broadway or on one of its off-off-off fringes. Well, it isn't so; here are some perfectly good plays that originated 3,000 miles away where the continental shelf drops off toward Hong Kong and the marvelous.

All of my plays—or at least the earlier versions from which some of them have sprung—were written for production by two San Francisco theaters—The Interplayers and The Actor's Workshop. Both of these companies are now long defunct: not to be wondered at, since playhouses of ideas are ephemeral fowl, short-lived for all their gaudy plumage and protestations of perdurability. Both these companies shared a dislike of plastic commercial realism and were devoted to theater as a way of life to be followed with Taoist fervor. The Interplayers were perhaps the more international in flavor; its leaders were pacifists, vaguely Existentialist, and sensitive in particular to the winds from the Continent: Anouilh, Giraudoux, Cocteau, Saroyan and Shaw were the names to conjure with there. My first four plays were added to their repertory.

The Actor's Workshop, the more famous of the two, has been described in detail by Herbert Blau in his book, *The Impossible Theater*. Its organizing principles were roughly those of the Strasberg-Clurman Group Theater; its literary tastes tended to be those of Blau himself and were a good deal more ideological (and dare I say sombre?) than those of the catch-as-catch-can bohemian company from which I had come. Their production standards—supervised by the late Jules

Irving—were also far higher than anything San Francisco had hitherto seen. For eight or ten years the company breathed theatrical excitement, and I am sure that if I have learned anything about practical stagecraft and the art of directing (and without some knowledge of these the playwright is truly at sea) I owe it to my five years of work with these masters. *Prometheus Found* and *The Busy Martyr* were written for this company, and I think it testimony to the careful critical attention Irving and Blau gave these scripts in rehearsal that I have found so few revisions necessary in preparing them for this book.

Ultimately, of course, The Actor's Workshop came apart. The leaders succumbed to the siren song of the establishment and left to manage New York's Lincoln Center—a big plum, no doubt, but one that proved impossible to digest. New York gained little and San Francisco lost a lot.

Of the plays here, *The Busy Martyr* has had the longest life on stage. It won the Stanley playwriting award and has since seen over a dozen productions, chiefly in university theaters. Particularly memorable presentations were those by the Tufts Summer Theater in Boston and the Circle Theater in Nashville. The text here is reprinted from *First Stage*, a Purdue University publication. *Prometheus Found* is reprinted from the *San Francisco Review*.

Finally, a word of affectionate appreciation for the many actors who helped bring these entertainments to life. Theater, as we all know, is a collective venture, and until a script takes form through voice, body, and spirit of the actor it cannot presume to true existence. Thus I recall particularly Tom Rosqui in *Prometheus* and later as Muscari in *The Martyr*, Peggy Doyle, Alan Mandell and Rudy Solari in *Prometheus*, Robert Symonds, again as Muscari; and Adrian and Joyce Wilson for their constant encouragement in the beginning. To them and the hundreds of others who shared in the adventure, and particularly to the memory of Michael O'Sullivan and Jules Irving, who believed—my gratitude.

For the rest—the play's the thing!

—GH

❧ PROMETHEUS FOUND

A Tragicomedy In Two Acts

The text of *Prometheus Found* is as first presented by The Actor's Workshop in San Francisco, July 21, 1958, and September 5–19, 1958, with the following casts:

Prometheus . . . . . Rudolph Solari
The Guardian . . . Alan Mandell
Meg . . . . Jinx Hone, Margaret Doyle
Harry . . . . Tom Rosqui
Rasmussen . . . . . . Robert Symonds, W.R. Jonason

ACT ONE
Scene One

A mountaintop: volcanic rocks. Beyond, a gun-metal sky empty of everything. At the rear a great wheel against which the naked PROMETHEUS *is chained as if crucified. His head hangs forward and it is only by its intermittent movements that we see that he lives.*

THE GUARDIAN *sits on a rock a little distance apart. He is an inconspicuous man of middle age clothed in a shabby serge suit. He smokes a pipe. After a moment* THE GUARDIAN *knocks the coal from his pipe, arises, steps downstage and speaks.*

THE GUARDIAN: *(Unemotionally)* This is Prometheus, imprisoned here because in disobedience to the will of Zeus he carried fire to Man. I do not know any other details of his story. It all happened thirty thousand years ago, and thirty thousand years is a long time, even to immortals. I have been here less than three hundred and already I am thoroughly tired of it. I have nothing against the prisoner. I simply carry out orders: discipline must be preserved and, after all, Zeus is Zeus.

Today there has been more excitement than usual. A plane passed overhead at 08:00 and after lunch there was an electrical disturbance. *(PROMETHEUS moves on the wheel.)* He is restless. Usually at this hour he catches a few winks of sleep. There is no way of finding out what he feels. He does not talk to me and when he screams I find it pleasanter to stop my ears. This has been a very lonely station for me.

I hear it rumored about that his term of punishment is very nearly over. It's said that Hercules is coming to rescue him. Of course, that's just hearsay. I don't object. I prefer a station where there is some company, even if it's only the company of mortals. And if they try to rescue him Zeus must have foreseen it. Probably he approves. Anyway, it will all come out the way he planned it. I shan't interfere. I am only an inferior god. It doesn't do to show *hubris*. It's safer to let events take their course. *(He goes off.)*

MEG *enters from the other side and assumes a pose against a rock. She is 23, handsome, suntanned and dressed in hiking shorts and a white blouse. She has an intelligent face with signs of tension in it. She has been hiking and carries a light rucksack.*

HARRY: *(Voice offstage)* Hold it. The light is too strong.
MEG: Don't you have a filter?
HARRY: *(Offstage)* K-3. Dark yellow. It brings out the sky tones. At this altitude I should have ultraviolet.

HARRY *enters bearing a light meter which he holds against* MEG'S *face.* HARRY *is an athletic young man of perhaps 25, unmistakably American. He too is dressed in hiking shorts; on his back he carries a packsack on a Norwegian packboard with bedroll attached. Around his neck and from his belt hang pieces of photographic equipment, a hunting knife, etc. When he speaks, it is in a strong, pleasant, Midwestern voice, which is suffused with almost permanent enthusiasm. It is obvious that he has few doubts about the world or his place in it, but all the same his brashness is generally inoffensive since it is tempered by a boyish delight.*

HARRY: I can get by without it. *(He gives* MEG *the end of a tape measure.)* Hold this a second. *(He paces away from her.)* I'll focus at 16 and stop down to f-11.
MEG: Sounds complicated.
HARRY: *(Rolling up the tape.)* Not really. Below f-11 you lose the shading. Ready?
MEG: *(Neither of them have observed* PROMETHEUS.*)* Ready.
HARRY: *(Kneeling)* Nothing but the sky beyond. *(He snaps a picture.)* One more. Lean back against the rock. And raise your arm just a bit.

MEG: There isn't too much glare?

HARRY: It's all right. *(They stand with their backs to* PROMETHEUS.*)* Now I want to get one of the valley.

MEG: We've come a long way.

HARRY: Tired?

MEG: A little.

HARRY: It was a stiff climb. You're a good sport.

MEG: Do you suppose the others will make it?

HARRY: No, they turned back. They didn't have the endurance. And that's what it takes. Endurance. *(He removes his pack.)*

MEG: *(Seated)* My shoes are full of volcanic ash. *(She takes one off and shakes it.)* Frankly, I'm just as glad. If there's anything I detest it's conducted tours. And I had about all I could take of those mousy school teachers with their stupid questions about Byzantine art.

HARRY: I'm glad you feel that way. I'm the lone wolf type myself.

MEG: Oh?

HARRY: Now don't get me wrong. I think it's perfectly all right to go places in groups. I just don't think the group ought to be too large.

MEG: *(Changing the subject)* Is that the railroad?

HARRY: Where?

MEG: Over there. Just below that strange-looking cloud.

HARRY: *(Looking along her arm)* I don't see it.

MEG: It's out of sight now.

HARRY: I guess so. *(He has obviously enjoyed being close to her and it takes an effort of his will to break away.)* Like I said, it's all just one flat plain laid out in sections.

MEG: What?

HARRY: Nebraska. And all the roads run at right angles. *(He sits.)* That does something to you, growing up where the roads don't wind. It's like living on a checkerboard. Where are you from?

MEG: New England.

HARRY: Oh. *(He pauses and searches for a new opening.)* Say, you're not from Brockton, Massachusetts, by any chance? *(She shakes her head.)* I suppose that sounds like a peculiar question, but the reason I asked is because my father's company has its main office there and a lot of people from Brockton, Massachusetts are always visiting us on their way out to the Coast. *(Pause)* They make fiberboard.

MEG: What?

HARRY: Fiberboard. You know, out of asbestos and glass. It's for sound-proofing things.

MEG: It sounds like an admirable product.

179

HARRY: Sure, sure. *(Suspiciously)* You from Boston?

MEG: No. Vermont.

HARRY: Oh.

MEG: But, quite frankly, I've been away to school for so long and then traveling that home seems like a strange country to me.

HARRY: I guess I'd feel that way, too, if I went back to Nebraska, after this. After traveling over most of Europe and Asia, I mean.

MEG: Yes, it does alter your perspective, doesn't it?

HARRY: It sure does. Look, if you'd rather, I'll keep quiet. I know how you must feel.

MEG: You do?

HARRY: Sure, when you're alone like this in the back country or on some mountaintop you want to appreciate nature in silence and there's nothing more irritating than somebody yak-yakking all the time when all you want is to be left alone. I feel the same way myself plenty of times. It's like when you've spent all day hiking up to some place you really thought was remote and when you get there you find a lot of empty beer cans and newspapers lying around. It really disgusts you. So, if you want, we can just sit quiet and not say anything for a while.

MEG: All right. *(They sit. MEG takes out a cigarette. HARRY attempts to light it but she forestalls him. He thinks of a number of things to say but controls himself.)* Frankly, it was better when you were talking.

HARRY: *(Jumping into the breach)* That's because you've had too much loneliness.

MEG: How did you make that discovery?

HARRY: Oh, I can tell. All the way up the trail I was watching you. When you are hiking you hold your hands in like this, with your fingers bent into your palms. That's the way lonely people walk.

MEG: Really, that sort of theory went out with phrenology.

HARRY: No, it didn't. I've made a study of gestures. You can always tell what a person is by what he does with his body. You bend over forward when you're climbing—that means you're impulsive. Here, let me show you something. *(He takes her hand.)* Look at your thumb, it won't bend backward—that's a sign of stubbornness and a strong willpower.

MEG: Flattering but completely untrue.

HARRY: Then why did you keep on up the mountain when all the others turned back?

MEG: *(Hesitantly)* I suppose I had to prove something to myself.

HARRY: What?

MEG: Nothing in the least important.

HARRY: *(Triumphantly)* Anyway, it took willpower, didn't it?

MEG: Really, I've already been psychoanalyzed. By a Jungian. Don't you think it's rather late for palmistry?

HARRY: And you hold your cigarette right at the tip of your fingers—that means you're fastidious.

MEG: Why fastidious?

HARRY: Because you don't want to get nicotine stains on your fingers.

MEG: Believe me, I've never given it a thought.

HARRY: It's subconscious. That's the beauty of it, it's subconscious. But you don't perspire in your palms, that's lucky. It means you're not anxious.

MEG: *(Disengaging her hand)* I have a presentiment that I am not going to like you.

HARRY: Yes, you will. Strong-willed, fastidious and lonely girls always like me. Although at first they generally deny it.

MEG: *(With feigned shock)* No!

HARRY: I'm just being perfectly frank.

MEG: Are you?

HARRY: *(Sure of himself now)* At first they always think I'm dumb and when they find out that I'm not it's a big surprise and that pleases them. Then I'm strong—physically *and* morally. I know just what I want and I go after it without a lot of beating around the bush. Do you want to hear any more?

MEG: Not particularly.

HARRY: Okay. There are some things you can't say with words, anyway. *(He kisses her—she neither resists nor reacts; she has suddenly seen PROMETHEUS for the first time.)*

MEG: Harry! There's someone here! Someone watching us!

HARRY: What?

MEG: *(Breaking away from him)* Look!

HARRY: *(Running toward PROMETHEUS)* My God! They left him here to die!

MEG: Don't touch him!

HARRY: Why not?

MEG: Those sores. He may be a leper.

HARRY: He's trying to say something. *(To PROMETHEUS)* Do you speak English? We want to help you.

MEG: He doesn't understand. Perhaps he wants water.

HARRY: Give me the canteen.

MEG: We'll have to boil it afterwards.

HARRY: Never mind that. *(He holds the canteen to PROMETHEUS' lips.)* Sorry, old fellow. It's only Choco-malt. That's all we have.

MEG: Can't we get him loose?

HARRY: I need something to pry with. My geology hammer.

MEG: Where is it?

HARRY: In my pack. Hurry.

MEG: *(Handing it to him)* Here.

HARRY: I may be able to spring the chain with it.

MEG: If only he weren't so diseased-looking.

HARRY: That's not his fault. But Meg—

MEG: Yes?

HARRY: We ought to discuss this.

MEG: Discuss what?

HARRY: Well—everything.

MEG: Can't we get this over with first and then talk about it later? I'm beginning to feel sick.

HARRY: That's not the point. Once we take him down we're responsible for him.

MEG: All right. But let's not talk in front of him.

HARRY: What difference does it make? He can't understand us.

MEG: I can't stand the way he's looking at us. So expectantly.

HARRY: Okay. *(They walk downstage and lower their voices.)* There's something weird about this whole thing, Meg. Someone must have put him there. And they must have had a reason. We have to take that into consideration. If we were at home I wouldn't hesitate a moment. But this is a foreign country. Perhaps he is some oddball like those Indian fakirs—you know, the ones who lie on a bed of nails just to prove how strong they are.

MEG: But this isn't India.

HARRY: All right, all right. Then maybe he's a criminal.

MEG: But such a cruel punishment!

HARRY: I know. But they do things like that here.

MEG: Even so, we can't let him stay there.

HARRY: Of course not. But if there's trouble with the police we have to agree on what to say.

MEG: Do you suppose there will be?

HARRY: I don't know.

MEG: Look! Someone is coming.

HARRY: Perhaps he can tell us what this is all about.

THE GUARDIAN: *(Entering hurriedly)* If you have come to rescue him, I shan't interfere. I am unarmed. I bow before superior force.

HARRY: But who is he?

THE GUARDIAN: *(Surprised)* You don't know?

HARRY: No.

THE GUARDIAN: Then there has been a mistake. You are not the one I took you for. I am sorry but there has been a mistake. *(He pulls a screen across the rear of the stage, concealing* PROMETHEUS. *On the screen is painted an appropriately banal classical landscape.)* Casual visitors are not permitted. It was a mistake. Few people come here. Those who do always prefer something agreeable. Pleasant, isn't it? Not inspired, but pleasant. Ah, you think it out of place on a mountaintop? I can see that you do. I quite agree with you. It is in bad taste. I have often thought so myself. Now, what can I do for you? You'll find the best view from the western promontory. Takes in a great deal of picturesque country. On a clear day you can see the ocean. This way, please, and watch where you step. Many of the pebbles are jagged and bruise the feet. *(He offers to lead them off—they do not move.)* I like company. Young girls don't often come here. When the sun passes its zenith it is shady and cool on the other side of the crest. We could sit and converse. *(They do not move. He pleads.)* There is a glacier on the north slope. Not a big glacier but it is worth seeing. *(Silence: he gives in.)* All right. He is a troublemaker. I don't know the details. It all happened a long time ago.

HARRY: He's a criminal?

THE GUARDIAN: If you wish, a criminal.

HARRY: But why do they torture him?

THE GUARDIAN: He is not being tortured. He is being punished.

MEG: That's no justification for cruelty.

THE GUARDIAN: You are quite right. But what can we do? There it is.

HARRY: Who are you? An official of the government?

THE GUARDIAN: *(Modestly)* My name would mean nothing to you. Shall we look at the glacier?

HARRY: *(Outraged)* And leave him to suffer?

THE GUARDIAN: He is used to it. It is only the novelty of pain that is annoying. It's like living in water. If you don't drown you grow gills. *(*PROMETHEUS *coughs.)* Furthermore, he enjoys being disagreeable. In all these years he hasn't said a dozen words to me. If you set him free, he won't thank you for it. He is a troublemaker. You will find him very unpleasant company.

HARRY: But we can't leave him here to die.

THE GUARDIAN: He won't die. You don't understand these things. No matter how much he is hurt, the wounds all heal the following day. That is the restorative power of suffering.

HARRY: Take the screen down!

THE GUARDIAN: Take it down yourselves. You have been warned. If there are reprisals it is you who will suffer them. I wash my hands of the whole thing. *(He goes. Silence.)*

HARRY: *(Takes out a map and studies it.)* We're only five degrees from the equator. How could there be any glacier?

MEG: *(Sitting, her hand to her stomach)* I think I'm going to be sick.

HARRY: You can't trust these native guides about anything. It's too hot here for any permanent formation of ice.

MEG: *(Her eyes closed, in a tense, automatic monotone.)* The quick brown fox jumped over the lazy dog. The quick brown fox—sonofabitch, sonofabitch, sonofabitch—

HARRY: *(Alarmed)* What's the matter?

MEG: *(Under iron control)* There. It's better. *(She gets up and walks about.)*

HARRY: What?

MEG: The nausea.

HARRY: *(Solicitously)* Hadn't you better lie down?

MEG: *(Pacing)* That doesn't help. I've got to keep my mind off it. Say something.

HARRY: What should I say?

MEG: *(Explosively)* Anything! For God's sake, just start talking! That shouldn't be too difficult.

HARRY: *(As he talks she continues her pacing.)* Okay. I was thinking how we would have to carry him when we got him down because he'll be too weak to walk by himself so I thought of the Fireman's Lift and I tried to remember how we did it when I was at Scout camp on the Platte River only it came out all confused. Let's see. *(He demonstrates.)* You take your left wrist in your right hand and the other fellow takes his right wrist in his left hand and then you take his left wrist in your right hand—no, that must be wrong; you take his right wrist in your left hand and he takes your left wrist in his right hand then the fellow you have to carry sits on your hands and puts his arms around your shoulders and you carry him down the trail. Feel any better?

MEG: Not much.

HARRY: Well, there's an even better way. We can make an Indian litter—I learned how to do it up in the Michigan woods. Here, I'll show you. *(He undoes his pack.)* You take a single blanket and spread it out on the ground and then you fold it over so that it's double. Then you take your sheath knife and stab six holes in the blanket like this, one in each of the four corners and one in the middle of the left-hand side and the right-hand side. If you've got time you reinforce the holes with leather thongs so that they won't tear but it'll work pretty well without that if the person you have to carry isn't too heavy. Then you run two long poles through the slits and you have a litter. I take the front end and you take the back end.

MEG: Where are we going to get the poles? There isn't a tree for twenty miles.

HARRY: *(Who obviously hasn't thought of this)* There must be some poles around somewhere. There always are.

MEG: In Michigan, perhaps. But this isn't Michigan.

HARRY: Well, anyway, you feel better, don't you?

MEG: Some.

HARRY: It's probably just mountain sickness.

MEG: No it isn't.

HARRY: If you're not used to the altitude it plays tricks on your stomach.

MEG: I've been through this before. I know all about it.

HARRY: Loosen your shoulders. Like this. Just let your arms hang down like dead weights and move your shoulders up and down, forward and back, up and down, forward and back, up and down—

MEG: What for?

HARRY: It relieves tension.

MEG: Have you got any exercise to relieve cowardice?

HARRY: What?

MEG: Cowardice. That's my trouble. All the time you were talking to that guide I had just one impulse. To run away. As fast and as far as possible.

HARRY: But you didn't.

MEG: No, I didn't.

HARRY: Don't you see what that proves?

MEG: *(Sitting on the blanket)* Of course. That I've got rubber legs and would never make it down the mountain by myself.

HARRY: No, it doesn't. It proves that you've got real courage. Who do you think are the bravest men in a war? Not the ones who aren't afraid, but the fellow who knows how scared he really is but conquers his fear and doesn't run away.

MEG: You're really very sweet.

HARRY: I told you you would like me once you got to know me.

MEG: You talk as though the world had just been discovered yesterday.

HARRY: Now you're laughing at me.

MEG: No, I'm not. Not really. I mean, essentially I really do admire strong people, even if I don't always believe in them. In their motives, I mean. This is very confused.

HARRY: No, it isn't.

MEG: I suppose it's a form of compensation.

HARRY: What?

MEG: Compensation. What I mean is, basically we know so little about our inner drives and I think that's a shame, don't you?

HARRY: Sure, sure.

MEG: I'm not making myself at all clear.

HARRY: Oh, that's all right. You've just got to learn to relax.

MEG: I doubt if that will help.

HARRY: Of course it will. And cut down on the smoking for a week or two. You'll notice the difference right away.

MEG: But when I stop smoking I always gain weight.

HARRY: Not with a high-protein diet you won't. Have you tried that?

MEG: I was on the *Good Housekeeping* diet for a while. Is that the same?

HARRY: Pretty much. Lean meats, cottage cheese and leafy vegetables with a high sunshine content. No potatoes or starchy foods. You have to realize that one of the basic troubles with modern man is that he eats too much.

MEG: And the wrong things.

HARRY: Sure, and the wrong things. *(Rising)* Well, what about it?

MEG: What about what?

HARRY: Shall we take him down?

MEG: Now?

HARRY: Why not?

MEG: All right.

HARRY: Sure you feel up to it?

MEG: That doesn't make any difference. It's got to be done, hasn't it?

HARRY: That's the spirit.

MEG: Only you've got to help me.

HARRY: Sure. Any way I can.

MEG: Lift me up. *(She holds out her hands to him. He takes them and starts to pull her to her feet.)* No, not that way. *(Gently but insistently she pulls him toward her.)* This way. *(She throws her arms about him and kisses him fiercely.)*

Blackout.

Scene Two

The same as Scene One save that the blanket has been put away and there are now a bridge-table and two folding camp-stools downstage. MEG and HARRY are playing cribbage as the lights come up.

HARRY: Ten.

MEG: Twenty and a pair.

HARRY: Twenty-eight.

MEG: Go.

HARRY: Thirty-one for two.

MEG: Eight.

HARRY: Fifteen-two.

MEG: Twenty-one. Twenty-six and one for last.

HARRY: *(Picking up his hand)* Fifteen-two, fifteen-four, and a double run is twelve.

MEG: Fifteen-two, fifteen-four and a flush is eight.

HARRY: Your crib.

MEG: Harry.

HARRY: What?

MEG: I'm cold.

HARRY: You're sitting in the sun.

MEG: Just the same, I'm cold.

HARRY: Take my sweater, then. *(He takes it off.)*

MEG: Sure you don't need it?

HARRY: Of course not. I like this mountain air.

MEG: Well, if you're sure...

HARRY: I'm sure. Count your crib.

MEG: *(Struggling with the sweater)* How can I?

HARRY: Warmer now?

MEG: Some. Fifteen-two.

HARRY: Where?

MEG: The six and eight.

HARRY: That's fourteen, not fifteen.

MEG: All right. Nothing then. *(Pause)*

HARRY: If only there was some way to get in touch with the American consulate!

MEG: Could we send the guide?

HARRY: I don't trust him.

MEG: Frankly, I don't either.

HARRY: What do you mean by that?

MEG: Just what I said.

HARRY: He'd report us to the police. And then we'd be in serious trouble.

MEG: Why?

HARRY: Why? Because it's just the sort of thing that starts an international incident.

MEG: A what?

HARRY: An international incident. They're always being started by seemingly unimportant things. You know, the Archduke at Sarajevo, that sort of thing.

MEG: But we would only be doing the right thing.

HARRY: The man who shot the Archduke thought he was doing the right thing, too. I read about him. His name was Gavrilo Princip.

MEG: How did we get on this subject?

HARRY: But of course we have to do something. We can't just sit here.

MEG: All right. Let's take him down, then.

HARRY: You're sure we ought to?

MEG: *(Weakening)* I don't know. What about you?

HARRY: I'm willing if you are.

MEG: All right. Let's do it.

HARRY: Now?

MEG: *(Rising)* Yes, now. Let's get it over with.

HARRY: *(Rising slowly)* All right. *(They take a step toward the screen.)* Meg.

MEG: Yes?

HARRY: There's no point in going off half-cocked about this. Suppose he should die. I mean, after we took him down.

MEG: Don't say things like that!

HARRY: But supposing he does. Then we'd be responsible.

MEG: I don't see why.

HARRY: Yes, we would. There was a case just like this in Omaha. Some man fell down in the street with diabetes—you know, insulin shock. The people who picked him up thought he was drunk and took him to the police station. They were just being Good Samaritans. But he died in jail and his family sued them and got a judgment for fifty thousand dollars.

MEG: I don't see the parallel.

HARRY: The point is, they were responsible. It didn't make any difference that they thought they were doing him a favor.

MEG: But what should they have done? Left him lying in the street?

HARRY: I'm not saying that.

MEG: What are you saying, then?

HARRY: I'm just pointing out that from the legal point of view your intentions don't count. The law says that if you interfere you are responsible for what happens.

MEG: We've got to make up our minds. It'll be dark soon and we can't stay here all night.

HARRY: Don't get so excited. Of course we're going to take him down. But there's no harm in studying all of the angles, is there? *(MEG returns to her chair and sits down despairingly.)* I mean, if we're going to have a lawsuit on our hands we ought to be prepared for it.

MEG: Who could possibly sue us?

HARRY: I'm not saying that anyone would sue us. I'm just saying that it's a possibility, that's all. *(Silence)*

MEG: It's your deal.

HARRY: *(Shuffling the cards.)* You've got to be careful. There was a professor my father knew who signed some sort of manifesto clear back in 1936. To get milk for the Spanish Reds or something like that. That was all he did—just that one little thing. Twenty years later he was working for the State Department. Along they came—*(He riffs the cards.)*—that was it. He was out of a job.

MEG: That's terrible!

HARRY: *(Dealing)* Sure, it's terrible. I agree. But what does it prove? That you've got to be careful. You heard what the guide said. Suppose this fellow is a political prisoner?

MEG: That wouldn't make a bit of difference to me.

HARRY: No?

MEG: *(Firmly)* No.

HARRY: You a radical?

MEG: No.

HARRY: A liberal?

MEG: I guess so.

HARRY: That's all right. I am too. A conservative liberal. Your play.

MEG: Ten.

HARRY: Fifteen-two. *(Scores)* What I mean is, I may not agree with his opinions but he's got every right to have them.

MEG: Twenty and a pair.

HARRY: That's fundamental. But if we interfere, it goes into our records. Twenty-eight. They put every little thing down, things you never even remembered, And then some day it pops up to confront you. Go?

MEG: What?

HARRY: I asked, is it a go?

MEG: Go.

189

HARRY: Thirty-one for two. *(Pause)* And all the governments have extradition treaties now. It isn't like it was twenty years ago when a Samuel Insull could go abroad and practically thumb his nose at a federal indictment.

MEG: Who?

HARRY: Samuel Insull.

MEG: Who in God's name is he?

HARRY: A utility magnate.

MEG: We're getting off the subject. Far off.

HARRY: It was just an example.

MEG: Of what?

HARRY: *(Irritably)* Do you want me to go back and repeat it all over again?

They glare at each other. RASMUSSEN *enters. He is a pink-cheeked old man dressed in a neatly pressed suit and carrying a physician's bag. He is the perfect picture of the amiable, warmhearted and gruff small town family* G.P.

RASMUSSEN: Good morning. Beautiful stretch of weather, isn't it? Puts the springtime in these old bones, puts springtime in 'em. *(He puts down his bag and stretches his arms.)* Aaah! Aaah! That does it! Does me good to breathe that pure mountain ozone. Nothing like it. Nothing like it. God's own remedy. Wonder people don't realize it.

HARRY: *(Eagerly)* Are you a doctor?

RASMUSSEN: Physician and surgeon—obstetrics, gynecology, intestinal disorders.

MEG: There is a man behind that screen—

RASMUSSEN: Don't have to tell me. No hurry, though. You get out of breath after that climb. *(He sits.)* I suppose you came up the south slope?

HARRY: Our compass is broken.

RASMUSSEN: Easy to tell. On the south slope your back is to the sea. Now I generally take the north trail myself. It's steeper and there's danger of falling granite, but the shade is a compensation—

HARRY: Then you've been here before?

RASMUSSEN: Although in the winter there's more snow on that other side. *(He opens his bag, takes out a bottle, and gargles.)* You will pardon me. Antibiotics. Bacteria in the air. You'd think at this altitude they'd find it hard to live, wouldn't you? But that's not the case. *(PROMETHEUS can be heard to sigh.)* All right, all right, I'm coming. *(But he does not rise.)* You're a photographer? So am I, in a way. Would you care to see some pictures of my children? *(He takes pictures from his wallet.)* Of course, I don't have your sort of equipment. Just snapshots. This one was taken by a Brownie. It's Ella at Camp Larrabee—the one on the left—the other girl is her swimming instructor—

MEG: She is lovely. But, doctor, there is a man there in terrible agony—

RASMUSSEN: This one is my son James, James Junior. It was taken the day after his graduation. That's the Grand Canyon in the background. It's blurred, of course, as I had to focus on the close-up. I only wish I had the equipment for color photography. You have no idea how lovely it is—shades of mauve and pink all turning to purple where the shadows fall across them. It's like a fairyland.

HARRY: I know. Only I saw it in wintertime.

RASMUSSEN: This one I took sailing. In the Mediterranean. The chap at the tiller is a young Dane we met in Nice. That's my wife with her head behind the sail. We had just jibbed the moment before I took it.

MEG: Doctor, you must do something for him.

RASMUSSEN: I know, I know. But don't be alarmed. I've been treating him every day for ages.

MEG: But if he is ill, why do they leave him on that wheel?

RASMUSSEN: Why? My dear young lady, ask me why the moon rises by night and the sun by day. They never give me any sensible answers. I requisitioned a hospital bed for him months ago. Do you think I got one? But that's the way things are here. Inefficient. Hopelessly inefficient.

HARRY: What's the matter with him?

RASMUSSEN: *(Putting on his spectacles)* I'll read you the diagnostic report. Of course, it's all rubbish, but it's what they gave me. *(Reads)* "Paranoia, messianic delusions. Patient convinced he is chosen to save mankind. Irrational fantasies. Delusions of persecution by unnamed spiritual being—" et cetera, et cetera. What am I to make of that lingo? These diagnosticians are all infatuated with psychosomatic medicine, simply because it's the latest craze. Everything must have its psychological explanation. Balderdash! Would you believe it, they sent a consultant down here last week who tried to convince that poor devil that his chains were only "the externalization of psychic reality!" I must say that when I hear gibberish of that sort I blush for the whole medical profession.

HARRY: But what is the matter with him? In your opinion.

RASMUSSEN: My opinion? There's no opinion about it: It's liver disease. The pancreas is damaged, too, but the infection is mainly in the liver.

Yellow skin, palpitations, jaundiced condition, it's perfectly plain.

MEG: But isn't there something we can do to help?

RASMUSSEN: *(Drawing on a pair of surgical gloves)* Help? What do you want to help for? What you mean is, you want to mind someone else's business for him.

MEG: That's not—

RASMUSSEN: *(Interrupting her)* Yes it is. We've turned out a generation of bleeding-hearts. They can't manage their own affairs and they think that gives them the right to manage the other fellow's. No thank you. If I need your help I'll call for it. *(He disappears behind the screen. There is silence.)*

MEG: Harry.

HARRY: Yes?

MEG: I'm frightened, Harry.

HARRY: What for? He knows what he is doing.

MEG: But did you see what was in his bag when he opened it?

HARRY: Oh, the usual thing.

MEG: No. Scalpels. Knives. Dozens of them.

HARRY: Why shouldn't he carry them? They're part of a doctor's equipment.

MEG: I feel sick.

HARRY: Of course, he doesn't know anything about photography. Everything he showed us was over-exposed.

(There is a long, agonized scream from PROMETHEUS.)

MEG: I can't stand this, Harry.

HARRY: Hold my hand. There is nothing we can do about it.

(They stand in silence. Then there is another scream, even more intense than the first: then silence.)

MEG: We shouldn't have let him do it.

HARRY: There's no point in being hysterical. If you can't trust the doctor then there is no one you can trust.

MEG: But I don't think he is a doctor.

HARRY: That's ridiculous, Meg, and you know it. I'd know that man was a doctor if I met him anywhere.

MEG: Why?

HARRY: Why? Because—oh, don't ask silly questions. Because anyone can see he is a doctor.

MEG: Don't shout at me. I can hear you.

HARRY: Sorry. *(Pause)* I need a drink. Is there any whiskey left?

MEG: *(Handing him a flask)* A bit.

HARRY: *(Holding it up)* For snakebite. *(He drinks, then passes her the flask.)* Here.

MEG: You finish it.

HARRY: I thought you wanted a drink.

MEG: I've changed my mind. *(RASMUSSEN can be heard shouting in Greek.)*

HARRY: What's that?

MEG: I don't know.

THE GUARDIAN runs across the stage speaking in Greek. He disappears behind the screen and RASMUSSEN'S angry voice can be heard berating him. Then silence.

MEG: Me, too.

HARRY: It's all gone. *(He holds the flask upside down.)* You know, I used to throw the discus at college. I bet if I threw this as hard as I could it would land at the bottom of the mountain.

MEG: Don't.

RASMUSSEN: *(Reentering, taking off his gloves)* Still here, I see.

MEG: What did you do to him?

RASMUSSEN: Are you staying long?

HARRY: What language were you speaking to the guide?

RASMUSSEN: There's a chalet a few miles down the east slope. You'll find it more comfortable at this time of the year. Rather like a hostel— informal singing, supply your own bedding, that sort of thing. But clean, no insects, and a tree on the grounds. *(He starts to go off.)*

MEG: Doctor! Wait a minute!

RASMUSSEN: It's your own fault if you don't enjoy it here. *(He goes.)*

MEG: *(Turning back)* It's no use.

HARRY: You can't make him stay if he doesn't want to.

THE GUARDIAN: *(Who enters wiping his hands on a towel)* Has he gone?

HARRY: Look here. Who is he? Is he a government physician?

THE GUARDIAN: He left his forceps. He always leaves things. *(MEG starts to take the instrument from his hand.)* Don't touch it, signora, you'll get blood on your hands.

MEG: *(Crying out)* Harry! Pull back that screen!

THE GUARDIAN: No, no! It is not permitted! Visitors are not allowed!

HARRY: Get out of my way, you little wop! *(He strikes THE GUARDIAN and advances to the screen.)*

THE GUARDIAN: *(On his knees)* Zeus! Zeus! Have you forgotten your servant? Is it for this I have served you? To be beaten and reviled? Give

me a sign, Zeus, let me know that you have not deserted me!
(There is a roll of thunder. Harry pulls the screen aside, revealing PROMETHEUS *on the wheel with a great gash across his abdomen from which blood pours.)*

MEG: Harry! They've killed him!
HARRY: The barbarians!

Blackout.

ACT TWO
Scene One
At curtain rise the stage has been changed in the following details: the screen has been closed, there are tin cans, empty cigarette packages and candy wrappers on the ground, and women's panties and bra are spread on one of the rocks, drying in the sunlight. Over the arms of the camp chair are towels neatly labeled "His" and "Hers." HARRY *stands down-stage leaning on a golf club.* MEG *sits on a rock. She is now dressed in slacks and blouse and is filing her fingernails.*

MEG: It would be a hospital for children. And every little kid that was sick or undernourished or wanted to run away from home because her parents didn't love her could come there for free, and instead of stairways there would be banisters and slides from one floor to the next, and the waiting rooms would all be laid out in gold mazes with yew trees growing in the center and... and the gardens would be on three levels with pathways through the air among the branches and down below through the roots of all growing things, and no violins, no potted plants, no calla lilies, but sunlight and all the chairs made out of yellow straw, and no Sundays or Mondays but just the middle of the week from one year to the next, and the nurses all African women dressed in apple green and—and—*(She breaks off.)* And that's all. Ridiculous, isn't it?
HARRY: No, it's beautiful. It shows the kind of person you really are.
MEG: But I'm not like that at all. It's sheer fantasy.
HARRY: You shouldn't be ashamed of it.
MEG: I never finish anything I start. When I was fifteen I ran away from home. I was going to the Belgian Congo.
HARRY: Why the Belgian Congo?
MEG: To join Dr. Schweitzer. I got as far as Boston.
HARRY: We all have to have our dreams—or nothing would ever be

accomplished in the world. Every time there's a great improvement, like the electric light or the automobile or penicillin, it's because someone had the courage to dream about it. Now watch this one. *(He takes a stance and swings.)* I've got to correct that slice. I bring my shoulder up a little too far every time.

MEG: Harry.

HARRY: *(Taking a stance again)* Yes?

MEG: Are you glad?

HARRY: *(His eye on the ball)* Huh?

MEG: About us, I mean.

HARRY: Sure, sure. *(He swings again.)* Damn it! Did it again. It starts perfectly straight but it always ends in a slice.

MEG: And you don't think I am frigid?

HARRY: Ahh, you know I was just kidding when I said that. It was just kidding around, you know that. You were swell. Now keep your eye on this. The stance is the thing you've got to watch. You have to have your feet equidistant from the ball. Start with the body weight on the right foot and then as your swing comes down the weight is transferred forward onto the left foot. *(He swings and then waits for her comment.)* What's the matter?

MEG: I just thought you might say you liked me.

HARRY: Of course I do. Lots.

MEG: Thanks.

HARRY: Don't be sarcastic. What do you want me to say? All right. You're Cleopatra and Lady Godiva and Marilyn Monroe all rolled up in one. Does that make you any happier?

MEG: No, it doesn't.

HARRY: Then put your bra back on before that little Greek comes back. I can see him undressing you every time he looks at you.

MEG: I don't care.

HARRY: *(He puts the golf club back in the bag.)* Well, you ought to.

MEG: I wonder what it's like down there.

HARRY: *(He looks for a rag to clean his clubs and, finding none, appropriates the towel marked "Hers.")* Down where?

MEG: In the glacier. There are caves there, you know.

HARRY: I wish you would stop harping on that subject. It's all in his imagination. There isn't any glacier.

MEG: How do you know?

HARRY: In the first place because we're practically on the equator. And in the second place, I went and looked.

MEG: When?

HARRY: Yesterday. When I went for firewood.

MEG: And you didn't see anything?

HARRY: No. I thought I did. At first.

MEG: What was it like?

HARRY: Just a big patch of dirty ice. Only when I got there it was gone.

MEG: Oh.

HARRY: It must have been the sunlight reflected on the mica.

MEG: On the what?

HARRY: Mica. It's crystallized potassium silicate.

MEG: Thanks. *(Silence)*

HARRY: Well, what about a game?

MEG: All right. *(Listlessly, they take their places at the table.)*

HARRY: Cut for deal?

MEG: You deal. I don't care.

HARRY: No, it's fairer to cut. *(He cuts.)* Nine of spades.

MEG: *(Cutting)* Deuce of hearts.

HARRY: My deal. *(Shuffles)* That reminds me, I found something down there.

MEG: What?

HARRY: *(Taking a stone from his pocket)* See that? You know what it is?

MEG: A rock.

HARRY: No, those red streaks on it. That's ferrous oxide. Iron ore. There's a cropping of it nearly a hundred feet long down there.

MEG: Deal.

HARRY: Just a minute. I estimate that it runs at least fifty percent pure iron. Hold that rock.

MEG: Frankly, I don't want to.

HARRY: But see how heavy it is. And it's lying right out on the surface. The only thing that's needed is some good, cheap way to get it down to the railroad. *(He consults a scratch pad.)* You owe me three thousand, four hundred and sixty dollars.

MEG: I'll write you a check. On the Burlington First National.

HARRY: Want to play one game, double or nothing?

MEG: If you want.

HARRY: *(Dealing)* That makes it more exciting, everything on one game.

MEG: Harry.

HARRY: Yes?

MEG: *(With a glance toward the screen)* Do you suppose he...?

HARRY: I thought we agreed we weren't going to discuss that subject any more.

MEG: What good does that do if you can't stop thinking about it?

HARRY: It's just a question of willpower.

MEG: Is it?

HARRY: *(Firmly)* Yes, it is. Make your discard. It's my crib.

MEG: *(Playing)* Ten.

HARRY: Fifteen-two.

MEG: Twenty-three.

HARRY: Twenty-nine. Go?

MEG: What?

HARRY: I asked, is that a go?

MEG: Yes.

HARRY: Well, that's all I asked. It's your play.

MEG: I don't want to play any more.

HARRY: You can't quit in the middle of a game.

MEG: Why not?

HARRY: You just can't.

MEG: *(Throwing her cards down)* Oh yes, I can. *(She gets up.* HARRY *starts to follow her and then, seeing that she is in a temper, thinks better of it.)*

HARRY: Okay, have it your way. *(Pause)* What's for lunch?

MEG: Van Camp's pork and beans.

HARRY: Again?

MEG: Again. And it's your turn to get firewood.

HARRY: I got it yesterday.

MEG: No, you didn't. That was the day before yesterday.

HARRY: Always right, aren't you? *(He goes off.)*

When he has gone, MEG *goes swiftly to the screen and draws it back.* PROMETHEUS *is revealed chained to the wheel and so haggard as to appear almost lifeless.* MEG *takes a jar of water and holds it to his lips. He drinks and then thanks her with a wan smile. Alternately attracted and repelled, she finally touches his wound to see if it has stopped bleeding. He winces. She dips her handkerchief in the jar and cools his forehead with it.*

MEG: *(Softly)* It doesn't make any difference what I say, does it? *(He attempts a smile.)* Yet you like to hear a human voice, don't you? If you knew how vile and cowardly we really are you wouldn't say so. But you can't know that, can you? I suppose not. If only you didn't smell so much! Don't be offended, I'm sure you can't help it. *(She takes the moist handkerchief and commences cleaning his calves and feet, kneel-*

ing before him. THE GUARDIAN *enters unobserved.)* Why are you here? Are you a murderer? Did you strangle someone in the night? Or perhaps poison your wife? Never mind. I understand. I forgive you. I forgive you everything if you'll only stop staring at me. I can't sleep any more because of your staring, did you know that?

THE GUARDIAN: *(Coolly)* Where is your husband?

MEG: *(Jumping up startled)* He went to get firewood. And he is not my husband.

THE GUARDIAN: Then the signora is a signorina?

MEG: Yes.

THE GUARDIAN: Let me show you the glacier.

MEG: No, thank you.

THE GUARDIAN: The ice is very beautiful. Deep blue.

MEG: I'm not interested.

THE GUARDIAN: *(Taking up the lingerie from the rock)* Very pretty.

MEG: Put that down. *(THE GUARDIAN laughs.)* Please! *(He puts it back.)*

THE GUARDIAN: Why don't you go?

MEG: We are going today.

THE GUARDIAN: You say that every day.

MEG: Today we are going.

THE GUARDIAN: *(With a nod to PROMETHEUS)* And will you take him?

MEG: Yes.

THE GUARDIAN: *(Laughing)* He is no good for a woman. He is too thin. Take me instead. But no, your husband would not like that.

MEG: He is not my husband.

THE GUARDIAN: He will not take him, either. He sees that you love him: he is jealous. That is to be expected.

MEG: I love him? That wretched, diseased man?

THE GUARDIAN: Why did you come here, then?

MEG: By accident.

THE GUARDIAN: Indeed? And you stay—why?

MEG: We are leaving today.

THE GUARDIAN: How tender your fingers were on his wounds. Or are they your own wounds? *(He approaches her.)* Do not be alarmed. I have manners, I shall not harm you. *(He lowers his voice.)* However, I see everything quite clearly. You desire to take him in your arms. Just as he is, bloody and grimed as he is. You desire to kiss his wounds. To throw yourself at his feet. To worship him as one worships a god. Answer me, signorina! Is it not the shape of your dream? *(MEG stands as if transfixed.)* Are you angry? Strike me, then. Strike the little wop whom your husband has already insulted. *(He pauses: she seems incapable of motion.)* Then you are no longer capable of anger? The air is thin here. It is an effort to exert one's self. *(He turns contemptuously toward* PROMETHEUS.*)* You are foolish! He is not worth your adoration. He can show you nothing. It is I, signorina, who am the god here. It is I who can show you mysteries. In my fingers are the keys to these doors. *(Suddenly he becomes obsequious once more.)* However, I am patient. The signorina will still be here tomorrow. And when she grows tired of this show of suffering, the signorina can always rely on my discretion. *(He bows.)* In the glacier there are caves of great beauty.

He goes. HARRY *enters with an armload of thorns.*

HARRY: I found some grapes along the trail. *(He puts the brush down and searches in his pockets.)*
MEG: *(Motionless)* What?
HARRY: Grapes. Someone must have left them. They're Concords.
MEG: *(In fear)* Let's not stay here any longer, Harry.
HARRY: There was a yellow sparrow flitting around between the rocks.
MEG: All right, I believe you.
HARRY: It's just that it's interesting that they can live where there's hardly any vegetation. It shows how adaptable life is.
MEG: Harry, are we going to set him free or not?
HARRY: Don't look at me that way. Is it my fault that we've been held up?
MEG: I didn't say it was.
HARRY: But that's what you think. *(He goes to the screen.)*
MEG: What are you doing?
HARRY: *(Closing the screen)* I told you I don't like to talk about this in front of him.
MEG: I didn't know you were so squeamish.
HARRY: Meg, if there is one thing I don't like in you, it's that tone of moral superiority you adopt whenever this subject comes up. If you want to be a savior, why don't you go ahead and set him loose yourself? I won't stop you.
MEG: I'm not strong enough to pry the chains off, that's why.
HARRY: Have you tried?
MEG: Harry!
HARRY: Well, have you?
MEG: I meant to.
HARRY: But you haven't. So before you call me a moral coward, just take a good look at your own behavior.

MEG: Harry, let's not fight!

HARRY: And now you get the worst of an argument, so you say, "Let's not fight."

Silence.

MEG: I'm so tired. I think I could sleep for years.

HARRY: Well, build the fire first. It's your turn.

MEG: You do it this time.

HARRY: The one who gets the firewood doesn't have to build the fire. That was the agreement.

MEG: All right. But couldn't we just once forget the agreement?

HARRY: It was your idea.

MEG: Oh, all right. *(Listlessly she picks up some of the brush.)* Harry.

HARRY: Yes?

MEG: Harry, what is it like to make love in the ice?

HARRY: *(He is lathering his face to shave.)* In what?

MEG: In the glacier.

HARRY: Look, for the last time, I tell you there isn't any glacier.

MEG: I know. But suppose there were. And suppose there were caves deep down inside it, all blue and pure and shimmering. Would you make love to me there?

HARRY: Stop being morbid. We've got enough to worry about without you being morbid.

MEG: But would you, Harry?

HARRY: You disgust me when you talk like that.

MEG: Why? Is it any different than in a bed or on the beach or in an automobile?

HARRY: Stop this, Meg. You're heading for a nervous breakdown.

MEG: Do you care?

HARRY: Of course I do.

MEG: No you don't. No one cares.

HARRY: *(Outraged)* That's a hell of an unfair thing to say. What about your family? What would they say if they knew what you've been saying to me?

MEG: Oh, they'd be horrified, all right. But they don't care either. Not really.

HARRY: Well, I do. You've gotten to be someone very close to me. I mean really close. And I don't like to see you being so morbid.

MEG: Oh. *(Silence)* Harry, let's go.

HARRY: All right. After lunch.

MEG: *(With sudden, furious energy)* No. Not after lunch. Right now.

HARRY: I've got to shave.

MEG: Why?

HARRY: Because I started to.

MEG: We've got to get out of here!

HARRY: And leave all that firewood? We may not find any more for miles.

MEG: Now! Right now!

HARRY: And what about him? We can't just leave him there.

MEG: Why not?

HARRY: You really mean it?

MEG: Yes, I really mean it.

HARRY: Well—

MEG: *(Fiercely)* We have to get out of this nightmare, Harry. I don't care any more for what's right or what's wrong. I simply know that if I don't leave here right now something awful is going to happen to me.

HARRY: Don't be melodramatic. We have to think this over.

MEG: I don't want to think it over! We've thought it over for days and what good has it done us?

HARRY: Well, we can't go just like that.

MEG: Why not?

HARRY: I've got to shave.

MEG: Why?

HARRY: Because I started to.

MEG: We've got to get out of here!

HARRY: And leave all that firewood? We may not find any more for miles.

MEG: Now! Right now!

HARRY: And what about him? We can't just leave him here.

MEG: Why not?

HARRY: Because I've got to shave.

MEG: Why?

HARRY: Because I started to.

MEG: We've got to get out of here.

HARRY: We can't go just like that.

MEG: Why not?

HARRY: *(Triumphantly)* We've got to pack! *(Pause)*

MEG: Why? Let's leave everything right here and go.

HARRY: Now you're being childish. *(He pulls out the card table and folds its legs.)* I'm perfectly willing to go but we can't leave all our things.

MEG: Why not? We can't take all this stuff, anyway.

HARRY: *(Commencing to pack)* Then sort out things and we'll decide what to leave behind. These are yours. *(He throws a pair of high-heeled slippers toward her.)*

MEG: Leave them. *(They run about the stage frantically picking up articles and cramming them into their packs.)*

HARRY: This goes.

MEG: That stays.

HARRY: Pick up your underwear.

MEG: Are these your socks?

HARRY: Whose *Time* magazine is this?

MEG: Where are my curlers?

HARRY: I dropped my fraternity pin someplace.

MEG: Hurry up!

HARRY: Now I can't find the cord to the electric razor.

MEG: You're not going to carry those clubs all the way down the mountain, are you?

HARRY: You don't expect me to throw them away, do you?

MEG: Well, at least leave the pressure cooker. I can't stand the sight of it.

HARRY: *(The tension between them is growing.)* It's perfectly easy to carry. You just tie it on the bottom of the pack.

MEG: Where did you learn that? In the Boy Scouts?

HARRY: Don't be sarcastic. What's this?

MEG: It's the halter to my sunsuit. What did you think it was?

HARRY: Well, put it away. I guess the card table will have to stay. It's a shame, though. It's aluminum and they're hard to get. And this parasol—we won't need it.

MEG: If you can find room for your golf clubs we can certainly take it, too.

HARRY: But what good is it?

MEG: It's mine.

HARRY: That doesn't answer my question.

MEG: Put it in your golf bag.

HARRY: It won't fit.

MEG: Simply because it's mine you think it's worthless.

HARRY: Look for yourself. If I take it I'll have to leave a mashie behind.

MEG: *(Shouting)* Leave one, then! You've twenty golf clubs and there's only one parasol!

HARRY: *(Furious)* You don't understand. The clubs come in a set. You can't break the set.

MEG: Isn't that too bad! The little Nebraska Babbitt with the do-it-yourself kit—somebody's going to break his set!

HARRY: *(In a rage)* Shut your damned mouth! I know all about you New England snobs. Intellectual thrills—you'd do anything for them, wouldn't you? And just because you can't feel anything decent or normal—

MEG: And what about you? I've met some windbags in my day, but when they start giving prizes for pretentious bullshit, brother, you're going to get the Oscar. *(There is a long silence during which they glare at each other.)*

HARRY: If you think apologizing is going to get you out of this, you're mistaken.

MEG: *(Icily)* I wasn't considering it.

Silence.

HARRY: *(Softening)* Meg. *(No answer)* Meg, why do we have to fight like this?

MEG: What difference does it make?

HARRY: *(Putting the umbrella into the golf bag)* Look. I'll carry the mashie in my hand.

MEG: *(Dryly)* Thanks.

HARRY: *(Attempting sweet reasonableness)* It's this place. We haven't been ourselves since we've been up here. *(Pause)* It will all be different once we get down below. I promise you it will. Look! Look at all that country spread out below us. Down there people are living, are doing things. Building railroads and running factories and writing poems and raising families, while up here we've just been stagnating. That's where we belong, Meg, down there where life is. It was a mistake for us ever to come up here, I see that now. We've done nothing but morbid introspection ever since we got here, and that's not for our kind of people. And as for him, we have to recognize that there has always been suffering and injustice in the world and there always will be. We can't change that. All we can do is make our own lives a little brighter and more fulfilled. And I sincerely think that in that way we will be building a better future for everyone, a future where everyone will have his own house and car and no one will go hungry. But we have to do it down there, Meg, down where we can get our feet on solid ground. Not up here in the clouds.

Silence.

MEG: *(Slowly)* Do you really believe all that?
HARRY: *(After a long pause)* No.

Silence.

MEG: Then why did you say it?
HARRY: *(In a voice that is little more than a dejected whisper)* Well, what can we do?

The lights go out slowly.

Scene Two

The same as before. The screen is closed and the stage is littered with piles of rubbish. THE GUARDIAN *sits alone on a rock.*

THE GUARDIAN: This is certainly a red-letter day for me. To think that at my age I could be so fortunate! You wait and wait. Then something drops in your lap when you least expect it. Yet I knew today would be different from the other days. Last night there was a dust-cloud on the moon. And a wart on my finger was gone this morning. Today will be different, I said to myself. And it was. That's what comes of being patient. *(Meg enters.)* Signora! *(He rises and offers her his seat on the rock.)*
MEG: *(She speaks in an indifferent monotone; indeed, for the remainder of the play she acts as if drugged.)* You needn't be so polite.
THE GUARDIAN: But it is my pleasure. *(She sits.)* Are you comfortable?
MEG: No.
THE GUARDIAN: Perhaps my coat? *(He offers to take it off.)*
MEG: Please. Just leave me alone.
THE GUARDIAN: As you wish. I am old. But I have manners. With me there is no unpleasantness, no recrimination.
MEG: *(Shivering)* Just go, please.
THE GUARDIAN: If you should wish to see it again—
MEG: I don't.
THE GUARDIAN: *(With a bow)* Whatever you say. *(He goes.)*
HARRY: *(Entering from the other side of the stage with his pack)* What's he doing here?
MEG: *(Without looking at him)* Who?
HARRY: You know who.
MEG: Nothing.
HARRY: I don't like him hanging around you. Where have you been?

MEG: I went for a walk.

HARRY: All morning?

MEG: All morning.

HARRY: You might have brought some firewood back.

MEG: I didn't want to.

HARRY: You never want to. *(Takes his pack off)* It feels like I'd carried this all my life. *(Opens the pack)* Look.

MEG: *(Without interest)* What is it?

HARRY: Iron ore. I'll bet there's as much iron in this mountain as there is in the whole Mesabi Range.

MEG: The what?

HARRY: The Mesabi Range. In Minnesota. It's where fifty percent of the iron comes from.

MEG: What do we want with it?

HARRY: *(With an attempt at his old enthusiasm)* It's immensely valuable. I got samples from six different outcrops. I'm going to take them to an assayer.

MEG: *(Yawning)* Right now?

HARRY: When we get back.

MEG: And when is that going to be?

HARRY: Don't start on that again. We're going tomorrow.

MEG: *(In a monotone)* I know better. We're never leaving. We're going to stay here day after day. We're going to watch the world turn to stone around us and then to ash and then to stone again and see the snow melt and the water dry up and every airplane wither and fall out of the sky and still he'll be there and we'll be here.

HARRY: What's gotten into you?

MEG: Nothing. I wish there was some way to wash my hair. It's filthy.

Silence.

HARRY: I found a centipede. *(He takes it from his pocket.)* I thought you might be interested.

MEG: I'm not.

HARRY: Okay. *(He puts the insect down and watches it crawl away.)* That's the trouble with people. They don't pay enough attention to the world around them. *(He follows the insect with a stick.)* Ninety percent of the people are totally unaware of how interesting nature can be.

MEG: I have a splitting headache.

HARRY: Shall I rub the back of your neck?

MEG: If you want. *(She sits. Harry sits on a rock behind her and massages her head.)* Where is it?

HARRY: What?

MEG: The centipede.

HARRY: It crawled away. *(He rubs her head in silence for a moment.)* Does it help?

MEG: Some.

HARRY: Relax. Shoulders forward. You've got to be careful. Most head-aches are psychosomatic.

MEG: Mine certainly is.

HARRY: Where does it hurt worst?

MEG: *(Indicating)* Here.

HARRY: Take off your sunglasses. For example, it's only an accident of evolution that man is where he is today. In many ways the ordinary ant is better adapted to his environment.

MEG: The what?

HARRY: The ant. It is several times as strong as man is for his size and surprisingly intelligent.

MEG: How did we get on this subject?

HARRY: All right, if you're not interested—

MEG: But I am. Tell me all about the ants and the bees and worms.

HARRY: Don't be sarcastic. *(Silence)* We're out of firewood.

MEG: Well?

HARRY: It's your turn. I went yesterday.

MEG: No, you didn't. That was the day before yesterday.

HARRY: I distinctly remember it was yesterday.

MEG: And I distinctly—All right, have it your own way.

HARRY: *(Walking toward the screen)* Thank God he's been quiet today. Do you suppose he's still there?

MEG: Where would he go?

HARRY: *(His hand on the screen)* Do you want to see?

MEG: No.

HARRY: Why not? You ought to learn to face him without all these emo-tional reactions. That's the only way.

MEG: Leave me alone.

HARRY: You're shivering. *(He goes to her.)* What's the matter? *(He takes her hand.)* You're cold as ice.

MEG: Just leave me alone.

HARRY: But you're freezing.

MEG: *(Getting up)* Leave me alone, Harry.

HARRY: All right. But you've caught cold. *(Silence)*

MEG: What's for lunch?

HARRY: How should I know?

MEG: It's your turn.

HARRY: No, it isn't. I fixed breakfast.

MEG: I didn't have any breakfast.

HARRY: That's not my fault. I fixed it. Don't blame me if you didn't want any. *(He sits at the card table.)*

MEG: I wasn't hungry.

HARRY: A bargain's a bargain. That's one of your faults. You have to learn responsibility.

MEG: Don't lecture me.

HARRY: How about a game?

MEG: What?

HARRY: A game.

MEG: No, thanks.

HARRY: I just thought it would be more sociable if we both played.

MEG: Oh.

HARRY: *(Dealing a hand of Patience)* That's all I thought.

MEG: Harry.

HARRY: Yes.

MEG: I wish I were dead.

HARRY: *(Playing)* What brought that on?

MEG: Don't you care?

HARRY: Of course I care. But that's just an unrelated sentence. It's not related to anything.

MEG: I said what I meant. I wish I were dead.

HARRY: So?

MEG: That's all.

HARRY: You'll get over it. *(Silence)* My foot hurts. I think I've got a pebble in my shoe. *(He unlaces his shoe.)* Look, I've been thinking this over.

MEG: What?

HARRY: Why we don't leave here. *(He takes off his shoe.)* I think I found the answer. It's just guilt feelings. *(Shakes his shoe)*

MEG: What do you suggest doing?

HARRY: We've got to get rid of them. They're completely irrational. And as long as we feel this way we can't get anything constructive accomplished.

MEG: Did you find it?

HARRY: What?

MEG: The pebble.

HARRY: No, there wasn't anything there.

RASMUSSEN: *(Who enters smiling, with his bag)* Still here, I see.

HARRY: *(Hardly looking up)* Still here. *(RASMUSSEN goes behind the screen.)* What a bore that man is.

MEG: What?

HARRY: I said he was a bore.

MEG: Oh.

HARRY: What's the matter? Can't you hear me?

MEG: Yes, I heard you.

HARRY: Then why do you always say "what" every time I say something?

MEG: Do I?

HARRY: Yes, you do.

MEG: I don't know why. *(There is a terrible scream offstage.)*

HARRY: And he! Why does he scream like that? If he just clenched his teeth and kept quiet I'd have more respect for him.

MEG: I suppose it hurts.

HARRY: Of course it hurts. But what good does screaming do? That just makes it worse.

MEG: What?

HARRY: There you go with your "whats" again. I said it hurts worse if you scream.

MEG: Oh.

PROMETHEUS *screams again.*

HARRY: If you're a man you have to learn to face pain. When I was a kid the dentist used to work on my teeth without any anaesthetic.

MEG: And you didn't cry?

HARRY: No.

MEG: Why not?

HARRY: Because I had strength of will, that's why. *(Silence)* You haven't listened to a thing I said.

MEG: What?

HARRY: Look here. If you say "what" just once more, I'll strangle you.

RASMUSSEN: *(Appearing from behind the screen)* Still here, I see.

HARRY: You said that before.

RASMUSSEN: *(Pleasantly)* Did I? *(He takes off his gloves.)* Nothing holding you, you know. You can leave any time you like. *(Takes a deep breath)* This mountain air is so bracing. Gets into your veins. *(He goes off.)*

HARRY: The same thing, over and over again. *(He drums his fingers on the table.* PROMETHEUS *commences to groan. They are low, fitful groans but they give no promise of breaking off.* MEG *and* HARRY *listen to them for a long time.)* Meg.

MEG: Yes.

HARRY: We can't go on like this.

MEG: What?

HARRY: What?

MEG: I asked you what you said.

HARRY: And I said we can't go on like this.

MEG: I heard you. So?

HARRY: So. *(HARRY rises and goes behind the screen.* MEG *puts her fingers to her ears.)*

MEG: The quick brown fox jumped over the lazy dog. The quick brown fox jumped over the lazy dog. The quick— *(There is a pistol shot.)* Jumped over. Jumped over. Jumped over.

HARRY: *(Stepping from behind the screen with the pistol)* I'm not going to make any excuses.

MEG: Did he look at you?

HARRY: No. He didn't even see me. I don't think I could have done it if he had looked. *(Silence)* Well, shall we go?

MEG: Where?

HARRY: Back home.

MEG: It doesn't make any difference now.

HARRY: *(Explosively)* You know, the first thing I'm going to do when we get home is take a shower. As long as we've been here I've never found a place where the plumbing worked. *(He throws the pack of iron ore on his shoulders.)* Well, are you coming with me?

MEG: *(Leadenly)* Yes, I'm coming.

THE GUARDIAN *enters.*

HARRY: And you! While we're on the subject, there isn't any glacier.

THE GUARDIAN: *(Politely)* No?

HARRY: I just don't like to be lied to, that's all.

THE GUARDIAN: But then there is never any glacier for those who cannot see it.

HARRY: *(To MEG)* Come on. Let's get going. *(He goes resolutely, followed at a little distance by* MEG, *who walks as if dead.)*

THE GUARDIAN: *(Turning downstage)* The thirty thousand years are up. The punishment of Prometheus is over. Hercules returns to his home. I shall be transferred to a pleasanter station. Everything came out as Zeus foresaw. *(He drops to his knees.)* Hail to Zeus the all-powerful! Hail to Zeus, hail!

ZEUS *obliges with an answering peal of thunder.*

The End

❦ THE BUSY MARTYR
A Play In Three Acts

Characters:
The Mayor of Sandaraque in 1961
The drummer boy
An old woman
Etienne Concarneau, Mayor of Sandaraque in 1890
Mme. Concarneau
Alfred Concarneau, their son
Mme. Pichegru, the mayor's aunt
Alberic, her butler
Lesonge, the town banker
Emmanuel, his son
Poulette, the town grocer
Mme. Poulette
Gabriel, their son
Mathilde, their daughter
The widow Leclerc
Father Jarmian, curé of the parish of Sandaraque
Laboussère, a farmer
Annette Béchar
Jean-Baptiste Hippolyte Marie-Henri Muscari
The jailer
A veiled woman
M. Goularte, a lawyer from Toulouse
The executioner
His apprentice
Bonfils, the innkeeper
Various citizens of Sandaraque in 1890 and 1961

Scenes: Places in and about the town of Sandaraque in southwest France.
Time: The Prologue and Epilogue are laid in the present. The remainder of the action takes place in 1890.

PROLOGUE

A pedestal revealed on which stands a shrouded statue; beneath it a scroll reading "Pro Patria Pro Peternitas." Girls in Sunday attire run in, hotly pursued by eager young men. A boy enters beating upon a drum, followed by the elders of the town of Sandaraque. The MAYOR *and members of his council now enter, dressed in stiff Sunday black. Festive members of the crowd are shushed into silence. The* MAYOR *consults his turnip watch, then his notes, and commences to speak.*

MAYOR: Citizens of Sandaraque! *(A drumroll)* Citizens of the Republic! *(Another drumroll)* On behalf of the municipal council of Sandaraque I welcome you to this celebration of the one hundredth anniversary of the birth of the martyr to whose memory our community owes so much. *(Applause. Girls bring in a floral wreath that they lay at the foot of the statue.)* Is there a member of my audience today who is not acquainted with the life of the man to whom this statue is dedicated? Is there a Sandaraquian who has not thrilled to the story of his sacrifice? Is there one among us who has not drawn courage from his heroism? Indeed, where in France—I make bold to say, where throughout the length and breadth of the civilized world—is the name of Sandaraque known without in the same breath calling to mind that of its most revered citizen, the name of Jean-Baptiste Hippolyte Marie-Henri Muscari? *(Applause: drumroll)*

Citizens! We come here today from all walks of life, from all persuasions, laying aside for the moment that petty strife and discord that too often inflames certain of our citizenry, we come here, I say, with the olive branch of unity clasped to our breasts— *(A councilman draws his attention to the time.)* —we come here, I repeat, to pay tribute to the man who found Sandaraque languishing in the swamps of immorality and by his courage and moral probity gave a new birth to decency in our community. *(A girl in the crowd gives her young man a resounding slap in the face.)*

I realize that there is hardly one among you today who does not claim descent from our foremost citizen—generally without trustworthy evidence—but it is only under the administration that you have chosen me to head that just recognition has been paid to Jean-Baptiste Hippolyte Marie-Henri Muscari in the form of this beautiful statue which has been cast totally out of unalloyed bronze by M. Vergniaud who is a Parisian! *(The councilmen renew their appeals to their watches.)* Citizens! The fireworks display for which not a single franc has come out of the public funds will commence in just two minutes. I give you the founder of our liberties, *(Drumroll)* the true father of our community, *(Drumroll)* Jean-Baptiste Hippolyte Marie-Henri Muscari!

He pulls a cord: the shroud is drawn back revealing a small, quite ordinary-looking man elegantly dressed in the style of 1890; he holds a book open with one hand with the forefinger of his other hand pointing to the text; his face is set in an expression of angelic vacuity. Applause. There is a sudden glare offstage.

CITIZEN: The rockets! They're setting off the rockets!

The MAYOR and CITIZENS run off excitedly. In a moment no one remains save the DRUMMER BOY and one OLD WOMAN. THE DRUMMER, flushed by the importance of the occasion, goes to the statue and reverently bares his head.

OLD WOMAN: Well, you're all fools, that's all I can say.
DRUMMER: You've drunk too much, auntie. Go on home.
OLD WOMAN: A statue for him? Hmmph! Next they'll be raising a statue for that hatchet murderer in Grenoble who chopped his wife up and mailed the pieces to the dead-letter office!
DRUMMER: Auntie! Someone may hear you. *(Shouts offstage, and the glare of another rocket)* Did you know him?
OLD WOMAN: Did I know him? My grandfather was mayor when it all happened. Ah! You don't know what Sandaraque was like in those days. Quiet. Proper. The best grapes in the whole district. The young men weren't charging around the countryside on motorcycles in those days. And the girls! What seamstresses they were! The best in France. And proper? There wasn't a more proper town south of the Loire than Sandaraque. Devout and God-fearing. Do you know, for twenty years there wasn't a crime reported in the whole district, until *he* came?
DRUMMER: The great Muscari?
OLD WOMAN: Great, indeed! Oh, he changed it all; you have to give him credit for that. Although how decent people can mention his name without crossing themselves and crying, "Get thee behind me!" is more than I can understand. *(Another rocket flares. The DRUMMER starts to go.)* Wait! I'll tell you the true story—
DRUMMER: And miss the fireworks?
OLD WOMAN: You can see them just as well from here. *(The DRUMMER reluctantly comes back.)* And put down that drum. I never could stand

213

that hideous noise. *(They sit at the side of the stage.)* First there was my grandmother *(Lights dim)* Madame Concarneau, the mayor's wife, that is. You might say that she was responsible for the whole business...not that she meant any harm by it....

ACT ONE

Curtain opens revealing M. ETIENNE CONCARNEAU, *mayor of Sandaraque in the year 1890, who has been reading his newspaper but is now engaged in quarreling with his wife who sits opposite, sewing. Behind them is a music stand and metronome, at which their son* ALFRED, *a gangly youth of 17, is practicing for the choir. When he sings it is in a falsetto, but during most of the scene he is content to mutter the words of his part with artistic gestures and grimaces.*

MME. CONCARNEAU: *(Heatedly)* No, I won't!

CONCARNEAU: But you have to!

MME. CONCARNEAU: For the last time, no!

CONCARNEAU: But she is my aunt!

MME. CONCARNEAU: Every Sunday for four years at her house!

CONCARNEAU: And Alfred's great-aunt! His patroness!

MME. CONCARNEAU: I don't care. I shall have hysterics if I have to attend another of her séances!

CONCARNEAU: She will be insulted if we don't.

ALFRED: *(Singing)* Introibit ad altarem...

CONCARNEAU: And Alfred is her favorite grand-nephew. If we offend her she will leave all her money to those worthless Malmaisons and they will spend it raising orchids. Then who will pay for Alfred's music lessons?

MME. CONCARNEAU: We won't offend her. I shall simply invent an excuse.

CONCARNEAU: Invent an excuse? She won't believe you. She never believes anyone but that medium of hers.

MME. CONCARNEAU: Well, I'm not going to waste another Sunday at her house. Every time we visit her I have to sew new buttons on your overcoat. Her butler hangs it up and just as soon as the séance starts that precious aunt of yours sneaks out into the hall and clips the buttons off it.

CONCARNEAU: You imagine it. She is the wealthiest woman in Sandaraque.

MME. CONCARNEAU: Then why is she always stealing buttons?

CONCARNEAU: *(After a pause)* Well, if you give her an excuse, be sure that it doesn't make her angry.

MME. CONCARNEAU: Leave that to me.

ALFRED: *(Singing) Ora pro nobis...*

CONCARNEAU: That's a very sweet note, my boy. What is it called?

ALFRED: G natural, Papa.

CONCARNEAU: And will you sing that note with the choir?

ALFRED: Yes, Papa.

CONCARNEAU: In church?

ALFRED: Yes, Papa.

CONCARNEAU: But what's this you're practicing?

ALFRED: It's the Passion according to Saint Luke.

CONCARNEAU: Passion, eh? Don't you think that's a little extreme to sing in church?

MME CONCARNEAU: Don't be ridiculous, Etienne.

CONCARNEAU: I'm a free-thinker, but after all, Sandaraque is not Paris. We don't want any appeals to the baser emotions here. Our town has a wonderful reputation for purity and I don't see any point in putting ideas in people's heads. Who selected this piece of music?

ALFRED: Father Jarmian did.

CONCARNEAU: I thought that priest would be at the bottom of it. The Passion according to Saint Luke, eh? And what will come next, I ask you? Where will this lead?

MME. PICHEGRU, *a dowdy, yet magnificent dowager, sweeps in.*

PICHEGRU: Ah, my dear nephew and niece! Have I told you? M. Menton is coming from Toulouse for this Sunday's séance. You will be there, of course?

MME. CONCARNEAU: Auntie, the truth is—

PICHEGRU: *(Interrupting)* You really shouldn't leave so much thread lying about, my dear. *(She picks up snippets of thread.)* How are you, nephew? And Alfred, my dear?

ALFRED: Fine, Auntie.

PICHEGRU: *(Who never waits for an answer)* M. Menton has written me that there was an error in his arithmetic. The world is coming to an end some time in July of 1897, not in 1891 as he originally forecast. *(CONCARNEAU has brought her a chair.)* Thank you, my boy. *(To MME. CONCARNEAU)* What are you sewing, child?

MME. CONCARNEAU: A shirt for Alfred.

PICHEGRU: A shirt? How nice. If you don't mind my asking, will it have bone or metal buttons?

MME. CONCARNEAU: Neither. I am making it so he can slip it over his head. And Auntie, I think this Sunday will be quite out of the question—

PICHEGRU: I don't think Alfred will like that, my dear. A proper shirt always has buttons—mother-of-pearl or plain bone if you can't afford any better.

CONCARNEAU: Of course we can afford them!

PICHEGRU: You see! And I do expect you this Sunday.

MME. CONCARNEAU: *(Firmly)* I'm afraid this Sunday is quite out of the question.

PICHEGRU: Please don't bite the thread off, my dear, it sets my nerves on edge. Here, I'll lend you my scissors, I always carry a pair with me.

MME. CONCARNEAU: The truth is, we have hired a new gardener—

PICHEGRU: It's certainly about time. Your dahlias looked very shabby this year.

MME. CONCARNEAU: However, since he is employed during the week, he can only come to us on Sundays. So I shall have to spend the next few Sundays showing him his routine.

PICHEGRU: And miss M. Menton?

MME. CONCARNEAU: I really don't see how it can be avoided.

PICHEGRU: What a pity! Well, what's his name? I know all the gardeners in the district and, without exception, they're all thieves.

MME. CONCARNEAU: I wrote his name down. It's on my shopping list. Let's see—bulbs, watering-can—yes, here it is. It's Muscari.

PICHEGRU: Muscari? Never heard of him. Are you sure it isn't Mouget? I had a second cousin by that name who went into a drapery shop in Lyons and quite dropped out of the family.

MME. CONCARNEAU: No, the name is Muscari. *(Changing the subject)* Now, Alfred, aren't you going to sing for your aunt?

ALFRED: Does she want me to?

PICHEGRU: I do not. The boy's flat. He's always flat. And, besides, it couldn't be Mouget. He would never have become a gardener. He had hay fever.

The curtain closes. In a moment MME. CONCARNEAU *appears in a spotlight in front of the curtain to the left.*

MME. CONCARNEAU: God will forgive me, I know. It was such a very small lie I told about the gardener and I only told it to protect my son's inheritance. In a few days I had forgotten all about it. And that would have been the end of it if it hadn't been for Mme. Pichegru's miserliness.

A spotlight stage right reveals MME. PICHEGRU *with* ALBERIC, *her but-ler, a decayed old man in dirty livery.* PICHEGRU *is staring intently through her lorgnette.*

PICHEGRU: Curious. Curious. She has missed every séance for a month, yet her hedges still look as blowsy as ever and no one has clipped the ivy on the pergola. *(She passes the lorgnette to* ALBERIC.*)* Look closely, Alberic. Would you say that anyone had swept the oyster-shell walk?

ALFRED: I would not, madame.

MME. CONCARNEAU: *(Front)* She couldn't resist the temptation to steal anything that appeared to be of no value.

PICHEGRU: I know my nephew. He wouldn't spend a sou for a turnip unless he knew he could sell it for five times the price. And yet he hires this gardener who never does any gardening. What do you make of it, Alberic?

ALBERIC: Yes, madame.

PICHEGRU: You eternally agree with me, Alberic. I find it annoying.

ALBERIC: No, madame. I mean, I don't think so, madame.

PICHEGRU: And you're as deaf as a potato. *(Shouts)* Go into the village and inquire. Find out who this Muscari is and why he is so valuable. And don't come back until you can tell me everything about him. *(Observes* MME. CONCARNEAU*)* My dear niece! What a pleasure to meet you!

MME. CONCARNEAU: And you, Mme. Pichegru!

PICHEGRU: I have been admiring your garden. How beautifully it grows!

MME. CONCARNEAU: Thank you.

PICHEGRU: So lush and...tropical! *(Pause)* And how is dear Alfred?

MME. CONCARNEAU: *(Coldly)* He is at choir practice. Good day. *(She goes out.)*

PICHEGRU: She is hiding something from me, that's apparent. *(Spies a thread on the floor)* Ah! Good wool yarn! Who could have dropped such a fine piece? It's nearly six inches long! Well, if they think they can keep this Muscari all to themselves, they're mistaken. *(She goes.)*

ALBERIC: *(Alone)* My own part in this affair was extremely modest and I want no credit for it. I simply followed Madame's orders and if, as they say, I helped discover this great man, well, I wash my hands of it. In Sandaraque there was one man who knew everything. That was Lesonge, the banker. So I got on my bicycle and pedalled into town.

He steps into the wings. The curtain opens revealing LESONGE, *in shirt-sleeves and eyeshade, standing behind a high desk stamping due bills. After a moment* ALBERIC *enters.*

LESONGE: Ah, M. Alberic, come in, come in! What a pleasure to see you! *(Shakes his hand)* You've come about the paving bonds?

ALBERIC: No, no, I have nothing to invest.

LESONGE: *(Jovially)* It's not your money I want, M. Alberic—it's your help in averting a calamity. Here. Be seated. *(He pushes* ALBERIC *into a chair and unrolls a map before him.)* Look. The town council proposes to change the road here and shorten it so that it cuts across here. Clever of them, isn't it?

ALBERIC: M. Lesonge—

LESONGE: *(Interrupting)* Observe whose farms it will cut through. Medridec's, Laboussère's, Grimaire's. All opponents of the mayor and his Radical Party. Of course, Concarneau claims it's just an accident. An accident, indeed! Poor Medridec will be split in two!

ALBERIC: Eh?

LESONGE: If he wants to drive his cows from his pasture to his barn they will have to cross a paved road. And if it is rainy and they slip on the asphalt, who is to make good the damage?

ALBERIC: Yes, yes, that's serious. Cows are always falling down.

LESONGE: And the rock quarry! What a scandal that is!

ALBERIC: The rock quarry?

LESONGE: Exactly. They propose to open a new one to get the gravel for the road. And where will it be? On the mayor's property, of course. Think what it means, M. Alberic. *Thump, thump, thump,* day and night. Rock dust blowing through the air, sandstorms at night—a regular Sahara!

ALBERIC: And will the dust get into the wine?

LESONGE: Unless we defeat these paving bonds it will get into everything. M. Alberic, this has always been a quiet, respectable town where we could bring up our children without exposing them to carriage races and the like. This paved road is the thin edge of the wedge. If we don't defeat it, Sandaraque will be full of excursionists and riff-raff from all over France. We can rely on your vote?

ALBERIC: Eh?

LESONGE: *(Shouting)* Your vote!

ALBERIC: Well, I won't invest anything, but if the dust is going to get into the wine I shan't vote for it.

LESONGE: *(Rolling up the map)* Good. Now if there is something further I can do for you—

ALBERIC: Yes. Madame asked me to make inquiries about a man called Muscari.

LESONGE: Muscari? Glad to oblige. *(Calling)* Emmanuel! My son handles the deposit accounts. If this chap banks with us he will be able to tell you all about him.

ALBERIC: I don't think he does.

LESONGE: But everyone in the district deals with us.

ALBERIC: I think this fellow is an...itinerant.

LESONGE: Oh? A gypsy, eh?

ALBERIC: Possibly.

EMMANUEL enters, lost in a book. He is a pallid, bespectacled youth.

EMMANUEL: *(Reading aloud but to himself)* "Beware the invisible parallelograms of rectitude and the right angles of moral complacency. The Superior Man finds solace only in the parabola—"

LESONGE: What's that?

EMMANUEL: *(Putting the book in his blouse)* It's a book I'm reading.

LESONGE: He's always studying. Last month it was frogs and now it's geometry. *(To his son)* Do we have a client named Mascagni?

ALBERIC: Muscari.

LESONGE: Muscari, then.

EMMANUEL: I'll look and see. *(He exits.)*

LESONGE: *(Giving it thought)* A gypsy, eh? Wait a moment. Does he mend kettles?

ALBERIC: I really don't know, sir.

LESONGE: There's a fellow who lives out by Montfaçon that answers your description very well. He's red-haired, has a limp, and sells calendars in the marketplace.

ALBERIC: I think our man is more of a gardener, sir,

LESONGE: This fellow isn't above doing a bit of gardening if he has to. *(EMMANUEL reenters.)* Any record of him?

EMMANUEL: Muneville, Murat senior, Murat junior. Musette, Mutramont —no Muscari.

LESONGE: There. No bank account. What did I tell you? That red-haired gypsy is your best bet. Have you seen anyone like that loitering around, Emmanuel?

EMMANUEL: There was that man I told you about this morning, Father.

LESONGE: Yes, but you didn't say he was red-haired.

EMMANUEL: But he certainly limped. And he looked like a gypsy. He might have dyed his hair.

ALBERIC: Who is this?

LESONGE: We had a little theft here this morning.

ALBERIC: A theft—in Sandaraque?

LESONGE: Apparently. Someone entered the bank after the charwoman left and before my son arrived to open up. The cash-drawer was pried open and twenty francs were gone.

ALBERIC: And you think this Muscari might have done it?

LESONGE: I accuse no one. But my son caught a glimpse of the thief as he ran away and should be able to identify him.

ALBERIC: And he was really a gypsy?

EMMANUEL: I'm not sure. But I seem to remember that he wore a gold earring.

LESONGE: But this is only circumstantial evidence. It may have been an entirely different person. *(He gives his son a searching glance.)* In my business, M. Alberic, I have learned never to jump to conclusions. *(EMMANUEL goes out.)*

ALBERIC: All the same, I thank you for the information.

LESONGE: Not at all, M. Alberic. Any way I can be of help… *(Showing him out)* My regards to madame. And don't forget to tell her about the rock-crusher. When the wind is in the east it will cover her rose-garden with dust…

Curtain. PICHEGRU *enters before the curtain.*

PICHEGRU: Alberic! Alberic! You are not listening to me.

ALBERIC: *(Following her)* Yes, madame.

PICHEGRU: You don't use your head. He can't live on air, can he?

ALBERIC: No, madame. I mean, it isn't likely, madame.

PICHEGRU: Then the way to track him down is through the green-grocer's. If he is a gypsy he will eat cabbages; gypsies are always fond of cabbages. Go to M. Poulette and ask who buys a suspicious quantity of cabbages. What day was he born on?

ALBERIC: Who, madame?

PICHEGRU: Why, this Muscari, of course.

ALBERIC: That I have not yet ascertained, madame.

PICHEGRU: Well, I can't do his forecast without it. Have you asked the Ouija board?

ALBERIC: Yes, madame.

PICHEGRU: And what did it say?

ALBERIC: The Ouija board said sometime in the middle of summer, madame.

PICHEGRU: But what day of the week?

ALBERIC: The Ouija board was perplexed as to the day, madame.

PICHEGRU: How vexing! You'd think it might be more precise! Hmm—well, go to the greengrocer's. No—wait! I'll go myself. Have the horses hitched to the brougham. You never get anything right, you poor man.

ALBERIC: Yes, madame. *(They go out.)*

The curtain opens revealing POULETTE, *the grocer, his wife, his daughter* MATHILDE, *and his son* GABRIEL. GABRIEL *is sifting flour from a barrel.* MME. POULETTE *kneels with her ear pressed against her daughter's belly.*

MME. POULETTE: *(After listening in silence)* Appendicitis? *(She listens again.)* No, no my girl. That won't do.

POULETTE: *(Chronically choleric)* I knew it! I knew it! Those buggy rides to Montfaçon! That sudden interest in butterflying! Out at dawn with her net, hopping from hedge to hedge, God knows where, after a pair of wings. Treacle! It's all treacle in our eyes!

MATHILDE: Oh, Mama! I hurt so! I think my appendix is in a rupture.

MME. POULETTE: Sssh! It's stirring again!

POULETTE: It moves, your appendix! And soon it will kick and in three months' time it will learn to bawl and suck its finger!

GABRIEL: Can I stop now, Papa?

POULETTE: *(Whirling on him)* Sift! Sift! Every last maggot must go! *(Pause)* Do you think we have no regard for our customers? *(To his daughter)* And you! Sucking peppermint candy and pretending that it was the sugar that made you fat!

MATHILDE: Papa! Everyone will hear you!

POULETTE: And you wanted my brandy to preserve butterflies in, did you? There's ingratitude for you! *(To GABRIEL)* And afterwards you can wash the mold off the lentils. *(To his wife)* Bolt the door!

MME. POULETTE: We'll lose trade.

POULETTE: And what will we lose if this gets spread around town? *(His wife hesitates.)* Is a man not to be master in his own house? *(She goes.)* Now, my girl, who planted it in you?

MATHILDE: Oh, Papa, you are so coarse!

POULETTE: Who gave it to you? Was it that young devil of a Lesonge?

MATHILDE: Oh, Papa!

POULETTE: Or the miller's son who's always whistling to himself? Or that meek scoundrel Alfred Concarneau? Tell me who did it, I'll call for Father Jarmian, and there'll be a new son-in-law in the house by tomorrow morning.

GABRIEL: *(Assuming a fighting stance)* Just tell us who did it and I'll smash his face in!

POULETTE: You keep out of this. You'd do the same thing yourself if you had half a chance. Now sit and sift!

MME. POULETTE: *(Reentering)* Poulette! What are you saying?

MATHILDE: It—it wasn't any of them at all.

POULETTE: Then who was it?

MATHILDE: It wasn't my fault! I swear it wasn't!

POULETTE: Where did it happen?

MME. POULETTE: When?

POULETTE: Out with it.

MATHILDE: *(Faltering at first)* It… It was by the stone culvert—where the road leaves the poplar trees at Montfaçon. I was chasing a spotted orange butterfly and it flew down among the reeds. I climbed over the wall after it. It was such a beautiful butterfly, with big purple spots and—

POULETTE: Never mind the spots! What happened?

MATHILDE: *(Bouncing in a childish rage)* I'm trying to tell you!

MME. POULETTE: *(With apprehension)* Don't bounce, dear.

MATHILDE: I had my net just over it and my bottle in my other hand. And just when I was about to catch it, a man jumped out of the reeds! "Let me go!" I said but he wouldn't and I screamed and kicked and bit him on the hand but it was no use—he kissed me! *(Pause)*

POULETTE: Go on! Go on!

MATHILDE: *(Primly)* That's all.

POULETTE: *(Roaring)* That's all? This is no better than the appendicitis story!

MME. POULETTE: Don't torture the poor girl. She must have swooned.

MATHILDE: *(Eagerly)* That's it. I swooned. I swooned right away. And when I woke up he had run off.

POULETTE: What did he look like?

MATHILDE: *(With gathering enthusiasm)* He was a giant—over six feet tall and all tattooed and, oh yes, he had a black beard and curly moustaches. I think he must have been an Arab or maybe an Italian or Swede. He was horrible. *(Sobs)* And his moustaches were all bristly and *(brightly)* he was so strong! *(Sobs again)* Oh, Mama, I want to die of shame, right now. I want to die! How can I ever face anyone at choir practice again? *(Loud knocking on the door)*

POULETTE: *(To his wife)* Tell them we're closed for the day.

MME. POULETTE: My poor darling! What an experience! *(To her husband as she goes out)* Don't you dare touch her, you brute!

POULETTE: I? A brute? Am I to blame? What a thing to happen! And only two days before the Feast of the Blessed Virgin! *(He catches sight of his daughter again and holds his head in anguish.)* How can we sell candles with a clear conscience?

MME. POULETTE: *(Reentering)* It's that old Madame Pichegru. She got her foot in the door when I opened it and she won't leave.

POULETTE: *(To MATHILDE)* Quick! Hold a pan in your lap and pretend that you are shelling peas. We can't let that old gossip see how big you are. Here! Bend over it!

MATHILDE: But there's nothing in it.

POULETTE: Pretend! Pretend! *(To GABRIEL)* Sift! Sift! *(MME. PICHEGRU enters and he becomes all smiles.)* Ah, Mme. Pichegru, how good of you to honor our little shop with a visit. Gabriel, get madame a chair. And what will it be today? A provolone? *(Holds up a cheese)* We've a dozen just in from Genoa. Gabriel, a cushion, a cushion! *(He holds the cheese to her ear.)* Listen. Sound as a good melon. *(Raps)* Hear that? Firm all the way through.

PICHEGRU: Rubbish!

POULETTE: That's enough sifting, Gabriel. I'm sure you've gotten all the lumps out. We've been saving something just for you. Show madame the tinned sturgeon.

PICHEGRU: There's no need. I've told you, Poulette, I'll buy nothing in tins. If the manufacturers want my trade they must learn to pack everything in glass jars—or, better still, in little china pots with handles. There is nothing you can do with tins once you've opened them and you're put to the expense of having them carted away.

GABRIEL: It's very good sturgeon.

PICHEGRU: Nonsense. If it were good it would be properly packed. *(She eyes MATHILDE fixedly.)* You can always tell the quality of the goods by the way it's packed.

MME. POULETTE: *(Trying to get off the subject)* They say ribbons will be coming back on this year's hats.

PICHEGRU: *(Still staring at MATHILDE)* Eh?

MME. POULETTE: Ribbons.

PICHEGRU: They never went out. *(Silence)* May I ask what you are doing?

MATHILDE: I'm...shelling peas. *(Pause)*

PICHEGRU: Well, you should hold the pan more firmly on your, uh, lap, or you will spill them all on the floor. *(To POULETTE)* But why are you closed? Is someone ill?

POULETTE: It's...it's my wife's Saints-Day.

PICHEGRU: That would be Saint Anselm the Lesser, I suppose. Curious. *(Pause)* Poulette, I am looking for a certain unidentified man.

POULETTE: *(Grimly)* So am I.

PICHEGRU: I am informed that he is a gypsy and has been seen loitering around the fields near Montfaçon.

POULETTE: Eh? Is he interested in butterflies?

MATHILDE: Oh, Papa!

PICHEGRU: You know him, then?

POULETTE: Madame, I think I have an account to settle with that man. What is his name?

PICHEGRU: The name is unusual. It is Muscari.

At the mention of the name the actors freeze in tableau except for GABRIEL, *who steps downstage.*

GABRIEL: *(To the audience)* Well, that's the way rumors get started! Deplorable, isn't it? *(The curtain closes behind him.)* Is it any wonder that we of the younger generation don't believe in anything when we see what silly, half-baked stories our parents will swallow? *(As he talks he takes off his apron and dons a jacket.)* Is it any wonder that we are all cynical? Take my sister, for instance. She knows perfectly well that babies don't come from kisses, even from tattooed gypsies. But can you blame her for saying it if she knows that my mother will believe it? I think it is disgusting the amount of plain, downright ignorance there is in the world. And the worst of it is how it spreads once it gets started. Of course old lady Pichegru told everybody about what had happened to Mathilde and then there was nothing for it but for Father to go to the police and file a complaint. That started it! The next day that old widow Leclerc who lives back of the distillery reported that someone had broken into her henhouse—

WIDOW LECLERC: *(In spotlight)* Ever since Leclerc passed away I've been a light sleeper. Gone of the consumption, poor man, it took him off in his prime. Well, I had hardly settled myself in bed when I heard this clatter in the henhouse. "It's a fox," I said to myself and I put on my slippers and ran out with a lantern. And what did I see? This dreadful man with long dark hair down to his shoulders and a cape flying off him so he looked like a bat in the darkness. Over the fence he went, quick as a bird, and my three best layers lying strangled in their bran. Strangled, I tell you, citizens, and they'd never done anything to deserve it but cackle a bit perhaps and... *(Spot out)*

GABRIEL: And the same night old Laboussère set fire to his own barn for the insurance and by ten o'clock the next morning there were three eye-witnesses ready to swear they knew who did it—

FIRST WITNESS: *(In spot)* There he was in the hayloft. I saw him from where I was plowing. A gypsy-looking fellow with striped trousers and a nankeen jacket.

SECOND WITNESS: Climbed over the roof like a cat. It was Muscari; I'd know him any place from those yellow teeth of his. He was swearing and cursing at farmer Laboussère.

LABOUSSÈRE: I'd just finished milking the cows when I saw this man with a blazing torch in his hand. I tried to stop him but he ran up into the hayloft and the first thing I knew the whole barn was afire. "That's Muscari," I said. *(Spotlight out)*

GABRIEL: And within a week you couldn't go anywhere in Sandaraque without hearing something about this gypsy. It's disgusting. I mean, it's enough to make you lose your faith in justice and honesty, don't you think?

ALFRED CONCARNEAU: *(Running in)* Come on. The town council is meeting.

GABRIEL: I ought to punch you right on the nose.

ALFRED: What for?

GABRIEL: You know what for. If there is one thing I can't stand it's people who try to pass the blame off on other people.

ALFRED: I only kissed her once. And it was in the vestry room at church. You can't get babies there.

GABRIEL: I ought to punch you right on the nose, that's what I ought to do.

ALFRED: Have you heard the latest about the gypsy?

GABRIEL: No. What?

ALFRED: He broke into old lady Pichegru's house and stole six cases of cognac.

GABRIEL: No!

ALFRED: God's truth. Her butler surprised him in the cellar. He got hold of his shirttail but Muscari threatened him with a razor and ran out through the coal chute. The gendarmes are chasing him right now—twelve of them.

GABRIEL: Six cases! Wow! *(They run off.)*

EMMANUEL LESONGE enters and crosses the stage, reading intently from his book. He stops, draws himself upright, and throws his shoulders back.

EMMANUEL: Superior! *(He goes out, reading.)*

The curtain is drawn, revealing the Sandaraque town hall as if ready for a meeting. CONCARNEAU *is alone, his hands full of police reports.*

CONCARNEAU: What a mess this is! Everyone in town seems to have met this gypsy. Except for me. And it's "Catch him, catch him!" That's all I hear. Ai! What a headache I have! And how can I catch him when no two people agree on what he looks like? First he's tall, then he's short; now fat, now thin as a steak knife. This report says he has a beard and wears a checked vest; this one says he's clean-shaven and has pointed ears. Yesterday he was barefoot and today he wears cavalry boots with brass spurs. What can you make of it? I've sent for Father Jarmian. He's the most educated man in town—perhaps *he* can explain it.

FATHER JARMIAN: *(Entering)* You asked for me, M. Concarneau?

CONCARNEAU: Indeed I did. I need your advice.

JARMIAN: My advice, M. Concarneau? I have given it before but you did not often follow it.

CONCARNEAU: Well, I'll follow it this time, providing it's nonsectarian. What do you know of this Muscari?

JARMIAN: A great deal.

CONCARNEAU: Ah! You have met him?

JARMIAN: I have encountered him hundreds of times in the course of my work.

CONCARNEAU: He's not a taxpayer, I hope. That would be ticklish.

JARMIAN: M. Concarneau, I do not think that he is a person at all.

CONCARNEAU: But you said you had met him—Eh? You don't suppose it's Old Nick himself?

JARMIAN: No. Not in the literal sense.

CONCARNEAU: Of course, as a free-thinker I don't believe in that sort of superstition, but it's a relief all the same.

JARMIAN: I think rather that the Muscari is the spirit of guilt, or perhaps I should say the spirit of evasion of guilt. Has it not struck you as odd, for instance, that Mathilde Poulette would wait for six months before reporting her violation?

CONCARNEAU: Eh? I hadn't thought of that. Then her story is all moonshine?

JARMIAN: Completely. And the widow Leclerc's chickens. Have you examined them?

CONCARNEAU: Of course not.

JARMIAN: I have. There is not a mark on them.

CONCARNEAU: Then what did they die of?

JARMIAN: Who knows? Boredom, perhaps. But they were certainly not strangled.

CONCARNEAU: I can't be concerned about a lot of chickens. What I want is a summary of your opinion.

JARMIAN: My opinion is that the people of Sandaraque have invented a scapegoat, someone on whom they can lay their own misfortunes and sins. *(Sighs)* I understand them. Our district's reputation for virtue has no doubt gotten to be more than they can bear.

CONCARNEAU: I don't agree with you there. There can't be too much of a good thing, particularly when that thing is an honest pride in one's own native town.

JARMIAN: But it is such a heavy load to carry—the reputation for virtue! Particularly when one knows how little foundation it really has. *(He goes.)*

The councilmen and townspeople now enter. The MAYOR *greets them variously.* FARMER LABOUSSÈRE *enters grimly, a bucket in his hands.*

LABOUSSÈRE: Good morning, M. le Maire.

CONCARNEAU: Good morning, M. Laboussère. What brings you here?

LABOUSSÈRE: I have come to demand justice!

CONCARNEAU: And this bucket?

LABOUSSÈRE: *(With tragic intensity)* In this bucket is all that remains of my barn. Yesterday a splendid frame building with silo attached. Today—ashes! Nails! Three gate hinges! A horse shoe! The labor of years, M. Concarneau, gone in a moment! Look at my hands! See these calluses! I have worked hard, M. Concarneau, God is my witness. And for what? For ashes? For nails? I ask you, is that justice?

THE CROWD: No! No!

CONCARNEAU: M. Laboussère, this is a meeting of the municipal council. We have an agenda. We will discuss your barn under the heading of Unfinished Business.

LABOUSSÈRE: *(Indignant)* Unfinished? But it *is* finished! Utterly! Look for yourself! *(He slams the bucket down on the* MAYOR'S *table to the accompaniment of a cloud of ashes.)*

CONCARNEAU: M. Laboussère, remove that bucket from the council table or I will have you ejected.

LABOUSSÈRE: And what have you done? Have you caught the arsonist?

VARIOUS VOICES: What about Muscari? It's a scandal! *(Etc.)*

CONCARNEAU: *(Pounding for order)* Enough! Enough! Quiet, please! We will proceed with the regular order of business. Be seated, please. Be seated, everyone. *(Some sort of order is restored and the councilmen take their seats.)* The first point on today's order of business is discussion of the paving bonds.

POULETTE: *(Rising in outrage)* Paving bonds! M. Concarneau, have you no conscience? How can you speak of paving bonds at a moment like this? *(Tumult)*

CONCARNEAU: Sit down, M. Poulette! I am following the regular order of business.

LABOUSSÈRE: *(Reviving)* What about my barn?

WIDOW LECLERC: And my chickens? Before God, citizens, I swear that Muscari strangled them!

VOICES: That's right! We saw him! *(Etc.)*

CONCARNEAU: *(Pounding)* Order! Order!

POULETTE: Are you blind? Do you know that there is not a woman in Sandaraque who dares to walk in the dark after what happened to my daughter?

CONCARNEAU: *(Acidly)* What *did* happen to your daughter, M. Poulette?

POULETTE: *(Enraged)* What are you insinuating, you maggot?

CONCARNEAU: Why did she wait six months before reporting it?

POULETTE: *(Charging at him)* I'll break your jaw for you!

CITIZENS: *(Intervening)* Gentlemen! No violence! *(Etc.)*

CONCARNEAU: *(After POULETTE has been hauled back)* Order, please! In the unfortunate case of Poulette's daughter, the police have taken steps to capture the culprit. However, we do not believe that the gypsy was involved at all.

POULETTE: *(On his feet again)* So? Is my daughter a liar? Is that what you mean?

LABOUSSÈRE: And my barn? What about that?

WIDOW LECLERC: And my chickens! Strangled, I tell you, dear citizens, strangled in their nests!

CONCARNEAU: We are investigating! We are investigating! But I must tell you that there is some doubt whether there is any such person as Muscari.

A CITIZEN: *(Derisively)* No Muscari? Then who drank the six cases of cognac? Tell us that!

CONCARNEAU: Let me continue. Who has seen him?

MANY VOICES: I have! He has! We all have! *(Etc.)*

CONCARNEAU: Good. And what does he look like? *(Everyone talks at once and describes Muscari with widely dissimilar gestures.)* You see!

None of you can agree. How do we know that there is any Muscari if none of you can agree? *(The crowd is momentarily silent.)*

LESONGE: Citizens! This is a trick! Why should you agree! Indeed, it is precisely the virtue of our great democracy that you all have the right to disagree! Am I correct? *(Shouts of approval)* Then let us not be misled by demagoguery. As taxpayer it is my duty to point out that our present mayor has allowed law enforcement to languish and decay, while at the same time he and his colleagues of the Radical Party have approved staggering expenditures for such visionary projects as asphalting the market road and the construction of a post office—

CONCARNEAU: *(Breaking in)* I stand on my record. The people of Sandaraque voted for progress and I shall give it to them.

LESONGE: *(With oratorical indignation)* And you call the fumes of smoking asphalt progress? While justice sleeps? While bandits can in broad daylight force their way into the banks? No, M. Concarneau, you have not given us progress—you have given us anarchy! Asphalt and anarchy!

CONCARNEAU: *(Pounding)* M. Lesonge! Be good enough to sit down!

LESONGE: Not one franc for the paving bonds! That is my program. Arrest Muscari! And no more asphalt! *(He sits amid prolonged cheers.)*

CONCARNEAU: Order! Order!

GABRIEL and ALFRED enter, running.

GABRIEL: They have him! They have him!

POULETTE: Muscari?

GABRIEL: The gypsy!

CONCARNEAU: They've caught him?

ALFRED: Almost.

GABRIEL: They have him surrounded.

CONCARNEAU: Where?

GABRIEL: In the old windmill at Saint-Méro. He upset all the milk-cans at Trouvec's dairy and then ran up into the tower. The gendarmes have all the doors and windows covered. If he doesn't come out in ten minutes they are going to set fire to the windmill and force him out.

POULETTE: *(Shaking his fist at CONCARNEAU)* So there isn't any gypsy, eh? What do you say now?

CONCARNEAU: I say, M. Poulette, that the police are working under my orders. If Muscari is caught, he will be caught by my administration.

ANNETTE BÉCHAR: *(Running in, weeping hysterically)* The police! The police!

CONCARNEAU: What is it?

ANNETTE: Where are the police?

CONCARNEAU: At Saint-Méro. Why?

ANNETTE: *(With sobs)* I was stacking books in the library at Morillon. It was broad daylight.

POULETTE: How long ago? When?

ANNETTE: An hour ago. It was horrible! I'll never forget how horrible it was. But what could I do? What could I do?

CONCARNEAU: In God's name, girl, what happened?

ANNETTE: *(Hysterically)* There he was, standing in the aisle in front of me, and without a stitch of clothing on!

CITIZENS: Who? Who?

ANNETTE: Muscari! He didn't say a word, but his eyes—his eyes! I've never seen such eyes before! "Let me go! Let me go!" I screamed. I tried to run away but he ran right after me. I ran behind the dictionary stand, but he ran right through it as if it weren't there at all. I tried to hide in the periodicals—but my foot caught on a newspaper rack and I fell down and there was nothing more I could do—nothing! nothing! *(She swoons dramatically and falls to the floor.)*

POULETTE: *(In triumph)* Now do you admit the truth?

CONCARNEAU: But they have him trapped in the windmill!

LESONGE: Idiot! Can't you believe your ears? He has escaped again!

A VOICE: May I speak, please?

CONCARNEAU: Who is it?

The STRANGER *steps out of the crowd, he is a small, mild man dressed in a rather shabby suit, with unruly hair and a moustache that badly wants trimming.*

STRANGER: I don't think you know me in Sandaraque. But I have a statement I should like to read.

CONCARNEAU: How long is it?

STRANGER: *(Taking a document from his pocket)* Three pages. But it is extremely interesting.

CONCARNEAU: I shall cut you off if it's not to the point.

STRANGER: I don't think you will have to. Could I have a glass of water? My throat is rather dry.

CONCARNEAU: *(Pouring)* Here.

STRANGER: Thank you. *(He drinks leisurely, takes spectacles from his pocket, wipes them, puts them on his nose, unfolds his document and after clearing his throat and gazing amiably at his audience, commences to read in a dry, unemotional voice.)* Prompted by remorse and a sense of my own unspeakable depravity, and in order to make amends to the virtuous citizens of Sandaraque against whom I have transgressed, I offer the following statement: It was I who on the night of February 15, 1890, entered the hen-house of Angelique Leclerc and there laid hands upon and strangled three birds.

WIDOW LECLERC: What did I tell you, dear citizens? Not a peep, nor a chirp from any of them.

LESONGE: Arrest him! *(Tumult)*

STRANGER: Please! Let me continue. On the night of February 21, 1890, I poured kerosene in a hayloft belonging to one Arsene Laboussère and set fire to it, causing the destruction of the barn and all livestock quartered therein. *(Commotion)* I confess to robbing from the cellar of Madame Pichegru six cases of cognac and to threatening her butler with disfigurement by a razor in the course of this crime. *(Tumult)* I confess to stealing from the merchant Poulette—

POULETTE: What's this?

STRANGER: Twelve sausages and a keg of hard cider. *(Laughter at POULETTE'S expense)* I confess to assaulting the gendarme Armand Poitou in a drunken rage on the night of December 2nd, 1889, and to dropping his body into the well opposite the church.

LESONGE: Murderer!

CONCARNEAU: And everyone thought he had gone to visit his niece in Vichy!

STRANGER: I confess to the assault and seduction of the schoolgirl Mathilde Poulette on the riverbank near Montfaçon.

POULETTE: You bastard! You'll hang for this!

STRANGER: *(Unperturbed)* I confess to the rape of Suzanne Fabre on August 21, 1889, in the cemetery at Bignancourt. *(A general gasp)* I confess to the rape of the serving-woman Marie Deniz in the loft above the sacristy at Saint-Méro on the evening of last Bastille Day.

CONCARNEAU: What? Is not even our national holiday sacred?

STRANGER: I confess to the enforced seduction during the months of June, July and August of last year of the following women of Sandaraque: Annette Béchar, among the periodicals at the library at Morillon; Yvette Larun, on the back porch of her father's cottage at Montfaçon and four times in a rowboat on the neighboring stream.

A WOMAN: *(Rising, incredulous)* Four times? *(The STRANGER nods pleasantly.)*

STRANGER: Mme. Henriette Noirmontier, in a hedgerow at—

CONCARNEAU: *(Pounding)* Enough! You're a bluebeard! We've listened to enough of this!

STRANGER: But I've only just begun.

CONCARNEAU: Monster!

POULETTE: Where are you from?

LESONGE: What is your name?

STRANGER: I am a citizen of France and a servant of the Muses.

CITIZENS: Your name! Your name!

STRANGER: My name, citizens, is Jean-Baptiste Hippolyte Marie-Henri Muscari.

Quick curtain.

ACT TWO

PICHEGRU: *(Entering, before the curtain)* Well, have you found him?

ALBERIC: *(Just behind her)* Who, madame?

PICHEGRU: The gardener.

ALBERIC: Yes, madame, he has been found.

PICHEGRU: Well, it's about time. Do hurry, it's going to rain. And what are his special talents?

ALBERIC: It appears, madame, that he is a rapist.

PICHEGRU: A Papist? Nonsense. That's not a talent; it's a point of view.

ALBERIC: I said *rapist*, madame. A violator of women.

PICHEGRU: And they *pay* him for that? M. Menton was right, the world deserves to die. And just think, Alberic, my nephew's wife had him in once a week for months! And on Sundays, too! Did you ever hear the like?

ALBERIC: No, madame.

PICHEGRU: The world has certainly changed since I was a girl! Well, it's a good thing I made inquiries before I hired him. I'm much too old to be interested in that sort of service! *(They exit.)*

The curtain opens on MUSCARI'S *cell in the town jail.* MUSCARI *is on his knees, praying. The* JAILER *and* FATHER JARMIAN *appear at the grill.*

JAILER: I brought him his supper but he wouldn't touch it. "No," he said, "it's not right that a sinner like me should be waited on by such a good man as you." All he would take was a copy of the *Book of Martyrs* to console himself with.

JARMIAN: Let me speak with him. *(He enters the cell; the* JAILER *goes.)*

MUSCARI: *(Praying)* Give me the strength of Samson among the Philistines so that I may bear up under adversity.

JARMIAN: Muscari!

MUSCARI: You who raised up Jacob on a beam of holy light, speak to me!

JARMIAN: Enough of that, you rascal!

MUSCARI: *(Without looking around)* That isn't the voice of the Lord.

JARMIAN: No, it isn't. *(MUSCARI turns and attempts to kiss the hem of JARMIAN'S soutane.)* Get up off your knees!

MUSCARI: I am not fit to stand in your presence, Father.

JARMIAN: Get up! Get up! I'll have no more of this shamming! *(MUSCARI rises.)* That's better. Now, enough of this nonsense. I want to know why you confessed to all these atrocious crimes.

MUSCARI: Because I am guilty. I admit to everything.

JARMIAN: *(Sternly)* Do not lie to me. Remember, I am the priest of this parish and know the secrets of the confessional. There is not one in ten of these crimes of which you can possibly be guilty.

MUSCARI: *(Dropping his penitent manner)* No doubt. But you can't testify to that in court.

JARMIAN: I know that. But I rely on an appeal to your own conscience to tell the truth.

MUSCARI: To my conscience? If, as you say, you know the real criminals, why don't you appeal to their consciences?

JARMIAN: *(Sadly)* I have.

MUSCARI: And nothing came of it, eh?

JARMIAN: The spirit of evil is abroad in Sandaraque. I have urged every sinner to confess publicly. But there is reluctance.

MUSCARI: *(Smiling)* I could have told you that.

JARMIAN: No. Until your arrival I had hopes that they would accept responsibility for their misdeeds. But all that is changed now. No one will admit to anything. The confessional stands empty for days on end. People avert their eyes when they pass me on the street. My only hope is that you will withdraw your false confession.

MUSCARI: Well, I won't.

JARMIAN: And If I secure confessions from the real culprits?

MUSCARI: That will never happen. I know towns like this. There is not a person in them who will admit to anything unless he is forced to.

JARMIAN: Not even to save an innocent man from the guillotine?

MUSCARI: Especially not to save an innocent man. Towns like Sandaraque enjoy executions, and if the victim happens to be innocent that merely lends piquance to the occasion. However, I'll make you a bargain. If you can persuade a single one of your parishioners to come forward and confess, out of motives of Christian conscience, to just one of these crimes, I will tell the truth about all of them. Is that a fair proposal?

JARMIAN: It is a diabolical proposal.

MUSCARI: But will you accept the challenge?

JARMIAN: Of course I accept. I have been priest here twelve years and I know these people too well to be deceived by them. They may be weak, but they are kind, lovable, and generous at heart. *(MUSCARI smiles.)* But now tell me what prompted you to this monstrous imposture.

MUSCARI: Gladly. But, remember, I shan't admit to a word of this in court.

JARMIAN: I am a priest. I never bear witness.

MUSCARI: You are also an educated man.

JARMIAN: *(Modestly)* I have some acquaintance with the Muses—

MUSCARI: Have you ever heard of a little booklet entitled "The Anaesthesia of Necessity?"

JARMIAN: No.

MUSCARI: Or a book of essays entitled *In Defense of Arrogance?*

JARMIAN: No.

MUSCARI: *(Prodding his memory)* It was printed in an edition of one hundred and fifty copies on Japanese rice paper. With apple green covers.

JARMIAN: I am sorry. I don't recall it.

MUSCARI: *(A note of desperation)* But perhaps in your reading you may have, from time to time, come across poems over the signature "Invictus?"

JARMIAN: I don't think so.

MUSCARI: *(With explosive bitterness)* There! What does my life amount to? Wherever I go it is the same story. Not one reader! Not a single person who has ever heard of "The Anaesthesia of Necessity!" It has fallen like a pebble in the sea without leaving so much as a ripple behind. Ah, monsieur, you do not know how bitter it is to be ignored!

JARMIAN: *(Incredulous)* And you have confessed to these crimes solely in order to gain notoriety?

MUSCARI: But think what it means to pour out one's heart year after year and in the end to be utterly unnoticed! Now I promise you that they will notice me. I shall die a famous man!

JARMIAN: A famous scoundrel!

MUSCARI: *(With intense conviction)* That is better than oblivion! *(Pause)*

JARMIAN: But you are a stranger here. How did you come to know the details of all these crimes?

MUSCARI: By divine intervention. Or, if you like, by one of those accidents that make us believe in providence. I was standing on the street outside of the National Academy in Paris. It was March 20th, the anniversary of Napoleon's return from Elba—I had chosen the date intentionally. Under my overcoat I had twelve sticks of dynamite strapped to my body—

JARMIAN: *(Aghast)* You are mad!

MUSCARI: *(Modestly)* No, madness is not one of my gifts. I am merely persistent. I had mailed copies of "The Anaesthesia of Necessity" to the press, accompanied by a brief manifesto. It was my intention to wait until the street was clear—I have a horror of involving strangers in my personal problems—then light the fuse with my cigar—hurl myself against the portico—and pouf! I should join the Immortals.

JARMIAN: But this ghastly plan miscarried?

MUSCARI: Unfortunately. The bulge in my coat must have excited suspicion, for there was a man who kept loitering nearby. I could not bring myself to... let him share my experience, so I waited for him to leave. He persisted. An hour passed by. At last it began to rain. My cigar went out! In order to keep the powder in the fuse from getting wet I asked to borrow his umbrella. In getting it open I inadvertently threw back my coat and he saw the dynamite—

JARMIAN: Heaven be praised! And he turned you over to the police?

MUSCARI: No, he took me to a café and bought me dinner. "You are wasting your time on the Academy," he said. "It's merely the scum on the surface of the pond. If you want to use dynamite, you should use it where it will do some good." "And where is that?" I asked. "On the self-righteous smugness of the provincial middle classes. Without them the whole structure—academicians, pettifogging lecturers, dramatic critics—would fall of its own weight." *(Pause)* I must admit that I had never seen things in quite that light before. We spent the whole evening talking. And at last he told me about Sandaraque.

JARMIAN: What? Had he lived here?

MUSCARI: He had been the school teacher here for ten years.

JARMIAN: M. Pinneloup!

MUSCARI: You knew him, then?

JARMIAN: We played chess together for years. But he always seemed such a respectable man!

MUSCARI: Out of boredom here—with the town—he had compiled Sandaraque's secret history. He had meant to write a novel on provincial life, but when he saw how determined I was, he made me a present of his researches.

JARMIAN: And—the dynamite?

MUSCARI: I threw it in the Seine. *(Silence)*

JARMIAN: *(Rising)* I see. And you are quite determined to give up your life in pursuit of this insane scheme?

MUSCARI: What should I do? Hug life to myself like a miser his gold, and part with it spitting and coughing on some rented mattress? Who will then remember me? Who will read me? Monsieur, nothing is more important to a poet than the manner of his death. Shelley drowned, Villon in jail as a thief, Byron feverish in the swampy isles of Greece— they are my masters! They knew how poets must die!

JARMIAN: And you propose to follow their example?

MUSCARI: I propose to outdo them! *(He spreads his arms.)* I propose to die as only one other poet has done—for the sins of others! *(He drops his head. JARMIAN crosses himself.)*

JARMIAN: *(Intensely)* And I propose to see that you do not have that opportunity.

Quick curtain. After a moment the lights come up on the forestage and ALBERIC enters with an umbrella and camp-stool.

ALBERIC: *(Front)* I feel that I owe everyone an explanation about those six cases of cognac, particularly since some people are claiming that I drank it all myself, and that would reflect very unfavorably on me if I were to apply for another position. I admit that I told a falsehood when I reported finding the gypsy in the cellar, but as for drinking all that cognac myself—well, I am a decent, God-fearing old man, and six cases is seventy-two bottles and whoever started that rumor— *(He breaks off, then, more confidentially.)* It was all Poulette's fault. I told him to bill Madame for six cases of Vichy water and never mind delivering them, just pay me the wholesale price. But he would make it cognac instead of mineral water and when Madame read that bill I can assure you I had to think rapidly to explain what happened to all that brandy. Poulette is a fool. But I won't have it hinted about that I am a common drunk. *(JARMIAN enters.)* I have served in some of the best houses in France and the old Contesse de Rochambault when I left her because of the Conte's losing all her money at baccarat, said that—

JARMIAN: M. Alberic!

ALBERIC: *(Rising and bowing)* At your service.

JARMIAN: M. Alberic, an innocent man is going to die unless we take steps to save him.

ALBERIC: You mean this Muscari?

JARMIAN: Yes.

ALBERIC: And he is innocent after all?

JARMIAN: I am sure of it.

ALBERIC: What a surprise! I could have sworn that he was guilty. *(Hiccups)* What do you want me to do?

JARMIAN: Search your soul, M. Alberic. Are you certain that it was he who stole the brandy from madame's cellar?

ALBERIC: More or less.

JARMIAN: And what does this more or less mean?

ALBERIC: I mean more or less according to the circumstances. For example, I would be less certain of it if this Muscari turned out to be a gentleman in disguise or the secret heir to a fortune or—

JARMIAN: And if that isn't the case?

ALBERIC: Then I would have to rely on my eyesight. And my eyesight tells me that he is the one, all right.

JARMIAN: And your conscience? What does your conscience tell you?

ALBERIC: Monsieur, I am a retainer, the descendant of a family of retainers. My conscience never speaks unless it is spoken to.

JARMIAN: I see. And I needn't ask what is the language which your conscience understands?

ALBERIC: It would be most unfeeling to put such a question. A gentleman always knows how to manage these things without causing embarrassment to his inferiors.

JARMIAN: Of course. My apologies. And if your conscience isn't spoken to, you will be forced to testify against Muscari?

ALBERIC: With reluctance, but yes. Is it so important?

JARMIAN: A man's life is at stake.

ALBERIC: But he seems so eager to give it away.

JARMIAN: God will not forgive us if by our deceit we are accomplices in his self-destruction.

ALBERIC: And after all the felonies he has confessed to, they will hardly guillotine him for six cases of cognac. Indeed, it is likely to count in his favor. It was the best cognac—the judge will be impressed by his taste.

JARMIAN: And if he should be innocent of everything?

ALBERIC: *(Politely)* We are all going to die, Monsieur. It will be a comfort to him in his final moments to know that he is guiltless. Few will able to say as much. *(Exit)*

JARMIAN: *(Front)* Of course, I was aware from the start that Muscari was either a lunatic or a very dangerous man. But my faith has taught me that there is no human life so degraded or desperate that it is not worth the effort of saving. *(Pause)* But was this what I really felt? In looking back on it, I think there was an element of personal vanity in my stubbornness. I simply could not face the possibility that after a dozen years in Sandaraque my sermons had had so little effect. Surely there must be at least one culprit in my parish who would listen to the voice of his Christian conscience! Among all you good people assembled here tonight I know there are many who would step forward without hesitation to save a fellow human's life. *(Pause)* But Sandaraque was perverse and stubborn. As I went from person to person the thought at last grew on me that Sandaraque was uniquely damned. At last I called on Poulette and his family. They had been faithful members of my parish for many years. I had every hope that they would give a sympathetic ear to my counsel— *(He goes into the wings.)*

POULETTE'S grocery store. MME. POULETTE and MATHILDE are knitting. POULETTE enters, sees them, and shrugs in disgust. FATHER JARMIAN enters and the women hastily put away their work.

POULETTE: Ah, Father Jarmian, good morning!

JARMIAN: Good morning. *(He exchanges greetings with the ladies.)*

POULETTE: *(Jovially)* And what will it be today? Some of our Lisbon port? We've a case just in—clear and red as a ruby.

JARMIAN: Thank you, M. Poulette, but I have come to you on a matter of conscience. It's about this Muscari.

MME. POULETTE: Mathilde, leave the room!

JARMIAN: I should prefer that she remain.

POULETTE: *(To his wife)* Then close the shutters. I am glad that you came Father. We have been talking this over and we want your advice on the same subject.

JARMIAN: God be praised! Then mature reflection has led you to a change of heart?

POULETTE: It has. I'm a hot-tempered man, Father, but I don't want to see a man die because of a few mistakes. I know right from wrong and I'm willing to do the right thing—

JARMIAN: I am sure of it.

POULETTE: —just as long as the right thing is done by me. Please. Take this chair. Now you have talked to this Muscari?

JARMIAN: I have.

POULETTE: And is it true that he is an educated man and not a gypsy after all?

JARMIAN: He is a Frenchman, M. Poulette, as you and I.

MME. POULETTE: What a relief!

POULETTE: Well, that's one thing off my mind! Try the crackers, Father.

JARMIAN: Thank you. And there is no doubt that he has some education.

POULETTE: Maybe a university man?

JARMIAN: That's not impossible.

MME. POULETTE: How nice!

POULETTE: But what I really want to know, Father, is whether in your opinion could he be, perhaps, a gentleman?

JARMIAN: *(Shocked)* A gentleman?! How can you ask that?

POULETTE: But in the usual sense of the word—look here—what I mean is, does he come from a good family, does he have connections?

JARMIAN: Why is that important, M. Poulette? We are all subject to God's judgment and He makes no distinction between His children of low birth or high.

POULETTE: I know all that, Father. But the Good Lord doesn't have to make the practical decisions about His children that I have to about mine.

JARMIAN: Very well, then. I know nothing about Muscari's family, but he has the manners of what the world calls a gentleman.

POULETTE: You see, wife! I told you we ought to give this a second thought!

JARMIAN: What does this mean, M. Poulette?

POULETTE: Father, the rumor has been going around town that this Muscari is really the son of someone high up in the government—very high! Now I don't know whether it is true or not. But if it is true and he should be acquitted through his family's influence, there is one thing I do know—our Mathilde is carrying his child in her belly—

MATHILDE: Oh, Papa! How coarse you are!

POULETTE: Potatoes are potatoes. You don't change them by boiling them in perfume. Let me put it this way: No grandchild of mine is going to be born out of the church!

JARMIAN: What? Would you seriously consider allowing your daughter to marry a man who has admitted to such atrocious crimes?

MATHILDE: I would never, never do it. He's too ugly!

POULETTE: You keep out of this! This is no time for you to be choosey, my girl!

JARMIAN: But the violation of all those unfortunate women!

POULETTE: That's deplorable, I agree. But what's done is done. Furthermore, some of those women aren't as innocent as they pretend—

JARMIAN: And the burning of Laboussère's barn?

POULETTE: Oh, we all did pranks like that when we were youngsters.

JARMIAN: *(With growing amazement)* Well, what about the murder of the gendarme Poitou?

POULETTE: Who says it was deliberate murder? Pushing a policeman into a well is more the sort of thing a young gentleman might do for a lark. Not that I think it ought to be encouraged, mind you, but I'm sure he had no way of knowing that Poitou couldn't swim.

JARMIAN: And the thefts from your shop? Were they a lark, too?

POULETTE: No, no, that's the ticklish part, I admit. It's hard to believe that a gentleman would admit to being a common thief. But even that I couldn't hold against him if there were circumstances...

MME. POULETTE: There was that Baronet in Vichy who turned to thievery because his greyhounds were starving.

POULETTE: Yes, that's the sort of thing! It does happen. And then if his family hires one of those smart Paris lawyers and the word is passed along to the judge—you know how it's done—he may get off. What do you think, Father?

JARMIAN: I? I think he is innocent.

POULETTE: Ah, then you agree! So he will be acquitted?

JARMIAN: I didn't say acquitted. I said innocent.

MME. POULETTE: But what good will it do him to be innocent if he isn't acquitted?

JARMIAN: Perhaps he will also be acquitted. But to a large extent that depends on you. If you have the courage to examine your own consciences and act as they bid you, he may yet be saved.

MATHILDE: It isn't my fault!

POULETTE: Be quiet! The father wasn't talking to you!

JARMIAN: I was talking to each of you.

POULETTE: And I'll answer for all of us. We have thought it over, haven't we, wife? We want to do the right thing. And naturally we don't want to see anyone executed for what might have been—well, just high-spirited pranks. So if there is a way to pass the word quietly along to this young man, you can let him know that if he promises—

MME. POULETTE: In writing.

POULETTE: Of course. In writing. If he promises to make things right with our Mathilde, she won't press the charges against him.

JARMIAN: *(Icily)* And what about the theft from your shop that he admitted?

POULETTE: Oh, I'll throw that in, too. I couldn't hold a few sausages against my son-in-law.

JARMIAN: And if he is convicted in spite of this?

POULETTE: We will have tried. If it doesn't work out, neither of us is the loser. Mathilde certainly wouldn't hold him to his promise if he is going to be guillotined the next day. Well, what do you think, Father?

Will he agree to it?

JARMIAN: M. Poulette, I do not know what Muscari will say, but I know what I must say. This is without doubt the... *(He breaks off and struggles to control his rage.)* No, no, I have taken the vow of charity. *(Tableau.* JARMIAN *steps downstage as the curtain closes behind him.)* And so it was everywhere I went. No one would confess. Laboussère, whose barn had been burnt, took a practical view....

LABOUSSÈRE: *(In the spotlight)* Father, I admit I might have been mistaken. It was a dark night. But I've already filed for the insurance. If I change my testimony now their lawyers will take me to court and I'll never get a sou. Who will pay for my barn then? I ask you, is it fair?

JARMIAN: Others were more emotional....

WIDOW LECLERC: *(In spotlight)* I sinned, Father, I sinned! I knew my poor dear chickens had died of a gas leak in the incubator. I told a lie. I confess it. But you can't ask me to go to the police. Ever since Leclerc died I've had palpitations of the heart. And it was such a tiny sin compared to all the others. Solve one of the important crimes, then come to me!

A WOMAN: *(In spotlight)* You know what my neighbors are saying? Already they're saying I'm no better than a whore, that's what they're saying! And you expect me to say I'm a liar, too? Get out of here! Never mind, is it true or not. How am I going to face my neighbors after this?

ANOTHER WOMAN: *(In spotlight)* You can't ask me to do it, Father. If I said it wasn't Muscari in the hammock that night I'd have to say who it really was, and his wife would kill me, I know she would! *(Spots out)*

JARMIAN: But whatever the excuse, it amounted to the same thing. *(Pause)* I put off seeing the mayor until the last. He had not always been friendly to me and, as a free-thinker, he was opposed to clerical intervention on principle. But I hoped at least to appeal to his sense of justice....

JARMIAN *steps into the wings as the curtain opens on* CONCARNEAU'S *home.* MME. CONCARNEAU *is fitting a blouse on a tailor's dummy, while her husband rehearses a speech.*

CONCARNEAU: I do not hesitate to say, citizens, that in bringing this monster—this fiend in human form—before the bar of justice, your administration has once again demonstrated its devotion to liberty, equality and f-f-financial responsibility! *(He pauses for imaginary applause.)* I thank you, citizens. Your tribute touches me to the bottom of my heart. *(Offers to shake hands with well-wishers)* Thank you, thank you. *(Dropping his oratorical manner)* Will it do?

MME. CONCARNEAU: I don't know whether you should mention Lesonge and the Royalists by name.

CONCARNEAU: Why not? They've done nothing but sneer at this trial from beginning to end. But let me tell you, wife, once this Muscari is convicted—

MME. CONCARNEAU: *(Startled)* What did you say his name was?

CONCARNEAU: Who?

MME. CONCARNEAU: This criminal you caught.

CONCARNEAU: Muscari.

MME. CONCARNEAU: Muscari?

CONCARNEAU: Yes, Muscari. What's the matter with you, wife?

MME. CONCARNEAU: *(Covering her confusion)* I dropped my thimble.

CONCARNEAU: *(Suspicious)* Eh? Have you ever heard of him before?

MME. CONCARNEAU: The name is familiar. Never mind. Perhaps I read it somewhere.

PICHEGRU: *(Sweeping in, attended by ALBERIC)* Where is Alfred?

MME. CONCARNEAU: He's at choir practice, Auntie.

PICHEGRU: Well, fetch him at once. *(She plumps herself in a chair. MME. CONCARNEAU goes.)* I am going to change my will!

CONCARNEAU: Auntie, what do you mean?

PICHEGRU: Stop fussing around me, Etienne. *(ALBERIC hiccups.)* Alberic! Will you kindly stop making those noises. They're disgusting.

ALBERIC: Yes, madame.

CONCARNEAU: Auntie, you mustn't do anything hasty!

PICHEGRU: *(Pityingly)* You poor boy, you haven't the sensibility of an artichoke, have you?

CONCARNEAU: Eh?

PICHEGRU: All this lasciviousness going on right under your nose and you've never even noticed it, have you? Your dear mother was quite right. "My Etienne is a sweet boy," she used to say, "but he's so retarded that I can't trust him to hand out the wash."

CONCARNEAU: *(In desperation)* What in God's name are you talking about?

ALBERIC: *(Hiccups)*

PICHEGRU: Alberic!

ALBERIC: Yes, madame?

PICHEGRU: I thought I told you to stop that infernal cackling.

ALBERIC: I... can't.

PICHEGRU: Nonsense! You lack moral fibre, Alberic. With moral fibre you can do anything.

CONCARNEAU: Auntie! I insist that you make yourself clear.

PICHEGRU: Very well, Etienne. You have been cuckolded—I believe that's the term.

CONCARNEAU: Impossible!

PICHEGRU: And why is it impossible? Do you suppose that you are the only husband in Sandaraque to escape it? I tell you the man is a veritable bull. He is insatiable!

CONCARNEAU: Who?

PICHEGRU: Who? Why, this Muscari, of course. *(ALBERIC hiccups.)* Alberic! For the last time—

CONCARNEAU: But it's preposterous! They don't even know one another!

PICHEGRU: Open your eyes, Etienne. I know for a fact that she has had him here every Sunday for months. She had the impudence to boast of it to me. Where they had their...assignations, I leave to your imagination—no doubt in the garden house among the begonias. *(ALFRED and MME. CONCARNEAU enter.)* Alfred! What are you doing here?

ALFRED: You sent for me, Auntie.

PICHEGRU: Well, leave the room at once! *(To her nephew)* How do you dare discuss such matters in front of this child?

ALFRED: But you sent for me.

PICHEGRU: Speak when you're spoken to, child, and not before. *(ALFRED goes.)*

MME. CONCARNEAU: Auntie, dear, what is the matter?

PICHEGRU: *(Coolly)* There's a button loose on your dress, niece.

CONCARNEAU: Wife! Will you swear that you have never met this man?

MME. CONCARNEAU: What man?

CONCARNEAU: Muscari.

PICHEGRU: Be quiet, both of you. I am leaving tomorrow for Bayonne, to visit my cousins. They are building a new hot-house for their orchids and need my advice. But before I go I have asked my lawyer to meet with me. I am changing my will and naming M. Menton the new executor. If I should not live to see the end of the world, as now seems improbable as M. Menton keeps postponing the date, my little nest egg will be spent on astral research—

CONCARNEAU: *(Imploring)* Auntie!

PICHEGRU: Don't interrupt. Since dear Alfred can hardly be held responsible for the sins of his parents, I am leaving him my priceless collection of objets d'art, with the exception of the three gold buttons from Admiral Bougainville's dress uniform, which I have already promised the Louvre. That is final. *(Rises)* And as for you, niece, I have tried to be understanding. I am not completely old-fashioned. I realize how the... lusts of the flesh must torment you. But in the future I advise you to choose your... paramours from your own social class. *(ALBERIC hiccups.)* Good day. *(PICHEGRU and ALBERIC go out.)*

ALBERIC: *(At the door)* Pardon me.

CONCARNEAU: Do you know what just went out that door?

MME. CONCARNEAU: A foul-mouthed old woman.

CONCARNEAU: Our son's inheritance, that's all. His whole future.

MME. CONCARNEAU: She's leaving him her buttons. He should be able to set up a shop.

CONCARNEAU: How can you joke about it? And what did you tell her about you and this gypsy?

MME. CONCARNEAU: *(Indignant)* What? You mistrust me after twenty-three years in the same bed?

CONCARNEAU: I didn't say that. But she swore that you boasted to her that you had met this scoundrel every Sunday for weeks.

MME. CONCARNEAU: And you believed her, did you?

CONCARNEAU: Don't shout—the neighbors will hear.

MME. CONCARNEAU: Look. Do you know who this Muscari really is?

CONCARNEAU: Of course. He's the rapist we've got in jail,

MME. CONCARNEAU: No, no! He's the gardener I invented to get out of going to your aunt's séances. I remember it perfectly now. I took the name off my garden list. Muscari. It's a little blue flower that grows from a bulb.

CONCARNEAU: Have you lost your mind? First it's a rapist, then it's a gardener who doesn't garden, and now it's something that grows from a bulb. Where is this going to end?

MME. CONCARNEAU: But he's imaginary!

CONCARNEAU: And all those seductions—are they imaginary, too? Oh, my head! It's spinning like a Ferris wheel.

MME. CONCARNEAU: But it's just a case of mistaken identity. That silly aunt of yours has gotten the gardener confused with your prisoner.

CONCARNEAU: What gardener? We've never had a gardener.

MME. CONCARNEAU: The one I invented.

CONCARNEAU: The one that grows from a bulb, eh?

MME. CONCARNEAU: I'll call her back and explain everything.

CONCARNEAU: You do that. *(MME. CONCARNEAU goes.)* Although how you can make her see it when I can't understand it myself, is beyond me. *(Pause)* So! A little blue flower, eh? Growing from a bulb, eh? Mmmmhm. And she dropped her thimble and blushed when I mentioned his name.

ALFRED: *(Offstage)* No, no! He can't see you!

CONCARNEAU: What next?

MATHILDE: *(Pushing her way past ALFRED)* Yes, he will. Let me go, Alfred!

ALFRED: *(Trying to keep her out)* But he's busy, I tell you!

CONCARNEAU: *(Sternly)* Alfred! As mayor I am always at home to any citizen in distress.

ALFRED: Don't listen to her, Papa. She has the hysterics.

CONCARNEAU: Alfred! Now, my dear child, what is it?

MATHILDE: *(Tearfully)* M. Concarneau, I want to tell the truth.

CONCARNEAU: The truth? That's always commendable.

MATHILDE: What I told the police was a—a little white lie.

CONCARNEAU: Eh? That's just what the Curé said. So that whole story about the gypsy was moonshine, was it?

MATHILDE: Yes, M. Concarneau. *(MME. CONCARNEAU reenters with PICHEGRU and ALBERIC in tow.)*

PICHEGRU: I am listening to you only for Alfred's sake.

CONCARNEAU: Wife! It's all coming out now. The girl admits that she invented all that about Muscari.

PICHEGRU: She invented it? *(To MME. CONCARNEAU)* And you just claimed that *you* invented it. We shall have to consult the Ouija board to get to the bottom of this, shan't we, Alberic?

ALBERIC: Yes, madame. *(They start to go again.)*

CONCARNEAU: Auntie! Wait! She's going to clear everything up. *(He turns on MATHILDE.)* Well, go on. So this Muscari isn't the father of your child, is he?

MATHILDE: No, he isn't. The Curé said I should be honest and tell the truth and I am going to. And I will never, never marry that awful man no matter what they say.

CONCARNEAU: So you decided to come to the mayor and tell the whole story, eh?

MATHILDE: Oh, M. Concarneau, I didn't come to you because you are mayor.

CONCARNEAU: No?

MATHILDE: No, M. Concarneau. I came to you because you are going to be its grandfather.

CONCARNEAU: What are you saying, girl?

MATHILDE: That it is Alfred's child.

ALFRED: Papa! She's exaggerating!

MATHILDE: It's the truth! He made me swear not to tell because he is going to become a great tenor and he said that marriage would make his voice change. But I can't keep it quiet any longer. Not when the whole town is saying that its father is a Roumanian. I would die of shame!

CONCARNEAU: Alfred! Is this true?

ALFRED: No, it's not.

MATHILDE: *(Wailing)* Oh, Alfred, how can you? And after you said you loved me if only I would and we were going away to Paris together if only I would and I would become an artist's model and you a concert singer if only I would and I did! *(She throws herself on the floor in a tantrum.)*

PICHEGRU: Dear me! This house has become a positive brothel! Come, Alberic. *(At the door)* I certainly think it fortunate for all of you that the world is coming to an end soon. *(She exits with ALBERIC.)*

ALFRED: It isn't true, Papa! I didn't tell her all that!

MME. CONCARNEAU: *(To her husband)* Don't stand there like a post. Do something. If this gets out you are ruined.

CONCARNEAU: But what can I do?

MATHILDE: *(Screaming)* I'm going to tell Papa! I'm going to tell everyone!

MME. CONCARNEAU: *(Shaking MATHILDE)* That's enough of that! *(She pulls MATHILDE to her feet roughly.)* Now listen to me, Mathilde Poulette. When you went to the police to give evidence they asked you to put your hand on the Holy Bible and swear to tell the truth so help you God, didn't they?

MATHILDE: *(With a sob)* Yes.

MME. CONCARNEAU: And now you say that you lied to them?

MATHILDE: *(Sulkily)* It was only a fib.

MME. CONCARNEAU: Only a fib? With your hand on the Holy Bible?

MATHILDE: I just put two fingers on it.

MME. CONCARNEAU: But you swore, as God was your witness, to tell the truth. Do you know what that is?

MATHILDE: Fibbing?

MME. CONCARNEAU: No, Mathilde, it is perjury. And do you know what the penalty for perjury is?

CONCARNEAU: *(Getting the idea)* They die like flies down there.

MATHILDE: *(Alarmed)* Down where?

ALFRED: Devil's Island.

MATHILDE: Oh-h-h-h!

MME. CONCARNEAU: Do you want to go to prison, Mathilde?

MATHILDE: No.

MME. CONCARNEAU: That's what happens to people who lie in a

criminal case.

MATHILDE: Is it?

CONCARNEAU: It certainly is.

MME. CONCARNEAU: It was Muscari who did it, wasn't it?

MATHILDE: I guess so.

MME. CONCARNEAU: No, you are absolutely sure.

MATHILDE: I am... absolutely sure.

JARMIAN: *(Entering hurriedly)* M. Concarneau, my apologies for break-ing in like this— *(He sees* MATHILDE.*)* Ah, then she has come of her own accord! The Lord has shown her the way. I thank Him that there is at least one honest person in Sandaraque. So you know the truth at last?

CONCARNEAU: *(Grimly)* We know... the facts.

MME. CONCARNEAU: Mathilde, tell the Father how it happened.

MATHILDE: Must I?

MME. CONCARNEAU: Yes, Mathilde, you must.

MATHILDE: *(After long looks at* JARMIAN *and the* CONCARNEAUS, *she speaks as if in a dream.)* I was chasing a spotted butterfly and it flew down among the reeds. I climbed over the wall after it and just as I was about to catch it Muscari came after me out of the willow bushes. "Let me go!" I said... "Let me go!" *(She looks despairingly at* JARMIAN *and he casts a disgusted took to heaven as the curtain closes.)*

ACT THREE

The lights come up on the fore-curtain area. Several young women of the town run excitedly across stage.

YOUNG WOMEN: *(All more or less together)* Isn't he wonderful! What manners! I almost fainted! *(Etc.)*

The young women rush off. The curtain opens revealing MUSCARI'S *cell. But the cell has been transformed since we last saw it: there are ruffled curtains on the windows, a quilt on the cot, pillows and antimacassars spread on the bench, and against the rear wall there is a bank of potted plants and floral wreaths. After a moment, a lady dressed in black and heavily veiled enters, looks hastily about, gives a tiny sob, and hides herself in a niche on the far side of the stage. In a moment the* JAILER *enters, accompanied by the* EXECUTIONER, *a dignified craftsman in stiff black clothes.*

JAILER: Sit over there, sir. Monsieur should be back shortly.
EXECUTIONER: I hope I won't be in your way.
JAILER: *(Whisking the furniture with his duster)* Oh, not at all. Just a little light housekeeping. *(He turns to the flowers.)* Look at all these! Carnations! Lilies! Azaleas! Who would have thought he had so many admirers? Here's one that just came in. *(He reads a card.)* "Be Brave." That's all. And it's signed, "A Well-wisher."

MUSCARI *appears in the doorway. He is now dressed in the height of fashionable elegance; his hair has been trimmed, his moustache waxed, and he wears a boutonniere in his lapel. A girl follows him eagerly.*

GIRL: *(Almost breathless)* Oh, M. Muscari, may I have your autograph?
MUSCARI: *(Fastidiously removes his gloves and writes his name in the proffered book)* There you are. Pardon the penmanship. It has always been illegible. *(He pinches her cheek and she runs off, delighted.)*
JAILER: Just tidying up, sir. I thought your press interviews would take longer.
MUSCARI: *(Leisurely tossing his gloves on the table)* Any mail?
JAILER: It's in the basket, sir. Trial over already?
MUSCARI: *(Looking through the mail)* Yes.
JAILER: I do hope the verdict was agreeable, sir.
MUSCARI: *(Casually)* Guilty. On all counts.
JAILER: What a pity! Then you'll be leaving us soon, I suppose.

248

MUSCARI: Tomorrow morning. I am to be hanged by the neck until exhausted. I believe that was the phrase.

EXECUTIONER: Guillotined.

MUSCARI: *(Noting him for the first time)* Hullo! Who are you?

EXECUTIONER: You are to be guillotined, not hanged. France is a civilized country.

MUSCARI: That's an immense relief. But what are you doing here?

JAILER: *(Cheerily)* Oh, don't be alarmed, sir. It's only the executioner.

MUSCARI: The executioner? But our appointment is not until tomorrow.

EXECUTIONER: Right you are, sir. This is just a courtesy visit. No cause for immediate anxiety.

MUSCARI: I see. And to what do I owe the honor of this courtesy?

EXECUTIONER: It's the new spirit in penology, sir. Usually I don't meet a client until the actual hour of our appointment, but it often has a bad effect on him, you know, sir, first meeting me in my official uniform—he's likely to have difficulty in adjusting. So I said to the super, "Supposing I just drop in first for a little get-acquainted visit, just to ease the tension all around."

MUSCARI: That's very thoughtful of you, I'm sure.

EXECUTIONER: Thank you, sir. Decent of you to look at it that way. Do you mind if I smoke?

MUSCARI: Go right ahead.

JAILER: I don't suppose you will be needing the flowers much longer, will you?

MUSCARI: Do you want them?

JAILER: Oh, not for myself! That wouldn't be proper. But I thought I might send them over to the orphanage. Perhaps with a little card—something simple, you know. Just "Courtesy of Muscari," or "In Remembrance."

MUSCARI: Don't you think I've done enough for the orphanage as it is?

After a moment's pause, the JAILER *and the* EXECUTIONER *laugh.*

JAILER: That's what I like about you. Always ready with a quip.

EXECUTIONER: Being famous hasn't gone to your head like some I've known.

JAILER: One other thing, before I forget it. The barber wants to know, wouldn't you like to have your hair trimmed before your appointment?

MUSCARI: But I had it trimmed yesterday.

JAILER: I know, sir, but you will be doing him a great favor. The truth is that a number of young ladies have taken to wearing a curl of your hair in their lockets. And the demand has been so brisk that he has fallen a bit behind. So if you wouldn't mind—

MUSCARI: And leave me to die bald? Never.

JAILER: Oh no, sir, he's a very reasonable man.

MUSCARI: Reasonable? He's a ghoul. I'm not even dead yet and already they're dismembering me.

EXECUTIONER: Don't let it upset you, sir. It's the price you have to pay for popularity. Why I had a client once—he had murdered his mistress by putting poisoned bath salts in her tub—who was so greatly admired that he found it practically impossible to get near the guillotine. The crowd broke through the police lines and tore off every bit of his clothing for souvenirs. We had to postpone the execution, of course, for it wouldn't do for a Frenchman to go to his death naked. Set a bad example for the younger folk, you know.

MUSCARI: Can't we talk about this some other time?

EXECUTIONER: Not that anything of that sort is likely to happen in your case, sir. The mayor has very prudently called out the civil guard and a squadron of soldiers has been sent up from Bordeaux to see that the crowd doesn't get out of hand. Still, in my profession, you can't tell. *(Rising)* Well, sir, it has done me a world of good to have this little informal chat with you. Very relaxing, very relaxing indeed.

MUSCARI: Quite.

EXECUTIONER: And when we meet—out there—if there's any little consideration I can show to make you more comfortable, don't hesitate to ask.

MUSCARI: *(Edging him to the door)* Believe me, I won't.

EXECUTIONER: It's been a pleasure meeting you, sir.

MUSCARI: No, no, the pleasure was mine.

EXECUTIONER: Goodbye, sir.

MUSCARI: Goodbye.

EXECUTIONER: Or perhaps we should say... au revoir?

The JAILER shows the EXECUTIONER out and follows him off.

MUSCARI: *(Alone)* So this is what fame is like. *(He turns his attention to the flowers, picks up one of the bouquets, smells it appreciatively, and then opens the accompanying card. The VEILED WOMAN emerges from her hiding place and, opening her bag, takes out a tiny pistol.)*

MUSCARI: *(Reading)* "Dear M. Muscari. Don't lose hope. The younger generation is all behind you—"

VEILED WOMAN: *(After an emotional struggle she succeeds in pointing the pistol at him.)* Muscari!

MUSCARI: *(Without turning)* One moment, please. "We will save you from the guillotine." *(Turning)* Yes? What is it?

VEILED WOMAN: Just this. *(She pulls the trigger. The pistol emits a tiny pop! MUSCARI looks at her in stupefaction for a moment and then executes a perfect fall into the midst of the flower pots.)* That will teach you to involve a lady's name in a public scandal! *(She puts the pistol back in her bag.)*

JAILER: *(Entering hurriedly)* What's this? Entertaining ladies in your cell? You know that's strictly forbidden, sir. *(To the LADY)* Come, you'll have to leave. This is a prison, not a coffeehouse. Out with you! *(He pushes her out.)* And don't come back! *(He turns to the prostrate MUS-CARI.)* Repulsed you, didn't she?

MUSCARI: *(Dazed)* Something of the sort.

JAILER: That's the way it is with women, sir. Tease you and torment you and just when you reach out to take them in your arms—*smack!* They send you sprawling. *(MUSCARI anxiously pats his body in search of the bullet wound.)* What's the matter, sir? Lose something?

MUSCARI: I hope not.

JAILER: Look at this poor begonia! I'm afraid it's hopelessly bruised.

MUSCARI: I'd rather not. I'm feeling a little unwell myself. *(He is now satisfied that he is unwounded.)* To miss completely at ten feet! What resolution!

JAILER: The priest is waiting outside to see you, sir. With two other gentlemen.

MUSCARI: Well, show them in. But in the future please try to keep the door properly locked. I've had enough unannounced callers.

The JAILER goes. MUSCARI rises, takes a step, and nearly collapses again. He pulls up his trouser leg in alarm but to his relief discovers that it is only his foot which has gone to sleep. He slaps his ankle vigorously as JARMIAN enters. JARMIAN looks at him as if he suspects madness.

MUSCARI: Sorry. Restoring the circulation. *(JARMIAN sniffs the suspicious odor in the air. MUSCARI does likewise.)* Gun powder, isn't it?

JARMIAN: *(Sternly)* You promised me you would give up those methods.

MUSCARI: I have. One of the ladies I admitted seducing just fired a pistol at me.

JARMIAN: You are wounded?

MUSCARI: Unfortunately she missed. I should have preferred dying in her arms to the scaffold.

JARMIAN: You need not die at all. I have two gentlemen with me who wish to help you.

MUSCARI: *(Eagerly)* Are they publishers?

JARMIAN: No. *(He goes to the door.)* M. Lesonge, will you step in here please?

LESONGE: *(Entering)* Muscari, Father Jarmian has talked to me at length about your case. He has called my attention to many irregularities and discrepancies in the evidence that Concarneau has used to convict you.

MUSCARI: Indeed?

LESONGE: I do not say that he has convinced me of your innocence, but he has planted a doubt in my mind, a doubt which I cannot put to rest. I have, therefore, at my own expense, called in M. Goularte of Toulouse— *(At his signal GOULARTE enters. He is a blasé attorney with an immense conviction as to his own importance; he swings a gold watch from the end of its chain.)* —the distinguished criminal advocate. *(GOULARTE promenades across the stage, swinging his watch in leisurely arcs.)* M. Goularte has examined the transcripts of your trial and agrees with me that this is an obvious case of political oppression. Am I correct, M. Goularte?

GOULARTE: *(Without breaking stride)* Essentially.

LESONGE: It is our conviction, for example, that the Mayor of Sandaraque has brought undue pressure on witnesses to testify against you. Do you agree, M. Goularte?

GOULARTE: Intrinsically.

LESONGE: Furthermore, we have sworn testimony that he has boasted that your conviction is essential to the re-election of this Radical administration for another term. Do I state your views, M. Goularte?

GOULARTE: Substantially.

MUSCARI: Where is all this leading?

LESONGE: I am coming to that. M. Goularte has drawn up the necessary papers to carry your case to the higher courts. He feels that, prima facie, we stand on excellent grounds for a retrial with change of venire and that, in any event, he can secure a stay of execution while procedural issues are being argued on a writ of certiorari.

GOULARTE *stands over MUSCARI, draws himself up to his full height, and twirls his watch in his face.*

MUSCARI: And what do you want *me* to do?

LESONGE: Merely sign these documents. M. Goularte will take care of everything else.

MUSCARI: But why should I sign them? I am guilty. I confessed to everything.

LESONGE: Your confession of guilt is a damaging factor, we admit, but by no means fatal. The appellate judge will have to balance it carefully against all the other evidence before handing down his decision. All this will take time. If the case is managed skillfully there is no reason why you should not enjoy several years of relative comfort here before a decision is reached. Do you agree, M. Goularte?

GOULARTE: Unequivocally.

MUSCARI: And what is your interest in all this?

LESONGE: I am a Frenchman, monsieur. I share my country's devotion to justice.

MUSCARI: I see. And are you so devoted to justice that you would testify in court as to who actually broke into the cash drawer of your bank?

LESONGE: *(After a moment)* Believe me, if I knew the culprit I would not hesitate a moment.

MUSCARI: Get out of here!

LESONGE: What?

MUSCARI: I said, get out of here! You, your attorney, and all your papers! *(He drives them out.)* I'll handle my own appeals, thank you.

LESONGE: This is the conduct of an anarchist!

GOULARTE: Unquestionably! *(They go.* MUSCARI *turns to* JARMIAN.*)*

MUSCARI: Why do you plague me with these blow-flies?

JARMIAN: Is there nothing that will make you turn back?

MUSCARI: Nothing. I kept my bargain with you. All your sermons and appeals to conscience amounted to nothing, as I knew they would. Now let me die in peace.

JARMIAN: And this is the sort of fame you really want? That crowd out there? These half-delirious girls screaming for a glimpse of you? These imbecilic journalists writing down your every word as if it were the Sermon from the Mount? Muscari, deranged as you are, I thought you were a man of some principle. I see now that I was mistaken.

MUSCARI: I admit there are moments when all this attention is tedious. But I realized before I began that it was the price I would have to pay for success.

JARMIAN: Success? You call this success? You, a poet and man of letters? Not one of these so-called admirers of yours has ever read a single word you have written.

MUSCARI: *(Sadly)* I know. But that will come later.

JARMIAN: You delude yourself. What you have achieved is not honest fame, but a cheap notoriety which will be forgotten the day after your execution.

MUSCARI: We shall see about that.

JARMIAN: Very well. I am going to argue with you no more. You are a depraved, wicked scoundrel whom God in His wisdom will know how to punish for your blasphemies. *(Pause)* Muscari, if it is any satisfaction to you, I came here to tell you that I have asked my bishop to transfer me to another parish. I have failed in Sandaraque and in good conscience I cannot continue the Lord's work here.

MUSCARI: Where will you go?

JARMIAN: I do not know. Where he chooses to assign me. But I pray that it will be some place where the people are not so hopelessly corrupted by self-interest.

MUSCARI: *(With an ironic smile)* Then you too, monsieur, persist in your delusion? *(JARMIAN glares at him for an instant and then goes out in silence. MUSCARI goes to the window of his cell. As he appears in it there is a tremendous roar outside.)* There certainly is an immense crowd.

Cries of "Muscari! We want Muscari!" etc. MUSCARI bows in the window. The JAILER appears and silently ushers in EMMANUEL LESONGE, who is extremely ill at ease. The JAILER goes again.

EMMANUEL: *(After a moment)* M. Muscari?

MUSCARI: *(Irritably)* Well, what is it now? Who are you?

EMMANUEL: Lesonge. Lesonge Junior, sir.

MUSCARI: You are the son of that old jackass who was just in here?

EMMANUEL: Yes, sir. And I don't mind what you call him, sir. I am in rebellion against him myself.

MUSCARI: *(Surveying him)* You are?

EMMANUEL: Yes, sir. I am in revolt against the organized b-b-brutality of p-p-parental authority.

MUSCARI: Well, what do you want with me? If you want to shoot me, I'm not at home. And if it's my photograph, you'll have to get it from the jailer, he has a stock of them.

EMMANUEL: It's not that, sir. I want to confess something.

MUSCARI: The priest just left.

EMMANUEL: But I don't believe in sacerdotalism, sir.

MUSCARI: In what?

EMMANUEL: *(Taking a stance)* Sacerdotalism. That is, I think the Superior Man has no need of a priest. M. Muscari, I want to confess that it was I who broke open the cash drawer of my father's bank and stole twenty francs from it.

MUSCARI: *(Stunned)* You!

EMMANUEL: Perhaps you think I am not strong enough to? I pried open the lock with a pinch-bar.

MUSCARI: But why are you confessing, you little idiot? Don't you know that I have already admitted the theft?

EMMANUEL: Yes.

MUSCARI: Then why don't you keep your mouth shut?

EMMANUEL: *(Stammering)* Because it would be on my conscience if you were to die for something I did. And because I can no longer stand the hypocrisy of b-b-bourgeois morality.

MUSCARI: *(Suspiciously)* Where did you pick up all those words? Not in Sandaraque?

EMMANUEL: No, sir. It's from a book I read. A book that has changed my whole attitude toward life. It's called "The Anaesthesia of Necessity."

MUSCARI: *(Tremendously excited)* "The Anaesthesia of Necessity!" Where did you find it?

EMMANUEL: In a b-b-barrel, sir. Gabriel Poulette gave it to me. His father had bought a barrel of old papers to wrap fish in. Gabriel found this book in it. It has changed my whole way of life, sir. I am a Superior Man now, no longer bound by the Chains of Circumstance.

MUSCARI: And do you know who wrote that book?

EMMANUEL: Yes, sir. A Professor Invictus. Would you care to hear some of it? I've gotten the first chapter by heart.

MUSCARI: Please!

EMMANUEL: *(After clearing his throat)* "The Superior Man must walk upright amidst delusions and carry his conscience through the ambuscades of authority—" *(MUSCARI'S face lights up with recognition.)* "He who assumes the power of division lays on his soul the cost of multiplication—" *(MUSCARI takes up a flower pot and, with an ecstatic gesture, buries his face in the blooms.)* "I say unto you, be on guard against the satiety of forgiveness. Beware of the deflection of eclipses—"

MUSCARI: And to think that I wanted to die!

EMMANUEL: What?

MUSCARI: Nothing. Go on, go on!

EMMANUEL: "—the deflection of eclipses, the Gorgons which stir in the blood, and the consternation of Equinoxes. I say unto you, you shall only be free when you have freed your mind of longitudes. Parallel lines meet only in obscurity. Nothing remains of Heaven but our ineluctable mirages."

MUSCARI: *(Carried away with emotion)* To be alive! With the fragrance of flowers! And the sun shining! *(He skips to the window.)* And children! Yes, little children playing in the streets.

EMMANUEL: *(Amazed)* Shall I stop now, sir?

MUSCARI: *(Embracing him impetuously)* And you! A fierce young rebel with the courage of youth! You have saved me!

EMMANUEL: I?

MUSCARI: Yes, you! Jailer! Jailer!

JAILER: *(Appearing)* What is it now, sir?

MUSCARI: Call that lawyer back!

JAILER: He has left for Toulouse, sir.

MUSCARI: Then call the police! Call the mayor! I am going to tell the truth!

The curtain closes quickly. EMMANUEL *steps down to the forestage and speaks in a mature, unemotional voice.*

EMMANUEL: Naturally, I did the only thing an honorable man could. I went straight home to my father and told him that it was I who had stolen the money from the bank and that I meant to go to the police and make a clean breast of the whole thing. My father was very surprised. He immediately took me to the railroad station and put me on a train to visit my aunt in Normandy. I protested, of course, but it did no good. I don't judge him too harshly for it—he felt that he was protecting his family and, besides, he had no idea how a Superior Man should behave. I offer this not as an excuse, but simply to explain why you won't find me present at the next scene. When I got back it was all over. I was terribly upset, particularly when I learned that Muscari was really the author of "The Anaesthesia of Necessity." I have done everything I can to perpetuate his memory and pay him the honor he deserves. In later years, when I took over my father's bank, I founded the scholarship to the seminary which bears his name, and every year I have made substantial contributions to the fund for the Muscari Memorial Football Stadium. I apologize, I apologize sincerely, for that moment of weakness in which I gave way to my father—but since then I have, in the management of my bank and in public affairs—always tried to live up to the principles of the Superior Man. I hope you will understand and forgive me.

He steps into the wings. The curtain opens on a part of the town square. GABRIEL POULETTE *enters, pushing a wheelbarrow loaded with cushions and pennants. His father follows him.*

POULETTE: Station yourself over there. The crowd will have to pass by here on the way to the guillotine. Now, remember, one franc for the cushions and twenty sous for a slice of salami.

GABRIEL: *(Calling)* Cushions. Flags. Sausages.

POULETTE: Louder! Put some conviction in it!

GABRIEL: Salami! Cushions! Salami!

BONFILS THE INNKEEPER: *(Entering)* Ah! Good morning, M. Poulette! What a day for Sandaraque, eh?

POULETTE: There hasn't been anything like it since the Emperor Napoleon stayed overnight here.

GOULARTE *enters and walks downstage, swinging his watch and lost in his own importance.*

BONFILS: The inn is jammed. My wife and daughter had to sleep in the chicken shed to make room for the journalists who came in from London last night. If it keeps on like this, I won't have a drop of wine left in the house.

GABRIEL: Salami! Cushions!

POULETTE: A shame it has to be over with so soon, eh?

BONFILS: That's the way it is with executions, Poulette. With weddings one can always look forward to the christenings and all the trade they will bring, but with an execution, once it's done it's done.

WIDOW LECLERC: *(Entering)* Good morning, M. Poulette. Come to see the last of your son-in-law?

POULETTE: I ignore you, Mme. Leclerc.

WIDOW LECLERC: And what will you call your grandson? Anonymous Poulette?

POULETTE: Do you hear someone talking, M. Bonfils? Or is it the wind shaking an old dried bladder?

GABRIEL: Cushions! Cushions! Get your cushions here!

CONCARNEAU: *(Entering, followed by other citizens)* Good morning, gentlemen. *(They exchange greetings.)*

BONFILS: Is everything ready?

CONCARNEAU: They're bringing him from the jail now.

BONFILS: I hope there isn't any trouble.

CONCARNEAU: I don't think there will be. Last night he had a hysterical spell and wanted to withdraw his confession—

BONFILS: They often get that way the final night.

CONCARNEAU: —but I was firm with him. "It's too late for all that," I told him. "You'll just cause embarrassment for all concerned. Be a good loser," I said, "and we'll all respect you for it." He saw the point after a while and I don't think he'll give us any trouble now.

A roar offstage. Cries of "Muscari, it's him!" etc. LESONGE *runs on.*

LESONGE: *(To* CONCARNEAU*)* Are you going to let that rascal turn this into a Roman holiday?

CONCARNEAU: Who?

LESONGE: That Muscari. Do you know what he's doing now? He's standing on the steps of the jailhouse distributing pamphlets!

CONCARNEAU: Pamphlets? What's in them? Nothing seditious, I hope.

LESONGE: It's some rubbish about the necessity for anaesthesia.

CONCARNEAU: *(Relieved)* Well, if it's only a medical matter...

LESONGE: *(Catching sight of* GOULARTE*)* M. Goularte, what are you doing here?

GOULARTE: Substantially or specifically, M. Lesonge? Specifically, I am here because I boarded the 7:36 train out of Toulouse this morning. Substantially, however, I am here to represent my client, one Jean-Baptiste Hippolyte Marie-Henri Muscari, in a matter of terminal litigation.

LESONGE: Your client? But I thought I told you I had no further interest in this case?

GOULARTE: Indisputably, M. Lesonge. Your interest in this litigation has ceased. However, a Higher Person has deigned to intervene.

POULETTE: It's his family! I knew he was a nobleman!

LESONGE: But the case is closed, I tell you!

GOULARTE: *(Imperturbable)* Then there is nothing to be alarmed about, is there, gentlemen?

Cries of "Here he comes! Muscari! Make way!" etc. A photographer runs on, followed by the crowd, then by soldiers. A drum beats. At last MUSCARI *appears, flanked by guards. He is pale but he bears himself bravely and is, if possible, even more elegant than when we last saw him.*

GABRIEL: Cushions! Last chance for cushions!

A girl breaks through the cordon and runs to pin a flower on MUSCARI'S *lapel.*

MUSCARI: Thank you, my dear. *(He blows her a kiss.)*
CONCARNEAU: The prisoner has had the sentence read to him?
MUSCARI: A number of times, thank you.
CONCARNEAU: And does he have any final request?
MUSCARI: Is Lesonge here? Lesonge, Junior?
LESONGE: He is not. He is in Normandy visiting his relatives.
MUSCARI: And he left no message for me?
LESONGE: He did not!
MUSCARI: I see. Thank you. That will be all, then.

Silence. The drums roll again. The EXECUTIONER *enters, masked and followed by his apprentice, a boy of fifteen.*

MUSCARI: This is... the host?
EXECUTIONER: We meet again, sir.
MUSCARI: So I see.
EXECUTIONER: One final favor, sir, if you would be so kind?
MUSCARI: Yes?
EXECUTIONER: It's my apprentice, sir. You are the first notable person he has ever had the privilege of meeting. He would like to shake your hand before we go.
MUSCARI: I have no objection.
EXECUTIONER: Aristide! Monsieur has very kindly consented to meet you. *(The boy hangs back.)* Don't be bashful, lad. *(To* MUSCARI*)* This is his first time; that's why he's so shy.
MUSCARI: I sympathize. It's mine, too. *(The boy rushes forward and takes his hand, then bursts into sobs!)* There, there, don't be upset. You must get used to taking men's lives or you'll grow up to be a very poor citizen. *(The boy turns away.)* Now, M. Concarneau, shall we get on with our business? I don't want to keep posterity waiting any longer than necessary.
GOULARTE: *(In a commanding voice)* One moment, please!
LESONGE: Keep out of this, Goularte!
GOULARTE: *(Ignoring him)* There is not going to be any execution! *(General tumult)* Your attention, please! *(In his grandest oratorical manner)* I have, at an early hour this morning, interceded with the President of the Court of Cassation at Toulouse, Monsieur Rochard-Pratolin! *(Mention of this august name awes the crowd)* M. Rochard-Pratolin is, as you no doubt know, not only the permanent secretary of the Anti-Vivisection Society, but is also the author of many learned works on jurisprudence, which have earned him election to our

National Academy!

MUSCARI: *(With a dreadful grimace)* The Academy?

GOULARTE: Don't interrupt! I have brought it to M. Rochard-Pratolin's attention that the condemned man is himself the author of certain poetic effusions. M. Rochard-Pratolin has examined them and is pleased to announce that, while he finds them utterly devoid of talent, it is inconceivable that our great Republic should guillotine any man of letters. The execution then, will not take place. I have here M. Rochard-Pratolin's duly authorized commutation of sentence.

MUSCARI: Commutation? To what?

GOULARTE: *(Examining his document)* To... er... thirty years at hard labor.

MUSCARI: Thirty years imprisonment? That isn't jurisprudence—it's literary criticism.

GOULARTE: M. Rochard-Pratolin thinks it very generous.

MUSCARI: No doubt. *(He seizes the document.)* However, I must decline his kind offer. *(He tears up the paper.)* I prefer to be treated as an illiterate. *(Cheers and cries of Bravo!)*

GOULARTE: *(Aghast)* You are destroying an official document of the Court of Cassation!

MUSCARI: *(Sprinkling bits of the paper about)* Destroying it? Not at all. I am merely editing it. As a fellow author, I am sure M. Rochard-Pratolin will understand that. *(There are renewed cheers from the crowd. GOULARTE leaves in anger.)* And now, in the few moments left me I should like to add some additional details which slipped my mind in court—

A VOICE: Tell us about the girls!

ANOTHER: And how you pushed the policeman in the well!

CONCARNEAU: *(Thundering)* No! No more confessions!

MUSCARI: As you wish. Citizens, last night in a moment of pessimism, I thought I might like to go on living. *(Cries of "No! No!")* But I see now that if I did so, I should only begin to repeat myself, and that is the one sin for which no poet is ever forgiven. All right. I have said what I have to say and I owe it to my reputation to stop before I become boring. I thank you all for your many kindnesses. And now, shall we get on with the ceremony?

He turns and, flanked by the soldiers, goes off. The drum beats slowly; the townspeople crowd after him until no one is left save three girls scrabbling for the pieces of torn-up paper.

260

FIRST GIRL: And he dropped his flower here!

SECOND GIRL: The pieces of paper! We can put them back together!

THIRD GIRL: Give it here!

SECOND GIRL: It's mine! It's mine!

THIRD GIRL: Give it here or I'll scratch your eyes out!

SECOND GIRL: It's mine, I tell you, I found it first!

They start to fight. JARMIAN enters, carrying a valise and a rolled-up umbrella.

JARMIAN: You little savages! Have you no respect for anything? *(He separates them.)* Get up off the ground. You ought to be thrashed, every one of you! *(He threatens them with his umbrella. The drums are heard again and the girls run off. JARMIAN walks slowly down to GABRIEL'S deserted barrow.)* Barbarians! *(He kicks a cushion out of the way.)* Barbarians!

JARMIAN sits on the barrow and dejectedly holds his head in his hands. We hear nothing except the distant drum-beats and sighs of the crowd. At last MME. PICHEGRU enters from the other direction. She is followed by ALBERIC who is loaded down with suitcases, bundles, and potted plants. They are weary and have obviously been trudging some distance in the hot sun.

PICHEGRU: Put them down, Alberic. We'll rest a moment. But be careful you don't damage the orchids, you know how sensitive they are.

ALBERIC: *(Collapsing)* Yes, madame.

PICHEGRU: Curious! Curious! You don't suppose there's a plague in town, do you? Not a soul at the railway station! Not a hackney-cab in sight. And what is that dreadful noise? It's like the lions growling at the zoological gardens. What can it be?

ALBERIC: I really couldn't say, madame.

PICHEGRU: Ah, M. Jarmian. *(JARMIAN rises and bows to her.)* What a fatiguing railroad trip! Nothing but dust everywhere. But your bag? You're just returning too?

JARMIAN: No, madame. Our paths cross. I am leaving.

PICHEGRU: Leaving Sandaraque? *(JARMIAN nods.)* Forever? *(JARMIAN nods again.)* Well, you are extremely sensible. It's a hideous town. Not at all as it was when I first came here fifty years ago. There was some sense of style in those days, even in Sandaraque. Now it's become so dreadfully bourgeois. Alberic! You're letting the orchid stand in the sunlight. You must shade it or it will wilt. *(To JARMIAN)* I'm leaving, too, you know. I've just returned to clean up a few odds and ends, and then we are removing to Bayonne where at least there are some beautiful gardens. *(Pauses; again we hear the drum.)* But what is that exasperating hullabaloo? Are the Freemasons having another of their parades?

JARMIAN: No, madame, there is an execution.

PICHEGRU: An execution? That's novel! But whatever for?

JARMIAN: Listen. *(They are silent. The drum rises to a crescendo, followed by a distant sigh from the crowd.)* There. I'm afraid it's all over with the poor devil.

PICHEGRU: Eh? Which reminds me: one of the things I want to clear up before I go is the affair of that wretched Poitou.

JARMIAN: Poitou?

PICHEGRU: The gendarme, you know. Don't tell me you haven't missed him? Someone must have noticed that he was no longer swaggering about, rattling on people's doors with his night stick.

JARMIAN: Madame, what is it you want to tell me? Do you know what happened to him?

PICHEGRU: *(Practically)* Of course I do. I, M. Jarmian, am his assassin—at least I suppose you could put it that way.

JARMIAN: You?!

PICHEGRU: Well, don't act so astounded. Merely because I am no longer young, you mustn't suppose I am unable to protect my honor against the lewd embraces of a drunken gendarme. No doubt he thought I was defenseless, but he should have remembered that a virtuous woman, properly alerted, can always find a way out of any difficulty. I had left my hat-pin at home but I was not such a fool as to be out at night without my parasol. I caught him very neatly right below the Adam's apple. Unfortunately, he was standing next to the well at the time. I believe he grabbed at the rope to save himself but only succeeded in pulling all the buckets down on top of him.

JARMIAN: *(Fiercely)* And do you realize, madame, that an innocent man has just paid the supreme penalty for that crime?

PICHEGRU: What? Who?

JARMIAN: A poor misguided wretch named Muscari.

PICHEGRU: Muscari? Alberic, do you hear that? It's the gardener! You know, I wondered whatever became of him. You mean to say they have executed him merely for killing a gendarme?

JARMIAN: It was one of the charges.

PICHEGRU: Times certainly have changed! My great-uncle, the Marquis of Cleves, must have killed at least half a dozen gamekeepers, gendarmes and the like during his lifetime and he died a Marshal of France.

JARMIAN: But why? Why didn't you come forward and confess this at the time it happened?

PICHEGRU: No one asked me. And besides, at the time, M. Menton kept saying the world was going to end any hour, and I couldn't see that one gendarme more or less would make any difference. But believe me, M. Jarmian, I do want to get the whole thing cleared up. And if you want me to go to the authorities and explain just how it happened, I'm quite willing to.

JARMIAN: It is your Christian duty, madame.

PICHEGRU: Quite. Only of course, I am not a Christian, you know. I believe I am a Theosophist now.

JARMIAN: A what?

PICHEGRU: A Theosophist. It's extremely interesting and some time if you like I'll explain it all to you. Come, Alberic, pick up the orchid. *(To JARMIAN)* It's a present from my cousins in Bayonne. We must be on our way to the police. But you were leaving.

JARMIAN: *(Grimly)* I was. But I have changed my mind. There are some odds and ends here in Sandaraque that I want to clean up, too.

PICHEGRU: Good. Then I shall have time to explain the Doctrine of Transubstantiation to you, shan't I?

JARMIAN: Yes. We will have time.

They go out as the curtain closes.

EPILOGUE

In a moment the spotlight comes up on the DRUMMER *and the* OLD WOMAN.

DRUMMER: And that was it?

OLD WOMAN: *(Bitterly)* Oh, it was a fine scandal, believe me! They took it all the way to Paris, and the government appointed a special board of inquiry that came down to Sandaraque and turned everything upside down. And that devil Muscari had set such an example, that everybody else wanted to rush in and confess, too. It was a plague of confessions, like scarlet fever! And the Royalists claimed it was all the Radicals' doing and the Radicals swore the Royalists were to blame, and in the middle of it my poor grandfather, M. Concarneau, died of apoplexy so they settled by blaming it all on him. They took his name off the new asphalt highway—

DRUMMER: You mean Muscari Boulevard?

OLD WOMAN: Honest people still call it Avenue Concarneau. And my family was left without a sou, and my mother had to take in washing and my father give music lessons just to scrape by. And all because that scoundrel Muscari stuck his nose in where it didn't belong.

DRUMMER: Just the same, Auntie, he was a great man.

OLD WOMAN: Rubbish!

DRUMMER: I want to look at the statue again.

OLD WOMAN: Suit yourself. But I'd rather look at the hind end of a camel.

The DRUMMER *pulls back the curtain, revealing the statue of* MUSCARI *as before.*

DRUMMER: No, Auntie, you're wrong. If it weren't for people like him there wouldn't have been any progress in the world. That's why we stand for a moment of silence on his birthday, and that's why they built this statue to him. He taught us to admit things when we do them and not to pass the blame off on somebody else. And we can appreciate Muscari today because people are so much more honest now than they were seventy years ago.

This is too much for the STATUE, *who looks incredulously at the* DRUMMER *and then shakes his head in despair as the curtain closes.*

The End

ON KAYAK

☞ HITCHCOCK ON KAYAK
FROM CARLETON MISCELLANY

George Hitchcock's submission to "Concerning the Little Magazines: Something Like a Symposium, with Something Like Twenty Contributors or Combatants" in The Carleton Miscellany *(Spring, 1966, Vol. VII, No. 2).*

Kayak is edited upon the assumption which is, I should imagine, implicit in the manifestoes of most little magazines—that the editor knows what he likes and is prepared to print it come hell or high water. And it seems to me a perfectly healthy motivation behind the immense labor of editing, producing and distributing the literary magazine unblessed by institutional support. In fact, the small literary magazine is today virtually the only remaining example of what was once a noble American tradition—the tradition of personal responsibility in journalism. All else has been swallowed up by the faceless corporate entities devoted to providing what their managers conceive to be the requisite pabulum for this or that stratum of the reading public. Amidst the anonymous waves only a few dissident vessels are uneasily bobbing.

Kayak is one of these dissidents. It plies the freezing waters of American poetry, negotiating its narrow channels and hurling an occasional spear at the more preposterous icebergs and barking walruses which bar its way. As its title indicates, *kayak* is piloted by a single oarsman who is, indeed, not only captain and harpoonist but sculleryman, cook and armorer as well. *Kayak* exists in an epoch prior to the division of labor. It is, perhaps, an artifact.

Among the icebergs which *kayak* would dynamite as menaces to navigation there is, of course, the vast glassy hulk of Anglo-American metaphysical iambics. But then everybody is out to smash that icon: Yvor Winters and John Crowe Ransom have been fair game for a generation, and The Sons and Daughters of Wystan Auden are rapidly going the way of the Lindy Hop. More dangerous game is provided today by the stupefying eclecticism of *Poetry* (Chicago), the Suburban Sociologists who fill the space allotted to poetry in many of the university quarterlies, and that self-aggrandizing gang of unreadable and pompous hierophants, descended (sinisterly) from Ezra Pound, who worship Charles Olson as His Only True Hagiographer. From time to time *kayak* takes them all on.

Kayak's weapons in this running naval engagement are the bone spear, the carved walrus arrowhead, the leather amulet and the lethal concave mirror which focuses and directs the rays of the aurora borealis. Attacked by this arsenal, its victims suffer bizarre delusions and suffocate in clouds of dandruff.

The poetry I print in *kayak* is, quite naturally, the best that is being written in the United States and Canada. (Every editor who is worth his salt feels this about his own selections.) It is, for the most part Romantic poetry, although it's unlikely that Coleridge would recognize it. I believe that the most important Romantic mode of twentieth century poetry is the surrealist, although I also welcome imagist poetry— nor should, I hope, the pages of *kayak* ever be closed to another Dylan Thomas, were he miraculously to rise from Atlantis. But what most contemporary Romantics hold in common is a love of sensuous content, a feeling for the liberating image and a profound antagonism to the given data of our senseless society. Technically, the poets in *kayak* are likely to have more in common with Rimbaud, García Lorca, the Chinese, Breton, Éluard, Vallejo and Neruda than they do with Pound, Eliot, Dr. Williams or Mr. Frost. Yet there are always exceptions. Editing is an ever-renewed and renewing choice—it is not a profession of doctrine. And naturally none of *kayak's* contributors has voted me his proxy in this discussion.

Finally, *kayak* is interested in the political poem, a genre which has been neglected in America since the thirties, although Robert Bly has done yeoman service in reviving it during recent years. The poet today inevitably functions as an enemy—whether covert or avowed— of the society in which he lives, and expressions of that antagonism which do not sacrifice poetry to polemics are very much in order.

THE FIRST TEN ISSUES OF KAYAK

This essay by Robert Bly, published in kayak 12, *1967, sparked furious discussion in the correspondence section of subsequent issues of the magazine.*

I.

George Hitchcock asked me for some prose for *kayak*, and I asked if I might do an attack on his first ten issues. He thought that was a good idea.

Some people feel that criticism is always destructive, like an over-exposure to X-rays. That fear comes from concentration on criticism a decade ago. The Lowell-Shapiro generation were not good critics. They were always looking up into the sky: who was there? Yeats. His blazing rocket arching across the sky. His solitary rocket-like career was the only model they accepted for their own lives. They acted as if every writer was for himself. Each poet had his own rocket launching pad, separate from the other. It was important to keep the formula for your rocket fuel secret, otherwise the others might catch you! Your obligation to the other rockets was to throw off their timing. (Norman Mailer's gossipy sneers at his novelist friends is a good example of this.) The poet's criticism was either sheer gush (out of ignorance or guilt) or a transparent attempt to weaken competitors.

Partly out of reaction to this sterile and mutual hostility, the Black Mountain poets in the early fifties made loyalty into a heroic virtue. They still refuse to make judgments of anyone if he has professed loyalty to the Olson creed. Whatever their doubts in private, in public not a word of criticism falls from their lips. (Creeley's reviews in *Poetry* are examples of this.) They save all their hostility for outsiders. (Prose in the Grove Press anthology is an example of that.) But reviews by fine poets that keep mum on important flaws of their contemporaries confuse younger poets, who end up distrusting their own critical instincts. These two approaches to criticism, capitalistic dog-eat-dog competitiveness and corporative "don't knock the company" team spirit, both seemed good ideas at the time, but both approaches now seem big failures. There is a third possibility: those who are interested in the same sort of poetry attack each other sharply, and still have respect and affection for each other. I don't see why this approach should be impossible for Americans. Criticism does not imply contempt. The criticism of my own poetry that has been the most use to me has been criticism that, when I first heard it, utterly dismayed me.

Turning to *kayak* then, I think the first ten issues have been on the whole clogged and bad. As an editor, George Hitchcock is too permissive. Poets are encouraged to continue in their failures as well as their fresh steps. Sometimes I think George is more interested in printing four issues a year—he loves to see those wild looking pages go through!—than what is in the issues. Like the Provençal lover, he goes through incredible pains, but it's possible he is in love with the idea of having a magazine, as the Provençal poets were said to be in love with the idea of being in love.

Too much foggy stuff gets in: in *kayak* poems usually someone is stepping into a tunnel of dark wind and disappearing into a whistle; the darkness is always pausing to wait for someone. One gets the feeling that as long as there are a few skeletons of fossil plants in the poem, or some horses floating in the mind, or a flea whispering in Norwegian, in it goes!

The images even take on a certain grammatical skeleton of their own. For instance they are made of *a)* an animal or object, *b)* a violent action, *c)* an adjective (often tiny, dark, or great), and then *d)* the geographical location. "Lighted cigars fall like meteors on a deserted football field in Pierre, South Dakota (III, 17); "Birds fly in the broken windows / of the hotel in Argyle" (III, 32); "Black beetles, bright as Cadillacs, toil down / The long dusty road into the mountains of South Dakota" (V, 31). Sometimes the place comes first: "In Wyoming a horse dies by a silver river" (I, 7).

There get to be a lot of passives: "Policemen were discovered in the cupolas waving felt erasers" (VII, 37), and partial passives: "Hands are choking a cat in a small liquor store in Connecticut" (I, 7).

Often, to end the poem, an image with literary resonance will be followed instantly with an offhand remark from the world of truckdrivers. "I pick two apples, / then leave the cold park. / That's all I can do." "Another beer truck comes to town, / chased by a dog on three legs. // Batman lies drunk in the weeds." (III, 32). "At the farther / End of the mind, a farmer / Douses the lamp and climbs / The narrow stairs to sleep. // All night, under the window, / A horse gallops in the pasture." (V, 42).

Moreover, all *kayak* poems seem to take place in the eternal present: the poet uses the present progressive tense—past and future tenses have died out. As a result, those hands are still choking that poor cat in the liquor store, and the horse is forever galloping up and down in the pasture.

At the same time *kayak* is valuable, and a much-loved magazine. Unlike the *Kenyon Review*, which everyone for years has been hoping would kick off soon, *kayak* would be missed very much if it developed a leak and sank. George offers some kind of nourishment. Every hand of course is sometimes open, sometimes closed. As a fist, *kayak* is raised against stuff like this, crystalized flower formations from the jolly intellectual dandies:

> Mind in its purest play is like some bat
> That beats about in caverns all alone,
> Contriving by a kind of senseless wit
> Not to conclude against a wall of stone.
>   (Wilbur)

But *kayak* is also against the high-pitched bat-like cry of the anal Puritan mandarin:

> That I cannot take
> and that she will not
>
> not give, but will not
> have it taken
>   (Sorrentino)

This trapped, small-boned, apologetic, feverish, glassy, intellectualist fluttering is just what George hates. He has tried to provide a place where poems that escape from that glassy box can come. If you turn into a fish, he has a muddy pond, with lots of foliage.

Then too, the dark wells and wet branches and drunks-sleeping-happily-in-cellars images that we see so often in *kayak* say important things in themselves: they are hints to the mind that it can escape if it wants to. Of course adoption of a style cannot make a poet free. The mind has too many tricks in reserve for that—it hates change. In order to keep a restless poet quiet, the rational mind will even slide down to him some floating breast images and extinct dinosaur bone images, perhaps enough for a whole poem! But these images can

271

remain perfectly rational. When we read them, we feel something not genuine there. Poems of that sort are like movies of mountain scenery shown on the inside of a stationary train window.

So a lot of poems that *appear* to have escaped from the mind-walls really haven't escaped at all. A conventional form of the underground lakes poem is beginning to appear, and *kayak* publishes too many of them. Of course that is not all George's fault: he is publishing the best poems he can get, and he has published some marvelous ones, about fifty at least. In fact, some of the best poems he has published have nothing to do with what I have called here "the *kayak* poem": for example the wonderful poems by William Lane, "Green" in number IV, "Turning" and "What To Do Till the Answer Comes" in X; Jean Batie's poem "I saw my mother on the stair" in IX; David Ignatow's bagel poem in VII and "Political Cartoon" in X; John Ridland's "Yachting Scene" and "Sunkist Packing Plant" in V; William Pillin's frightening poem "Look Down!" in III; Richard Hugo's "Castel Sant'Angelo" in II; Bert Meyers' "A Tree Stump At Noon" and "They Who Waste Me" in V; Louis Simpson's "Progress" in V; and John Woods' "Some Martial Thoughts" in X. The truth is we don't write enough good poems to fill a large magazine like *kayak*.

II.

Turning to the poets then, if a poet has written a conventional *kayak* poem, what mistake has he made? First of all, I think he has mistaken a way of living for a style.

Looking through *kayak*, one sees many poems on trees, leaves, animals, plants, nature poems. But it is clear from reading them that the poet at the moment he wrote them was not really out in the field, he was not alone out there in the non-human, on the contrary, he was sitting at his desk, in his usual place. (The poems of John Haines are exceptions to this.)

Many *kayak* poets, turning away from the rhetorical verse of the Fugitives or the hairy wits, have aimed at a greater simplicity of style. But simplicity is a natural expression of solitude, just as cluttered complexity and rhetorical flourish are the natural expression of an over-socialized life, a life with too many people in it. So the next step for many poets who want to write better is not to learn more about the style, but to stop their usual sociability. That step is difficult for many American poets who are teaching in universities, where sociability is forced upon them by the nature of their work. Poets in artistic colonies or hippie colonies are better off, but still are within a sociable world.

Almost all American poets insist on their right to be sociable.

Bashō said, "To express the flavor of the inner mind, you must agonize during many days." That is a wonderful sentence! The purpose of it all is not to write long endless poems, but to express "the flavor of the inner mind." That phrase suggests how alive the senses must be to do that, and also suggests that we step into that mind through pain. Bashō thought the poet should be willing to live in solitude, which is occasionally painful and lonely. In one of his best poems, Bashō makes clear that the true poem is not associated with what Freud calls the "pleasure principle" (sociability, eating, consuming), but rather with the "pain principle":

> Dried salmon
> And Kuya's breakthrough into the spirit,
> Both in the cold time of the year!

(Kuya was a young monk of an earlier time who one day in December suddenly made the Zen "leap," and spent the rest of his life helping the poor.)

The Japanese say, Go to the pine if you want to learn about the pine. If an American poet wants to write of a chill and foggy field, he has to stay out there, and get cold and wet himself. Two hours of solitude seem about right for every line of poetry.

—Robert Bly

Sorry, but the editors of kayak feel that
your submission is not quite what we need
this season.   Thanks anyway.

George H. Kolar

𝒱 KAYAK REJECTION AND RENEWAL

INTERVIEWER: Can you tell me a little bit about your rejection letters?

HITCHCOCK: You can imagine them yourself. I'd assembled considerable sources of nineteenth century wood engravings and from time to time ran across one which seemed appropriately ghastly or ironic for a rejection. I had one with an executioner bringing an ax down on the head of the unfortunate victim and it said "The Editor regrets that your submission is not acceptable at the present time."... I had sufficient variety to keep people amused and I usually had about fifteen to twenty of them at the same time. Everyone remembers that. It was good for a laugh although some people were terribly insulted. But the ones who are terribly insulted you wouldn't want in the magazine anyway.

Dear George Hitchcock:

You sent me 2 rejection slips. That hurt, George. If you had accepted at least one poem I would have gone on and maybe made it as a human being... But you rejected (it was your signature that did it) and I've had it. In one half hour I'll suffocate in my Volkswagon.

Sincerely,
(name withheld)

Dear Sir or Madam:

The editorial board of kayak has perused your submission with the greatest of care and finds, on reflection, that it won't do.

Yours, etc.

George Hitchcock

Dear George Hitchcock:

I sit here gaping at your latest rejection notice wondering what kind of man could profess to be a poet and yet send me something like this...

Goodbye,

The editor of kayak regrets that he cannot oblige you by publishing your obviously meritorious work--
sincerely,

George Hitchcock

Sorry! *George H. Helvert*

for the editor, kayak

"Letter to the Editor"

Listen: this is
A punch in the nose

I enclose no
return postage

Take it for what it is
And for what I intended

Dear Mr. Hitchcock:

Have you ever considered sponsoring a contest wherein the individual with the largest number of *kayak* rejection slips would receive a free subscription to *kayak?*

The editor of kayak is, of course, grateful
for your submission but regrets that it is
not quite what he has in mind for its pages

Sincerely,

Dear Hitchcock:

Thanks for your signed rejection slip. And please tell the guy who got 2 of them from you and was going to kill himself that only tough poems and hardened poets deserve to make it. I have about 100 on my private Wailing Wall.

(unsigned)

so you won't think I'm brown-nosing.

The editor of kayak thanks you for your very interesting submission but regrets to report that it is not quite what he needs for his magazine.

Sincerely,

No room for your contribution just at present,

regretfully,

George H. Kelik Jr

editor of kayak

Dear *kayak*,

Here are some new poems. If, God forbid, you are so foolish as to reject me again, please send a new rejection slip. I already have Gentleman in Icy Crevasse (2), Wolf Attacking Innocent Youth, and Gentleman Being Forcibly Escorted Down Stairs. How many of them are there, anyway? I intend to collect them all like baseball cards.

Dear *kayak*:

...for at least three years I have been stabbed in the stomach, mutilated by mad dogs, castrated, upended, thrown to the lions, been devoured by plunging leviathans, bitten in the esophagus by slippery metaphors, strangled, defiled bodily and psychically by stalking demons unleashed by the editors of *kayak* from the ancient steel engravings that have arrived punctually month after month after month...

The editor of kayak regrets that your submission, although worthy, didn't quite make it.

Sympathetically,

Dear Mr. Hitchcock:

...your rejection slips; I have received so many... so many in fact that I believe this will be my last attempt to get an acceptance from you. In the interest of expressive graphics I have attached an illustration showing the writer's feelings after receiving one too many rejections:

Dear George:

   Don't be cross at the enclosed check—it's just blackmail, intended to force you to keep on putting out the magazine. But if you decide to suspend (don't!) before you reach the 70th issue, you need return nothing. And if you decide to raise the rates, that just means you'll come back to me (with your elegant menaces—Edwardian?) the sooner.

Kayak and therefore you, have given me much pleasure...

kayak
a magazine of poetry

requests you to renew your subscription which has unfortunately disappeared with this issue. $5.00 for the next four issues, please

George Hitchcock

Kayak Kohorts:

There are probably things worse than not having a subscription to *kayak* but I can't think of any of them.

Do people keep telling you that your work is provocative? That your work is appreciated? That you are making a valuable contribution to American literature? All of the above are true.

I'm giving this note teeth by enclosing my subscription renewal.

Your subscription to kayak collapses with this issue. We would, of course, be delighted to continue our ministrations to your fantasy life, but we'll need another $4.00 for the next four issues.

yours

George Hitchcock

HITCHCOCK ON KAYAK
FROM TRIQUARTERLY

Published in TriQuarterly *43, 1978.*

If there is any discernable trend in the publication of little magazines over the last decade, it is certainly only numerical: there are more and more of them. Because of the widespread availability of low-cost offset printing equipment and a newfound generosity on the part of the National Endowment for the Arts, small magazines have proliferated at an unprecedented rate. Is this boom growth a good thing? I am of two minds about that. Certainly from the political or social point of view it is preferable to have several thousand localized and generally anti-establishment voices, and any shift in that direction and away from the control of publishing by our great monopolies is desirable. Little magazines have come to be an integral part of the counterculture and, by their independence and intransigence, offer a really hopeful alternative to the increasing stranglehold the corporate marketing mind has over our traditional cultural outlets.

Yet at the same time I'm afraid the new wave of little magazines, by their very number and fundamental sameness, has created confusion and apathy. Who can possibly read more than a thousandth part of them? And isn't it probable that a sort of literary Gresham's Law has come into effect—bad writing driving out good, or at the very least inundating it in a surf of paper?

I have no real answers to these questions. Analyzing the state of the zeitgeist has never much appealed to me. Artists are usually better off leaving such questions to the sociologists and historians of letters. In what follows I shall merely offer a few opinions based on twenty years of independent publishing, both of books and magazines, appending some caveats for those who may be considering a similar plunge into the unknown.

In the late fifties, encouraged by the sparks from the bonfires of what was then called (in retrospect, a bit optimistically) the "San Francisco Renaissance," I shared editorial responsibility in the newly launched *San Francisco Review*. The magazine was the creation of Roy Miller, a San Francisco lawyer whose impulses were, I suspect, as much sociological as literary. At any rate, he had gotten an article by Bertrand Russell and poems from the ever-generous William Carlos Williams and e.e. cummings with which to launch his first issue. There was also, I think, a prose poem by Bill Saroyan and a two-act play of mine that had been recently premiered by Jules Irving at The Actor's Workshop. It was because he admired this play that I was invited to sign on as associate editor (no salary, of course). That was more than twenty years ago, and, once hooked, I've never properly been able to get away.

The *San Francisco Review* was rather ambitiously conceived and, I'm afraid, never quite lived up to its initial promise. For one thing, it was letterpress printed in England and shipped to its editors via book post; consequently, there were vast and irksome editorial and publication delays. Even more important, there was a very substantial deficit for each issue. The deficit was made up by the editors but, I hasten to add, not by the associate editor. And in any case, it didn't run to such astronomical projections of red ink as were incurred by the other San Francisco literary magazine of that period, *Contact*, whose editors, Bill Ryan and Evan Connell, the grapevine tells me, contrived to drop around $70,000 in the five or six years of the magazine's existence.

But I soon learned the number-one law of little magazine publishing: no literary magazine in America can hope to break even without either financial subvention from a patron or the discovery of some way to beat the printer's bills. Another lesson I also learned was that collective editorship, even with the greatest initial enthusiasm, has dreadful drawbacks. In fact, I should be inclined to think that more initially promising publications have been ruined by the multiplicity of ladles in the literary broth than by any other single cause. The three of us at *San Francisco Review* (very shortly a third editor who was prepared to assist in the financing was added) regularly disagreed. Of course, that in itself is not a bad thing, and I look back upon many of our fiercer arguments with a certain retrospective relish. But what invariably happens with an editorial board of equals is that either—to borrow Orwell's phrase—one becomes more equal than the others, or the acceptance basket tends to become filled with submissions which have as their least common denominator the fact that no one objects to them very strongly. And I am afraid any magazine edited along these lines is ultimately doomed to a tepid eclecticism. In any event, soon enough the money ran out. Roy Miller, the founding editor, went back to the law; he is at present compiling a parliamentary guide for, I believe, the

Library of Congress. June Degnan, on whose shoulders the lion's share of the financial responsibility had fallen, went on to the greener pastures as the financial consultant for Eugene McCarthy's presidential campaign. We had published twelve issues, some good authors, and a fair amount of rubbish, and had summed up the magazine by issuing, in collaboration with Jay Laughlin of New Directions, one paperback collection of which I am still quite proud.

But I had merely gotten my feet wet. I was convinced that the only effective way of publishing a little magazine was through an absolute dictatorship. This method of government, while certainly not to my taste in the commonwealth, seemed to me then, and still does, the only one that works in the world of art. An editor who is not prepared to be an autocrat in matters of literary taste, who is not ready to face with a smile the raucous cries of "Elitism!" would be better off somewhere else. Far too many editors or quasi-editors lack the courage of their convictions. Many go into little-magazine editing with the psychology of correspondents of a Pen Pal Club or a society of clock collectors: they want to get letters; they want to be liked. A mistake. I have met others whose activities are ruled by the conviction that their chief function is a philanthropic one toward young writers. Of course, a certain amount of vaguely diffused benevolence may be a by-product of the publication of a good little magazine. But it should always be viewed suspiciously as a by-product and nothing else. An editor who is also publisher, and thus undertakes complete responsibility for all aspects of his magazine, should, I think, have first of all a responsibility to himself—that is, to please himself and to meet his own highest artistic standards. His second responsibility, I should like to argue, is to his readership, not to an amorphous, anonymous "public" but to a readership made up of individuals, with each of whom the editor can envisage an enjoyable conversation. If such a readership does not exist, then it's up to the editor to invent it, and in time nature may come to imitate art and provide him with it.

Somewhere very far down the scale of responsibilities comes the welfare of novice authors. And even there, let us remember that patronizing other human beings, and particularly bad writers, is a crime which should be punished by immersion in boiling—well, perhaps a boiling puree of old rejection slips.

In 1964, alone and armed by my experiences with the troika at the *San Francisco Review*, I launched *kayak*. The title was not accidental; in the initial issue I defined a kayak as:

Not a galleon, ark, coracle or speedboat. It is a small watertight vessel operated by a single oarsman. It is submersible, has sharply pointed ends, and is constructed from light poles and the skins of furry animals. It has never yet been successfully employed as a means of mass transport.

It was my intention to publish chiefly poetry showing certain tendencies which I admired and felt to be gravely under-represented by the then existing poetry journals. These tendencies can, I suppose, be roughly defined as the various branches of contemporary Romanticism. Romanticism is, of course, a very loose term, perhaps exclusively associated with Coleridge, Keats, Swinburne, Rossetti, and their epigoni. However, specifically modern Romanticism seemed to me to be work in the imagistic and surrealist modes. In fact, I don't think it an overstatement to say that surrealism, in one or another of its forms, is the quintessentially modern guise of the Romantic movement. At the same time that I was prepared to flaunt my own predilections for imaginative and subjective poetry of this sort, I didn't want to shut any editorial doors on Romantic poetry in the English tradition where it was still alive. I thought when I started *kayak*, for example, that I should prove a very poor and imperceptive editor if I were to turn down the work, let us say, of a younger Dylan Thomas or David Jones simply because it didn't measure up to some pre-established canons of surrealist taste.

Anyway, in practice no editor worth anything creates his magazine on the basis of a priori considerations. Theories are interesting, but in artistic discrimination the viscera play an equally important part. So to the catalogue of preferences I've listed above I should add a list of my often irrational hates, particularly since by character and ancestry I have always been a rebel and tend to be provoked into action more by what I don't like than by positive affinities. Thus in 1964, listed in no particular order, I actively disliked neoclassicism, the neo-Hemingway "tough guy" posture, most of the New Criticism, the Vietnam war (already in its initial stages), the banal eclecticism of *Poetry* (Chicago), excessive academic analysis at the expense of feeling, our national administration, the pseudo poetics of Charles Olson and his Black Mountain disciples, the cliquish pretentiousness of many of the Beats, poets preoccupied with the trivia of suburban existence—in short, ninety percent of what was being written or done in my own time. Enough fuel to keep my critical fires burning for quite a while.

In the early sixties I was certainly influenced as well by Robert Bly and his rediscovery of what was then popularly referred to as "the deep image" of European and Latin American surrealist poetry. However, it was more than forty years ago that I first began to read Breton, Soupault, and García Lorca, to mention but three, so what may have been a discovery to Robert Bly was not exactly a novelty to me. I think Bly performed a great service, though, with the early issues of his magazine *The Fifties*—to become in later decades *The Sixties* and *The Seventies*—and for a number of years it was certainly a model to me of what could be accomplished by energy and cantankerous individual taste. Since Robert has apparently lapsed into unforeseeable depths of inwardness and Oriental mysticism, my own extrovert's empathies with him have diminished a bit over the years.

Still, if all this means anything it is that an editor or poet is capable of creating a magazine worth reading only if he feels passionately, if he brings to his work deeply held convictions and a taste founded upon something more committed than a desire for personal celebrity. And particularly in America, where getting ahead has been the major ideology for a century or more, this attitude is not found every day.

People sometimes ask me what they should do to make their forthcoming magazines successful. I think the only sensible answer I can give them is to start by forgetting about success. In our literary climate the only real successes are the honorable failures. Then, of course, they should read widely, learn about printing, and cultivate their own passionate prejudices. With these maxims in mind, they may find some joy in their work, and—who knows?—sooner or later they may earn the esteem of a few ardent readers. There are far too many magazines being published in America today that bring such stern joys to no one at all and fulfill no particular purpose unless it be to feed the editor's vanity or advance him up the ladder of academic promotion.

This of course brings me to the literary magazine spawned by a university English department or one or two ambitious creative writers within it. When editorial responsibility for such a magazine is turned over to students, it probably fulfills a sufficiently honorable pedagogical function and can be justified on those grounds. But when, as is more often the case, it is edited by a faculty committee with one eye fixed on the promotion and tenure committee and the other following the rise and fall of New York publishing reputations, then I for one can do without it.

Of course, there is nothing inherently wrong with university patronage of a literary magazine, but the university would be well advised to make sure that it is spending its money on the genuine living article rather than a mere eclectic grab bag and vehicle for faculty ambitions. I can think offhand of only two or three university-financed reviews in which the impact of a strong editorial personality has created a vital magazine. The examples that come to mind are those of David Ray and the strong social-radical consciousness he has brought to the editing of *New Letters* for the University of Missouri at Kansas City; of the elegant and rather patrician standards James Boatwright has given to *Shenandoah* at Washington and Lee; and of Robin Skelton, who has brought such a distinctively international flavor to the *Malahat Review* at the University of Victoria in British Columbia. In all these cases the magazines appear to be run on the autocratic principle, and their achievements are counterbalanced by the dead, doughy weight of several score of other magazines—which shall here be nameless—edited by faculty committees.

Of course, if one is going to edit without patronage—and that has always been my personal choice—then the prerequisites must be sufficient mechanical and printing skill and a great deal of free time. I have no advice as to how to secure the latter, but offset printing equipment is today so readily available at a reasonable expenditure that I am inclined to think the chief prerequisite for any editor is to learn to print. Of course one doesn't have to approach printing with the zeal of a William Morris at Kelmscott, although it is certainly a nice thing to be able to do beautiful printing; but some knowledge of offset processes, or at least of typesetting and paste-up, seems to me to be absolutely fundamental. Besides which, I am with Morris and Blake in prizing the written word that you have designed and made with your own hands over and above the product of alienated labor. In a factory-ridden world, the little magazine can be one of the rare creations in which thought and labor meet without the intercession of the impersonal processes usual in our society. And as for *kayak*, which is now publishing its forty-eighth issue [editors' note: *kayak* published a total of sixty-four issues], it is in its design and production—always with the freely given help of a sodality or brotherhood of poets—that the joy of the thing lies.

LIGHT POLES AND THE SKINS OF FURRY ANIMALS, OR HOW THE KAYAK WAS BUILT FROM CALIBAN

An interview with Lawrence Smith published in Caliban 1, 1986.

SMITH: When did you decide to start *kayak*?

HITCHCOCK: After the collapse of the *San Francisco Review* in 1963 (on which I served as an editor) I decided to try for a magazine which would reflect my tastes and avoid the defects of the editorial committee, which had become all too apparent during my years (1958–63) with the *San Francisco Review*.

SMITH: Even though *kayak* was clearly a one-man operation—in one issue you listed yourself as "dictator"—did you have advice and help from the San Francisco writers (or those from elsewhere) when you were starting up?

HITCHCOCK: No advice, no. However, I wrote many of the poets with whom I had worked during the *San Francisco Review* period and they responded most generously. San Francisco friends turned out to help on the collating and mailing, as they were always to do during the life of the magazine. Some of those early colleagues were Larry Fixel, Robert Peterson, Ray Carver, Lennart Bruce, Morton Marcus, et al. The poets who were most helpful in offering criticism and reviews were, of course, John Haines, Robert Bly, and H.R. Hays. It was understood from the beginning, however, that editorial decisions were never to be delegated.

SMITH: You proclaimed hospitality to surrealist, imagist, and political poems. Surrealist and political make sense to me, but imagist less so. By imagist did you mean what was being called "deep image?" Or did you mean the poetry which developed earlier in the century?

HITCHCOCK: By "imagist" I did not mean Amygism or any school of imagery, but simply poems which relied strongly on visual and sensual imagery, as opposed to the abstract Neo-Anglican-Rhetorical.

SMITH: Did you feel that any major American magazines were hospitable to surrealism in 1964 when you started *kayak*? Or did you feel you stood alone?

HITCHCOCK: Certainly Robert Bly's *The Sixties* was hospitable to surrealism, but I felt that it was published spasmodically at best and that what was needed was a journal published with great regularity and frequently enough so that various dialogues could be launched in its pages and relevantly discussed soon after.

SMITH: Bly states a preference for Spanish surrealism, but *kayak* seems to lean toward the French, verbally and visually. Was that conscious on your part? Were you making a choice?

HITCHCOCK: Bly is/was more doctrinaire than I. If you choose to call Max Ernst a Frenchman (that certainly was *one* of his passports) then I was subject to French influences. But I have never been a follower of Breton. I think I am to this day as much a painter as a poet and hence can hardly escape the influence of the Paris school. But I hope this has been a "digested" influence.

SMITH: Speaking of Max Ernst, how did you set about creating the visuals for a given issue? Did a theme come to mind or did the available "19th century pop art" material determine that? How conscious were you of linking the page illustrations with the poems and prose pieces?

HITCHCOCK: Occasionally a theme relevant to American poetry suggested itself. Before issue #2, for example, I found a book called *Boston's Main Drain*, with appropriate woodcuts, and illustrated the whole issue with it. Four or five years later in a Lexington, Kentucky, thrift shop I was lucky enough to chance on a 19th century treatise on plastic surgery which seemed appropriate to the issue being planned. But in general I relied upon Improvisation, my true *dueña*.

SMITH: Several times you had a single artist provide the drawings for the entire issue, but this was relatively rare. Did you make a decision to stay with collage, as opposed to free-drawn art?

HITCHCOCK: No decision, but a paucity of artists able to compose in a sufficiently playful spirit. When they came along I used them. But in general the scissors proved a more reliable ally.

SMITH: Although you included found poems through most of *kayak's* twenty years, there was always some controversy among the readers as to their value. One letter asked who had lost or mislaid them. Since you and Robert Peters did a whole book of them, you obviously had a commitment to the form. Did that commitment have a theoretical or historical basis? By what criteria did you judge found poem submissions?

HITCHCOCK: Found poems are constant testimony to the fact that wonder may still be found in places where you least expect it. The sign says "Entrance"; I am in the habit of reading that as a command. It is as simple as that. The criteria? Where, I think, the language was amazing and the form verged on stichomythia or wrapped itself up in oxymoronic robes of mystery, as in almost any application form or set of review questions to a text on beekeeping.

SMITH: Why the humorous and slightly insulting rejection slips that were a *kayak* trademark? Were you trying to tell the would-be contributors not to take it all so seriously?

HITCHCOCK: No doubt.

SMITH: During the early years you solicited "vehement and ribald articles on the subject of modern poetry." Why "vehement" and "ribald?" Did you feel that most critical exchanges were too polite and tame?

HITCHCOCK: Obviously.

SMITH: During the same period you also expressed interest in "political" poems. Did you see that as a category separate from "surrealist"? Shouldn't they ideally have been one and the same, as in many of your poems?

HITCHCOCK: A surrealist poem may be political and a political poem is occasionally surrealist, but the two are certainly not the same.

SMITH: In retrospect, do you think that the Che Guevara prize was a good idea? Many of the critical letters implied that government money was poison, regardless of the use to which it is put. Especially since you prided yourself on *kayak's* independence, did you ever feel such outside assistance might be a threat? How do you feel about the general proposition of the government as a patron of the arts?

HITCHCOCK: An excellent idea. Che Guevara was one of the authentic poetic heroes of our time and the prize (for the best poem on Guevara's life or death, as judged by W.S. Merwin, Tom McGrath and John Haines) still strikes me as a wonderful use of government money. The grant, incidentally, wasn't solicited but was proposed by Carolyn Kizer, then Literary Director of the NEA [National Endowment for the Arts], who was very supportive of what *kayak* was up to. It was renewed by her successor Leonard Randolph to enable me to print some thirty books, but, from beginning to end, *kayak* never *asked* for a grant from anyone. If money came we spent it, but we never thought twice about the psychology of grantsmanship or what any agency might or might not think of the magazine. Certainly government assistance or the hope of it can be a threat to editorial independence but not if you won't let it be.

SMITH: In creating a place for American surrealism, did you see *kayak* as a way of encouraging or strengthening the "movement," or did you see the magazine as simply serving a need that existed previously?

HITCHCOCK: In 1964 I found most American poetry magazines extraordinarily boring. I thought that *kayak* might relieve the tedium, *c'est tout*. After having been an active Communist for many years, I had grown skeptical of all programmatic art. I do not think the answer to Zdanovism lies with other exclusive programs and their manifestoes; if I have any fixed doctrine it is that of Keats: *negative capability*. No, I did not seek to create a movement: perhaps a meeting ground for friends with cognate vocabularies, nothing more.

SMITH: You never wrote essays nor developed any sort of manifesto. Did you consciously avoid that surrealist tradition. Why?

HITCHCOCK: Feeling as I do about manifestoes, I have never been eager to indulge myself in them. Anyway, the proof of the pudding, et cetera. What mattered were the poems themselves.

SMITH: One letter accused *kayak* of racial and gender bias and proceeded to do a census count of one issue. And in the correspondence page there was a running controversy over multiculturalism, whether or not it should be sought in magazines, anthologies, et cetera. What do you think about this? Did you make any efforts along these lines?

HITCHCOCK: Any white male Anglo-Irish atheistic middle-aged dictatorial editor is bound to be biased and would be a fool to deny it. In compensation, I have tried to admit my various biases freely (some might say, to parade them). They have never consciously included any form of racism or sexism; of what sins my subconscious has been guilty obviously I couldn't say but I hope that they are venial rather than mortal. As to the second part of your question, multicultural anthologies obviously have great value, but *kayak* was never organized along these principles and would have lost the cutting edge of its effectiveness the moment it attempted democratic gestures of this sort.

SMITH: As I was indexing the issues of *kayak*, I found that you included at least five or six new poets in every number. There clearly was a *kayak* circle, but you kept adding to it. Did you feel that this was vital to your undertaking—bringing in new blood?

HITCHCOCK: Yes, certainly. The flush of discovery is the warmest reward we editors attain.

SMITH: You published translations throughout *kayak's* lifetime, many from less frequently translated languages. Certainly *kayak* acknowledged foreign influences, but did you feel that translated work was also important in the poetic forum you created? Do you think, as Robert McDowell once suggested in an article you published, that translation has a negative effect on American writers?

HITCHCOCK: Yes, I thought American poets tended to be too parochial and that translations just might help overcome this. On the other hand, we had very limited space and the fatter academic quarterlies seemed the more appropriate place for the survey-of-foreign-lit type of thing. Ultimately, I always judged a translation by its qualities as a poem in English. If it didn't move me in that language it was out. What Robert had in mind I'm not at all sure; but I don't think he would mean to imply that good poetry could hurt any writer, whether from Urdu or Old Icelandic.

SMITH: How quickly did *kayak* become the "in" place for the new poetry?

Was it an instantaneous recognition or did it take a few years?

HITCHCOCK: The question implies that which may be true but which I cannot recognize. I have never tried to court fashion; she is far too fickle a mistress.

SMITH: How conscious were you of your geographical location, physically and spiritually? Did you feel that there was a "West Coast" quality to *kayak*?

HITCHCOCK: Well, I am a Northwesterner, with pretty much the same background as Ken Kesey or Gary Snyder, even though our aesthetics obviously differ. *kayak* was never programmatically Regional but I certainly doubt if its characteristic élan could have popped up in the East.

SMITH: One of the things that cannot be judged by reading the magazine is the amount of material that crossed your desk and was rejected. Letters you occasionally published indicated that you were proud of your high standards. Would we be surprised by the names of the people and the number of poems which were rejected in those early years? Did you make any major mistakes of oversight?

HITCHCOCK: For many years I received around fifty envelopes of manuscript a week. In the final years it fell off a bit. I certainly rejected work by a great many well-known poets; particularly in the early years I published a certain amount of work by poets who, on the face of it, would not appear particularly simpatico—I think offhand of X.J. Kennedy, A.R. Ammons, Dick Hugo, James Merrill, Karl Shapiro, Kenneth Rexroth and Richard Wilbur—but who offered their work out of general friendship. I remember that in one day's mail I received unsolicited manuscripts from Anne Sexton and Richard Eberhart. I liked (and published) the Sexton, but alas, with the best will in the world, I thought the Eberhart poem very weak and returned it.

SMITH: Bly's attack on the first ten issues of *kayak* accused you of having a weakness for formula surrealism. Did that seem a just criticism to you at the time? Did it affect you in any way?

HITCHCOCK: Bly's criticism was solicited and I was happy to publish it, since what he has to say is invariably lively and crotchety. I certainly didn't think *kayak* had any greater weakness for "formula surrealism" than Robert did himself. Perhaps it caused me to look a bit more carefully at pseudo-surrealist poems in the mail, but the magazine continued, as always, to publish a great deal of work that wasn't even marginally surrealist. (In passing, it's worth noting that the most published poet in the life of *kayak* was Herbert Morris, who if he acknowledges any influences at all, bows toward the French classicist St. Jean Perse.)

SMITH: In number twenty you dropped the proclamation of hospitality to surrealist, imagist, and political poems. Why? Especially in dropping the word "surrealist," did you want to widen the scope of the magazine?

HITCHCOCK: Perhaps. It was never my intention to create a typology.

SMITH: All during the history of *kayak* a number of regular contributors would suddenly disappear, never to reappear. Did you cease liking the work of some of these regulars? Did they tire of *kayak*? Were there some important fallings-out that weren't recorded on the correspondence page?

HITCHCOCK: Some poets fell through the ice and were eaten by narwhals, others got tangled in their skates and moved to Baltimore. In twenty years a lot can happen. A couple of good friends (Lou Lipsitz, Clemens Starck) quit publishing for a decade and then returned to *kayak* after the hiatus; others, no doubt, lost interest in the magazine altogether, but no one was ever excommunicated and what still amazes me is how many of the early contributors were still around with their support twenty years later.

✎ BIOGRAPHIES

GEORGE HITCHCOCK was born in Hood River, Oregon, in 1914. He graduated with honors from the University of Oregon and worked as a journalist, eventually moving to San Francisco to work as a staff writer for the *Western Worker*, then sports editor for the *People's Daily World*, where he wrote a regular column under the byline Lefty (and hired Kenneth Rexroth to write an outdoor column). Throughout the 1930s he wrote several novels, none of which survive. During World War II he joined the Merchant Marine as a 2nd cook and baker. After the war he traveled throughout California organizing dairy unions and was eventually invited to teach at the California Labor School. He held a number of positions at the Labor School, including teacher of philosophy.

During the 1950s, Hitchcock became active in writing and performing for the theater and worked with the Interplayers, The Actor's Workshop, and Oregon Shakespeare Festival, acting in over forty leading roles; his role of Creon in *Antigone* was recorded and published by Columbia Records. In 1958 he was called before the Un-American Activities Committee and his testimony was broadcast nationally; his response to the question "What is your profession?" became legend: "My profession is a gardener. I do underground work on plants."

From 1958–1963 he co-edited the *San Francisco Review* and in 1964 he founded *kayak*, a literary magazine "particularly hospitable to surrealist, imagist, and political poems." For the next twenty years, *kayak* would be one of the most important, and certainly the liveliest, magazines in the country. During this period, Hitchcock was invited to join the faculty at the experimental College V at the University of California, Santa Cruz, where he taught for nineteen years.

After *kayak* ceased operations in 1984, Hitchcock turned his attention to the visual arts, including stone carving, printmaking, and painting, and has exhibited his artwork in Mexico and the U.S. He lives with his partner, the poet Marjorie Simon, in La Paz, Mexico, and Harrisburg, Oregon.

As a teacher, publisher, editor, poet, storyteller, activist, actor, and playwright, George Hitchcock has strongly influenced the last fifty years of American literature. He is unforgettable, unique, and irreplaceable.

Editors

JOSEPH BEDNARIK is the editor of *The Sumac Reader* (Michigan State University Press, 1997), a contributor to *Conversations with Jim Harrison* (University of Mississippi Press, 2001), and is finalizing a comprehensive index of *kayak* magazine. His literary interviews and reviews have appeared in *Five Points, Northwest Review, The Oregonian,* and *The Seattle Post-Intelligencer.* He works at Copper Canyon Press and lives in Port Townsend, Washington.

MARK JARMAN has published seven books of poetry, including *Unholy Sonnets, Questions for Ecclesiastes,* and *Iris.* He is co-author of *The Reaper Essays.* He has won the Lenore Marshall Poetry Prize, The Poets' Prize, a Guggenheim Fellowship, the Joseph Henry Jackson Award, and three NEA Fellowships, and was a finalist for the National Book Critics Circle Award. He is a professor of English at Vanderbilt University and lives in Nashville, Tennessee.

ROBERT McDOWELL is the author of three collections of poetry—*Quiet Money, The Diviners,* and most recently, *On Foot, in Flames.* His essays, reviews, poems, and fiction have appeared in numerous magazines and anthologies. The editor of *Poetry after Modernism* and *Cowboy Poetry Matters,* McDowell has worked for the past eighteen years as founding publisher and editor of Story Line Press. He lives in Talent, Oregon.